EARLY

All In combines the complex, inner workings of the jewelry business, insurance nuances, and crimes with large payouts. Appleton, Wisconsin is about the last place you'd imagine a calculated heist of this magnitude. Nowitzke and Anissa find themselves fighting for their lives to solve a string of eerily similar burglaries and robberies. How are they connected? Who is the mastermind? And who survives the fast-paced investigation? *All In* is a heart-pounding race that will leave you absolutely dazed until the very last page . . . and craving more Nowitzke and team. J. P. Jordan is leaving his mark with expert subject matter and undeniable style.

- Sara Schultz, Insurance Professional

Everyone loves a good heist story. This is a great heist story. Jordan never fails to make me believe that I've got everything figured out before taking me on another twist. Overall, a fun read that expands the world Jordan began in *Men of God*.

- Robert W. Christian, author of *Unholy Shepherd*

The attention to detail in *All In* will keep you on the edge of your seat, waiting for every clue, the tension building as the story progresses. J. P. Jordan's writing style allows the reader to create a vivid, realistic picture of this story in their mind. Wonderful book!

- Queen Book Reviews

J. P. Jordan's latest mystery is an excellent read. He again uses his knowledge of insurance as the basis to weave a complex story of burglary, robbery, and murder. It features the police officers introduced in *Men of God*, Chuck Nowitzke and Anissa Taylor. Two seemingly unrelated crimes, a burglary in one jewelry store and an armed robbery in another have only one thing in common: their insurance company. They arrest one of the culprits only to have him murdered while in custody. The insurance underwriter starts getting cryptic texts about a future heist. They race to stop the next crime while trying to figure out all the pieces of the puzzle. It results in a surprising but very satisfying ending.

Mr. Jordan does a great job developing the relationship between the two detectives and providing more information on their backgrounds. I can't wait for a third book featuring these two characters. If you enjoy John Sanford, Earl Emerson, or JA Jance, you'll like *All In*.

- Bill Lebo, Retired Insurance Executive

In J. P. Jordan's second novel, *All In*, Detective Chuck Nowitzke turns his attention to the jewelry industry. Nowitzke investigates a major theft from a small-town Wisconsin jeweler. Meanwhile, a string of jewelry thefts and murders ensues, and Nowitzke's inquiry leads him to discover irregularities in the insurance business. Ultimately, he learns that greed can affect anyone.

All In is a fast-paced novel with an intricate plot. You may think you have it all figured out, but you will be surprised by the outcome. A very good read!!!

- Joann Kilgus

ALL IN

J. P. JORDAN

ten16press.com - Waukesha, WI

Also from J. P. Jordan:

MEN OF GOD

All In
Copyrighted © 2021 J. P. Jordan
ISBN 9781645382768
First Edition

All In
by J. P. Jordan

For information, please contact:

www.ten16press.com
Waukesha, WI

Edited by Lauren Blue
Cover design by Kaeley Dunteman

Dedication

There is an old saying that "It takes a village to raise a child." After writing my first novel, *Men of God*, I discovered a corollary: "It takes a family to sell a book!"

Over the past year, I have been grateful for the support of my wife, Nancy, as well as other family members and friends who have purchased copies of my book and gone out of their way to actively market *Men of God* on my behalf. Your help continues to inspire me to keep on developing my new craft.

A special shout-out goes to the MOG Marketing team (Jamie, Mila, Ivy, and Arie) for all their creative ideas and determination to make me successful! Keep up the great work.

Jim

CHAPTER 1

"Are you ready to get out of here, Fiona? C'mon. It's ten o'clock, and the party should be in high gear by now," implored the tall young man to his girlfriend.

"Just one more minute and then we can leave," she said, wrapping up the sub sandwich.

"You're doing it again, aren't you? I thought we talked about this. Your new friend will follow you like a lost dog and bug the shit out of us every time we close the store. You just never know about these guys. He might be mentally unstable, or on drugs, or have a knife or gun."

"Chad, don't be such a wimp. Yes, we had a conversation about this already, but apparently, we agreed to disagree. Besides, it's my money, and I want to do the right thing," said Fiona as she finished cleaning up. After everything was done, she grabbed the food and her jacket and said, "I'm ready to go," before heading toward the door.

"Well, it's about time. We've had no business for the past hour, and I was hoping to get out of here early tonight," said Chad impatiently, holding the door open for Fiona before snapping off the lights.

As Chad locked up the shop, Fiona skipped across the narrow cobblestone street of the up-and-coming business district and began searching the darkened doorways. She found the homeless man tucked in an alcove in front of a high-end kitchen store. "Here you go, sir," she said in a timid voice. "I made it for you. Enjoy, and please be safe." Keeping her distance, she tossed the food a few feet to the grimy old man, who caught it on the fly. He was wearing mismatched clothing and burrowed into a shabby sleeping bag for warmth. "I'm Fiona," offered the young woman.

"God bless you, Fiona," grunted the man as he tore open the white wrapper with his teeth. "You are my angel once more."

"What's your name?" asked Fiona.

"Henry," came the response between ravenous bites of the sandwich.

Still standing near the front door of the shop, Chad interrupted the conversation. "Fiona, say goodbye and let's go," he yelled impatiently.

"Sorry, Henry. I've got to leave," said Fiona to her new friend. But the old man did not reply, now wolfing down his food. With that, she turned on her heels back toward her boyfriend, who was still on the sidewalk. Locking arm in arm, the pair walked quickly down the quiet street lit only by decorative streetlamps and the stars.

Halfway down the block, a man sat in darkness behind the wheel of a large white-paneled truck, watching the proceedings. He couldn't hear the couple's conversation or figure out why the girl briefly moved onto the street before leaving. All he cared about was that they were gone. Interestingly, he had met both kids briefly one evening several weeks prior when he reconned the sandwich shop looking for dinner, along with any surveillance cameras. As the pair turned the corner, the driver spoke into his headset. "We're all clear on this end."

He heard a click with a monotone reply from his crew leader, known as Moose. "Bogdan, we're in place with our equipment and ready to go. Relax and wait for the designated time."

Two hours later, Moose contacted the driver. "Turn on your scanner and sit tight. The call will be coming in shortly. I'm on foot and moving to the back of the store to keep my timetable."

Through the windshield, Bogdan watched as Moose made his way to the door of the sandwich shop, taking his time to pick the lock. They had followed the same pattern for the past week. Then, just as on all previous occasions, Bogdan held his breath for a moment, until his partner disappeared into the structure. The driver exhaled deeply upon hearing nothing. Staring at his watch, he knew that Moose would again trigger the adjacent jewelry store's alarm at 12:18 a.m. precisely, sending a signal to the monitoring service. Hoping for the perfect result, his patience was finally rewarded.

In the truck, Bogdan heard the immediate burst of chatter on the scanner. The police dispatcher had been contacted by the central station alarm service monitoring Bateman Jewelers about a possible intruder. Given recent history, the dispatcher preemptively sent a cruiser in the direction of the business before contacting the owner of the store, Malcolm Bateman. However, rather than getting a thanks, she instead got an earful before waving off the squad car. "Unit Five, I've contacted the owner of Bateman Jewelers about the alarm condition. Apparently, this has happened for nine consecutive nights. He says the alarm company has been out to the store several times over the past week, but they can't find the source of the malfunction. He was perturbed that I woke him. Since we've dispatched cruisers for several evenings responding to other false alarms and started charging Bateman, he told us to forget it. He's not, I repeat *not*, coming down to the store. You can stand down."

"Fair enough, Dispatch," responded the patrolman. "Unless you've got something better for us to do, we're off to find some lunch."

"10-4."

The driver of the panel truck spoke into his microphone. "There's a ghost in the machine. We are a go."

"Got it," replied Moose. "Do you see any outside lights on in front of the store?"

"None."

"Great, we'll see you in a few hours when we're ready for step two. Let us know if anyone gets ambitious in the meantime."

"Will do."

With the all clear sign, a second white-paneled truck passed the first, pulling down the alley immediately adjacent to Bob's Sandwich Shoppe. After defeating the backdoor lock of the shop, Moose moved well into that portion of the building to trigger the alarm system of the adjacent jewelry store. Moose smiled to himself, recalling his first entry into the sandwich shop. On that evening, he had been particularly cautious, pausing briefly at the entrance, waiting for something unexpected . . . the sound of a newly installed local alarm bell . . . the snarling of a dog . . . or the cocking of a handgun. But, just as on the other evenings, he heard nothing but the sound of crickets chirping in the grass. Once in the store, he signaled his partners. The four professionals wore dark jumpsuits, ski masks, and headlamps to light their way. In short order, they emptied their vehicle, quietly carrying several heavy bags containing their equipment into the kitchen. Upon the final trip, they locked the door behind them. It was time to go to work.

Using a reciprocating saw purchased from Home Depot, one member of the crew created a new doorway from Bob's into Bateman's. Once through, the others quickly moved into the premises to locate the imposing safes in a back room of the store. Within minutes, they began their assault on the heavy boxes.

Moose made a final call to Bogdan. "Can you hear us out on the street?"

"Negative."

With no time pressure from the police or the alarm service and having ears on the street, the team meticulously went about their work. Moose mused rhetorically, "If a cutting wheel carves through a safe and no one is around to hear it, can we still get rich stealing the jewelry?"

At 5:00 a.m. sharp, their shift was over. Although it would not be light for at least another forty-five minutes, the crew had a timetable to keep. Three of the men repacked the van with their tools and equipment. They also carefully stowed five military-style duffel bags containing their plunder. Adrenaline coursed through their systems, giving each of them a high. As their excitement peaked, Moose contacted the driver. "Still awake?"

"Fuck you," came the reply.

"You need to switch to decaf, asshole. Any activity downtown?"

"None. Not even an early morning jogger yet."

"Okay, the boys have a load, and they're heading out with their truck. Pull up to the front door of the store."

Moments later, the vehicle rolled up the street before parking across from the sandwich shop. The driver quickly hopped out, opening both side doors as Moose casually stepped out of Bateman's Jewelers.

"How did it go?" asked Bogdan as his partner approached.

"Like clockwork. We thought we could get into three safes, but we were even able to hit number four with our plan." Moose coughed as, one by one, he hoisted two heavy duffels containing the goods into the vehicle. Sitting on the floor of the truck with his legs dangling, he caught his breath.

"Are you alright, Moose?" said the driver.

"Yeah, I think I'm just catching a cold," he shot back. "I feel like shit, and I'm kind of dizzy. May just be lack of sleep." He pulled off his balaclava, tossing it into the back of the truck before taking yet another deep breath. Steam rose from his sweat-matted salt-and-pepper hair in the cool morning air.

"What was the take?" asked the driver excitedly.

"All the high-end stuff. Diamonds and gold. Everything was exactly where we were told it would be."

"Any guess on the total?"

"Probably two to three million . . . for each bag."

"No shit," exclaimed the driver before letting out a low whistle as he calculated the total take. As they were set to leave, Bogdan noticed one of Moose's arms glistening in the twilight. "Are you hurt? Your arm?"

"No," replied Moose reflexively as he began to check himself, eventually finding several rips on the left arm of his jumpsuit. Feeling his body, Moose fingered a couple of deep scratches near his shoulder where blood had seeped through. "Shit, I must have caught myself on something sharp when we entered the store. I didn't even feel it. It doesn't look like a big deal though. Maybe a couple of stitches at worst. Let's get the merchandise to the airport, ditch the vehicles, and get some breakfast. I'm starving."

As the driver completed the math about his cut, he hit the gas harder than intended, squealing the tires briefly before moving down the street in the still-quiet neighborhood.

CHAPTER 2

Malcolm Bateman was not like his father, and everyone pretty much agreed. Though, for Malcolm, any such comment served as a biting criticism. The only son of Grace and Julian Bateman, Malcolm was born into a life of privilege through the hard work and sacrifice of his father and mother. His parents saw to it that he had every advantage in life, positioning him for success. Part of that effort included an expensive Ivy League education, even though Malcolm never fit in with the East Coast elite. Aside from a couple of minor scrapes with the law involving alcohol during his school years, the only serious bump in Malcolm's road came with an early morning call from his father. Months later, his mother passed away from pancreatic cancer while he was away at college. Malcolm was devastated by his mother's death, withdrawing from the few friends he had. Of his two parents, he was always closest to Grace. She had been his confidant, listening when no one else would, especially when other kids, and later adults, referred to him as peculiar, or worse. Even though he loved his father, Malcolm feared Julian, worrying he would never measure up to the old man's standards.

Nonetheless, Julian began grooming his son at an early age to take over the family business. Built from the ground up in Appleton, Wisconsin, the incredibly successful jewelry store had been Julian's other baby, his firstborn. Truth be told, Malcolm was unsure at any given time whether he rated ahead or behind the company. Still, he showed early promise and a flair for the glamour and flash connected to the industry. Upon graduation, he went to work at J. Bateman Jewelers.

By all outward appearances, Malcolm was a second-generation success. A handsome young man, he took to wearing three-piece suits and heavy gold watches borrowed from the store to present a professional image. However, appearances can be deceiving. Despite having a gift for many aspects of the jewelry business, Malcolm had another set of proclivities that worked against him. Even as a relative novice in the business, Malcolm could astound his father by making difficult decisions about a marketing campaign or the future direction of the business. Then, in equally astonishing fashion, Malcolm would defeat all his good works with a single critical blunder. The errors ranged from missing the simplest and most straightforward data points to making an off-putting comment to a long-valued customer. This flaw set him apart from his father, and it didn't go unnoticed.

In Julian's world, the customer was always right, even when they weren't. According to the old man, a professional jeweler always knew when to talk and when to shut up. "Once the piece is on someone's body, be quiet, and let it sell itself," he often repeated. A lesson pounded into Malcolm's head early on in his career.

Julian also explained to his son that prior purchases made by a customer should never be mentioned. Malcolm looked at his father incredulously. "Why wouldn't we want to bring up a past purchase? It seems like a good thing to build a personal relationship with the client."

"Because, Malcolm, if a man purchases an expensive necklace, we never know if it was given to his wife or his girlfriend. And we don't care." The elder Bateman explained it as a cardinal rule of retail jewelry, akin to attorney-client privilege. However, on more than one occasion, Malcolm violated the tenet, placing the customer in an awkward position, much to his father's chagrin.

As Julian approached retirement, he saw Malcolm's development continue with a pattern of earning fifty "attaboys" before burning them all in one inglorious "oh shit" moment. Julian was concerned the stakes would only rise as his son took on an ownership role in the business. The elder Bateman even went so far as quietly looking for an outside buyer to protect his nest egg. But when no realistic offers materialized, and with no alternatives, Julian worked out a transition plan for Malcolm to take over control of J. Bateman Jewelers.

Almost immediately, Julian realized he had made a grave mistake. Even though he knew Malcolm absolutely loved the glitz and glamour of the jewelry, Julian recognized his son had not developed any business savvy required to run the operation over the long term. Malcolm started offering steep discounts to an extensive list of new friends, losing money on each transaction, not understanding that it was impossible to make it up in volume. Then, Malcolm shunned several of the business's primary suppliers, changing the makeup of the store's inventory, moving from traditional items to selling primarily diamonds, watches, and heavy gold pieces. In making this shift, Malcolm had miscalculated, not anticipating how many of the business's long-time customers would be alienated. And, contrary to Julian's practice, Malcolm did not stand by his merchandise. If a customer returned an item as being scratched or damaged in some way, Malcom viewed it as the customer's problem. Contrarily, for years, Julian had always given the benefit of the doubt to his clients, even when they did not deserve it. Malcolm regarded such a policy as foolhardy.

As another part of the ownership change, Malcolm invested heavily in marketing and advertising his store. Even though this created new opportunities for the business, he covered the additional costs by cutting corners in other critical areas of the business, such as insurance and security. Within fifteen months, Julian could not bear to come to his store any longer to watch the daily implosion of his business.

Two years removed, the store was on the financial ropes. However, Malcolm had a grand plan to have the largest jewelry sale north of Chicago, bringing in what his advertisements said was more than $10 million in unset diamonds and gold pieces. With creditors breathing down his neck, it was a Hail Mary pass to save the business. The promotion caught everyone's attention, and it was around this time that Malcolm began to experience false alarms with his security system.

CHAPTER 3

Despite another midnight call from his alarm service, Malcolm had a good night of rest before waking in good spirits and diving into his morning ritual. A creature of habit, he rose early and went to the gym. Thirty minutes on the same rowing machine each day, followed by thirty more on a treadmill. On his way home, he stopped at his favorite local coffee shop for a latte and a bagel, spending an hour lingering over *The Wall Street Journal*, mentally gearing up for work. Aside from his typical challenges, he added the ongoing unresolved issue with his alarm company, becoming more and more perturbed as he thought about it. *How many nights with false alarms without the damn company fixing it?* Following an extended shower and taking time to choose the right suit from his wardrobe, Malcolm exited his house at exactly 8:35 a.m. for the fifteen-minute trip to work. On the short drive, he resolved that his first order of business would be to call the alarm company and give them another piece of his mind.

Malcolm's Jaguar pulled up to an open parking space directly in front of the store. Although buoyed by the prospect of his big sale, he felt an inexplicable shudder after hearing the chirp from his car signaling the doors locking. His meticulous nature suggested something was wrong. Striding up the walk to the store, he stopped short on the stoop's dark red pavers when he realized the front door was askew. Every cautious step forward felt like he was walking in wet concrete. He gave the heavy door a shove so that it opened a crack as he yelled "Hello?" into the building. His hopes that one of his associates had arrived at work early faded as he heard only the reverberation of his voice on the walls. Summoning the courage to step inside, Malcolm immediately saw that the interior of his showroom was covered in dust and debris. With a growing panic, he charged through the store into the safe room. After calling 911, he barely made it back to the store's front lawn before throwing up, managing to miss hitting his expensive shoes.

****

Morning was not Chuck Nowitzke's best time of day. He had an ongoing battle with his snooze button, sometimes hitting it up to seven times before conceding yet another loss. It was even worse if he was out on the town the night before, which seemed to be more and more the case lately. However, for reasons he could not comprehend that morning, he woke up with a clear head, feeling good. He had just ordered his large coffee and breakfast sandwich from McDonald's when he received a call from his partner, Anissa Taylor. "Yeah, what's up?"

"Where are you, Chuck?"

"Getting ready to enjoy a heart-healthy breakfast and take on the day," replied a snarky Nowitzke.

"We got an emergency call half an hour ago about a break-in at J. Bateman Jewelers. We have uniforms on the scene, but this is a big deal. Chief Clark wants us to take the lead on the investigation."

"I know the place. The asshole who owns it profiled me. Ran me off because it didn't look like I could afford anything in the store."

"Well, Chuck . . . I would guess you probably can't," came a sheepish reply from Anissa. "I'll meet you at the scene. Oh, and please pick up a McMuffin for me?"

"Since when do you eat McMuffins? The way you eat, you wouldn't even enjoy it before sticking a finger down your throat to yack it back up," said Nowitzke as he clicked off his phone. The surly detective climbed into his old, rusted, blue Ford Taurus, managing to squeeze the cardboard coffee cup hard enough for the plastic cover to pop off, spilling the hot liquid onto his hand and the front seat of his vehicle. *Shit.* Biting his lip, he toughed out the burning sensation before pulling the lone napkin from his McDonald's bag, swabbing the area as best he could. Yet, even after it had been cleaned, he heard an audible *squish* as he settled into the car. *Thank God for black pants.* Placing the portable police light on top of the dashboard, he made his way to J. Bateman Jewelers. By the time he arrived, the tie he was wearing picked up a permanent grease stain courtesy of the cheese that fell from his breakfast sandwich.

Now in his mid-forties, Nowitzke had been with the Appleton Police Department for almost two years. He had come north from the Milwaukee PD to restart his life after one too many murder investigations and yet another failed marriage. Standing a shade under six feet tall, he was a paunchy man with a shock of brown hair, a thick mustache, and a perpetual three-day beard. Nowitzke's typical look was that of someone who dressed in the dark at a thrift store. In fact, many of his colleagues wondered if he was color-blind or just simply had no fashion sense. The growing consensus among his peers was the latter. And, like the tie that had just become another casualty, by the end of most days, whatever he wore picked up a stain of some sort, including on the odd days when he shaved. Inevitably, he would manage to cut himself, allowing a trickle of blood to spot the collar of his shirt.

His overall look was even more jarring when standing next to his partner, Anissa Taylor. In her late twenties, she was best described as statuesque, pushing six feet tall, with a lithe athletic body, shoulder-length blonde hair, and smoky eyes, combined with a sharp intellect. Typically, she dressed fashionably, looking more like a runway model than a criminal investigator. That was again the case as they met outside Bateman's: Anissa in a sundress with a blazer and heels compared to Nowitzke's red-and-black checked sports coat, khaki pants, and worn loafers. They had met by happenstance at a murder investigation handled by Nowitzke shortly after she graduated from the academy. Although they were clearly the odd couple, Anissa quickly learned that, despite Nowitzke's fashion gaffs, he was an outstanding detective who had trusted her when he had no reason to. That trust was being repaid with her loyalty and friendship.

Seeing Taylor at the front door, Nowitzke ducked under the yellow police tape that cordoned off the area. As he approached the entranceway, he stopped and did a slow 360-degree turn, taking in the scene and its surroundings.

"What do ya know, Nis?"

"Not much. Based on what the first uniform on scene told me, he arrived to find the owner on the front stoop crying. Apparently, the jeweler, Malcolm Bateman, found his front door open when he came to work today. After going inside, he saw that several of the safes had been forcibly opened. Basically, the burglars picked the lock at Bob's Sandwich Shoppe next door to gain entrance into the jewelry store."

"Didn't the jewelry store have an alarm system?" asked Nowitzke.

"Yes, but it had been disabled . . . by the owner."

"Huh?"

"Bateman told the officer he had been getting false alarm signals every night for at least the past week. He'd had the alarm company out here to check several times, but nothing was ever found. However, the false alarms continued. After so many, we start charging to respond to calls."

"Who's *we*?"

"Us, Appleton PD."

"No shit. Wow, to protect and to serve. Let me tell you what happened next," replied Nowitzke with a wry smile.

Anissa looked perplexed. "What do you mean?"

"Nis, this burglary was done by pros. They created the alarm problem and were ready to go last night when the jeweler decided he wasn't coming to the store."

"How would they know that?"

"After Bateman decided not to come down to the store to check the system and save himself a few bucks, someone on the burglary crew was listening on a police scanner. When he or she heard Bateman and the cops weren't coming, it was go-time for the burglars."

"Seriously?" she questioned, her eyebrows raised. "You've seen something like this before?"

"Yeah, several times when I worked in Milwaukee. There was a string of unsolved jewelry store burglaries using the same MO. Pros would gain easy access to an unprotected business next to a jeweler, then set off a false alarm by creating vibrations through an adjacent wall that would be picked up by the system protecting the safe. The bad guys would do this for several nights in a row, wearing down the owner. Eventually, the proprietor would become frustrated and call off the dogs," he concluded. "It's basically a waiting game, and the burglars generally seem to have nothing better to do."

Anissa shook her head in disbelief. "It just amazes me that people even think like that. The way you described it sounds like someone has this down to a science."

"No shit. Highly skilled folks that are not into confrontation but looking for big paydays. Let's have a look around and then we'll talk with the jeweler."

As Anissa and Nowitzke walked through the store toward the back room, they saw a distraught Malcolm Bateman sitting at his desk in his office drinking tea while being consoled by several members of his staff.

Nowitzke whispered to Anissa as they passed through the area, "Yeah, that's the asshole that brushed me off. Wonder if he'll remember me?"

Upon entering the spartan back room, the first thing Nowitzke noticed was, of the total eight safes, only four had been compromised. In addition, the burglars were not systematic in their attacks, starting at one end of the room and working down the line. Rather, the safes on each end of the row had been passed over. Of the six remaining boxes, the third and fourth from the left had also been spared for some reason.

Observing the large row of safes, each standing six feet tall, Anissa exclaimed, "Look at the size of these things. They're as tall as me. How would anyone ever get into one of them, let alone four in an evening?"

"Well, these boxes are about the best money can buy. Assuming they're all identical to those opened, you can see from the label inside the door that they are rated TRTL 30x6," explained Nowitzke, slowly walking down the line and examining the damage.

"Okay . . . explain," answered Anissa with a questioning look on her face.

Nowitzke stopped and pointed to one of the tags. "See here. The TR means 'torch.' The TL means 'tool.' The other numbers mean all six sides of the safe are torch and tool resistant for thirty minutes."

"Wait, you mean you can get into one of these safes in thirty minutes?"

"Well, I couldn't. But, in theory, with the right tools and know-how, that's the minimum time they should be able to withstand an attack, according to their rating. However, even a pro might need some more time to get into one . . . let alone four."

"What kind of tools are we talking about?" asked Anissa.

"Diamond-cutting wheels that fit on a circular saw, like you could buy from any hardware store, would be my guess. Look at all the dust covering every surface around here." His arms swept around the room. "What you see are bits of the safe and the used cutting wheels all over the place. It also looks like the burglars used an oxyacetylene torch to attack this one. Look here," he said, pointing to a hole in the door of one safe. "You can see burns on the walls of several boxes with black scorch marks on the carpet where the sparks flew. Imagine a torch that can cut this thick metal like a hot knife going through a stick of butter."

Anissa pulled her dress around her to keep it from dragging on the dust on the floor and squatted onto her haunches to get level with the hole in the door, peering inside. Then she carefully reached out with one hand, feeling for heat. Eventually, after giving the door several quick pats to test the temperature, she touched the melted area of the now cooled safe. "Is that a potential lead, Chuck? I mean, how many places sell a torch like that?" asked Anissa as she stood.

"It's right thinking, but unfortunately not much of a lead," he replied. "You can buy torches like this at pretty much any home improvement store."

"Amazing," she replied.

"Looks like the burglars were well-prepared. Considering the amount of time involved, this must be a pretty sophisticated crew."

Anissa scanned the room, looking for any other evidence. "Aside from some used grinding wheels, there are no tools left here."

"Yeah, all the tools are very portable. Like I said, the people involved were professionals. I would guess the burglars had a van or some sort of covered vehicle to conceal them while moving them around."

"So, these bad guys had some serious balls," Anissa commented.

"Yeah, certainly bigger than the average pair anyway," offered Nowitzke, continuing his look around the room. "After Bateman told his alarm company and the police to take the night off, this crew had all night to work." He paused. "I noticed cameras in the showroom, but none back here. I'll bet any recordings of what took place here are gone too. Do we know when the alarm call was made?"

Anissa paged through her notes taken from her conversation with the initial officer. "Yes, 12:18 a.m."

"This is a business district. By the look of it, the burglars must have been in the store for several hours," concluded Nowitzke.

The pair traced their way toward a closet in the safe room. Flipping on the lights, they entered the door to see a large mess, created by the owner, not the burglars. The small room looked like a poor man's rummage sale, holding shelves of extra jewelry boxes, wrapping paper, Christmas decorations, seasonal trinkets, and old promotional advertising pieces waiting to find their way to a dumpster. From the other side of the small room, the officers saw sunlight streaming through the crudely cut entranceway into the sandwich shop. Just as they were about to poke their heads in to have a look, Anissa shouted for Nowitzke to stop.

"Chuck, there's a roll of old carpeting on the shelf to your right with tacks and staples sticking out. I don't want you to rip your sports coat."

"Thanks, Nis. Got it," he said, freezing in place then turning to locate the problem.

"But look here," said Anissa. "You wouldn't have been the first victim." She pointed to several staples that had strips of dark cloth caught on them along with some bloody residue.

"Nice catch," retorted Nowitzke. "I think you just found a major piece of evidence. Get your camera and photograph the general area. And get samples of the cloth and the blood. Maybe we'll get lucky with a DNA match."

Stepping through the makeshift doorway into the kitchen of Bob's, they were confronted by an unknown voice. "Who the hell are you, and what are you doing in my store?"

Nowitzke and Anissa looked up to see a slightly built man entering the back door to begin his day. Both pulled out their shields as Nowitzke answered, "We're Appleton PD investigating a burglary of your neighbor." Looking at the thin, balding man, he then asked, "Who exactly are you?"

"I'm Robert Massey, a.k.a Bob, as in Bob's Sandwich Shoppe."

"Well, Bob, your sandwich shop was the point of entry for a crew of burglars who got into Bateman's sometime last night."

"No shit," said Bob, now examining his new doorway.

"By the looks of it, the burglars must have helped themselves to a midnight snack in your place while they were working," Anissa chimed in, pointing to several half-eaten sandwiches lying on the counter. Then all their eyes were drawn to a bite mark out of a two-foot-long stick of summer sausage hanging from the ceiling.

"Wow, I wondered why Fiona and Chad left such a mess," said Bob after quickly scrutinizing the store.

"Who are Fiona and Chad?" asked Nowitzke.

"My employees. They closed up last night."

"What time was that?"

"Should have been at ten o'clock."

"Where might we find them?" asked the detective, cocking his head while scratching his scruffy beard.

"They're both students. I'll get you their phone numbers and info," said Bob, heading to his small office.

"Nis, can you take Bob's information and then gather the rest of the evidence while I go talk to Bateman?"

"Sure. Do you want me to swab Bob's salami for DNA?" she said with a smirk.

"Didn't think you made friends that fast, smart-ass," he chuckled, shaking his head.

CHAPTER 4

It had taken more than an hour and several cups of Earl Grey to calm Malcolm Bateman's nerves. Now alone behind his desk in the well-appointed office, the jeweler loosened his tie, staring transfixed at the ledger on his laptop. The staff largely avoided Bateman's office while the police conducted their forensic work, staying in the showroom, unsure of what to do. It seemed clear they were not opening for the day, but everyone steered clear of their boss, who had suffered multiple crying jags throughout the morning.

Nowitzke knocked on the heavy door as he entered the room. "Mr. Bateman, I'm Detective Nowitzke, lead investigator on your burglary."

Bateman seemingly ignored the officer, muttering to himself, "Did you see what they did to my new rugs? Ruined. Thousands of dollars down the drain."

"Sir?" said Nowitzke patiently.

Bateman refocused, looking up from his chair to see the grizzled detective standing in front of the desk. After a moment, Bateman made a face as if he recognized the officer, straightened his tie, then said, "Do I know you? Are you a customer?"

Nowitzke hemmed and hawed, searching for a polite response. "No. I guess I would technically qualify only as a window shopper."

"Okay," said the still dazed jeweler. "What can I do for you, Detective?"

"What can you tell me about the burglary?"

"Nothing. I thought it was your job to figure this out," said Bateman brusquely.

"Yeah, it is," replied Nowitzke. "But I'd like your side of the story. You've been getting false alarms?"

Bateman exhaled loudly as if being inconvenienced. "I've already told your officer about this, but yes. For the last nine nights at exactly 12:18 a.m., the central station alarm has malfunctioned. For the first eight of those nights, I had to get up in the middle of the night, get dressed, and come downtown to meet the alarm people and police. However, there was never any break-in. I was all over the alarm company to find out why *their* system was malfunctioning. They sent out technicians several times over the last week but found nothing. Incompetent assholes. I'll sue them for everything they have for their malfeasance. I'd also been told by your colleagues that I would be charged for responding to any additional false alarms. God knows what else the police have to do at that hour that might take precedence over checking on a taxpayer's store. I can only guess it must have had the importance of breaking up fights between drunks or ordering a fresh batch of donuts at one of the local bakeries," he opined, looking up at the ceiling. "When I got the call from the alarm company early this morning, I told them to get screwed. I wasn't coming down . . . again."

"I don't think your system was malfunctioning," replied Nowitzke, doing his best not to lose his patience with the rude jeweler. "Probably been tampered with by the burglars." Just then, there was a light knock at the door, and an exotic, dark-haired young woman with deep blue eyes, a tight white blouse, and a very short skirt entered the room.

"Mr. Bateman, would you like some more tea?" she said with an accent Nowitzke could not place.

"No, thank you, Nadia," said Bateman. "Detective Nowitzke, with all the commotion, I've been impolite. Can we offer you some tea or coffee?"

"Nah, I'm good," responded the officer.

Bateman continued, "Nadia, with the burglary and the mess, I think you can go home. Would you let the rest of the staff know too? I'll call everyone tomorrow about our next steps."

Nowitzke's eyes followed Nadia as she left the room, closing the door behind her. "What's the story on Nadia, Mr. Bateman?"

"She is our top salesperson. She connects well with female customers, and men literally cannot say no to her."

"Go figure."

"Now, you were saying about my alarm system . . . ?" asked the jeweler.

"Yeah. I think the burglars set you up. I would guess they broke into your neighbor's store every night for the past week and beat on the wall adjacent to your safes. Your alarm company picked up the vibration and reported an intrusion."

"Marvelous," replied Bateman in a dour tone that matched the look on his face. "When I came to work this morning, I was shocked to find the front door open, several of the safes opened, and a big goddamned mess."

"Any idea about what was taken or how much?"

"The burglars took diamonds and gold. Until I complete an inventory and reconcile sales and the like, I don't know exactly."

"Ballpark?"

"Well, with our big sale just starting, it could be as much as $8 million or more."

Nowitzke's eyes opened wide upon hearing the number. "Tell me about your safes."

"Sure, they are top of the line."

"Noticed that. But I also saw that only four of the safes were opened and the thieves didn't start at the end of the row."

"Okay . . ." said Bateman questioningly. "What are you getting at?"

"Any idea why they took that approach? I mean, if all the safes are identical, why wouldn't they be more systematic, you know, starting on one end and continuing down the line?"

"How the hell would I know, Detective?" Bateman snippily replied. "Are you insinuating something?"

"Nothing. Just asking for your opinion. Since the four we talked about are empty, can you show me what's in the other safes?"

"Sure," said Bateman, getting up from his desk. As they got to the first safe, he explained, "We always put our repairs in this one." The jeweler completed the combination, and the heavy door swung open. Nowitzke eyed the contents organized in small cardboard boxes, each holding numerous labeled clear bags.

"This safe's less than half full," commented Nowitzke. "Any idea on the amount of value stored in here this morning?"

Looking into the safe, Bateman's eyes moved back and forth, searching for an answer. "Roughly a quarter million? You must remember, repairs fluctuate. At times, this safe has been jam-packed full. It's kind of a cyclical thing," explained the jeweler.

Skipping past the safes that had been compromised, Nowitzke asked Bateman to open the next in line that had been untouched. As the jeweler worked the combination, Bateman offered that this safe was largely for overflow. He explained that the store was preparing for a big sale. While this box might be light with contents, he anticipated it would be brimming soon when everything arrived. As the door opened, Nowitzke saw only a smattering of jewelry.

"What kind of value would you guess is in this one?"

"Probably a couple hundred thousand, tops. Pretty much the same for this one too," added Bateman, referencing the next safe as he opened it. "Not much here, but again, we planned ahead, anticipating storage for additional goods that continue to arrive."

Nowitzke's face remained stony while he continued to do the math in his head about the total of the burglar's take. Moving to the final untouched safe, Nowitzke saw several brands of luxury watches inside, including Rolex, Omega, and Tag Heuer. But again, barely half-full and hardly at capacity.

"What's the average value of a watch like this?" asked Nowitzke.

"It depends. You can get a starter watch from some of these companies for a couple thousand dollars, but these can quickly get to $50,000 or more. Like anything else in the world, you can spend as much as you want on something."

"No shit," said Nowitzke. "How often do you sell one?"

"Every day, all day. They are extremely popular with businessmen who want to make a statement. Unfortunately, they're also very popular with thieves too, who have little trouble fencing them. However, watches of this caliber are numbered. Any watches that are sold or are in for repairs also have owners' details on file with the company. If they ever get stolen, the watch company keeps a record of that as well. I've read about people who've sent their Rolex in for service years after receiving it as a gift only to find out it had been previously stolen."

The detective eyed the rows of boxes of luxury watches in the safe and shook his head. *Goddammit. Where does all the money come from for people to buy watches like this?* Just as Nowitzke was about to close the safe's door, something caught his eye that seemed out of place. In the midst of hundreds of thousands of dollars of expensive timepieces sat a tattered, yellow cigar box centered on a shelf in the upper portion of the safe. "What's in there?"

Bateman lowered his head, a bit embarrassed. "Baseball cards."

"Baseball cards?"

"My personal collection. I've been saving them since I was a kid. I've got some very rare cards. A Hank Aaron . . . a Mickey Mantle rookie card. An autographed Topps 1952 Willie Mays rookie card too," Bateman said excitedly. "My collection is valued between $50,000 and $75,000."

Nowitzke's mind was grinding. *Fucking baseball cards in this safe?* "Mr. Bateman, what was your total store inventory as of yesterday?"

"Roughly $12 million," responded the jeweler without hesitation.

"Okay. But what you've shown me in terms of the remaining goods is around $1 million."

The jeweler was paying rapt attention to the detective, listening intently, trying to understand where Nowitzke was headed.

"So, unless you've got anything else of real value hidden in the store elsewhere, some quick math puts your loss at closer to $10 million plus. I'm no expert, but wouldn't it have made more sense to spread the values more evenly across all the safes?" asked Nowitzke as tactfully as he could.

"I guess," pondered Bateman, still trying to grasp the numbers and the idea offered by the detective. "Here at J. Bateman Jewelers, we have our procedures. My father did things a certain way, and I've continued his tradition. And, Detective, as you said yourself, you're not an expert about the jewelry industry."

"True," said Nowitzke. "However, I am familiar with the theft industry. You got insurance?"

Upon hearing the detective's question, Nowitzke's point finally hit home for Bateman, who began to hyperventilate as his face turned white. "Oh my God. I do, but with all the hubbub with my upcoming sale, I forgot to call the insurance carrier to increase my limits. I've been carrying coverage for $5 million. Do you think they'll be willing to overlook my error and pay the difference?" asked Bateman, with tears forming again in his already swollen eyes.

"Yeah, I'm sure . . ." said Nowitzke, ". . . just like every other insurance company. Who's your carrier so I can get in touch with them if needed?"

"Wisconsin Specialty Underwriters. They have an outstanding program for jewelers, or so I am told by my more astute friends."

As Nowitzke jotted down the additional details on a small pad pulled from his jacket pocket, he paused. "A couple of final questions for you at this point, sir. Tell me more about Nadia," he asked after a distant memory popped into his head.

"Is this business or personal?"

Nowitzke laughed. "All business. I'm already paying for two prior mistakes, and I'm not looking to split up my stuff a third time. Plus, she's clearly in the majors, and I'm lost somewhere down in Single-A ball."

Bateman yawned as Nowitzke finished his story. "She's an immigrant who came to me looking for a job. She had all the proper legal documentation, knew the language and the jewelry. She's easy on the eyes and dresses the part. Frankly, Nadia might be the best hire I've ever made," he said smugly.

"How long has she worked for you?"

"Just about eight months."

"For the record, what's her last name?"

"Belushi," responded Bateman.

"You mean like the old comedian?"

"I guess?"

"Do you know where she emigrated from, by any chance?"

Bateman thought briefly. "I think she said she was from Albania."

As Nowitzke gave the jeweler his card, something else clicked with Bateman's answer. Finally, the detective asked the jeweler to contact him about the actual extent of the loss after the inventory was taken.

Anissa had finished gathering evidence and found Nowitzke in front of the store. The two of them stepped out onto the porch, alone. "What's the story on the jeweler?" she asked.

"I'm not sure. Bateman runs hot and cold but strikes me as a major dickhead starting with his crying jag. He doesn't see himself as being responsible in any way for the loss. Blames the alarm company. Then, there's the actual burglary. According to my math, the take was at least $10 million, of which he's insured for about half of that. But he seems more concerned about several thousands of dollars of damage to his rugs and the safety of his baseball cards. The whole safe thing bothers the shit out of me too. Almost all his value was in four safes. For some reason, the burglars didn't enter any of the half-full ones."

"You don't think they're exceptional guessers then?" asked Anissa.

"Negative, unless Superman with his X-ray vision was part of the crew. Somebody knew something. Did you see that little dark-haired hottie running around the store?"

"She was kind of hard to miss," conceded Anissa.

"Bateman said she's an immigrant from Albania. I need to make some calls down to my former boss who also worked on some jewelry thefts."

"You recognized her?"

"No, but believe it or not, there are some ethnic groups that target jewelers. It might be nothing at all. Just want to be thorough."

Anissa nodded, processing yet another piece of new knowledge. "Do you think Bateman might be in on the theft?"

Nowitzke contemplated the question momentarily, scratching his gut. "Nah, he's pretty shook up about the whole experience. But I'm curious about how his business is doing. He already told me he's underinsured. I'm no expert, but if you're going to stage a burglary, wouldn't you over-insure and try to build your claim?"

"That makes sense," said Anissa.

"Something's not right here," concluded Nowitzke. As his brain began to sort through what he knew of the burglary, his next steps, and Bateman himself, he blurted out, "Man, that guy is a squirrel."

"A pink squirrel?" cracked Anissa.

"Hey, you should be ashamed of yourself," he said, chiding her. "Who have you been hanging out with to make such an insensitive comment?"

"You."

Nowitzke laughed. "At least you're paying attention. Oh, and you were right. Short of me selling a kidney on the black market, there's nothing in that store that I can afford."

CHAPTER 5

After dropping off the evidence gathered with the forensics unit at APD, Anissa pointed her silver Audi TT Coupe in the direction of the local college's student ghetto in search of Fiona Gibson and her boyfriend, Chad Howell. Leaving his rust bucket to further decompose in the department's parking lot, Nowitzke occupied the shotgun seat, marveling as Anissa deftly guided the sports car through midday traffic.

"How do you afford this kind of car on a cop's salary?" asked Nowitzke.

"You don't," countered Anissa, "unless you have a former boyfriend that works at a dealership."

"Former?"

"Don't ask," said Anissa. "It's a long story. My lease was the only thing that survived the relationship."

"Wasn't going to, aside from wondering if he treats all civil servants the same way in terms of discounts or just works with the good-looking ones."

"Trust me, it wasn't worth it," said Anissa, brushing Nowitzke off. "By the way, how's your personal life these days?"

"For shit. Thanks for reminding me. My exes have joined forces taking turns calling to harass me for money and to suck the life out of me."

Anissa snickered. "I thought you settled with both?"

"I did with the first Mrs. Nowitzke. Got a meeting with number two and our attorneys in the next couple of days. My final lap dance with the stripper."

"Your second wife is a dancer?" queried Anissa.

"Yeah. When we first met, she went by the name Mercedes. But I didn't figure out until too late that she started going by Chlamydia," he said with a laugh that Anissa joined in on. "For some reason, both of my exes think I've got some treasure buried on one of the local beaches around here. I've paid alimony through the nose until the judge finally told number one to get a job. Number two makes more than I do . . . she just gets paid with a lot of singles. But even though my 401(k) has been drained, twice, I should get a raise in about ten days when my second error in judgment comes off the dole."

"No child support payments?" asked Anissa.

"Thank God, no. None of my swimmers ever completed the journey." Briefly taking stock of his situation, Nowitzke exhaled as he looked out the window. "Jesus, I'll be working until I'm seventy-five, unless my long-term investment comes through."

"What long-term investment?"

"I buy a lottery ticket every week."

"That's solid financial planning, Chuck."

To Anissa's relief, Nowitzke's tale of woe ended as the Audi's GPS system guided them to Gibson's address. Adjacent to the community college, the young woman lived in a two-story Victorian that had clearly seen better days. It was one of several in the once grand neighborhood that were all now roughly in the same poor condition. Surrounded by a decomposing wooden fence and several overgrown evergreen trees, the large home was covered in chipping lime green paint.

"Man, there's enough lead floating around the house to give everybody living here brain damage . . . along with their kids," offered Nowitzke.

The old structure had been carved up into multiple units by a local slumlord destroying the final vestiges of any elegance the house might have once had. In doing so though, he had increased his earning potential. His crowning achievement was squeezing in one additional rental unit by converting the attic into an apartment.

Fiona lived in that third-floor walk-up, much to the chagrin of Nowitzke, who left a river of sweat up the steps of the warm building. For her part, Anissa bounced up to the top floor in her heels like she was warming up for a marathon. The younger detective knocked on the door with the tarnished brass "8" as Nowitzke completed the journey, hands on his knees and out of breath.

"You could use some more cardio in your workouts," commented Anissa.

"I prefer strength training . . ." gasped Nowitzke, ". . . twelve-ounce curls."

A small, perky girl with curly black hair answered the door with a bubbly greeting, introducing herself as Fiona. However, all the air left the room when Anissa announced that she and her partner were detectives investigating a burglary at J. Bateman Jewelers, the neighboring business of Fiona's employer. "Oh my God, a burglary," she exclaimed before inviting the officers into her home.

The distinguishing feature of Apartment 8 was the low doorway. Although it was not a problem for Fiona, both officers needed to duck to enter the tiny space. "Jesus, Bilbo Baggins couldn't get into this place without hitting his head on the frame," whispered Nowitzke to Anissa. Given that the ceiling of the apartment measured only to six feet, neither Nowitzke nor Anissa could fully stand, remaining uncomfortably hunched over until being invited to take a seat.

Despite the decaying structure, the apartment was neatly kept. *Wish my place looked this clean*, thought Nowitzke.

The main room of the studio apartment was painted in contractor beige with barely enough space for three folding chairs, a dorm-sized refrigerator and comparable stove, a small, scuffed wooden table holding a laptop, and a futon that was currently occupied by a sleeping red-haired young man whose feet protruded at least a foot off the end of the couch. Snoring heavily, he was undisturbed by the arrival of the two officers until Fiona gave him a shove.

After Nowitzke finally caught his breath from the trek up the stairs, he began the conversation. "Fiona, I understand you work at Bob's."

"Yes, Chad and I closed last night around ten. Oh, and that's Chad by the way," she said as an awkward introduction, pointing toward her bleary boyfriend. "He had a late night partying and can't handle his liquor very well," she offered, her tone rising.

"At least I didn't barf," countered Chad with a scratchy deep voice as he struggled to sit up.

Nowitzke thought Chad looked roughly the same color as the exterior of the house. He continued. "How often do you two work at Bob's?"

"We generally work together a couple nights a week. We're both students and need the extra money," offered Fiona.

"Have either of you noticed anything peculiar about the place lately?" asked Anissa.

Fiona and Chad paused for a moment, exchanging confused looks before replying simultaneously, "Like what?"

"Anything out of the ordinary?"

"No . . . nothing," the students agreed, again in sync.

"We believe the burglars probably watched the sandwich store for a couple of days. Then they simulated alarm signals before breaking into the jewelry store, which they did by cutting a hole in an adjacent wall," said Nowitzke.

"My God, were we in danger?" asked Chad, who suddenly was more engaged in the conversation.

"Don't think so," Nowitzke replied. "The burglars were pros. They did it after hours. Basically, they aren't into confrontation."

Fiona exhaled a deep breath. Looking at Chad, she asked, "You don't think my new friend had anything to do with this, do you?"

Anissa and Nowitzke exchanged glances. "What new friend?" asked Anissa.

"Well, Chad and I closed the shop several nights this past week. I noticed a homeless guy sitting in the doorway across the street from Bob's. Anyway, I've kind of gotten into the habit of making a sandwich and giving it to him when we leave."

"Fiona, I told you that was a bad idea," said Chad.

Seizing on the moment, Nowitzke peppered Fiona with a series of questions. "What's his name?"

"He told me his name was Henry."

"What does he look like?"

"Like a homeless person. I don't want to sound insensitive, but they all pretty much end up looking the same to me. Henry was covered in filth. He wore grubby clothing. He's a white guy. Beyond that, I can't give you much more of a physical description. He was sitting under a sketchy sleeping bag trying to stay warm, so I couldn't guess height or weight. But he was very polite to me."

"Henry?" asked Anissa. "Any last name?"

"I didn't ask," said Fiona.

"Where did you find him last night?"

"He's generally in one of the doorways in the area. Last night, he was in front of the kitchen shop across from Bob's. I really don't know anything else about him," offered Fiona. "I'm sorry if I caused a problem," she added contritely.

"Are there a lot of homeless people living on that street during the evening?" asked Anissa.

"No. If there are, I haven't seen any. Henry seems to be the only one in the area," said Fiona. "I was just trying to help out another human being."

"Well, maybe you just did," countered Nowitzke.

CHAPTER 6

Anissa's Audi came to rest in roughly the same parking stall that had been used by the burglars the night before. It was a few minutes before 10:00 p.m. when she and Nowitzke exited the vehicle and began walking down the alley to the paved street that fronted Bateman's and Bob's. Turning onto the avenue in search of Henry, Anissa patted her large leather purse while both detectives also unconsciously touched their respective side arms as a matter of reflex, just in case.

"How do you want to do this?" asked Nowitzke.

"Exactly the same way Fiona did. I brought some bait along," said Anissa. "Let's walk up and down the street to see if we can find this Henry. If and when we do, maybe he'll respond to some food in exchange for answering our questions."

"Well, watch your ass, Nis. The homeless range from those who are just down on their luck to assholes with some serious psychological issues," said Nowitzke.

"Thanks for the tip," replied Anissa, who then pulled a large flashlight from her bag.

Nowitzke shook his head. "Jesus, were you a girl scout?"

"No, just being practical since our little recon trip is in the pitch-dark, Chuck."

The detectives walked slowly down the side of the street in front of the jewelry store, straining to get a look at the doorway of the kitchen shop mentioned by Fiona. However, the ambient lighting created just enough shadows for someone to hide in the recesses. After strolling to the nearest corner, they crossed the street and began to work their way back toward where they believed Henry might be located. Taking their time, Nowitzke and Anissa closed in on the target doorway and initially thought they had come up empty. However, before they could even see him, they heard snoring coming from under a grubby sleeping bag exactly in the space Fiona described. Trading looks about next steps, Anissa motioned for Nowitzke to step back.

Keeping her distance and staying on the sidewalk, Anissa whispered, "Henry?"

After listening to thirty seconds of snoring with no response, Anissa made a second try with a louder, "Henry?"

The snoring stopped immediately, yet the sleeping bag did not move.

"Henry," said Anissa in a normal tone. "Your friend Fiona said I might find you here. I have some food for you."

At the mention of either Fiona or food, the sleeping bag peeled back to expose a grimy face.

"Who are you?" came the terse reply.

"My name is Anissa."

"What do you want from me?" the man rasped.

"Just some answers to a couple of questions. I'm a detective . . ."

"You're with the police?" squawked the man. "Hey, bitch, leave me alone and get out of here."

A confrontation brewing, Nowitzke stepped between Anissa and the homeless man. "Asshole, we've got some food for you if you're willing to answer some questions," he interjected sternly. "Otherwise, we can arrest you and put you in jail for vagrancy. What's it gonna be?"

Silence came from the sleeping bag for a moment as the man seemingly thought through his options. "What kind of questions?"

"Someone burglarized the jewelry store across the street last night," replied Nowitzke.

"What kind of food did you bring?"

Anissa chimed in with her softer approach. "Tell you what, I've got a bag of sandwiches, brownies, sodas . . ."

"Damn, I'd kill for a brownie," replied Henry, pulling himself upright to a sitting position while using a portion of the sleeping bag to wipe his face. "You know, I thought something weird was going on across the street. In fact, it seemed like there were people here several nights this week. But last night, every time I fell asleep, something woke me up."

Anissa asked, "For the record, Henry, what's your last name?"

"Webb," came the reply.

"What are you doing here?"

"Well, it's a long story. But the bottom line is I lost my job, then my marriage, and what I knew as my life in record time. I was a laborer who was making good money. However, the company I worked for was bought out by a larger one. I got laid off along with about eighty other folks and told not to come back. I couldn't find another job, and before I knew it, I just ended up in this doorway," he said, taking a breath. "Where's that brownie you mentioned?"

"I'm sorry," said Anissa, handing a large bag of food to Henry.

Nowitzke chimed in, "What'd you see last night?"

Henry looked up at the detective from his seated position, chomping on his brownie while thinking. "Stuff started happening this past week. I noticed a white-paneled truck parked down the street with a guy just sitting in the driver's seat doing nothing. I thought it was odd that someone was just sitting there around midnight, but I wasn't looking for trouble. At first, I wondered if there was a drug deal going down. But no one ever approached the guy in the truck, and he always left around one in the morning or so."

"Did you get a make or model on the vehicle?" asked Anissa.

"Or a license plate number?" probed Nowitzke.

"No, I was too far down the street to see too much. But last night was different."

"How so?" asked Anissa.

"The truck parked in its normal spot around midnight. Same old, same old. But when 1:00 a.m. came, the driver just sat there . . . all night. I guess I nodded off until I heard the vehicle start after several hours, and it woke me up. Then, after the truck pulled up almost next to my doorway, I saw a guy with a mask come out of the front door of the jewelry store carrying two duffel bags. A short, stocky dude. Kind of swarthy-looking. After the driver pulled up, they had a conversation, and the stumpy guy pulled off his mask."

"You get a good look at him?" asked Nowitzke.

"No, it was still dark. Plus, I knew something big had gone down at that point and was scared that these guys would find me and kill me. I stayed pretty much under my sleeping bag and didn't move. Thank God they couldn't see me." He paused.

"Keep going, Henry," said Anissa.

"When the dome light of the truck came on, they tossed the bags in. But then I heard the driver tell the stocky guy that he was bleeding, like he'd been cut somehow. I couldn't see very well, but there was a dark wet spot on the arm of his jumpsuit."

Both detectives looked at each other knowingly.

"Go on," said Anissa.

"Well . . ." said Henry, "the stump and the driver talked about stealing millions of dollars in diamonds and gold. Then I heard one of them say they were going to the airport and then to breakfast."

"Okay, you've been very helpful," replied Anissa excitedly, looking at Nowitzke and seeing a similar reaction about their next lead.

"One last thing," said Henry. "The driver must have been pretty jacked because he peeled out of here fast. I would bet money he left some tire marks on the road."

"Can you show us exactly where?" asked Nowitzke.

The answer required Henry to rise from his comfortable spot. Stretching to a full six-foot-three, he towered over both detectives. Dressed in heavy, mismatched clothing against whatever Wisconsin spring weather might bring, Henry's pants would barely stay on his hips since he was little more than skin and bones. Walking deliberately onto the pavers, Henry paused for a moment, searching for the spot, and then pointed down. "Right here," he said.

Pulling out her flashlight, Anissa scanned the area. Sure enough, there were two tire marks on the pavement. More evidence to process on-site and potential video to gather from the local airport. She handed him the last of her food. "Henry, is there any place we can take you to get some help?"

"No," replied Henry, and then said to no one in particular, "You know, if I could just get a job, I could get back on my feet."

"I'm not sure what we can do for you there," said Nowitzke, "but if it helps, take this." The detective slid a $100 bill into Henry's shirt pocket.

"Oh my God, thank you, Detective."

"Henry, how can we get in touch with you if we need to?" asked Anissa.

"That might be tough. My secretary is in Barbados this week, and I don't have a forwarding address," joked the man, eliciting a laugh from Nowitzke. "I generally stay in this neighborhood, unless one of your patrolmen decides to run me off."

The conversation ended in an awkward fashion, with Henry taking his food and finding his way back to his doorway as the police officers called a squad car to bring a camera and some external lighting. Although both Nowitzke and Anissa realized that any tire evidence had probably degraded after a day of traffic, they nonetheless wanted to document their findings with photos.

As they waited, Anissa leaned over to Nowitzke. "Chuck, you're quite the soft touch after all."

"What do you mean?" he growled.

"You gave Henry a $100 bill."

Nowitzke stammered. "Well, he'll make better use of it than either one of my exes."

CHAPTER 7

The bad luck started early with their trip to the airport. Nowitzke and Anissa tracked down the airport manager, Heather Curtis, just as she got to her office door. Juggling keys, coffee, and her briefcase, she handed the latter to Nowitzke so she could open the door without spilling her drink. Entering the office en masse, and before Heather could take off her coat, Nowitzke flashed his badge and took the lead, explaining their need to see the early morning video from the day of the jewelry theft. After Heather booted up her laptop, she looked at the calendar, hesitated, and mumbled somberly.

"I thought so," she finally said out loud to herself. "On the date in question, the airport's support systems went through their monthly backup cycle from midnight until seven in the morning."

Both detectives looked at Heather as if she were speaking Greek.

Heather translated. "Essentially, during a backup cycle, nothing can be captured by the system. For that morning, we have no video of anything."

"How is that possible?" asked Anissa, trying to remain calm.

"Ma'am, we have to back up our data sometime," she said snippily. "Like every business, we have a cycle. We scheduled it based upon our assessment that the midweek overnight timing offered the least risk. I'm sorry, but there's nothing I can do. However, you're more than welcome to look at the balance of the video that we did capture before and after the time you asked about."

While both Nowitzke and Anissa took Heather up on her offer, they already knew that the vehicle in question would not show up, at least not on the front end of the video given the time of the alarm call. In a small office adjacent to Heather's, Nowitzke and Anissa drank bad airport coffee and scanned the recording from the time it came back online until the running internal clock in the corner of the screen read 10:00 a.m. As anticipated, there was no van. A dead end.

****

As they made their way back to the office, Anissa was fuming.

"Nis, we got several leads to follow up on. Just relax. We'll get these guys."

"I know that."

"Then what's wrong?"

"That bitch called me 'ma'am.' I'm still in my twenties."

"Don't take it personal. She did it just to tweak you because we were pushing her. Who knows what she would have referred to me as?"

After buzzing in both officers through the secured entryway of their department building, Officer Marlene Benson, who was the gatekeeper working the front desk, pulled them aside. "Detective Nowitzke, you have a visitor in your office waiting to see you."

"And he is?" asked Nowitzke, feeling like he was using up the first of his twenty questions as part of an ongoing skirmish with Benson. Benson, who monitored the entry into the building, had numerous prior disagreements with Nowitzke about who she had granted access to his office.

"Sean Cook," replied the middle-aged woman, taking a sip of her coffee.

"And who the hell is he?"

"An insurance guy. Says he works for Wisconsin Specialty Underwriters. Here's his card, sir," said Benson. "Even though he didn't have an appointment, he said it was very important to see you."

"Dammit, Benson, I've told you before to keep these people in the holding pen unless I want them in my office. The last thing I would do with my time is schedule an appointment with an insurance agent. Jesus, I'm in the middle of a big investigation," he replied, the volume of his voice rising. "Tell you what, though. If he's here to sell me life insurance, I swear you will be my first referral." Nowitzke jammed the card into his jacket pocket.

Hearing the discussion between Nowitzke and Benson, Anissa excused herself. "Chuck, I've got some calls to make about this investigation," she said, smiling.

"What kind of calls?" questioned the senior detective with a skeptical look on his face.

"Important ones," she replied, leaving Nowitzke to go one-on-one with the unwanted visitor. Then as a parting shot, she offered, "Oh, I'll be in shortly, in case you need me to witness any forms about the type of risk you are."

"Thanks," replied Nowitzke, sneering at Anissa as she bolted down the hallway.

Entering his office, the detective found a well-dressed, sandy-haired young man scrutinizing Nowitzke's collection of snow globes on the credenza behind his desk. In fact, he was holding one up to the light, examining a young woman wearing a Santa hat on a stripper pole surrounded by elves holding dollar bills. The rest of the globes were stationed on hallowed ground just below a wall displaying photographs of Nowitzke with friends taken over his career. Most of the rest of the office was buried in mounds of paper stacked on the desk and around the room. Grunting a "hello" to signal his visitor, Nowitzke served notice to the stranger to clear out from his personal space. "Put it down, please, and park it over there," he said, gesturing toward one of the chairs on the other side of the desk.

Undeterred by Nowitzke's brusque manner, the visitor slid the globe onto the edge of the sideboard. However, it was not safely in place and the globe fell, hitting the floor with an audible crack. "Shit," he said, bending over to pick up the dome, which now had a deep fissure in the glass and a minor leak. “I’m sorry, Officer.” He handed the damaged piece to the unsmiling Nowitzke. “A helluva way to start a relationship.” He laughed nervously before gesturing to the rest of the globes. “It’s quite a collection. Where did you get them from?”

“Everywhere,” came the terse reply from the still-annoyed Nowitzke, rifling through his desk looking for something to soak up the leaking liquid. “Started collecting them as a kid, and things just took off. People started buying them for me as gifts when they were on vacation. I bought a couple too. For some reason, they relax me. Overall, I think I have about fifty of them . . . well, forty-nine now. You’re lucky. The one you cracked is from my second wife, soon to be divorced.” Water still trickled through Nowitzke’s fingers from the globe as he found an old coaster in his bottom drawer. He set the damaged dome on the cork mat, returning it to the credenza. After wiping his hands on his pants, Nowitzke began rearranging stacks of files, moving them from his desktop to the floor to clear a line of sight between his chair and the one now occupied by his guest. “And who are you exactly?”

“Excuse me, sir, I’m Sean Cook,” said the young man, immediately offering his hand. “I am a vice president with Wisconsin Specialty Underwriters . . . WSU for short.”

Cook was of average build and height, with a closely cropped beard and smartly dressed in a black suit with a deep blue tie. Nowitzke’s first reaction was that Cook looked like an amalgam of every sketch artist’s wanted suspect . . . the type when the alleged witness was otherwise unremarkable.

“I’m here about the J. Bateman Jewelers burglary,” said Cook, sitting forward in the uncomfortable industrial chair. “I understand you are the lead detective on the investigation.”

“Yeah,” said Nowitzke, relieved he was not going to get a sales pitch.

“Detective, WSU insures Bateman, and this is a huge loss for us. Based on the initial indications, the owner will make a claim for roughly $9.5 million. Do you have any suspects? Have you been to the scene?" asked Cook nervously.

The detective studied Cook, gauging what he was willing to tell the young man. Even though they weren't exactly on the same page, they seemed to have some parallel interests. "Yeah, Mr. Cook, I've been . . ."

"Please, call me Sean."

"Alright, Sean. Yes, I've begun investigating the burglary. Before I get too far into what I know, can you help me with some background information first?"

"Sure," said Sean, who seemed to relax a bit, sliding back from the edge of his chair.

"How long have you insured J. Bateman Jewelers?"

Sean opened a portfolio on his lap and perused his notes. "About two years. I was the underwriter on the account when WSU took it from one of our national competitors. It was a major new client for us, especially since my employer was a newbie in this niche of the business."

"What does that mean . . . niche business? Aren't all insurers pretty much the same?" asked Nowitzke.

"All insurance companies do basically the same things in terms of their operations. However, not all carriers necessarily compete against each other. WSU specializes in insuring jewelry, fine arts, museums, and the like. We operate in specific segments that are different than what companies in the primary market might insure, such as mainstream businesses, small retail, car dealers, that type of thing. In fact, what our company insures might be viewed by other carriers as being high-risk."

"Apparently so, given the size of the loss. So, you're not interested in giving me a competitive quote on a late model Ford Taurus?"

"No, I'm sorry, sir. That's just not our focus."

"Thank God. When did WSU decide to start insuring jewelers?" asked Nowitzke.

"Well, I was hired to build the program from scratch four years ago.

It took some time to get things off the ground before we earned the trust of the jewelry community. But, over the past couple of years, we've made great strides with annual increases in both growth and profits."

"Interesting," said the detective, thinking Sean sounded like one of the financial talking heads on a late-night infomercial. "You said this is a high-risk type of business. Where did *you* learn how to do it? Excuse me, but you look like you were the captain of a high school JV football team a couple of seasons ago."

"I'm older than I look," laughed Sean. "I have an unusual background. My mother and father divorced when I was very young. When they split, I was living with my mother in London, since she was originally from Great Britain. Before I went to university, my mother arranged for me to get a part-time job where she worked, which was for one of the syndicates at Lloyd's. The underwriters I worked with insured fine arts, jewelry, and other high-risk items. I just loved the idea of it all and learned the business from the bottom up. That included the insurance contracts, security systems, and how everything works together. Later, I heard that WSU was looking to expand into the jewelry segment. I contacted them, pitched my ideas, and discussed my background, and I was hired to get the company into that business. It's been a quick four years."

Before Nowitzke could pick up the discussion, Anissa entered the office. "I hope I'm not interrupting your risk assessment, Detective?"

Nowitzke gave his partner a dirty look but remained seated behind his desk, handling introductions from there. However, upon seeing the comely blonde enter the room, Sean took the initiative, literally jumping out of his chair. Even Anissa blushed at Sean's reaction to her as they shook hands before she sat and joined the conversation.

"Anissa, Mr. Cook here is a vice president of the insurance company that insured Bateman's Jewelers," said Nowitzke, trying to get the discussion back on track.

"Really. A vice president?" said Anissa, looking impressed at the young executive.

"It's not that big of a deal," responded Sean sheepishly. "Everyone who's anyone at a bank or an insurance company seems to be a VP. We certainly have more than our share at WSU." He handed his business card to each detective.

"Sean was giving me some of his personal background, and we were about to talk a little more about the burglary. But first, Sean, can you tell us about Bateman's current financial status?"

"It's probably not as up-to-date as it should be," conceded Sean, who looked down at his file. "When I originally underwrote the account, the father, Julian, was in charge. At that point, the books were solid and the account had been highly respected for decades. However, recently, I found out that Malcolm, the son, is now running the business, and that is a cause for concern."

"How so?" asked Anissa.

"With any management change, even from a father to a son, people want to make their mark on the world. In my experience, family transitions can be among the worst changes to a business. Sometimes the next generation doesn't appreciate or respect the hardships of the father, literally taking the business's success for granted. The younger generation never had to make payroll, taking care of the employees before the owners got whatever was left. All the hard work was done to establish the business, but the next generation didn't really know or understand the effort required. Now, don't get me wrong, I've seen these changes work well too, where the kids bring new energy into the business. The question becomes *when* the king decides to put his son on the throne, as it were. The other issue is that when this type of ownership change takes place, the people involved don't necessarily call their insurance company."

"You got any reason to believe that Bateman was involved in the theft?" asked Nowitzke point-blank.

Sean considered his answer for a moment, his eyes rapidly moving left and right. "Probably not, although I would still like to have a forensic accountant look at the books and records. But no, I really don't think so." He looked at both officers. "What about you, Detectives? Do you think Bateman is in any way responsible for the loss?"

Anissa turned toward her boss, deferring to Nowitzke. "Not at this point . . . but it's early," he replied.

Sean nodded, then shifted in his chair. "I do have some questions about the loss though."

"Like?" asked Nowitzke.

"I understand the business has been having issues with security. A series of false alarms and then the lack of response by Bateman."

"Anything else?"

"Is there something you're not telling me?"

"I take it you haven't visited the scene yet?" replied the senior detective.

"No. The business is still not open . . . it's surrounded by yellow police tape."

"We can get you in shortly, but I'll give you a heads-up on a couple of curious details," said Nowitzke. "First, the perpetrators broke into a sandwich shop next door to Bateman's. For several nights, they simulated an intrusion that was picked up by the alarm service. However, when no one could find any malfunction, the false alarms continued until they wore Mr. Bateman down and he chose not to respond. When the burglars knew they were clear, they cut a hole in the wall and entered the jewelry store. In all your experience, have you ever had a loss similar to something like that?"

"No," said Sean hesitantly, shaking his head. "Never."

"How long have you worked in the jewelry insurance industry?" asked Anissa.

Sean searched the ceiling, doing the math. "Ten years total, including when I worked across the pond."

"Okay," said Nowitzke. "There is another little item. Of the eight safes, only four were attacked. Interestingly, they were the only ones with some serious value in them."

"Really?" exclaimed Sean. "That seems suspicious."

"Doesn't it, though?"

Anissa chimed in, "How much insurance coverage did Bateman have?"

"Well, Mrs. Taylor . . ."

"It's Ms. Taylor, but call me Anissa."

Nowitzke rolled his eyes while Sean's face brightened. "Alright, Anissa. That is the strange thing. Bateman is claiming about $9.5 million in losses but has only $5 million in coverage. If he were involved, you'd think he would have had higher limits."

"That's the way we saw it too," responded Anissa.

Nowitzke's desk phone rang. Picking up the receiver, he listened to the voice at the other end as both Sean and Anissa sat quietly, hearing only half of the conversation. Then Nowitzke stood, hung up the phone, and straightened his stained tie. "Wow, we've got royalty on the premises."

Both Anissa and Sean looked bewildered.

"The FBI is in the building wanting to discuss the Bateman case," said Nowitzke.

"Well, I should get going," said Sean, who stood and began moving toward the door. "Thank you both, Detectives."

Both Anissa and Nowitzke shook Sean's hand. "Nis, can you give our friend here our business cards and make arrangements to let him view the scene?"

"Sure, I'd be happy to do that."

Sean was halfway out the door when Nowitzke stopped him. "Wait, one last question before you leave."

"Yeah, sure."

"What do you know about YACS?"

Sean cocked his head, looking totally baffled. After a brief pause trying to gather himself, he responded. "You mean the animal? Like the yak, Y-A-K? Kind of like an ox?"

Nowitzke said nothing for several awkward moments, studying

Sean's face. "You better get going. Let me know about your opinion of the Bateman burglary when you get a chance."

Sean quickly excused himself and was halfway down the hall to the front door while Anissa lingered behind briefly, looking puzzled. "What the hell was that all about?" she asked.

"Tell you later. If you see a lost fed wandering around the building looking for my office, point him my way."

CHAPTER 8

Louis Russell was the epitome of what people envision when they hear the term "FBI agent." Standing at six foot two, Russell had a wiry, muscular build that was covered by an unremarkable, but pressed, brown suit as he entered Nowitzke's office. A born and bred Texan, the agent had twenty years of experience with the Bureau. He had earned the gray hairs on his temples one by one, which stood in sharp contrast to his otherwise jet-black hair that was combed and glued in place by some sort of product. Even though he presented a friendly demeanor, the sharp features on Russell's hawkish face, combined with his personal aura, gave him an intense look. A "fuck with me at your own risk" look. Most of Russell's customers picked up that message loud and clear, except for the occasional miscreant who got a remedial lesson.

Russell's presence was enough to levitate Nowitzke out of his chair and have him standing ramrod straight, like when he had married . . . the first time.

"Detective Nowitzke, it's a pleasure to meet you," said the agent in a thick drawl, extending a hand in greeting while also deftly providing the officer with his business card. "Call me Russ. Everybody does."

"And please call me Chuck. What brings you to Appleton?" asked Nowitzke, sitting back into his desk chair and gesturing Russell to do the same in the chair across from him.

"U.S. Code, Title 18, Part I, Chapter 113, section 2314," said Russell matter-of-factly.

Nowitzke considered the agent, trying to determine if he was serious or having some fun. "Okay . . . please refresh me, if you would?"

"Certainly," said Russell. "It is a federal law regarding the transfer of stolen property across state lines with values of $5,000 or more. Of course, I'm referring to the Bateman burglary. Based upon the FBI's experience with this type of crime, the perpetrators will begin to fence whatever they've taken within hours, generally in places like Miami, Houston, Chicago, or New York. As I understand it, the Bateman loss is in the millions, and the working assumption is that the burglars have already crossed the state line with the stolen merchandise."

"You here to take over the investigation?" Nowitzke asked.

"Hell, no, I've already got a full-time job," said Russell, a smile now appearing on his face. "The lead agent running the FBI's Gem and Jewelry program in New York became aware of the large loss and asked me to contact the local police to offer any assistance. I was in the greater Green Bay area investigating a string of cybercrimes when the Bateman burglary took place. Is there anything I can do for you?" he questioned in a much less official tone.

Nowitzke took the opportunity to bring the fed up to speed on the progress he and Anissa had made. The detective referenced the specifics of how the unusual break-in occurred, the remaining questions around why only those safes with the highest values were attacked, and the conversation with Henry. "We're still in the process of running down several leads," offered the detective. "Would you like to see the scene?"

"Sure. I've got some time."

Russell and Nowitzke arrived at Bateman's in the fed's car just as Anissa was about to return to the office. After introductions were made on the street, the three poked their heads into Bateman's. Sean had already completed his once-over of the premises and left. "When the insurance guy saw what had happened, he was white as a ghost," said Anissa. "I suppose he is responsible for the loss to his company."

Nowitzke served as tour guide, leading Russell through the store and pointing out where access to the store had been gained. A pair of carpenters were busy making final repairs to the wall. The detective then led the agent to the back room to examine the compromised safes, completing their walk-through in ten minutes. Malcolm Bateman was nowhere to be found. However, several members of his team were still cleaning the store. Then Nadia, wearing a black leather miniskirt and tight white top, caught everyone's eye as she zipped between rooms, apparently working on a pending sale. Russell took everything in but remained quiet during the entire visit.

Once outside the store, Nowitzke asked Russell if he had time for lunch. The agent nodded but said little, his brain seemingly elsewhere, as if sorting out all the information he received from Nowitzke and the site. He remained stoic until the three were seated at an outside restaurant down the street, enjoying sweet tea, sandwiches, and the noon sun.

After the waitress left the table, the agent took a long pull of his drink before speaking. "Chuck, have you ever heard of the YACS?"

The question surprised Anissa. She turned to Nowitzke, who was ready with an answer.

"Funny you bring that up. 'YACS' is an acronym for Yugoslavian-Albanian-Croatian-Serb. The YACS was a group of professional technicians who could beat high-quality alarm systems and crack safes. I know they were into stealing cash from ATMs, but I remember them being mostly after diamonds and jewelry."

"You're pretty good, Chuck," replied the surprised fed. "But you used the past tense when referring to this group. Ten or fifteen years ago, they were a much bigger deal, doing major jewelry thefts in New York City on incredibly sophisticated security systems. More than once, the YACS took millions of dollars in gems and jewelry from a single store. Then, when the pickings got slim in the city, they branched out, hitting some jewelers in Chicago."

"I know of them because they also went after some stores in Milwaukee," added Nowitzke. "When I first became a detective there, my boss and I were investigating a couple of big-time burglaries. Once we saw a pattern of how the group entered the various premises and what they could do, we talked with someone at the NYPD about the burglaries. That was the first time I heard anyone use the term YACS. I spent much of the past day trying to remember the acronym, but it finally hit me earlier today."

"The YACS remain active," said Russell. "Their MO is exactly what we just saw at Bateman's. Not too much has changed; however, I would say that this generation of the gang may be less sophisticated. It doesn't take a genius to simulate a series of false alarms to a burglary system. Further, given the availability of tools today, anyone with some level of skill who understands how safes are built can get into them . . . given enough time. However, the one constant is that they are still drawn to big values."

"Russ, did you say that one of the nationalities of the YACS is Albanian?" asked Anissa.

"Chuck did, but yes, ma'am," replied the agent politely with his distinct Texas drawl.

"Chuck, didn't you tell me that Bateman's little sales muffin, Nadia, had immigrated from Albania?"

Nowitzke nodded. Russell chimed in, "Isn't that an interesting coincidence?"

"It's another one of those open items on our list. I don't think there's a huge Albanian population in the greater Appleton area. Based on the look of her fingernails though, I'm guessing Nadia hasn't used a cutting saw lately. However, her being a sales associate in and around a major jewelry theft is curious. Betcha she knows which safes stored the heavy values. In fact, it might be an answer to the mystery about why only certain safes were attacked. But I don't want to jump to any conclusions."

Russ looked back at the detective and nodded his head in agreement. "It definitely deserves some attention though. Frankly, you both sound like you're on top of this case," responded the fed as he finished his lunch. "The FBI is always available to provide you with any assistance. Let me make one additional suggestion that might help relative to the missing diamonds. Ask Bateman for his inventory of lost merchandise that included any diamonds larger than, say, a carat or more."

"Okay?" responded Nowitzke in the form of a question. "How does that help?"

"Generally, those are the stones that may have been printed."

"Printed?" questioned Anissa.

"Well, each diamond essentially has its own fingerprint based on its size, weight, and internal imperfections," explained Russell. "Some, but not many, go through the process where they are certified and registered in the industry. If someone is trying to fence the larger diamonds, we might get a positive hit. If that takes place, the FBI might be able to assist you in finding out how the diamonds moved from Appleton to points unknown and potentially generate another lead. Or we could make a recovery."

"Seriously? This never came up on any of my prior cases. This has worked for the FBI?" questioned Nowitzke.

"Yes. But like I said, it generally only works with larger diamonds. Of course, it's not something that works every time either. A fence might choose to recut a very large diamond, for example, if there was something like a five-carat stone that would stand out from the rest or may be even recognized in the jewelry community. Recutting it into a pair of two-plus carat diamonds diminishes the size of the resulting stones, but also destroys the original fingerprint, making the new ones untraceable. The fence is also willing to take less in profit since he's paid only pennies on the dollar for the diamond in the first place. He still comes out way ahead while minimizing his risk."

"Unbelievable. So basically, the fences are jewelers too?" asked Nowitzke.

"Pretty much. They know the product, the value, and all the tricks of the trade to make money while not getting caught. At the same time, it doesn't take a rocket scientist to know who is likely doing the fencing either."

"What is a fence likely to get for a stolen diamond?" asked Anissa.

"Of course, it depends on the quality of the stone. But you can figure roughly about twenty to twenty-five cents on the dollar. However, the fence then sells those diamonds gradually, working them back into the legitimate jewelry world. Remember, for the most part, they are untraceable."

"Thanks for the primer," said Nowitzke.

Russell picked up the tab and excused himself, needing to get to Milwaukee for a late afternoon meeting, leaving Nowitzke and Anissa to ponder their next steps over another glass of tea.

"When should we talk with Nadia?" asked Anissa.

"When will you be ready?" answered Nowitzke.

"Me? Why me?"

"Listen, based on what I've seen of this young lady, I'm concerned I'll become distracted, to say the least, if I sat down with her. She is a potentially important witness, and sending me in to talk with her is like shipping me back to junior high school. But she's got no power over you. I will be your second at the conversation though."

"Marvelous," said Anissa disgustedly.

"Look, this is important. I think you're our best option with Nadia. What, are you pissed off that Russ called you 'ma'am'?"

"You caught that too, huh?" said the agitated detective. "It's becoming a trend."

"Jeez, Nis, it's a Texas thing . . . combined with FBI politeness. Nothing more. What's bugging you?"

"Nothing I want to discuss today."

Nowitzke rode with Anissa in silence back to their office. As she pulled into the parking lot, Anissa spoke with resolve. "Let's catch Nadia cold tomorrow at the beginning of the day."

"Fair enough," replied Nowitzke. "That will give me time to reach out to my old buddy, Arturo."

"Who?"

"Arturo Copeland. My boss in Milwaukee when I started my career. He's had some jewelry cases over the years, and I'd like to see what he remembers about the YACS, if anything."

Nowitzke excused himself, moving to his office. After making several calls to both Milwaukee PD and Copeland's cell without connecting, he left a message, telling Copeland that he would be in town the following week and asking about getting together for dinner.

Nowitzke closed his office door, took a large crystal snow globe of a German village off the cabinet, and sat back in his chair. Giving the globe a shake, he put his feet up on the desk and began to study how the glitter swirled and collected. It was as close to Germany as he would ever get. Nowitzke replayed in his mind the various interviews of those involved with the case, the evidence, and findings to date. He also had a mental punch list for follow-up items. He was pleased Anissa had made the connection between Nadia and the YACS. Proud like a father whose daughter had blossomed into what he knew she could become. His protégé had grown significantly over the two years they had worked together. He was also ashamed of himself for thinking he might not be professional enough to conduct an interview with Nadia. This had never been an issue before. Maybe it was just his mental state given his pending divorce. Anyway, the facts seemed reasonably straightforward, even though there was much work to be done. To some extent, he always hated the feeling of not knowing something early in an investigation.

Nowitzke replaced the globe on its shelf and began to restack the files he had moved from his desk to accommodate his meeting with Sean. Halfway through the process, Anissa knocked, entering the office. Her demeanor seemed much improved after their most recent conversation. "What's up?" he asked his young partner.

"Nothing much. Sorry for being a bitch earlier today."

"No problem. I was just worried about you. You know if I can ever help you out, all you gotta do is ask."

"I know." Anissa hemmed and hawed, looking around the

detective's office like she was trying to summon the nerve to tell her father something he didn't necessarily want to hear.

Dropping the last of the files on the desk, Nowitzke straightened up and begged the question. "Alright, what's on your mind?"

Anissa closed her eyes and sucked in a deep breath. "I just got a call from Sean Cook. You know, the insurance underwriter. He asked me out to dinner tonight."

Nowitzke sat back down and studied the ceiling while Anissa remained standing nervously by the door. "Nis, you don't have any conflict seeing Sean off duty. You know the rules if he's looking for any information." He hesitated for a moment, then asked, "Why him?"

"Well . . ." she said, gathering herself, "he's single, and so am I. I just thought he was interesting."

"So, why are you telling me this? You don't confide anything else about your personal life to me."

"Frankly, I don't know. I guess I just wanted you to know. I got the impression you didn't like him."

"It's not that. It's just szosty zmysl."

"Not your stupid Nowitzke Polish sixth sense." Anissa rolled her eyes.

"Yeah, well, you asked. Can't put my finger on it, but I got some questions about Mr. Cook. Something about him sets off alarm bells in my head."

"Seriously," replied Anissa. "But Nadia didn't?"

"No. Nadia set off alarms bells in a different part of my body."

Anissa returned a nauseated look. "Great, I just threw up in my mouth," she said.

"Listen, have your date with Sean," he replied, tossing her a pack of breath mints. "Just remember, it's a school night and you're our ace interviewer in the morning."

Anissa smiled at the comment and left, just as Nowitzke's phone rang.

"Arturo, thanks for returning my call . . ."

CHAPTER 9

Anissa arrived at the office the next morning to find Nowitzke with his head down over his laptop, using the hunt-and-peck method to complete his notes from the prior day. She stood quietly in the open doorway, watching him struggle. According to her math, Nowitzke was averaging five keys before looking for the backspace button to fix at least two strokes. She also noticed that Chuck's large Dunkin' coffee cup was sitting in its own puddle and the detective had dragged his arm through the wash, staining the right sleeve of his previously clean shirt.

"Morning, Chuck," she said cheerfully. "Do you want me to drive?"

Still looking down, Nowitzke was a mix of concentration and cursing amid his whirlwind twelve words per minute before barking, "One second." Anissa patiently stood in the doorway, smiling, her presence putting even more pressure on the struggling detective to complete his work. After making a final keystroke and closing the laptop, Nowitzke stood and stretched.

"The second time went much better." He had failed to save version one of his work that morning.

Nowitzke pulled on a brown sports coat with felt elbow patches. The jacket looked like it had once been owned by a university professor. Anissa did give her boss points, however, for the matching black pants and tie. He had roughly three days' growth of beard, and his hair had not seen a comb in at least that long. With the late spring day, Anissa wore a conservative black-and-white striped dress with black high heels. Her 9mm Beretta pistol fit comfortably in her large Shinola bag. After entering her Audi, they had traveled less than a mile before Nowitzke broke the silence.

"How was your date with Steve the insurance nerd?"

"His name is Sean," she corrected.

"Okay. So, how was your date with Sean the insurance nerd?"

Anissa smiled and shook her head. "I had a great time last night. He was a gentleman, and I'm not going to take the bait from you this morning."

"Did he dazzle you with talking about actuarial tables and premium calculations? Or his excitement about reading Harry Potter?"

"Hey, shut up. I like Harry Potter. This from a guy with a snow globe collection. If you must know, we went out for Italian, had an after-dinner drink, and I went home."

"Alone?"

"Don't be such a dickhead," she responded as she pulled to the curb in front of the jewelry store.

Bateman's had officially reopened that morning. As the officers entered the store, Malcolm spotted the pair and made a beeline for them. "Detectives Nowitzke and Taylor," he greeted them cordially, looking primarily at Anissa. "To what do I owe this honor? Have you made any recoveries of my merchandise yet?"

"Good morning, Mr. Bateman," said Anissa on cue. "And no, we haven't. We'd like to have a moment with Nadia, if she's available."

"Nadia?" questioned Bateman. "Why Nadia?"

"It's part of our investigation. Is she here?"

"Of course. Let me get her. She's in our stock room."

Both officers perused the men's watches case as they waited, trying to guess the cost of each.

After a minute, a sultry woman's voice said, "Can I take something out for you, Officer Nowitzke?"

The officer bit his tongue, stifling a snappy comeback before Anissa intervened on his behalf.

"No, we simply need a little bit of your time," said the female officer.

That did not stop the beautiful young sales consultant from stepping behind the case. As conservatively as Anissa was dressed, Nadia was at the other end of the spectrum. She wore her shoulder-length dark brown hair parted down the middle, setting off flawless skin and pouting lips that were painted bright red. Wearing a short grey skirt, matching high heels, and a white blouse with a plunging neckline, Nadia put on quite the show as she bent down to reach the front of the display before pulling out a Cartier watch and placing it on Nowitzke's wrist. As the detective considered the timepiece, he also was transfixed by Nadia's blue eyes. Anissa waited patiently for her turn as Nadia went through her pitch, showing off the features of the gold watch and explaining the movement and construction.

"You have such a thick, manly wrist," she said. "It looks perfect on you, Detective."

Knowing that if you have to ask the price, it's too expensive, Nowitzke finally crumbled. "How much?"

The young woman paused as if she was planning on making a sale to the police officer. "$33,000 plus sales tax. But for you, Detective, I could let you have it for $31,000," she said proudly.

In an instant, Nowitzke wanted nothing more than to have the watch taken from his wrist as Anissa intervened again. "Nadia, we have some questions for you."

"I know. Mr. Bateman said we could use his office." After replacing the watch in the showcase, Nadia grabbed Nowitzke by the arm, leading him to the luxurious office. Once inside, she looked at him and ignored Anissa. "What can I do for you, sir?"

Feeding off all the energy provided to her by Nadia, Anissa took control. "I'll be conducting the interview," she said, gaining the full attention of the saleswoman. Nowitzke dropped into one of the heavy leather side chairs as his charge took over. He feigned disinterest while listening intently.

Nadia sat opposite Nowitzke and crossed her legs. Anissa started slowly, confirming information about how Nadia had emigrated to the country from Albania and taken the job at Bateman's. Nadia calmly and coolly answered all of Anissa's questions. Yes, she had worked on the day of the burglary. Yes, she had put the merchandise away that evening because it was her turn to close the store. Yes, the alarm system was activated when she left the premises.

Halfway through the interview, Nowitzke's phone rang. Excusing himself, he left the room, moving to the front porch of the store to take the call.

"Chuck, it's Teddy Shaw from Forensics calling about the blood sample from the jewelry burglary the other night. First, we got a viable DNA sample. Unfortunately, we didn't get a match from the National DNA Database. We did, however, turn up something unusual with some other testing. The suspect's blood type is AB negative, which is very rare. In fact, less than one percent of all Caucasians and even fewer African Americans have that type."

"Interesting," said Nowitzke. "Nice work."

"There's something else. Through our testing, we found that your perp has aplastic anemia."

"Huh? Aplastic what?"

"Aplastic anemia. It's a disease that requires someone to get regular blood transfusions. Actually, a lot of them because their bone marrow isn't doing its job. This disease was once considered fatal, but now with the different kinds of treatments, most people who contract it can now live a long life. But this blood type might be an issue in finding a long-term strategy to manage the problem because getting a matching marrow donor might be hard."

Nowitzke sat on the top step of the porch, scribbling furiously to keep up with Shaw. During their conversation, several of Bateman's customers had to step around the detective to enter or leave the store.

"What kind of symptoms would someone with aplastic anemia have?"

"Probably things like nausea, shortness of breath, chest pains, weakness, dizziness, and bruising and bleeding."

"Thanks, Teddy. I owe you one."

After the conversation ended, Nowitzke mulled over this newfound knowledge as he found his way back to Malcolm's office, where the conversation between the two women continued. Nowitzke dropped back into his chair as Nadia smiled at him before she recrossed her legs.

Anissa asked some point-blank questions of the saleswoman.

"Did you participate in the burglary?"

"No," responded Nadia, whose previous answers had been more expansive. Now, she replied curtly, largely in single words.

"Do you know of anyone who was involved with the theft?"

"No."

With the meeting now pushing an hour, Anissa motioned for Nowitzke to step out of the office with her. Finding themselves back on the front porch, Anissa looked at her partner. "Nadia's a pretty cool customer. After you left to take your call, she denied everything about being in any way connected to the burglary, but . . ." she said, hesitating.

"But . . ."

"But the little woman in my head keeps telling me that Nadia is holding back."

"Well, how hard can you push her? Or should we tell her we're done for now but may have questions later?" asked Nowitzke.

"Let's do the latter," Anissa concluded. "Maybe we'll get some additional information as we proceed with the investigation."

"By the way, I got a call from Teddy Shaw about the DNA you recovered from the scene," said Nowitzke. The senior detective briefly stopped talking, his brain sorting out what Shaw had just told him. "Let me throw a couple of questions at her. I'd like to catch you both cold. Watch her closely and follow my lead."

When the detectives reentered Bateman's office, Nadia had not moved. She still looked calm and collected when Nowitzke sat down in front of her. Anissa remained standing off to the side to watch the balance of the proceedings.

Nowitzke took Nadia's hand, looking into her eyes contritely. "Ms. Belushi, we appreciate your candid answers. Also, we're sorry if we've inconvenienced you in any way. Just trying to do our jobs."

Nadia stood, pulled her hand away, and straightened her skirt. "No apologies are necessary, Detective. If you are ever in the market for a luxury watch, please make sure you see me," she said as she glanced toward the door.

"I will," replied the detective as he rose to his feet. "By the way, I think we just got a break. The call I just got was good news. We're a big step closer to catching the burglars. One of them was scratched on some carpet staples after they cut through the wall into Bateman's. We got an excellent DNA sample. And we got even more. Turns out, the person involved has a rare blood type, AB negative."

"Oh," said Nadia, sitting back down as the detective continued to provide details.

From her vantage point, Anissa wondered why Nowitzke would disclose these facts about the suspect to Nadia, who remained a person of interest.

"Yeah, our forensics team found that this particular person has a potentially fatal blood disease called... aplastic anemia," said Nowitzke, glancing down at his notes. "Based upon what I was told, the suspect will need several transfusions and soon. The person might also have nausea, bleeding, headaches, and dizziness. It's just a matter of time before this person develops some serious health issues. Anyway, you can see we're working hard to bring the bad guys to justice. Thanks again for your help." He put his notebook into his jacket pocket.

Nadia lingered in her chair for a moment, thinking through what Nowitzke had said. "Thank you, Detective," she said absently as she stood and left the room.

Nowitzke motioned towards Anissa, and the two of them walked out of Bateman's and back to the Audi. Once in Anissa's car, she looked at her boss. "Chuck, why the hell would you disclose that kind of detail to Nadia when we still haven't cleared her as a suspect?"

"Tell you what. Pull your car around the back of the jewelry store. But stay a good distance away, and then I'll explain."

Anissa circled the block and found a parking space on a crowded street but with a sightline to Bateman's back entrance.

"Sit tight for a moment and watch," said Nowitzke. At 11:00 a.m., ten minutes after their departure, both officers watched as Nadia left Bateman's and climbed into a silver Toyota Prius. She pulled out of the parking lot and turned in the same direction that Anissa's car was pointed. "A little early for lunch. Tail her, Nis, but keep your distance. Let's see where she's going."

"You set her up, Chuck. Didn't you?"

"I took a flyer on the Albanian connection. Considering our little corner of the world, having a young Albanian woman this close in proximity to a professional burglary by the YACS is too much of a coincidence. Everything I told her is real, though. But for all I know she might be going to her boyfriend's house for a quickie. I assume Nadia is not heading home?"

"No, unless she's taking the long way. According to what she told me, her address is in the opposite direction."

"Where are you taking us, Nadia?" Nowitzke asked rhetorically.

Anissa kept her distance, following Nadia for twenty minutes before she pulled into a complex of newer condominiums on the north side of town. Each structure appeared well-maintained, a combination of red brick veneer and white vinyl siding. Based on what the detectives could see, every condo on the main floor had a patio while the units on the second level had small decks. The grounds boasted young maple trees placed around broad lawns that had been recently mowed. Still watching from Anissa's Audi, the officers saw Nadia park and walk to the entrance of a building distinguished by a large 42. She paused.

Then, after hitting a buzzer, she waited briefly before pulling open the glass front door and stepping inside.

"Any chance she might walk through one building to get into another behind it, just to throw us off?" said Anissa to Nowitzke.

"I'd say no. This type of building looks like it has just enough security to keep out your garden variety bad guys and Jehovah's Witnesses. My assumption is you probably have to know someone to get buzzed in."

Roughly a half hour later, the officers observed Nadia exit building 42, enter her vehicle, and leave. Even from where they sat, it looked like she had been crying.

"Should I follow her?" Anissa asked.

"No, I think we have enough information if we need to find her again. I'm more interested in who lives in the building. My impression is we just moved up the suspect ladder to someone more important."

"How should we go about screening the residents of that condo building?" questioned Anissa.

"Let's see if we can find the super or whoever's in charge."

CHAPTER 10

Thirty minutes later, Anissa and Nowitzke were sitting across a desk from Ben Crawford, who was responsible for the entire eight-building campus. The office was a cookie-cutter special with cheap modern furniture. The only distinguishing features decorating the small space were a print of wild geese hanging on the wall behind Crawford and a fake fern on a stand in the corner. Although he was the manager, Crawford was not the stereotypical "super" that Nowitzke had become acquainted with from his experiences in Milwaukee. Eschewing the dirty white tank top and a back covered in thick hair, Crawford was professionally, but casually, dressed in a black golf shirt, khaki pants, and boat shoes. After seeing each detective's creds and learning the reason for their inquiry, Crawford pulled up the particulars on the residents of building 42.

"We have six condos in that structure, all of which are occupied. There are two families who have been here for several years, each in their own unit. Neither have ever caused a problem." Scrolling down through the occupant list on his silver laptop, Crawford studied the details of each, trying to help the detectives. "There are two single females, each in their own condos, with a disabled man in a first-floor unit. Each of those residents have lived in the complex for at least two lease cycles. Oh, and the final unit is occupied by a young single man."

"Can you give us more details about a couple of the residents, Mr. Crawford?" asked Anissa. "Tell us more about the single women."

Crawford replied with a laugh. "Detective Taylor, if you're investigating a jewelry store burglary, I don't think they're potential suspects."

"Really? Based on what?"

"Well, given that both are widows. Mrs. Morton is in her eighties and just had a hip replacement. Mrs. Crist is also approaching her eighties and unable to climb stairs. Probably not your expert safe crackers . . . even fifty years ago," said Crawford smugly.

"What's the story on the single guy? The one who's not disabled?" asked Nowitzke.

"He's in Unit Four, located on the second floor. Been in the condo for about six months. Pays his rent on time. Seems nice, very polite, and extremely quiet."

"You know, that's pretty much what they say about every serial killer after the fact," offered Nowitzke.

Crawford paged down, concentrating on the notes in the man's original application. "I believe this guy works at a local hardware store."

"And does he have a name?"

"The name on the lease is Musa Besnik."

"What does he drive?" asked Anissa.

"Besnik owns a red Chevy Malibu. License number HU6 8138 according to his condo application."

"Do you know Besnik's nationality?" asked Nowitzke.

"No. We don't ask for that information, and we don't discriminate against anyone," said Crawford exactly as he had been trained by the condo complex's lawyers.

"Yeah, I know. We're all God's children," replied Nowitzke. "How many entrances to each condo?"

"Just one."

"Can you give us the building access code so he doesn't have to buzz us in?"

"Sure."

As Nowitzke and Anissa walked across the parking lot back to the car, they pondered their next steps.

"What's the plan, Chuck? Should we confront Besnik?" asked Anissa.

"I think we have to. After I gave Nadia the details about our suspect, I pretty much boxed us in. However, since Nadia's first instinct was to leave work to see Besnik, presumably to warn him, there's gotta be some sort of relationship between the two. When we saw her crying after leaving his place, that cemented a connection for me. Let's poke the bear and see what happens."

Nowitzke punched in the code provided by Crawford and held the door for Anissa. As he climbed the stairs toward Unit Four, Nowitzke concluded that every multiunit apartment or condo was essentially the same. Perhaps the only point of differentiation was the smell, whether it was food being cooked by one of the residents or the level of mustiness in the hallways. Not knowing exactly what to expect from Besnik, Nowitzke pulled his Glock 19 Luger from his holster. Anissa pulled her Beretta from her bag and moved right of the doorway. Standing to the left of the frame, Nowitzke knocked on the door, announcing, "Appleton Police Department," and waited.

Nowitzke gripped his gun a little harder as he waited for a response. He could hear activity coming from inside the condo but no rustling moving toward the door. "Nothing," he said to Anissa. "Shit, someone's in there, but ignoring us." Looking at his partner, Nowitzke rapped harder the second time, accompanied by an amped-up, "Appleton PD, Mr. Besnik. Please open up!" The reaction was the sound of more indistinct activity from inside the apartment. "Nis, call for backup. Since you've got heels on, looks like I'll be our door kicker today."

Nowitzke sized up the quality and heft of the door, mentally walking through how he would kick open the entrance while keeping his gun at the ready. Having made the commitment, the clock in his head began to count down. *Three. Two. One.*

As Nowitzke's foot slammed open the door with a heavy thump, he heard breaking glass, a sickening crunch, and then a man screaming. His brain running on overdrive, the detective stepped into the room and followed his training, visually sweeping the apartment to assess any threats. Moving in the direction of the screams, he fast-walked across the main room of the apartment to the patio window and yelled to Anissa, who was clearing the back rooms of the place. "Nis, Besnik just jumped through the second-floor patio window!" he yelled. "Get down to the front lawn *now*." As he turned toward the apartment door, Anissa sprinted past him after kicking off her shoes, taking two and three steps down at a time. Stepping closer toward the window, Nowitzke felt the breeze of the warm air entering the condo as the drapes billowed. The detective remained cautious about Besnik until he saw the man lying on the manicured lawn fifteen feet below, now unconscious.

By the time Nowitzke made it to the lawn, Anissa had cuffed the jumper, who was now coming to. Anissa quickly searched Besnik for weapons but found none. She then realized Besnik had broken both of his legs with his leap; the sight of the bone protruding through the skin of the suspect's lower left leg drew most of her attention. Moving into shock, Besnik's yelps mimicked the siren of the approaching ambulance.

"Well, I don't think Besnik's a flight risk any longer," said Nowitzke, looking up to the second floor. "We'll need to get a warrant to search his place. By the way, I don't see either of your feet bleeding. How did you miss all the glass?"

"Beats me. I'd write it off to clean living, Chuck!" she said with a grin before turning her attention back to her suspect. She studied Besnik as the first responders arrived and began their work. Fortunately, they gave the man a painkiller to dull his excruciating pain and quell his screeching. Using surgical scissors, the EMTs cut off Besnik's jeans and his t-shirt to get a better look at his wounds.

"Chuck, check out Besnik's upper arm. He's covered in deep scratches and cuts that are still reasonably fresh, but not from this fall."

"Besnik just became our prime suspect," said Nowitzke. "Read him his rights and find out where they're transporting him. He'll probably need surgery to fix that leg and be out of commission for a while."

Taking in Nowitzke's assessment, Anissa looked from the lawn back up to the height of the second floor of the apartment building. "Maybe . . . maybe not. I'm sure you weren't expecting Besnik to do a cannonball out his patio window."

"You're right. Give Chief Clark a heads-up about posting a uniform outside Besnik's hospital room." Nowitzke continued his stream of thought. "I'll get a couple of patrolmen over to Bateman's to pick up Nadia. She's involved in this somehow. At a minimum, she must have given Besnik some insider information about the store before the burglary. If she's not there, we'll post an all-points bulletin to locate her."

CHAPTER 11

Although Nowitzke's game plan seemingly covered all bases, the outcomes were far less than expected. Anissa trailed the ambulance to Hobart Thompson Memorial Hospital to keep an eye on Besnik while a warrant was delivered to Nowitzke, who remained on the scene. However, the subsequent search of Besnik's condo yielded no evidence of any crime or anything incriminating to the suspect. Following the search, Nowitzke received a call from one of the uniforms at Bateman's Jewelers.

"Detective, Officer Hicks here."

"Yeah, Kenny. What's up?" asked Nowitzke.

"We went to Bateman's Jewelers to pick up your suspect. Looks like we missed her, Chuck. Her boss, Malcolm Bateman, told us that she returned from lunch in tears, quit her job, and just left. He seemed pretty upset by what happened too."

Fuck, fuck, fuck!

"We asked Bateman for Ms. Belushi's address, and I went directly to her apartment to see if I could catch up with her there."

"And?" asked Nowitzke, listening intently as he sat on the front steps of the apartment building.

"When we got there, the front door was open, and it looked like the bedroom had been ransacked, you know, kind of like she quickly packed a bag and bolted. She's disappeared."

Son of a bitch! "Thanks, Kenny. I appreciate you busting your ass to cover all the bases."

"Sorry, man. Do you need anything else?"

"No. I'll post an APB for the woman shortly," said Nowitzke, clicking off his phone with a sour look on his face. *Where have you gone, Nadia?*

The only upside for the detective was that they had their guy in custody. DNA evidence should confirm Musa Besnik as being part of the crew that took down Bateman's. With the end of the day looming, Nowitzke called Anissa to update her and see how things were progressing at the hospital.

"Nis, what's the story on Besnik?"

"He just went into surgery. Based upon the conversation between the doctors, Besnik will be under the knife for hours. A significant penalty for not sticking the landing."

"You okay with overwatch on him for now? Has the chief assigned someone to back you up?"

"Yes, I've got it covered. You're out of town tomorrow for your final divorce hearing in Milwaukee, right?"

"Yeah. Can't wait. With all the lawyers working the clock and spending a day with my soon-to-be ex, having surgery for a compound fracture sounds like an upgrade to me."

Anissa laughed. "Well, take care. I'll see you in a couple of days," she said from the hospital's waiting room. She planned to pass the time with a Starbucks and the new edition of *Condé Nast*, hoping to find a remote destination for a fall vacation before her relief officer arrived later that night.

CHAPTER 12

After a long day, Nowitzke slogged up the exterior stairs of his place, carefully balancing his pizza on a brown paper bag containing a six-pack of beer. The best seven-course meal he could afford. Aside from a rescue cat he named Sinker, Chuck Nowitzke lived alone in a walk-up apartment over the now ramshackle home of an elderly woman named Alma Thornton. Alma and her husband, Fred, built the home together after he returned from serving in the European theatre in World War II. Fred, a laborer at a local paper mill by day, constructed the house as his second job, taking three years to finish the task. When complete, the structure was magnificent, containing features and design elements far beyond those in the basic tract homes purchased by most returning GIs.

However, within five years of completion, Fred passed away from cancer. With Alma having no children or means, the home fell into disrepair over time. To survive, she had the house reconfigured so that she could take in boarders, albeit one at a time. Most people who lived in the apartment lasted an average of just under a year, given Miss Alma's stringent set of rules.

When she first talked with Nowitzke by phone on a Sunday afternoon about renting the upstairs room, Alma was thrilled by the potential of having one of Appleton's finest living above her. She was barely able to conceal her disappointment, though, when the paunchy and unkempt officer arrived for a showing. Nonetheless, she was willing to trade off her vision of a dashing detective for Nowitzke, deciding that having the protection of any officer was worth it, assuming the man would abide by her rules.

From Nowitzke's point of view, Alma fit the profile of having an undetermined, yet strict, religious affiliation. In his mind, this blue-haired woman, who stood just short of five feet tall, could easily have been a yardstick-wielding nun in a prior life.

The apartment was shabby, having been last painted during the Eisenhower administration. But it was furnished and included heat, a big plus for Nowitzke, considering Wisconsin winters. Nowitzke told his potential landlord that he liked the setup of the place since he sometimes worked odd hours and could come and go without disturbing Miss Alma, as she liked to be called.

Then came the terms from Miss Alma. Nowitzke did his best to focus and not utter a peep as she laid out her rules to the hungover detective, who managed to keep both glazed eyes open and not puke on her gladiolas as she talked.

"Detective, I don't believe in leases. But I want the rent paid to me promptly on the first of each month."

Nowitzke nodded blankly and agreed to an amount that was well below the going rate. *What's the catch?*

"There will be no smoking in my home."

"Miss Alma, we're off to a good start. I quit several years ago." Nowitzke relaxed but reached for the phantom pack of cigarettes in his breast pocket, suddenly feeling the need as his new landlord continued.

"Like many of the public buildings in the area, I have a no-gun policy. However, as a peace officer, I understand that you need to carry a weapon. Is that correct?"

"Yes, ma'am." Nowitzke pulled out his Glock to show the old woman.

"Please put it away. It scares me to think people need to carry handguns."

"Yes, ma'am. Me too," said the officer as he replaced his weapon.

"Detective, I want to make this clear. You are not allowed to have any women in the apartment."

"None? Not even my niece?" offered Nowitzke snarkily, even though he had none.

Miss Alma stammered briefly. "You know what I mean. No girlfriends. There will be no fornicating in my house."

Nowitzke gave Miss Alma as thoughtful a look as he could muster as he considered his pending divorce. "Right now, that's not a challenge for me."

Then, Miss Alma scrutinized the face of her potential tenant and cocked her head. "I will tolerate no alcohol of any kind in my home."

Nowitzke gulped. *There has to be an exemption for police officers, especially since this isn't Lent.* He considered the rule briefly but said nothing. Throughout his life, he generally thought of rules as merely guidelines, and this one seemed to have all the markings. With that, he looked at Miss Alma, who was waiting for a response, and mustered a nod, not wanting her to smell the booze still on his breath from the prior evening.

"Finally, Detective, no pets are allowed."

Nowitzke thought this through. Just a week prior, he had been walking on an avenue in downtown Appleton when he heard a weak distress cry coming from a storm drain. Looking into the sewer, he saw a scared and drenched kitten splashing and fighting for its life in a growing pool of water. The officer bent down, putting his stubby arm into the opening as far as he could. Not because he wanted a cat. He wasn't a cat person. But he couldn't just stand by and watch a living thing drown either. Eventually, he was able to reach far enough to pull the scrawny tabby from a watery grave. Naming it Sinker, he resolved to turn the animal over to a shelter the following morning. However, overnight, he became enamored with the kitten's purring as it snuggled against the hardened officer for warmth. Sinker became a family member and Nowitzke's first pet. Upon hearing Miss Alma's final rule, he mentally vowed to get a sweater for Sinker with the word

"Service" printed on it if push came to shove. Nonetheless, Nowitzke again nodded silent assent to Miss Alma.

They had come to terms, in theory. Just like the United States and Russia, neither on the same page. But despite Miss Alma's early suspicions about Nowitzke, things seemed to work out between the two, over time.

****

As Nowitzke contemplated what was about to happen the next day, he drained the last of his beers, crushing the can. Finally, the resolution of his second divorce. He would become a two-time offender. However, after running the gauntlet tomorrow, he would also finally be free of his last ties to Milwaukee. He had no fond memories of the place, even though he had grown up there. Time to pull the plug.

Nowitzke found Sinker on his way to his bed, stripped down to his underwear, and wrapped himself in a quilt before snapping off the cheap light on his headboard, resolving to get up early and pack before heading south to Milwaukee.

CHAPTER 13

Nowitzke loosened his tie as he quietly sipped his second beer, relaxing on the outdoor patio of his former preferred watering hole in downtown Milwaukee. It was a combination of big-time chic and Wisconsin cheese, as evidenced by the hanging owl lamps strung on the outdoor wooden posts surrounding the beer garden. Following a brutal winter and what passed for spring in Wisconsin, he closed his eyes, letting some of the first warm breezes of summer float through him and on down the avenue. Located literally just off the street, the outdoor seating area was an assault on the senses of its patrons. Traffic noise ebbed and flowed as vehicles moved down the avenue, generating a smell that was a potpourri of diesel fuel, exhaust, and cigarettes. A part of Nowitzke was the big city, but enough was enough, and he felt no qualms about leaving it.

Considering it was a Friday afternoon, the coming weekend seemed to have energized the businesspeople that were escaping from their offices and emptying out of the high-rises directly into street bars, seeking an adult beverage or two before heading home. Nowitzke loved the summer. As a trained detective, he was the consummate people watcher. Well, mostly a girl watcher. *Summer brings shorter skirts and higher heels.* But he was just a watcher, especially now. He couldn't afford to be much more.

After spending the bulk of the day with attorneys, this was easily the high point. Nowitzke's first drink was a rescue beer going down so fast he barely tasted it. His ex's lawyers peppered him with questions, assertions, and bullshit allegations, as the detective called them. However, the matter was now resolved. No more payments to his ex-wife. No more dealing with attorneys and their fees, aside from the eight hours of time on the spinning wheel incurred by his lawyer for the day's work. A small price to pay for his freedom. Nowitzke had presented himself well, proudly standing his ground. Now was a time to celebrate.

As he sipped beer number two, he reflected on where life was taking him. He enjoyed the slower pace working with the Appleton Police Department. Although Appleton had its share of homicides, deviants, and major crimes that challenged him as an investigator, it was somehow different. Maybe it was the attitude? People from the smaller town were friendly, smiling when they said hi. The locals also didn't seem hell-bent on achieving an annual personal best in murders, unlike the sense he got from those in the larger metro area.

Memories, good and bad, filled his head. Shortly after joining MPD, the young Nowitzke had set his sights on moving from patrol officer to becoming a detective. It was a dangerous route for the young man, who volunteered for every risky assignment. He had always done his best to follow procedures as closely as he could, sometimes incurring the wrath of his superiors when he didn't. However, what he lacked in attention to internal details, Nowitzke made up for with results, making numerous high-profile collars. In doing so, he caught the eye of a rising detective named Arturo Copeland. Copeland became Nowitzke's mentor, helping him move quickly through the ranks before earning the detective shield he coveted. Copeland also moved up in the internal structure, becoming MPD's most decorated detective and earning honors for his work.

The two men became fast friends and drinking buddies. Copeland was with Nowitzke when he met Susan Foster, a vivacious and quick-witted barmaid at their favorite tavern after work. Later, Arturo served as Nowitzke's best man at his wedding to Foster, as well as his confidant when the marriage went down in flames eighteen months later. Nowitzke often referred to Susan as his trophy wife, his "best in show."

Copeland was also with Nowitzke when he met his second wife on the rebound, Andrea Bennett, a buxom redhead who worked as a stripper in a local gentlemen's club. After weeks of plying her with twenty-dollar bills, Andrea agreed to see Nowitzke off the clock. Following a whirlwind courtship of thirty days, they were married in Reno within a day of Chuck's divorce, with Arturo again serving as his best man. Unfortunately, Nowitzke's marriage to Andrea literally went tits-up months later, as he joked. As his second marriage circled the drain, Nowitzke likened Andrea to a classic car. Fun to ride, but expensive, especially considering that the closer you got, the more you could see all the scratches and dents. But clearly the relentless schedule and demands of being a homicide detective would have been enough to kill off a legitimate marriage.

Now that chapter of his life was over, and he was excited to get a fresh start. And who better to begin a new phase with than his old buddy, Arturo.

Watching the Brewer game on multiple screens, Nowitzke smiled, especially when the busty young waitress asked if he wanted another beer. "Absolutely," replied the detective. He had another hour to kill before meeting his friend for dinner. It would be a night for the ages.

CHAPTER 14

Riley Britten, owner of Lockett's Jewelers, didn't know what was going on, but the result was palpable on his daily sales. Wedging open the front doors of his store just before noon, the warm air entered, bringing with it a steady supply of current and new customers. Britten's commissioned staff of six recognized the opportunity, skipping lunch to handle the flow of business. But the people in the store were more than just lookers. They were buyers with available credit card limits. Even several of those who shopped hard and decided to wait to make a purchase did so for no more than an hour before returning to spend their rent money for the next six months on the bauble of the moment.

Lockett's was an old-line Milwaukee jeweler. Under new ownership, the store got a facelift, transforming itself with chrome, glass, and special lighting along with a new approach to appeal to young up-and-comers. Britten, a third-generation legacy from his grandfather, Oscar Lockett, maintained the high-traffic location and expanded sales lines with luxury watches, rings, and diamonds. But Britten went on to make some more notable changes. He insisted that his staff be professionally dressed and groomed. Then, he expected that each member of his team be educated in the various lines of jewelry and stones. Britten even pulled a page from Las Vegas, offering complimentary wine and drinks to his clientele as they made their purchasing decisions.

Whatever was taking place that Friday was generating sales like a Saturday during the Christmas season, and Britten was on a mission to figure it out and bottle it for the next day. As five o'clock approached, he and the staff were approaching exhaustion. However, there were still another twenty-some customers in the store. Then the attack came.

Precisely at closing time, a white van double-parked directly in front of Lockett's. Four masked figures, three of whom were carrying AK-47s, stepped out of the vehicle and walked through the front door. As they entered, gunfire erupted without warning, assailing the senses of all those in the store. The burst continued for thirty seconds before a reprieve allowed the screams of those trapped inside to be heard.

"Everyone to the vault," ordered the leader. With that, the AKs again exploded as the robbers herded the employees and customers to the back of the store while passersby on the street scattered in all directions.

Once the employees and patrons were in the main vault, the next command came. "On the ground!" yelled the leader, followed again by another burst from the assault weapons. Shrieks and crying were the universal responses from those stuck inside. More than one person lost control of their bladder at the deafening sound of the machine guns and the fear of being killed.

Grabbing Britten by the scruff of his neck, the leader pulled him to the separate diamond vault. "Open it, or we'll start executing people one by one," he said coldly. Then, more gunfire from the leader's associates to make the point, imploring the owner to work quickly. Britten remained as calm as he could considering the circumstances. However, with his hands shaking, it took three attempts to solve the combination lock before the vault door opened. The leader quickly and carefully scanned the contents, pulling out several large drawers of both uncut and finished diamonds, placing them into an oversized brown briefcase.

With the crew now focused on their retreat, the leader grabbed Britten by the collar, wrenching him back to the main vault with the others before bellowing a final command. "Stay on the floor and keep your heads down. Count to one hundred slowly before you come out of the vault. If you come out too soon and we're still here, you will be killed. Oh, and thank you for shopping at Lockett's." Another hail of gunfire followed as the four robbers hastily exited the store and returned to their vehicle.

The initial roar of the AKs dispersed the crowd on the previously busy street, with bystanders running in every direction to seek cover. However, for whatever reason, the sight of masked people carrying large weapons and leaving the store never evoked a peep, let alone a scream, from anyone nearby. One brave soul held up his phone to take a photo of the robbers and their van as they prepared to leave. The photo opportunity was met by the muzzle of a weapon pointed in the direction of the would-be hero, who promptly dropped the phone and had it crushed by the heel of the leader, who had stepped out of the vehicle. As quickly as the robbery took place, it was over. For those inside the jewelry store, they found out just how long an eternity lasts. As the van door slid shut, the driver coolly pulled into the flow of traffic and merged onto the adjacent interstate highway, leaving confusion in its wake.

Three blocks away, Nowitzke recognized the clatter of heavy weapons. However, with the shots echoing off the canyons of the surrounding buildings and him operating at less than one hundred percent courtesy of the beer, the detective strode onto the street to get a fix on where the sound had come from. Masses of people were moving in every direction, offering no clues. Nowitzke held up his badge and yelled loudly, "Where did the shots come from?"

A distraught young woman in a business suit stopped running. Out of breath and with tears streaming down her face, she mustered up the courage to yell back, "Lockett's Jewelers! They're in Lockett's!" Slipping into shock, she mindlessly rambled on. "I was coming home from work and walking next to the store when several men with guns went into the building and just began firing. Someone told me there are mass casualties. My God, I just need to get home." Gathering herself, she rejoined the mob, running in her original direction away from the chaos.

Gauging the direction to the store, Nowitzke began to run, fighting the crowd. After two blocks, he was wheezing and sweating profusely. With hands resting on his knees, he realized his beer and pizza diet had caught up with him. He was still gulping air when his phone rang.

"Where the fuck are you, Chuck?" asked the familiar voice of Arturo Copeland.

"Damn, Art. I'm about a block away from the shooting. Apparently, someone robbed a Lockett's Jewelers in broad daylight."

"No shit. Already on my way," said the Milwaukee detective. "But with traffic, I can't get there for another ten minutes."

"Short of having a goddamned heart attack, I should beat you to the scene. See you in ten," coughed Nowitzke as he clicked off the call and resumed what others might have considered to be a fast walk.

CHAPTER 15

Picturing the worst in his mind, Nowitzke was surprised by the relatively calm demeanor of those in and around Lockett's Jewelers when he arrived. Taking some time to recover with several deep breaths outside the store, the detective saw that the first arriving officers had already cordoned off the area with yellow crime scene tape. Several ambulances had arrived and were treating those who Nowitzke believed were employees and customers with oxygen. And aside from one or two IVs needed to stabilize the more panic-stricken, the detective was shocked to see no bodies or blood, *anywhere*. No blood on the survivors, the first responders, none. *Thank God, but what the fuck?*

Nowitzke had expected carnage in the store but again saw nothing after being allowed to enter by a uniformed officer who recognized the former MPD detective. Although there was no blood, the store reeked of salty sweat and pungent urine. Nowitzke surveyed the scene, making general observations as Copeland arrived.

"Jesus, Chuck. Good to see you. Did you stop to take a shower on the way over?" asked Copeland, noticing that Nowitzke had sweated through his shirt and the droplets were now pooling on the floor.

"Fuck you, Art. Made it here before you."

"Listen, I'm glad you're here. I can use your help."

Nowitzke shook his head as he continued to scan the jewelry store. *Something here is off.* Rubbing his chin, he remarked, "The whole scene doesn't make sense."

"How so?" asked Copeland.

"To me, it looks more like a drill than the real thing. Like the robbery was somehow staged, you know, like actors playing a part. I'm glad there are no bodies. On the way here, a young woman said that a group of men just opened fire. She talked about casualties, but thankfully, that's not the case."

"That is good news. The paperwork would have been a nightmare. Let's find the person in charge and figure out what happened," said Copeland.

"That would be me," came a muffled voice. Sitting behind his desk, Riley Britten was wearing an oxygen mask while being attended to by an EMT. "I'm the owner." Still shaken, Britten continued. "Four men came right through the front door and began shooting. That was before they even told us what they wanted."

"Which was . . ." asked Nowitzke.

"Diamonds. Cut and uncut. We always have heavy inventory on hand, and they seemed to know that. After several volleys, the leader got down to business and took me to the diamond vault. He threatened to begin killing people if I didn't open it quickly. Frankly, I'm surprised I held it together and got the vault open."

"Any idea on the value they got?" asked Copeland.

Britten pondered the question. "We'll need to do a complete inventory . . ." he began.

"Yeah, yeah. An estimate?" asked Copeland, growling impatiently.

"I would guess maybe $10 million. We're insured. I'm just glad that no one was hurt or killed," continued the manager. As Nowitzke listened to the exchange, he drifted off, scrutinizing the scene more closely. *No real injuries. No deaths. All this glass, but no damage? Why doesn't this make sense?*

Nowitzke interrupted the back-and-forth between the owner and Copeland. "Mr. Britten, how many guys did you say came into the store?

"Four?"

"How many were carrying weapons?"

"Three."

"And what kind of weapons did you say?"

"AK-47s. I was in the Army when I was younger and recognized them immediately."

"Okay, and where did the robbers shoot when they were getting everyone's attention?"

"Everywhere. Mostly into the air, I guess, because no one got shot. Ask any of our associates or customers about what happened."

"I will," said Nowitzke. "One last question for you, Mr. Britten. If three robbers opened up with assault rifles in your store, where are all the bullet holes and broken glass?"

Britten looked curiously at Nowitzke, cocking his head. "What do you mean?" He paused, glancing around the store, then focused upward toward the ceiling. There were no bullet holes. Nothing was amiss. There was no damage. "Oh my God. Are you saying the robbers used blanks?"

CHAPTER 16

The internal video from Lockett's told the exact same story as Britten, his employees, and customers. The total elapsed time between the robbers entering the store and leaving with millions of dollars in diamonds was two minutes and thirty seconds on the button. As Nowitzke and Copeland studied the tape, they concluded that the robbery must have been quite the ordeal for those at the end of the muzzle, not knowing the perpetrators were firing blanks. Both detectives recommended that the city offer counseling to the victims to address any potential PTSD issues.

Based on the tape, the four suspects were of average height and weight, looking like interchangeable parts of the same team. They were all masked, wore sunglasses and gloves, and were dressed in identical grey jumpsuits with black Nike high-tops. Even a close examination revealed no distinctive differences between the robbers, such as birthmarks or tattoos. According to the staff, the leader had no discernable accent.

The forensics team spent considerable time at the scene but came up largely empty. There were no slugs, and the robbery crew had touched little inside the store aside from the door handles on their entry and exit. But wearing gloves, they left no fingerprints. There was no DNA or any other apparent physical evidence.

Copeland asked to review video of the interstate around the time of the theft from Department of Transportation traffic cameras. However, any findings were inconclusive since they did not have a clear description of the vehicle or the direction it was traveling. Ultimately, he concluded that white vans must have been on sale at some point as the vehicle of choice for all contractors, based on the video. After brainstorming for any other leads, Nowitzke suggested listening to 911 tapes reporting the crime.

Both detectives walked down to the 911 dispatch center. There were three reports. The first from a male caller at 4:55 p.m., who calmly reported the armed robbery of Lockett's but gave an address for the premise on the opposite side of the Milwaukee River from where the actual theft occurred. The second and third reports came from frantic female callers almost simultaneously at 5:02 p.m., imploring the police to respond immediately, the sound of heavy gunfire in the background.

"That's quite a disparity in the timing of the calls," said Copeland. "A gap of seven minutes with nothing in between?"

"Wait . . ." replied Nowitzke, "when did Britten say the robbers arrived?"

"He said closing, but he had people still in the store," responded Copeland, flipping through his notes. "Here it is . . . Lockett's closed at 5:00 p.m."

"So, the first call came in roughly five minutes before the robbers actually showed up?" questioned Nowitzke. "That and the caller directed the dispatcher to send cruisers to the wrong address, diverting them from the actual scene. We need to listen to a tape of the call."

Moments later, the officer on duty booted up the recording. Nowitzke and Copeland listened intently as they heard the first robbery report from what sounded like a young man. "He gave an incorrect address of the location and didn't provide a name," concluded Copeland.

"Go figure," said Nowitzke as he pulled out his cell and dialed the number captured by the system. However, the officer was rewarded only with a busy signal. "You want to bet the guy who made the 911 call was part of the crew and used a burner phone?"

"I wouldn't put money on that," said Copeland. "The phone was probably at the bottom of the Milwaukee River even before the robbery started. Think about how gutsy these assholes were. I'd have to assume they had more than blanks available. What if Milwaukee PD had responded and cornered the robbers while they were still in the store? What would they have done in the alternative? Surrender? They couldn't have shot their way out with blanks in their guns. Maybe we dodged a potentially serious hostage situation?" Copeland shook his head, still pondering what might have been. "You know, Chuck, the other complication is that MPD has a shift change at 5:00 p.m., meaning our coverage was thinner than the norm. Do you think the bad guys had insider information on our procedures?"

"Don't know, Art. But these guys were good. Very focused, and professional. I don't think you can beat yourself up about them having that type of info. They took advantage of every break."

By 11:30 p.m., Nowitzke was exhausted from his long day. Before departing for his hotel, he asked Copeland about meeting for breakfast the following morning.

"I'm sorry, Chuck. I've got some early morning business that simply can't wait. How about a raincheck for dinner the next time you're in Milwaukee? I'll buy."

A disappointed Nowitzke agreed and quickly refocused on a drink at the hotel bar before heading up to his room.

CHAPTER 17

As Nowitzke was heading off for his nightcap, Anissa arrived at her condo building from the hospital. It had been approaching midnight before she was finally relieved by an officer who would guard access to Besnik. She entered her apartment and placed her keys and purse on a table in the foyer, intent on collapsing in her bed, when her cell phone buzzed. Swearing to herself, she recognized the number as Chief Clark's.

"Good evening, sir."

"Anissa. Sorry to have to call you at such a late hour. I understand you had an interesting day. How is your suspect, Mr. Besnik, doing?"

"He's out of surgery. The doctors thought everything went well. However, when I saw him briefly, Besnik was babbling about needing his phone and being released from the hospital. He was pretty worked up, worried about something. But that might have just been the anesthetic talking."

"Where's Nowitzke?"

"He's in Milwaukee finalizing his divorce."

"Oh, that's right. I've been trying to contact him for the last hour," said Clark. "I keep getting his voicemail. Anyway, since I can't reach him, you're next in line."

"Okay?" she said apprehensively.

"I would guess that the Besnik case is your first experience with arresting a suspect who required medical attention before being booked and held in jail." Before she could acknowledge Clark's inquiry, he continued. "Sometime this evening, I was contacted by a new assistant district attorney, F. Terence Stokes, Esquire. Stokes is a recent graduate from Marquette Law and an ambitious little asshole who is being a stickler for policy."

Anissa was doing her best to pay close attention to her boss's boss but was finding it difficult due to fatigue.

"According to state law," Clark continued, "when law enforcement from a municipality arrests a suspect requiring medical attention, that jurisdiction is required to pay for all treatment received by that person. So, this ADA told the hospital the city had released Besnik so that Appleton taxpayers wouldn't have to pay a small fortune for his surgery. Then, after the fact, he called me, leaving a message on my phone explaining what he had done. The voicemail said we would need to rearrest Besnik after he was released by his doctors. Of course, I was out with my wife tonight, turned off my phone, and never got the message until an hour ago."

"Alright," said Anissa, trying to figure out the next turn of the story.

Although he generally maintained a level of decorum, Clark was unable to hide his growing anger. "I'm not sure if this little prick lawyer tried to contact Nowitzke or not. Since Stokes couldn't connect with anyone, he called the third shift watch commander, explaining the city's position. Then he told our guy we were wasting our time guarding Besnik since he couldn't run anyway."

"But that's not his call," said Anissa, who was now steaming. "Stokes has no authority to make that decision."

"I agree. However, after you left the hospital, the lieutenant in charge followed Stokes's orders and contacted the patrolman who took over for you. The LT told him to get himself back on the streets immediately, so for the moment, Besnik is not being guarded at the hospital. I just wanted to let you know when I finally put all the pieces together. Oh, and as an FYI, I plan to raise hell with the DA tomorrow morning."

"So much for communication from our department partners," replied Anissa. She clicked off the call from Clark, now trying to figure out what to do.

Resolving to take a quick shower and load up on caffeine before returning to the hospital, Anissa heard a knock at her door.

"What the hell?" she asked rhetorically, pulling the Beretta from her bag as she looked through the peephole. "Unbelievable," she exclaimed to herself and leveled her weapon, preparing to fire as she opened the door.

Nadia was standing on the other side.

CHAPTER 18

Bateman's top salesperson was wearing a baseball cap, a silk jacket, and black leggings, and was carrying a small backpack. Based upon the condition of her makeup, she had been crying. There was a momentary stalemate at Anissa's door as she processed what was taking place. She had several important questions for this suspect, not the least of which was how Nadia had found her apartment.

"Nadia, what are you doing here?" said Anissa, training the handgun on her. "You understand we have an all-points bulletin out for your arrest in connection with the Bateman Jewelers burglary, don't you?"

"Ms. Taylor, that is the least of my problems. People are coming for Moose. I can't stop them, but maybe you can."

"Who is Moose?"

"I'm sorry," replied Nadia. "Moose is my brother, Musa Besnik. I thought you knew."

Anissa lowered the pistol to her side, motioning Nadia into the apartment and closing the door behind her. "We didn't know the exact relationship, but Nowitzke made an educated guess that you and Besnik were somehow connected," she replied. "Besnik's your brother? Why don't you have the same last name?"

"Before I came to your country, I took my mother's maiden name. I didn't want any association with my father. He was a criminal, and then he took Musa down the same path, whether he wanted to or not." Nadia paused. "Can you help my brother? He's in the hospital and is very worried. Actually, he became extremely nervous when I told him what Detective Nowitzke said about his DNA being found at Bateman's."

"Nadia, there's very little I could do. I don't know that much about aplastic anemia or why you'd even think I could help . . ."

"Moose isn't afraid of any stupid disease, or your police or prisons," she said, cutting off Anissa. "He and the other members of the crew were contracted to break into Bateman's. His only concern is about his employer's reaction to finding out he left DNA evidence behind. He was upset enough to jump out of a second-floor window," she concluded. "I can only guess that Moose assumed his employer had sent someone to kill him."

"Who is Musa's contract with?"

"I have no idea. Moose won't tell me, aside from jabbering on and on about . . . Katallani," she said with an exhausted look on her face. Moving into the great room, she put her backpack on the floor and slumped heavily into a leather chair.

"Who?" Anissa followed Nadia's lead into the apartment, sitting on an ottoman directly in front of her guest, now wide awake and listening intently.

"For Albanians, Katallani is a monster spoken of by parents to make their kids go to sleep at night. Katallani is very primitive, but like a blacksmith with a crazy wild look. Supposedly, it eats people."

"Musa is concerned about the equivalent of an Albanian boogeyman?" she said facetiously.

"Yes. All I can tell you is that Musa is terrified of Katallani. He said the man was not to be trifled with. In fact, Musa told me a friend of his warned him that he should not take the contract with Katallani because any reward wasn't worth the risk." Nadia hesitated. "Then Musa told me I might be in danger too since I knew about what took place at Bateman's. He was so scared, it convinced me. I went home, packed some things, and left."

"How were you involved with the burglary, Nadia?" asked Anissa.

The question drew another awkward silence from Nadia. Choosing her words carefully, she continued. "Technically, I wasn't."

"Bullshit! You pretty much just told me you knew something. If you want any help from me, you better answer my question."

After another gap in the conversation, Nadia responded, "I started working at Bateman's several months ago. I found a great job on my own and was making more money than I had ever dreamed of. Then one day, Musa called me, asking questions about Bateman's and the store layout. I knew he had been involved in many jewelry store burglaries over the years, but I thought he was no longer a thief. He said he needed this one last job so he could retire and start his own business. Musa told me he had insider information about the type of safes, what they held, and how much value was stored in each at night. The only thing he asked me to do was to let him know if anything had changed procedurally during the time they planned the burglary."

"How was that supposed to happen?" asked Anissa.

"Musa told me roughly the week it would happen and that if there were any internal changes that I should leave the outside front streetlight on as a signal. He explained people would be watching and that was all I needed to do. And so, I did as he asked. But when I left that day, I turned the lights off."

"You obviously know about the YACS?"

"Yes," said Nadia. "Musa is a part of that group. As I said, he learned what he knew from our father. I begged Moose to pick a different store because Mr. Bateman had been so good to me. However, he said it was not his choice. Katallani made the selection for whatever reason."

Anissa stood from the ottoman and walked toward the large picture window, processing what Nadia had told her, trying to decipher fact from fiction. It was a wild story with potentially a scintilla of truth. *A fucking boogeyman somehow scaring the shit out of a career criminal?* But Nadia told it with conviction, and she was clearly rattled. The detective scratched her head and turned back toward her uninvited guest before asking a fateful question. "What do you want from me?"

"To protect Musa. He's my only brother. I feel that something terrible is going to happen to him. I don't know who Katallani is, but he sounds like a person intent on keeping his identity a secret."

"Only if you answer one final question," Anissa replied.

"Sure," said Nadia, feeling some hope.

"How did you track me down to my apartment?"

"When you were in the store, I noticed you had a new phone," replied Nadia matter-of-factly. "The current generation of mobiles has a GPS locator. Using the phone number that you gave me off your business card and a program from the internet, I was able to track you within a radius of one hundred feet," she summed up as if this was common knowledge to everyone. "Once I found your building, the directory on the main floor told me the apartment number."

Unfuckingbelieveable, thought Anissa. After wrestling with that thought for a moment, she said, "Well, Nadia, you're in luck. I was heading back to the hospital when you knocked on my door. I'll see what I can do."

"Would you call me if you find out anything more? I'm afraid to go home tonight and will be out looking for a safe place to stay."

"Of course."

Nadia turned to leave, opening the front door. But Anissa stopped her. Against her better judgment and with a potential major Nowitzke admonishment ringing in her head, Anissa offered, "Nadia, you look exhausted. Why don't you stay here? I've got a second bedroom."

Nadia began to cry again. "Thank you, Ms. Taylor. I don't know what to say but thank you."

"First of all, please call me Anissa," she said. Grudgingly believing Nadia's tale, the detective decided to take a risk. Showing her new roommate to the guest room, Anissa pointed out where the soap and towels were kept. She left the room and refocused on her shower, thinking about where to get coffee at that time of day. Following the quick blast of cold water, Anissa quickly dressed in a white warm-up suit, then grabbed her gun and bag. Moving down the hall, she quietly tapped before opening the door to Nadia's room. Nadia was asleep on top of the bed, out like a light. As she left her apartment, Anissa decided to call Nowitzke. However, she was taken directly to voicemail. "Goddammit, Chuck, where are you?"

****

One hundred miles away, Nowitzke tried to plug in his phone before remembering that he had left the charger on his kitchen table at home. Still wearing his clothes, sans socks, he succumbed to his final beer, falling onto the bed and snoring to the sound of the late local news.

CHAPTER 19

Catching her second wind from the shower, Anissa spotted a Dunkin' Donuts and ordered two large coffees at the drive-thru. Although she hesitated briefly, her resolve recovered in time before adding donuts to the order. *A cop and donuts. I'll never understand that connection.* With nonexistent traffic, Anissa's vehicle glided through the empty city streets as she took a periodic sip from the warm brew. She could feel the caffeine taking hold in her system by the time she arrived at the hospital. As luck would have it, she took the exact parking spot that she had left an hour before and stepped into the quiet of the very early morning. The air was still warm as she walked through the night entrance of the facility, balancing the carrier holding her coffees and her heavy purse. Anissa recalled the map of the hospital from memory and retraced her steps through the lobby, passing the empty security stand while she made her way to the elevator. Punching the six with her elbow, the lift began to rise silently.

Stepping off the elevator, the long floor of rooms took on a spooky quality that raised the hair on her neck. The hallways were darkened, with the only ambient light coming from select overhead fixtures supplemented by the glow from computer kiosks in workstations dotting the corridor. In contrast to the sounds of normal daily traffic of hospital employees and visitors, Anissa was greeted by relative silence, hearing only muffled late-night television infomercials coming from patient rooms along with the periodic "beep" of monitoring equipment cutting into the eerie quiet. The floor was a ghost town.

Moving down the corridor, most of the nursing staff seemed to have disappeared, leaving her feeling like the only person on the floor. While somewhat disconcerting, she reasoned to herself that a lower employee headcount made sense since it took fewer people to attend to patients overnight.

Besnik's room was located at the far end of the floor from the elevator. As Anissa approached the room, she could see the now vacant chair outside the door that had previously held a friendly uniformed officer. Again, she felt an unnerving chill, her limbic brain flashing an internal yellow caution light. Carefully placing the coffee on a small table next to the chair, Anissa drew her Beretta and opened the door to Besnik's room.

Stepping over the threshold into the darkened room, she fumbled to find a light switch. She could see the outline of Besnik's face with the rest of his body covered by blankets. Then, it dawned on her that she could not hear any of the medical monitoring equipment in the room. Finally locating the switch, Anissa flipped on the subdued lighting in the room. As her eyes adjusted, it was a matter of seconds before she saw Besnik's face frozen in horror with a single neatly round bullet hole directly in the middle of his forehead. With her pulse quickening and the shock of the scene sinking in, Anissa suddenly felt a sharp sting to her right shoulder accompanied by a strange *pfft* sound emanating from behind her. A second *pfft* followed immediately, along with a burning sensation on the right side of her lower abdomen.

Adrenaline surged through her system. Anissa moved her hands toward her right hip, feeling the warmth of blood flowing from the pass-through wound. Then she heard rustling behind her, but could not see the face of the person that pulled the trigger. Sliding toward shock, she did the calculus. *Oh my God, I've been shot!* Before losing consciousness, Anissa dropped her weapon and made a final desperate lunge over Besnik's body, managing to punch the blood-spattered call button on the wall behind the bed. *At least I'm in a goddamned hospital.* Then, just as everything went black, she heard someone running.

CHAPTER 20

Nowitzke began to stir sometime just after 7:00 a.m. He had fallen asleep on his chest, remaining facedown in the same position all night. One eye opened as he peeled his tongue off the pillow and took in his surroundings with his alcohol-addled brain. It took a couple of moments to register that he was in a hotel, although he wasn't entirely sure exactly which one. While he didn't frequent hotels, those he could afford all looked essentially the same. Then, he recalled the prior day of endless meetings with the army of lawyers, followed by the jewelry store heist at Lockett's.

From what seemed like another room, Nowitzke heard the upbeat chatter of a television news anchor, whose cadence and staccato were like every other morning newsperson trying to become an evening newscaster. Sitting up, the din of the television was only white noise as he stood, carefully padding his way to the bathroom to pee. Even though he was alone, he closed the door by force of habit as the background babble continued. However, as he slowly woke up, his conscious brain picked out several individual words and phrases from the television. Based upon the scramble of words, Nowitzke assumed the report was about the non-shoot-out at the downtown jewelry store. But as he focused, he heard something unexpected. "Appleton . . . shooting . . . the suspect Besnik killed . . . detective shot and in intensive care . . ."

The details of the story had moved onto the local weather by the time Nowitzke left the bathroom, barely completing his first order of morning business. He zipped his pants and bolted back into the bedroom, searching frantically before finding the remote hopelessly lost in the twisted sheets and blankets on the bed. He scanned the dial for other local morning coverage but frustratingly heard the tail end of the same story several times before locating his cell phone to resolve the mystery.

Ready to punch in the code to enter his phone, he realized the battery was dead when the screen remained blank. Picking up the landline in the room, Nowitzke gathered himself and dialed the hotel operator, telling a polite young man named Ted that he was an Appleton detective before using the words "police emergency." While the young man worked to make a connection to a local Milwaukee operator, Nowitzke explained that his phone battery had died, taking all his contact information along with it, that his partner had been shot, and he needed to talk with the powers that be in Appleton. Within several minutes, Nowitzke finally reached the main number of the Appleton Police Department. But the desk officer who answered could not connect Nowitzke to Clark, did not know Clark's personal cell number, and had no idea about the condition of Detective Taylor. "Fucking A!" he screamed in his room. He resolved to take a quick shower, load up on caffeine-laced coffee, and double-time it home.

After stepping out of the tub, Nowitzke heard a knock at his door. Wrapping himself in a towel and pulling the Glock from his holster, the wary detective held it behind his back as he looked out the peephole. Standing outside was a clean-cut young man dressed in a hotel uniform holding a large box and a cup of coffee. Puzzled, Nowitzke opened the door. "Can I help you?"

"Detective Nowitzke, I'm Ted . . . you know, the guy on the hotel phone. You mentioned your phone charger problem."

A dumbfounded Nowitzke, standing halfway into the hall still dripping on the carpet, could only respond, "Yeah?"

"Well, the hotel ends up with tons of lost chargers left behind by our guests. Please take one that connects to your phone. It might take a half hour or so for your battery to charge, but then you can at least access your directory and make a call. Oh, and I brought you some coffee for the road."

"Jesus, Ted. Thanks. You'll probably manage a place like this someday."

"I hope to do better than that, sir," Ted whispered back. Quickly searching the cardboard box, he found a cord that fit Nowitzke's phone before returning to his post at the front desk.

Minutes later, the detective was pointed north on Interstate 41. And even though he was far out of his jurisdiction, he placed the emergency bubble on the dash of his beat-up Ford, clearing a path for himself in morning rush-hour traffic. Nowitzke pushed the limits of his vehicle, cruising at ninety miles per hour, when, as Ted had predicted, the phone chirped, signaling that its mechanical heart was beating again. Juggling his phone while handling the steering wheel, the officer punched in a "1" on his directory, taking him directly to Clark.

The first ring was barely over before Nowitzke heard the perturbed voice of the chief on the other end. "Jesus, Chuck, where the hell are you?"

"Speeding back from Milwaukee to Appleton," he said. "What's the story with Anissa?"

"So, you've heard. I spoke with her late last night, letting her know that one of our young ADAs pulled the guard on Besnik. She must have gone back to the hospital after that. As far as we can tell, Besnik was dead when she got there . . . one shot to the head execution-style, with a suppressor. Very professional. The shooter must have still been in the room when she entered. Anissa took two to the back. For what it's worth, Besnik's murderer could have easily killed her. Thank God for small miracles. Anyway, Anissa managed to hit the nurse call button before losing consciousness and received immediate attention. It probably saved her life."

"How's she doing now?" asked Nowitzke as he fought back tears, hoping his emotion wasn't coming through the phone.

"She's still in surgery. We just don't know."

There was a long silence before Nowitzke asked his next question. "You got an ID on the shooter?"

"No. We pieced together the video of a suspect entering the hospital and followed his path by CCTV up to Besnik's room. There is little doubt it was a male. The issue is he wore a fedora and positioned himself in a such a way that we didn't get a look at his face. Most of the hospital hallway's lighting was muted. We got really nothing in the way of useable video. However, the dude looked like a brick, pretty stocky, probably under six feet tall. But there was nothing distinguishable about him. Because the tape was so grainy, we couldn't even tell what race our man was."

"Marvelous. Is Anissa protected?"

"Yeah. The hospital is crawling with our people, inside and out. But I don't think anyone was out to get her. The target was Besnik. Anissa was just collateral damage."

"Be there in the next twenty minutes," replied Nowitzke, punching off the phone.

CHAPTER 21

Rolling into the parking lot, Nowitzke thought about how many years it had been since he had seen such a police presence at a hospital. Early in his career in Milwaukee, two patrol officers had been ambushed on the streets by gang members using automatic weapons. Each of the uniforms had taken at least five bullets. One eventually succumbed to his injuries after several surgeries and days in limbo. The second survived, unfortunately, never to be the same person after taking a bullet to the brain. Nowitzke recalled seeing the man's young wife and small children in tears claiming their husband and father without any real ongoing help. It had been an eye-opening event for the young Nowitzke. Something he didn't want to contemplate, then or especially now.

The Appleton PD formed an impressive perimeter around the classic stone structure of Hobart Thompson Memorial Hospital. As he walked through the ring of blue, Nowitzke was acknowledged by several officers who knew his partner was inside. He found his way into the building before eventually arriving at the waiting area outside the surgical unit. The sterile room, heavy with the smell of antiseptic, was painted beige and covered with motivational posters with inspiring art and meaningless statements. Clark was the lone occupant of the space. Seated in a stylish but uncomfortable wooden chair, he was busy working the phone. Aside from Nowitzke, no other department personnel were allowed in the area.

"Chuck, glad you're here. I just got off the phone with Anissa's grandmother in northern Michigan. She and Anissa's father are making the trip here, but it will take them several hours."

"Any update on Anissa's condition?" asked Nowitzke.

"Yes, she'll be fine," interrupted a youthful-looking doctor, still wearing scrubs as he entered the waiting room. "I'm Dr. Fitzgerald," he added, introducing himself. "Gentlemen, if you didn't already know it, Ms. Taylor is one tough young lady. She lost a lot of blood as a result of the wounds, but she tolerated the long surgery remarkably well. The nursing staff should be wheeling her through here shortly before getting her placed in a private room."

Both officers responded simultaneously, "Thank you."

"She will be out of commission for some time though. Just wanted you to know," responded Fitzgerald. "Oh, and thank you for your service," the doctor continued as he moved quickly out the door and down the hall.

Nowitzke could have cared less about when Anissa would come back to work. She was alive. It was all he could ask for. Even though he had no children, the grizzled detective had a soft spot for his young protégé. He judged his feelings for Anissa as what a father would feel for his daughter. *If I'd been here, this wouldn't have happened*, he kept telling himself. This protective nature was rarely seen in him by others, and it surprised even him. He thanked God for answering the many prayers of an atheist for sparing Anissa.

As promised by Fitzgerald, Anissa rolled through the area on her way to her room with an entourage of nurses and miscellaneous healthcare providers. Amid a tangle of wires and tubes attached to her, the semiconscious Anissa managed a drowsy smile directed toward Nowitzke before falling back to sleep. The detective stopped the procession briefly and leaned over Anissa, whispering something only she could hear before gently kissing her on the forehead. Nowitzke and Clark followed the train to Anissa's room, meeting two uniforms who were sitting in chairs waiting for instructions outside the door.

Once Anissa's parade passed, Nowitzke pulled the young officers aside. In the presence of the chief, the detective took charge. "Gentlemen, that's my partner in there. She was shot largely because of some incompetent asshole at city hall. Make sure Detective Taylor remains protected. No one touches a hair on her head. Got it? It's your only priority. When you have a shift change, make sure the replacement team gets the same message. No one is allowed in that room aside from family, the medical team, Chief Clark, or me. If anyone anywhere says otherwise, you call me. This is an important assignment. Don't fuck it up. If you do, I'll kick the shit out of both of you."

Typically, such a threat from the fleshy detective would have been laughed off by either of the athletic-looking officers. However, the ferocity of Nowitzke's tone and his commanding presence left each uniform wondering just a bit. As the detective lumbered down the hall, both uniforms stood a little taller.

CHAPTER 22

While he would have much preferred to remain at the hospital, Nowitzke knew there was nothing he could do for Anissa for the time being. He resolved to return to his office and fight crime by returning the emails that had accumulated in his account. Entering his office, he recognized a familiar silhouette waiting in one of his office chairs. The man was engrossed in one of Nowitzke's treasured snow globes.

"Agent Russell. To what do I owe the pleasure of another visit?"

Russell shook the globe a final time before placing it on the edge of Nowitzke's desk and watching the snow inside fall on a large glass Buddha. "I didn't realize Buddhists celebrated Christmas," commented the fed.

"They don't," said Nowitzke, snatching up the globe and safely replacing it in its spot on the credenza. "I have no clue why Buddha is in the globe. Someone got this for me as a joke."

Russell slid forward to the edge of his chair. "What's the story on the half-filled one with the stripper held together by duct tape on the outside?" asked Russ.

"Don't ask," Nowitzke replied.

After a brief pause, Russ's tone changed. "I'm sorry to hear about Anissa. How's she doing?"

"Just came from the hospital. The docs say she'll be fine. She'll need some time to get back on the job though," said Nowitzke. "But I imagine you're not here to talk about Detective Taylor."

"You're right. I'm here about your involvement in the heist at Lockett's Jewelers yesterday, and . . ."

". . . and The Hobbs Act 18 U.S. Code § 1951?" finished Nowitzke. "Would you care to refresh me, Detective?"

"Why certainly, even though you already know that The Hobbs Act is a federal law from 1946 prohibiting robbery or extortion, or attempted robbery or extortion, that affects interstate or foreign commerce."

"You know more than you let on, Chuck."

"Keeps people underestimating me," reflected Nowitzke. "Anyway, my old mentor, Detective Copeland from Milwaukee PD, was on-site and completed the initial report. I was in the area celebrating my divorce when the supposed shooting started. Made it to the site and helped out with the investigation as a favor to Copeland."

"I saw the report. What can you tell me about the scene?"

"It was just bizarre. When I got there, people were screaming and afraid, but I had this strange sense that something wasn't right . . . it almost looked like a staged drill to me. That's what I told Copeland, anyway. After talking with the owner and hearing the details of the robbery, I expected to see more damage and blood. But, looking around, there weren't any bullet holes, anywhere. Have you ever heard of anything like that?"

"Actually, there was a similar case at a jewelry store in France years ago. Same MO with the robbers using heavy weapons and blanks. According to our Jewelry and Gem Unit, the total take yesterday was about $12 million. Add that to the Bateman's loss, and we're well into the $20 million range. Two major jewelry thefts in such a short time? What the hell got into the water in Wisconsin?"

"Beats me. Wondered the same thing this morning on the drive back. I was thinking about jewelry crimes from my early experience. Even though they're both major losses, isn't the psychological profile of robbers different from burglars?" Nowitzke asked, a dead serious look on his face.

"Yes, you're absolutely right," agreed Russell. "In theory, there should be no connection between these types of crimes. However, I just can't get over the coincidence of two large losses like this taking place in less than a week. This would even get people's attention in New York, let alone here," concluded Russ. "What can you tell me about Musa Besnik?"

"He couldn't fly very well," offered Nowitzke, earning a chuckle from Russ. "Remember we talked about another coincidence with the smoking-hot Albanian saleswoman working at the place that was taken down by the YACS?"

"Yes, another coincidence for people like us that don't believe in them. I assume you followed up?"

"Absolutely. Anissa took the lead in talking to the woman, Nadia Belushi, and did a great job. She confirmed Nadia was from Albania. Of course, she showed us all her paperwork documenting she was in the country legally. Nadia also told us about how much she enjoyed her job at Bateman's. Been there eight months. But she swore up and down that she knew nothing about the burglary. Interestingly, while Nis was questioning her, I got a call from our forensics unit about the DNA we found at the scene. Forensics found the suspect had a rare blood type. They also noticed the suspect had a disease called aplastic anemia. Something, I guess, that could kill a person who's not receiving treatment. Anyway, when Anissa got done with the interview, I took a risk and dropped that little health bomb on Nadia before we left. We waited outside. Sure enough, she left the building shortly thereafter, heading straight for Besnik's apartment."

"Where is Nadia now?" asked Russ.

"I'm not sure. We were so focused on cornering Besnik, she managed to get back to her apartment, pack a bag, and drop off the grid. We have an APB out for her but have yet to catch up with her."

"Is she afraid of us or ending up as another dead Albanian?" asked Russell.

"Good question. Probably a little of both. Any ideas about who shot Besnik or why?"

"Not yet. But it seems clear somebody was pretty pissed off about us finding a member of the burglary crew."

CHAPTER 23

At 1:00 a.m., the truck stop located in the middle of nowhere off Interstate 41 was surprisingly busy with activity. It was a clear night with a crescent moon that shone over semis of all sizes and shapes filling the yard. The pumps were busy with drivers making quick stops for fuel, heavily caffeinated coffee, and to relieve themselves. For other drivers, it was a chance to pull off the road and catch up on sleep. Others were there for a hot shower and either breakfast or dinner, based on their individual body clocks.

The main dining room was about half-full at that time of day. Best characterized in design as low-budget industrial, the large expanse was a mix of booths, tables, and barstools bolted to the floor in front of the deep green counter. All the seating had been coordinated with the counter with a similar-color faux leather, providing continuity in the room. The tables were covered with tablecloths, and each, along with the booths lining the wall opposite the counter, held a small glass vase containing plastic flowers to provide some level of ambiance. However, none of the design touches, from the white sound-deadening ceiling tiles to the indiscriminately arranged industrial tiles on the floor, really mattered to the clientele. They were there for the food. Well-larded with all the essentials for the working men and women. Eggs. Bacon. Potatoes. Grits. Tough steaks for the hearty eaters. And coffee by the gallon. To its patrons, it was the smell of heaven.

A nervous-looking young man entered the dining room, making his way to a booth far away from any other customers. Wearing a blue baseball cap with a farm seed logo on the front along with a black t-shirt, jeans, and a leather jacket, he chose the seat against the wall. From a strategic perspective, he arrived early to pick a chair so he could keep everything in front of him. In addition, it would allow him to more easily spot the older gentleman who would be arriving shortly. It had been well over a year since they first met and months since they had physically seen each other. Their preferred form of communication was by email and burner phones. All in all, their plan was progressing well, aside from the little hiccup that took place earlier in the week.

"Can I help you?" asked an earnest, obese waitress named Ruthie, according to her name tag. Ruthie's light green uniform and apron were covered in stains, advertising the daily specials.

"Just coffee, ma'am. Black," he said without looking up or making eye contact.

"For one?"

"No, I'm expecting one other person tonight . . . er, this morning. Thanks."

Moments later, Ruthie returned with two mugs and poured one, leaving a carafe on the table. The young man was surprised at the quality of the coffee, wondering if it contained more caffeine than a normal cup. Given the early morning, he began an internal debate about whether he would be able to fall asleep later, either due to the coffee or the topic of discussion. Fifteen minutes passed before his counterpart arrived. For whatever reason, the guy looked more like an executive than anyone who had ever seen the inside of a truck stop before. And he didn't seem to care whether he blended in with the crowd or not. From the kid's perspective, the most obvious faux pas was the flash of a solid gold watch on the man's left wrist. The expensive haircut and the finely cut suit did not help matters either. Certainly not close to the official uniform of the day of flannel and jeans.

Ruthie spotted the new arrival moving toward the table. Seeing the well-to-do man, she took a moment to straighten herself up before going to the booth. Having gone through a recent breakup, she considered herself an eligible bachelorette ripe for the picking. Who better than a rich man to take her away from spending her evenings with a constant flow of truckers playing grab-ass?

The waitress barely got to the table when the gentleman announced tersely, "Just coffee." Then, all her hopes were dashed when he added, ". . . and a little privacy." Ruthie poured a cup for the man and left to service other prospective eligible bachelors.

"What the fuck happened this week?" asked the young man.

"Keep your voice down. Our boy Besnik left DNA at the scene, and the police were on the verge of arresting him. If he talked, he could have pointed the police toward us. So, it was taken care of," he said matter-of-factly.

The young man took a sip of his coffee. "When we planned this originally, I was told there would be no violence. Now, there's a dead body associated with the burglary, and with you . . . and me. Oh, and a cop got shot," he said. "This is a shitstorm. Where's Besnik's sister?"

"I'm working on it. She's gone. Dropped off the face of the earth, for now. The guy that was sent for Besnik checked her apartment, but it looked like she left in a hurry. He spoke to the neighbors and is working on a couple of leads."

"Fabulous. Aren't you worried Nadia would run to the police?"

"No. The FBI and local police think she's in on the burglary. She's in no-man's-land. At least until we catch up with her to tie up that little detail."

The young man's head spun. "Seriously? Another murder? I didn't sign up for this."

"Too late now, kid. Wrap your head around the fact that we're each looking at serious prison time if we get caught," said the executive. "With one murder already, a second count along the way really won't make much difference to a judge and jury. By the way, you're getting paid handsomely, I might add. Don't worry, our backs are covered. You do your work, and I'll take care of mine. Besides, we only have two more jobs and the plan is complete. Then we can go our separate ways, each buy our own island, and retire."

"Wait," said the kid. "We said only one more."

"You said one, I said two. I need the info on the big diamond. You know the one."

"Yeah, I know. I also know that to get that stone, more people will likely be killed."

"I need everything. Who, what, when, where. Oh, and some details about the bodyguards," replied the exec.

"There should only be one for you to worry about. I've already fixed that."

"Even better, kid. Up until now, you've done everything that's been asked of you. There's no way we could have made this work without the specifics you've provided. But we need to see this through. I don't need that diamond. I want it. Get me the details I need in the next day. I insist," said the well-dressed man, exposing a revolver tucked in the waistband of his expensive trousers.

"Cover that up before someone sees it. I'll get you what you need by the end of the week. The guy has a trip coming up. Oh, and if you're going to do this, make sure my cut arrives in my account twenty-four hours later. After that, we have one final gig, and the partnership will dissolve. Correct?"

"Agreed. Don't worry," he said, flipping a hundred-dollar tip on the table as he left.

"What a dumbass," concluded the kid, shaking his head in disbelief as he watched his partner leave the dining room. He could not get a read on the man after their few meetings. However, he felt safe from the apparent violent whims of the executive only as long as he controlled the flow of information. With the man's departure, the kid glanced around the dining room, noting the few truckers there who could have cared less about him, engrossed in their own conversations or their meal. Once the kid hit the parking lot, Ruthie gave all the patrons a start that morning with her loud yelp upon discovering the tip of her life.

CHAPTER 24

Nowitzke was not sure exactly how to proceed. He knew what he wanted to do but struggled to get the order right. His preference was to spend time with Anissa and let her know that things would be fine, yet with other demands on his time, he couldn't keep a vigil either. The Besnik murder and Bateman's investigation were foremost in his mind. But the Lockett's robbery was stuck in his brain too. Even though it was not his problem, his head insisted on playing back the details of that crime. Sitting in a Dunkin' Donuts drinking his first morning coffee, he made a to-do list on a napkin. From a professional standpoint, he had to interview Anissa about what she remembered about the night of the shooting. Any details would be helpful. However, the question was timing. Nowitzke recognized that there was the practical matter about when Anissa would feel up to answering questions. He certainly did not want to push her or intrude on her recovery. In fact, he would bend over backward to avoid adding any stress to her life.

Then, there was the open question raised by Russell about the coincidence of the two losses. Was there any correlation? Like everyone else, Nowitzke knew that jewelry stores were prime targets for criminals. Aside from the big values involved in each theft and the tight time frame between the two, this would all be yesterday's news in another week or so. On the surface, it didn't seem that there should be a link, but something in Nowitzke's ample gut told him otherwise. He resolved to delve back into his notes and Copeland's findings from the Milwaukee shoot-out to see if he missed anything. And where was Nadia? Did she have any more information about what went down with Musa Besnik and Anissa? *Besnik and Nadia have to be connected somehow. How is she involved in all of this?* Finally, and most importantly, who pulled the trigger on his partner?

Wiping powdered sugar off his tie, Nowitzke grabbed the box that originally contained a dozen donuts, minus the three cream-filled ones he had for breakfast, and made his way to the hospital. *Maybe the smell alone will rouse Anissa.* On his drive, he resolved to make a goodwill gesture by moving Anissa's Audi back to the garage at her apartment. He did not want her new expensive ride to get vandalized or be exposed to the elements while she remained hospitalized. While at the apartment, he would also pick up her mail before Ubering his way back to the hospital.

The same officers Nowitzke had charged the day before were back on duty. Each jumped off their chairs, standing tall, when they saw the detective approaching Anissa's room from down the hall.

"Gentlemen, how are we doing this morning?" asked Nowitzke.

"Good, sir," said the senior uniform. "It's been quiet here aside from doctors and nurses entering and exiting Detective Taylor's room. I believe she slept most of the night, but I don't know that there has been any change in her condition either. Also, two members of the detective's family are inside," he concluded, holding the door. Nowitzke left the donuts with the officers, who he felt had earned them.

Anissa's room looked different than the prior day. She remained unconscious, appearing almost angelic despite the rhythmic beeping of the machinery attached to her body. However, rather than showing shadows, the large windows bathed the area in warmth and sunlight. As Nowitzke entered, he immediately noticed a huge bouquet of multicolored roses at the end of her bed, courtesy of Sean Cook. An elderly, white-haired woman and a physically imposing man about his age were in the process of rising from their chairs when the door opened, hoping for a doctor to provide a positive update about Anissa. The diminutive woman was wearing a plain blue dress and clutching a white leather purse to her chest with both hands. The thickly built gentleman wore jeans, a button-down shirt, and a sports coat, his shoes polished to a high sheen.

The detective held out his hand in greeting, introducing himself to the visitors. Both relaxed, exhaling at once after taking in the heavy officer wearing a threadbare blue blazer, light blue shirt, and wrinkled khakis. Nowitzke immediately regretted not shining his worn brown loafers in the past six months. With his hand still out, the older woman pushed it aside and wrapped her arms around Nowitzke in a bear hug with an intensity that surprised him. "I'm Virginia Taylor . . . Anissa's grandmother. We're so happy to finally meet you, Detective."

Nowitzke, now worried about the death lock the muscular man might put on him, was relieved to be offered only a handshake. That was, at least, until the detective's hand was enveloped in a crushing vise grip from the man, who shook it vigorously like a dog shaking a bone into submission. "I'm Matthew Taylor, Anissa's father. We've heard so much about you."

Well, maybe we can still be friends, thought Nowitzke as he flexed his hand, checking to see if it was still fully functional. "Heard you had a long trip in from Michigan?" he responded.

"Yah, Negaunee. Small town USA. I'm with the local police there, eh," Matthew said excitedly. Nowitzke suddenly felt sorry for the criminals in Negaunee. "Chuck, I just don't understand. I did numerous tours as a Green Beret all over the world. I was on shit details, worked as a sniper, and have been in firefights in countries most Americans couldn't find on a globe. Never once got much more than a scratch. And here, in the States, some motherfucker shoots my baby girl . . . in the back, no less?" said the former Special Forces operator, tearing up.

Nowitzke was unsettled by the emotional display from the professional soldier for his daughter.

"What's wrong with the world?" asked Matthew, shaking his head. "Do you know who did this to Anissa?"

"We're on it," said Nowitzke. He went on to provide a courtesy overview for the Michigan officer about the Bateman burglary, the DNA left at the scene, the Besnik arrest, and Nadia. "Don't worry, we'll get the shooter. I want him as bad as you," he assured Anissa's father. Then Nowitzke waxed on to Virginia and Matthew about Anissa's professionalism, how she had handled Nadia's interview, and how far she had come as a detective in such a short time. "I'm proud she's my partner," he concluded.

Virginia stepped back in front of the much larger detective. "Please get the bastard that shot my Anissa. She's my only granddaughter," she said before giving him another hug. "God bless you, Detective Nowitzke."

Matthew chimed in. "I know it's probably not possible, but if there's anything I can do to help you, Detective, all you have to do is ask."

Nowitzke thanked the small-town officer, filing away the offer for future reference and taking his business card. Now, wanting to be almost anywhere else, Nowitzke went into the closet, found Anissa's purse, and fished out her keys, explaining to the pair that he would move her vehicle back to her apartment building. Before leaving, he gave Matthew and Virginia his personal cell number, urging them to call him anytime. As they each went back to their chairs to continue their watch over Anissa, Nowitzke walked over to the bed and squeezed her hand. Taking a moment, he discreetly wiped away tears when he felt Anissa give him a gentle clutch back. A sign of acknowledgement and life. *She will be fine*, he told himself again. Then, he bent at the waist, kissed her forehead, and whispered, "You hang in there, Nis."

Once in the parking lot, Nowitzke pushed the button on the key fob, and the Audi responded in kind with a beep, unlocking the doors. He slid into the driver's seat of the sports car, taking a moment to adjust it to accommodate his frame and to scan the layout of the dashboard. After shifting the vehicle into reverse, Nowitzke decided to get the vehicle washed and cleaned for Anissa. He found a full-service car wash and downed a free cup of putrid coffee as he waited, walking parallel with the vehicle on the other side of the glass window as it worked its way through the cleaning process. When the car emerged from the machine, a pimply-faced teenager jumped in, moving it ahead to an area for hand drying. "Nice car, sir," said the kid.

"No shit," replied Nowitzke as he crushed the cardboard cup, launching it in the general direction of a trash bin.

"Pine or new car?"

"Huh?" asked the detective.

"What scent would you like for the interior of the Audi?" asked the kid earnestly.

"Who doesn't like new car?" Nowitzke mused at the irony that even the new car scent came in the shape of a pine tree as he hung the air freshener from the rearview mirror before taking off for Anissa's apartment.

CHAPTER 25

Twenty-seven years earlier

At twenty, Karolyn Decker had more going for her than should have been legal. Genetics had blessed the blonde-haired girl with large green eyes, high cheekbones, and a Junoesque body that intimidated men three times her age. In addition to what God had provided, man had also chipped in good fortune in the form of a seemingly bottomless trust fund. However, despite her physical gifts and financial situation, Karolyn would have been on a most wanted list if underachieving was a crime. Although she was reasonably intelligent with passable grades in high school, Karolyn had no focus and little ambition to pursue a traditional path.

Nonetheless, at her parents' urging, Karolyn was gifted with a route to attend a well-respected state college. She naturally assumed her parents would take care of everything, from completing her application to sending the required checks. But they did not, and she missed her filing deadline, which she did not really see as a problem. Compounding the issue, she became distracted on her way to the standardized testing facility. By chance, Karolyn ran into several friends at a local coffee shop and frittered away her morning, drinking lattes while her peers were providing answers to obtuse questions about math and science. Karolyn's distraction was not revealed for several months until her attorney father followed up with several calls to the powers that be, only to find out that his daughter had not participated in the process.

During her freshman year at a small community college, Karolyn decided that school was not for her and dropped out to pursue a modeling career. Although she landed some local gigs with car dealers and catalog shoots, Karolyn's new calling gained no traction. She also saw what little money she made on her own but did not consider it a problem given her parents' wealth. With no direction in her life, Karolyn convinced her parents that spending six months in Europe would be just the ticket to help her achieve her dreams. They relented, in part because they needed a break from the Karolyn issue of the moment. They also believed the experience might provide her with a lesson in learning responsibility. Unfortunately, their thinking could not have been further from the truth.

Karolyn enlisted two friends to accompany her to carve out a new life in Paris. She found a small flat in the 7th arrondissement in the center of the city. While she had no concerns about splitting the high rent like her peers did, Karolyn wanted their support until she could establish a network of new connections. Her first month in The City of Light was spent partying at the local nightclubs. Thirty days in, one of her roommates was tapped out of money with barely enough to return to the States. Her second roomie lasted another sixty days, finally becoming disgusted with Karolyn for not taking any responsibility for the upkeep of the apartment. But for the young woman who had been born with a silver spoon in her mouth, this was not an issue either. In her short time in France, Karolyn had made some professional connections in the fashion world, and Daddy's checks would simply have to take up the slack in covering the monthly rent.

She quickly found that her looks opened the door to several low-level assignments with smaller agencies. Her face had a magical quality that literally jumped off of every photo. That, and a body that screamed sex, caught the attention of several art directors. The early consensus was that Karolyn had a bright future. Then her flighty ways came back to haunt her.

Karolyn began to arrive late for assignments after drinking and dancing into the early morning, drawing the ire of both her colleagues and photographers. She was unprepared for shoots, cancelling at the last moment because she was hungover. In the relatively small community that was Paris modeling, Karolyn was deemed too high maintenance to be worth the trouble. As quickly as her career seemed to be gaining momentum, it flamed out even faster.

Left without a job or any real friends, Karolyn began spending her time with freelance photographers and wannabe models all seeking to catch their big break. An informal group typically gathered around noon at an outdoor cafe, whiling away their afternoons over expressos and conversation before switching to wine. After dinner, they would hit the local clubs, drinking and dancing well into the morning before the cycle repeated itself. And the clique grew larger, as long as Karolyn was footing the bills.

During that time, Karolyn met Alex Veil, a struggling photographer from a small town in the Normandy region of the country. Veil's work had been used in several European magazines, but his high-strung nature eventually got him blackballed from the best agencies. He still worked regularly but was left to take on only those assignments that others had already passed on. But, considering himself to be an artiste, Veil supplemented his income by doing what he called glamour work. Although he was taken with Karolyn's beauty, he was also puzzled about her endless supply of money. Early on in their relationship, Veil tried to convince Karolyn that she would become a star if she posed nude for him. The young woman had serious doubts about doing so but reluctantly agreed to see his studio and his previous work. The studio amounted to nothing more than a drab one-room flat containing lighting equipment and a bare draped set. Adorning the walls were large photos of stunning models in various forms of undress. While Karolyn had never done that type of work, she did not dismiss it out of hand, particularly after seeing the quality of Veil's effort.

The following day, Veil met with Karolyn for lunch, which devolved into several shots of absinthe. With the green fairy urging her on, the young model decided to pose for Veil. Although not a virgin, she wondered how many of the women in the photos had sex with Veil as she stripped down to only a robe in his bathroom. She had no interest in such a relationship with him. Her only hope was that the photos would jump-start a second chance at fame. To her surprise, Veil conducted himself professionally during the several-hour shoot, alternately coaching and praising her along the way. When completed, Veil proclaimed that Karolyn's photos were the best work he had ever done. In fact, he asked Karolyn to dinner so they could talk about the day and the plan to get both of their names back in circulation.

Feeling a sense of relief, Karolyn went home, took a shower, and chose an eye-catching red dress for dinner. She walked to the quiet neighborhood gastropub to meet Veil.

The quaint restaurant was dark, but charming, with small tables for two covered in white linen underneath colorful hanging glass lanterns. The maître d' escorted the pair past a long brass rail bar to a quiet corner. As Karolyn twisted her way through the small space, she made extended eye contact with a handsome, muscular gentleman who was sitting alone at the bar eating dinner. Aside from the gentleman and the wait staff, the only other patron was a dark-haired man wearing a blue sweater sitting at a table in the corner opposite the couple.

As Veil and Karolyn enjoyed a glass of wine, she took several glances towards the muscular man, catching him staring back at her in the large mirror behind the bar. And throughout her conversation with Veil, she continued to discreetly watch this man, unable to take her eyes off him. As best she could tell, he had finished his meal and was nursing a beer while chatting with the bartender.

After ordering more wine and dinner, Karolyn excused herself to use the ladies' room. Once she had left, the man wearing the sweater approached Veil. The two had a short conversation before the sweater went back to his seat. When Karolyn returned, she stole another glimpse of the man at the bar as she took her chair. She also saw him rise from his stool and make his way toward her table.

Veil was focused again on Karolyn but felt the presence of the large visitor lording over them.

"What did you put in the drink?" asked the man point-blank, directing his question to Veil. Receiving no response, he asked again in a louder voice. "What did you put in the lady's drink?"

Veil's eyes began to twitch as the stranger waited for an explanation, along with a confused Karolyn.

"I did nothing of the sort, you fucking American asshole," responded Veil indignantly, picking up on the man's accent. "Now leave before I call the police."

Karolyn was stunned at both the insinuation and the confrontation, swiveling her head back and forth between the stranger and Veil.

"Hey, I saw you in the mirror when you and the prick in the corner put a drug or something in this young woman's drink."

Veil did not move, but his eyes flashed toward the opposite corner of the room, catching the attention of the American. The sweater had pulled a switchblade from his pocket and was approaching from behind. In a split second, the American quickly pivoted towards his attacker, delivering a healthy kick to the sweater's groin. As the man groaned in agony, the American grabbed the arm holding the knife and twisted it grotesquely until there was an audible snap at the elbow. With the attention focused on his partner, Veil used the opportunity to stand, pulling his own knife to end the skirmish.

The American looked towards Veil, who froze. "Listen, Frenchy, if you don't put that knife away, you're going to look pretty funny walking home tonight with it sticking out of your ass." Veil stiffened as if thinking through that mental picture. "Did you put something in the woman's wine or not?"

Veil shrank back, looking at his friend writhing in pain on the ground and not wanting the same for himself. "Yes . . . we did," he finally confessed.

Karolyn began to shake and cry as the reality of the situation sank in. "My God . . ." she gasped. "I thought we were friends?"

"And what was the plan? After you drugged her, were you and your friend going to rape her?" asked the American.

Veil was silent, unwilling to make eye contact with Karolyn, before nodding with a modest, "Yes."

The American pressed. "Have you and your buddy done this before to other women?"

Veil offered another weak nod.

"Give me your knife, asshole."

Veil handed the switchblade to the American.

"I should cut off your balls with this, you fucking rapist bastard," said the American in a low but controlled voice, flashing the blade in Veil's face. "If I ever catch you again, you can be sure I will. But tonight, you're going to get off easy." He paused, then asked, "What hand do you jerk off with?"

The question stunned the photographer, who cocked his head sideways as if thinking through the alternatives. Reluctantly, he held out his right hand.

"Put it flat on the table," commanded the large man. "If you were looking for a new sexual experience tonight, you're going to get your chance." He drove the switchblade through Veil's hand well into the table. Veil screamed, but no one in the restaurant moved. "You'll have to use your left hand for quite some time, dickhead."

The American calmly looked down at Karolyn and took her hand. "We need to leave," he concluded, taking the distraught woman by the arm and leading her out of the restaurant onto the street. After walking a block, Karolyn stopped. "I need to sit down," she said, almost hyperventilating, horrified at the thought of what could have happened. "Who are you?" she asked in a shallow voice.

"Just a tourist on leave. Matthew Taylor," he said, extending his hand.

"On leave? You're a soldier?"

"Yes, ma'am. I'm with the Army. A Green Beret stationed in Germany. Just in Paris for some R&R." He paused. "Are you alright?"

"I don't know," she replied, still trying to put things together. "I'm Karolyn. Long Island, New York. I just can't believe what happened and that you stepped in on my behalf. Thank God for the Army. Why were you watching Veil?"

"Who? Oh, your friend? I wasn't watching him. I was watching you," he confessed. "I couldn't take my eyes off you. I've never seen another woman as beautiful as you. May I walk you home?"

"Yes," said Karolyn. "But before that, I could really use a drink."

The couple spent the rest of the evening at an outdoor café, sipping coffee and talking. Within a day, they had slept together at his hotel, setting off a torrid romance. In fact, they did not emerge from his room for several days. Within a week, Matthew moved into Karolyn's flat for the rest of his leave. Then, before Matthew needed to report back to his base, Karolyn realized her six-month tour was almost up and made an important call. After living lavishly on Daddy's dime, the rebellious Karolyn contacted her parents and told them she was not coming home anytime soon. She had decided to remain in Europe and live with an American soldier in Germany. Furious, Karolyn's parents threatened to cut off her money flow if she did not come home immediately. Faced with the ultimatum, she hung up, choosing to stay with her Green Beret.

When summer morphed through the seasons into the following spring, Karolyn found herself pregnant. Immediately after delivering a full-term healthy daughter, Anissa, the impetuous Karolyn announced to Matthew that she had become bored with him and was not ready to be a mother. She made another call to her parents, telling them about her latest faux pas and the birth of a baby girl before pleading for them to send her a first-class plane ticket home. Karolyn's parents acquiesced but were also dismayed, not so much caring about their grandchild as the well-being of their daughter.

Karolyn's attorney father decided to make things right by setting up a trust fund for the baby. In addition to the impressive monetary arrangement, the document came with a nondisclosure agreement and provisions that Karolyn had given up all her parental rights to the child. In addition, no member of the Decker family would have any further contact with the infant. Although she was set for life financially, Anissa would never know her mother.

Faced with a serious dilemma, Matthew made the long trip home to Michigan's Upper Peninsula with his new love in tow to ask for his mother's help. Virginia become Anissa's de facto parent with Matthew's absences during year-long deployments to parts unknown. Virginia was determined to raise Anissa in a comfortable and loving environment, much like she had done with her own son. Once Matthew completed his service with the Army, he retired to his hometown where he became a police officer. Anissa was a daddy's girl, thrilled when Negaunee became his permanent residence.

Even though she wasn't a top student, Anissa did well enough to finish in the top twenty percent of her high school class. From a physical and emotional standpoint, she hit the genetic lottery from her parents' pool with the perfect combination of only their strengths. Anissa was blessed with her mother's physical beauty and attributes. She also had the confidence of her Special Forces father, never self-conscious about wearing high heels, which made her taller than any of the boys she dated.

Upon graduation, Anissa chose to stick close to home, attending Northern Michigan University down the road in Marquette, where she studied Psychology. Yet, despite her degree, Anissa remained intrigued by her father's job in law enforcement. Following several family discussions, both Matthew and Virginia encouraged her to take the leap and attend a Wisconsin-based police academy. Even though both hoped she would return to her roots in Michigan, Matthew and Virginia were honored to sit in the first row at graduation, pleased that Anissa had accepted her first job as a patrolwoman with the Appleton Police Department.

Highly motivated, Anissa combined brains with ambition, rising quickly through the ranks. In fact, she progressed so rapidly that she became a target of jealousy and bullying from a handful of older and more experienced male officers, who believed time and service should be the only qualification for promotion. While most of the staff applauded her progress, naysayers chirped that Anissa's promotion was either because she was a woman or a public relations ploy.

Then, early one morning, Anissa responded to the scene of a brutal homicide where she met and assisted a newly hired detective, Chuck Nowitzke. As part of that murder investigation, she was permanently assigned to Nowitzke. By distinguishing herself on that case, Anissa was promoted to full-time detective while still in her twenties. Any of her detractors were told to answer directly to Nowitzke. When the loudest of the bunch was confronted, any additional squawking was quelled by the visual of Nowitzke's bruised hands and the other officer's broken jaw.

CHAPTER 26

Even though Nowitzke knew Anissa's address, he had never been to her condo. He was familiar with the general area, quickly finding her building on the edge of an expansive park on the far west side of town. The three-story luxury red brick structure featuring boxy turrets was known as van Berlage, the first of several planned buildings in a larger development. An homage to the work of Hendrik Petrus Berlage, the founding father of modern Dutch architecture, the developer sold prospective owners on the idea of cultural flair combined with walkable dining, bars, and diverse retail shops in the style of Amsterdam, sans canals. Tacking on a European-sounding name to the building allowed the owner to command premium pricing for each unit from those with means.

Nowitzke located the underground garage and clicked the entry remote on the driver's visor, gaining entrance before finding Anissa's assigned space. He was impressed by the elevator car alone with its dark wood and high ceiling even before stepping into the main lobby of the building to collect Anissa's mail. Featuring high-paneled oak walls, the atrium had the feel of an upscale airport lounge with polished tile floors, leather couches, chairs, and end tables holding designer lamps. A silent large-screen television hung on one wall, tuned to a continuous news and weather channel. Several original pieces of art and sculptures were placed throughout the room, finishing the space.

Nowitzke collected the mail from one of the keyed steel boxes before getting back in the lift to go to Anissa's floor. The third-floor foyer was smaller but equally impressive, holding another leather couch and table surrounded by expansive windows, taking advantage of the sunlight and the view overlooking the park along with the ongoing construction of the complex's promised amenities. *New car smell my ass. Next time make it new condo.*

With only four units on each floor, Anissa's door was steps away. Nowitzke struggled to find the key before realizing, by accident, that the door lock was electronically triggered by yet another fob on her ring. The detective heard a short buzz and the faint metallic clunk of the mechanism unlocking the door. Nowitzke turned the knob to find an open living space heavy with granite, black stainless steel appliances, and comfortable furniture surrounded by more floor-to-ceiling windows. Nowitzke knew Anissa came from money, but he couldn't recall the exact story. Clearly, Anissa's lavish apartment did not fit with Nowitzke's impressions of her father and grandmother, who projected being of more modest means. He made a mental note to ask Anissa after she recovered.

Nowitzke dropped the mail on the kitchen island and turned to leave when he heard a sound. In the otherwise quiet space, Nowitzke froze. Cocking his head, he listened intently, trying to determine whether the sound came from a neighboring apartment or from inside Anissa's unit. *White noise?*

Thirty seconds later, his brain dialed it in. *Running water.* Then it stopped, replaced by singing coming from down the hall toward the back of the condo.

Nowitzke carefully pulled his Glock. Holding his breath, he moved slowly and quietly down the darkened hallway, trying to rationalize the sound. Did Anissa have a roommate? A housekeeper?

He heard a door open and focused on a long hallway. Steam rolled out of what he guessed was a bathroom. He stalked closer and closer as the singing grew louder. Leveling his pistol down the hallway on the chance it was the person who killed Besnik and injured Anissa, Nowitzke took a combat stance with his feet apart, grasping his

Glock with both hands. Then a woman came dancing out of the door wearing only a towel on her head. Nadia turned the corner towards the detective but did not notice him. With her eyes closed, she continued singing until she sensed another person's presence. She stopped abruptly, opening her eyes to see Nowitzke gawking at her nude body with a gun pointed at her.

There was a thirty-second standoff while Nowitzke and Nadia each mentally sorted out what was taking place.

"Don't shoot me, Detective," implored the young woman.

Deciding between her modesty and his safety, Nowitzke went for the latter, commanding, "Nadia, you need to keep your hands where I can see them."

"Can I at least pull the towel off my head to cover up?"

The senior detective could only muster a nod in the affirmative. From a strategic standpoint, the small towel forced her to make a choice of where to cover.

"What are you doing in Anissa's apartment, Nadia?"

"Would you let me put on a robe, please?"

"Where is it?" asked Nowitzke.

"In my bedroom, around the corner."

"Do you have a gun?"

"Do I look like I have one?"

"Well, not one on you that I can see. Come toward me slowly and stay in my sight," commanded Nowitzke. "I don't trust you and don't want to get shot. I would also prefer not to shoot you either."

The two did an awkward and deliberate dance down the hallway. Nowitzke closed the distance at the door to the bedroom where he saw a white terrycloth robe lying on the bed. Using his gun, he motioned her to put it on. "But keep your hands where I can see them." Dropping the towel, she turned away from the officer, quickly pulling on the robe before tying it off at the waist. "We need to talk," said Nowitzke, pointing her toward the kitchen.

He debated handcuffing Nadia while they sat at the table but decided against it. It was clear she had no weapons on her, his mind going back to the mental picture of her body. Also, he didn't think she would run from him wearing only a robe. He had no doubt she could outrun him, but it would only be a matter of time before she was picked up again. Studying her demeanor, Nadia came across as self-assured and relaxed, sitting on her chair with her legs crossed. Calmly, he looked at the woman and talked in a flat voice. "Nadia, you're in a big effing legal mess. You're implicated in a burglary. At worst, you aided and abetted your friend Musa. If you were found guilty of such a crime, you could be sentenced to serve years in an American prison before being deported back to Albania. You also could be charged as an accessory to the death of Besnik and aggravated assault of a police officer."

Nadia sat motionless for a moment, trying to comprehend what the detective had said. Then, her body stiffened in the chair as her hands gripped the rails. Her head tilted, her eyes widened, and she began to shake as tears streamed down her face as she put things together. "Musa's dead?"

"Yes. He was murdered at the hospital last night."

"And a police officer was shot too?"

"Anissa took two bullets to the back trying to protect him."

Nadia's brain quickly processed the news. "Oh my God!" she screeched several times. Covering her mouth with both hands, she wailed, her body going limp. She slid off the chair onto her knees on the floor, where she remained, crying unconsolably. Her reaction to the news was disconcerting, even for a hardened detective, who was unsure of exactly what to do or say. Nowitzke chose to do nothing for several minutes before Nadia composed herself and pulled herself back into the chair. For his part, Nowitzke spotted a box of tissues on the counter and handed several to the young woman.

Still whimpering while drying her eyes and wiping her nose with a tissue, Nadia asked, "Is Anissa alright?"

"She needed surgery, but she'll live," replied Nowitzke. "Nadia, who are you to Besnik?"

"He was my only brother," she said, dabbing her eyes.

Although Nowitzke had surmised a connection between the two, he could not hide the "aha" moment on his face at the revelation and paused before proceeding. "I'm sorry for your loss," continued the officer. "Musa must have been involved with some bad people."

"He was. I know it. I told Anissa last night before she went back to the hospital. According to my brother, he was contracted by a man he called Katallani."

"First name or last?"

"Neither. As I explained to Anissa, Katallani is an Albanian term for a devil. I don't know the man's real name."

"That sounds like a load of bullshit to me, Nadia," exploded Nowitzke. "You need to come clean and tell me about Musa's involvement in the Bateman burglary."

The young woman closed her eyes briefly and took a deep breath. "Musa was a long-time member of the YACS, who had been contracted to do the theft. He understood how security systems worked and knew how to use tools to enter high-security safes. Something he learned from our father. Bateman's was supposedly his last job. To be honest with you, I don't know anything about the actual burglary or his crew. When I saw him yesterday, I told him what you said about his DNA being found at the scene. He immediately became afraid that Katallani would kill him for leaving behind any evidence . . . which is exactly what came to pass at the hospital."

"What was your role in the theft?" asked Nowitzke.

"Nothing really. I did know a burglary would happen, but not when. My only involvement was to turn on the outside light of the store during a period of a week to give a signal if any security procedures changed. But nothing did." She began to cry again.

"Do I look like I'm fucking stupid, Nadia?" Nowitzke said, his voice rising again. "Tell me how you were involved, goddammit. You knew the layout of the store, including which goods were stored in each safe."

"I *am* telling you the truth," she insisted, the sound of her voice rising to match Nowitzke's. "Musa told me he had information about Bateman's from another source. I loved my job. I was making good money before Musa and his crew screwed up my life," she said through her tears. "I told Anissa the exact same thing . . . before asking for her help to protect my brother at the hospital."

Nowitzke studied Nadia's face as he pulled more tissues from the box and handed them to the young woman. Despite the questioning look he gave her, Nadia held her ground.

After a long pause, Nowitzke asked, "What the hell are you doing in Anissa's condo?"

Nadia relaxed. "Musa warned me to leave my apartment and go into hiding. Even though he knew I had nothing to do with the burglary, he was concerned Katallani would assume otherwise. I didn't want to wait around to find out if I was on his list, so I bolted. But I had only a little cash and nowhere to go. Then I remembered Anissa's business card." She explained how she tracked the phone to Anissa's home via the internet. "I knocked on her door late last night, about the time she was going to go back to the hospital. I told her my story. She made me answer all the same questions you just asked me again." Nadia smiled. "Anissa has a good heart. With no other place for me to go to aside from a jail cell, she took pity on me and offered me a bed. Then I begged her to protect Musa. But she never came back. I was hungry but afraid to leave. I didn't know what to do. Stay here, or leave and have Katallani find me and kill me. I'm so sorry for everything that's happened, Detective . . . especially to your friend."

Nowitzke took in everything Nadia had told him. He would confirm her story with Anissa once she regained consciousness. Although he tended to believe Nadia, he remained wary of being duped by the beautiful woman. He also had a problem. If he charged Nadia with a crime, she would be taken to jail, and if Katallani was after her, he might be able to have her killed there. Worse, Nadia could make bail and be released. Nowitzke's witness might easily leave the area or the country for fear of being murdered by Katallani, whoever he was.

Nowitzke stood and shook his head, pondering his dilemma. Still not totally sold on a course of action, he considered Nadia once more. "Okay . . ." he began. "I have to talk with Anissa about what you told me. But that can't happen for a while. However, I do have a few more questions for you, and you need to tell me the truth so I can decide what will happen to you."

The young woman uncrossed her legs and sat up straight, looking attentively at the detective. Although Nowitzke was hardly a human lie detector, he had worked at his craft long enough to watch for certain cues from those being questioned that hinted deception. Specifically, he was interested in eye movement, body language, and whether Nadia's nonverbal behavior matched her verbal responses. He sat down directly across from her, taking her hands, and stared into her face.

"Nadia, were you involved in the planning or execution of the Bateman burglary?"

"Detective, I've already told you," she protested, shaking her head. "I knew none of the particulars aside from a period of time when it would take place and about leaving the outside light on for the crew."

Truth.

"Were you in any way associated with the death of your brother or the shooting of Detective Taylor?"

Nadia began to tear up at the suggestion before shaking her head and offering a forceful, "No."

Truth.

Nowitzke decided to take a long shot. "What do you know about the robbery involving Lockett's Jewelers in Milwaukee?"

Nadia looked confused. "I don't know what you're talking about."

Truth.

"Have you ever seen or met the person you called Katallani?"

At that question, Nadia became very still and pulled her hands back from Nowitzke. Looking panicked, her eyes moved back and forth as if searching for an answer. "I don't know, Detective," she conceded. "I may have. Shortly after I found out Musa was going to do one last burglary, a couple of months ago, we were having dinner with some friends, and as we were eating, a man I didn't know stopped by our table. He was distinguished, well-dressed, and seemed friendly. He tapped Musa on the shoulder and asked him if he had a moment. It was clear that Musa knew the man but seemed nervous as they walked off toward the bar. I could see them having a conversation but couldn't hear any of the discussion. Musa never told me who he was, and I didn't ask. It was all very weird. But I don't know if it was Katallani or not."

"Could you identify the guy if you saw him again?" asked Nowitzke.

She sat back in her chair as she shook her head. "I don't know. It was a while back. I only saw him for a moment," she said. "Maybe . . . but I just don't know."

Truth.

Although Nowitzke wasn't ready to trust Nadia to watch his wallet if he stepped out of the room, he believed what she had told him. And if she had really seen Katallani, she would become a valuable witness, one of the few people that might be able to identify him. Also, if Katallani knew her, she could easily be on a hit list. Nowitzke made a decision, though it was definitely not by the book.

"Nadia, get dressed and pack your things. We can't stay here, but I have a safe house in mind. Oh, and if anybody asks, you're my niece."

CHAPTER 27

With Nowitzke on alert for a potential shooter waiting for Nadia to return to her apartment, they made a brief stop there to pick up more clothing and personal belongings. After clearing all the rooms, the detective proclaimed a one-suitcase limit to be filled in fifteen minutes or less upon seeing her closet bursting at the doors. However, his decree became a point of furious debate between the pair, one which Nowitzke ultimately conceded. As the detective stuffed the second bag into the trunk, he realized he had nothing in the house to eat. He stopped at a local market to load up on provisions but needed Nadia to take the lead since he was unaccustomed to buying anything edible that did not already come warm and in a box. By the time Anissa's Audi arrived at Nowitzke's apartment, the car looked like it had been taken over by a hoarder.

The van Berlage it was not. If Nadia assumed all American police officers lived in high-end condos, she voiced no disappointment in her reaction to Nowitzke's place. She showed no emotion as she began lugging her belongings up the creaky wooden back stairs. The third trip up and down was enough to draw the attention of Miss Alma, who was waiting for the pair at the bottom step when they returned to empty the car. Nadia, who was wearing white shorts and a red blouse with sandals, stood waiting for an introduction. Over the course of his career, the beefy detective had been shot, stabbed, involved in numerous fistfights, and was not cowed by the worst offenders on the street. But for some reason, Nowitzke had a healthy level of fear for his miniature landlord.

"Hello, Miss Alma. I'd like you to meet my niece, Nadia. She'll be staying with me for a couple of days until her apartment becomes available."

On cue, Nadia gave Miss Alma a big hug. "It's nice to meet you. You have such a lovely home," she said in an unfamiliar accent. "Uncle . . ." she stammered, realizing she didn't know Nowitzke's first name, ". . . has told me so much about you."

Miss Alma squinted, looking the striking young woman up and down, did the calculus on her body, face, and exotic accent, but failed to solve the equation. Ultimately, the shrewd old lady concluded that Nadia might be Nowitzke's niece, for the time being anyway. Otherwise, short of paying by the hour, there was no way the paunchy detective would be with such a woman. "Welcome, Nadia. I've been baking bread this afternoon. Would you and your uncle like some?"

"Thank you, Miss Alma. Yes, how can I help you?" replied the young woman, charming the old lady.

Nowitzke watched warily as they wandered off, leaving him to finish unloading the vehicle. *Maybe sheltering Nadia at my apartment is a bad idea*. But now he had taken on the obligation to protect her. A witness who may or may not be able to identify Katallani. And there was the question of when this might happen. Without more information about this Katallani, there was no telling if an identification would even come to pass, ever. Nowitzke concluded he had done the right thing but now realized he had not built an exit strategy into the plan.

Once Nadia's belongings were in the apartment, Nowitzke waited for his new roomie to return, hoping Miss Alma did not break the young woman under interrogation.

Twenty minutes later, Nadia returned with a smile on her face. "Miss Alma seems very nice."

"Yeah, but she's pretty shrewd too. Oh, and she has these rules that we need to talk about." Nowitzke ran down the list. Yes, he knew he had already broken several. But he asked that Nadia do her best to abide by them. Nowitzke also told her that since he was the only police officer providing protection, there was no backup, short of an emergency. As such, Nadia was basically grounded, restricted to the property. Nowitzke asked that she call no attention to herself and to be on the alert for any suspicious people. Finally, he explained that he would have homework for her every night for the foreseeable future looking through volumes of mug shots in hopes of identifying Katallani. The young woman stood mute, her eyes not betraying her thoughts. She stared at the drab and dirty place, accepting what the detective said without any objections or questions. She had no choice. As the lecture concluded, Nowitzke's cat sauntered into the room, purring and rubbing himself on Nadia's ankles. "That's Sinker. Another stray," explained Nowitzke. "Yes," he said preemptively, "me not following the rules . . . again."

"What a beautiful little kitty," cooed Nadia in a childlike voice, picking up the cat. As she stroked Sinker, he purred even louder. Cradling her new friend, she strolled toward the kitchen. "Let's get you some milk."

"Great," muttered the detective. "A rescue who now likes her better than me."

When Nadia returned to the living room still caressing Sinker, Nowitzke announced that she would take over the only bedroom while he would sleep on the couch. The single bathroom would be shared on a first-come basis. Again, Nadia stood mute at the threshold of the detective's room until she opened the door and uttered an audible gasp. It was clear that the room had not been cleaned in months. Clothes were strewn about the space, hanging indiscriminately on a chair, the small desk, or collected in piles. On the stained mattress sat a twisted mishmash of sheets and blankets while empty food wrappers and beer bottles littered the floor. Still, after taking a breath, she concluded she had stayed in far worse places over the course of her life. At least now she felt safe.

CHAPTER 28

The following morning, Nowitzke rose early, hitting the snooze alarm only twice as a courtesy to his new houseguest. He showered with as much hot water as Miss Alma's system could muster to help loosen his stiff back after a fitful night on the uncomfortable couch. He decided to first go to the hospital to check on Anissa before heading to the office. The detective's day improved dramatically when he heard talking and laughter coming from her room as he walked down the hall. It was a welcome change considering the past couple of days. Passing the two officers still on watch, Nowitzke even mustered a smile at them before entering.

Anissa was sitting up in bed, looking like a princess who had awoken from an evil witch's spell. Virginia and Matthew were in their respective positions, again rising from their chairs on cue as Nowitzke entered the room, their formerly dour looks now replaced by broad smiles. The room was particularly fragrant with the addition of several new floral arrangements, including an impressive display courtesy of Sean Cook, who was seated in a third chair.

"Jesus, Nis, between Mr. Cook and the department, you could open your own flower shop. How are you feeling?"

Upon seeing the detective enter the room, Anissa turned toward him and beamed. "Great, Chuck. I'm ready to get back to work."

"Well, hold on. You're going to need a permission slip from your doc to make that happen," said Nowitzke. "Take it easy. I haven't been able to catch all the bad guys out there since you were laid up."

"Thank you, Detective," said Virginia. "We told her the same thing. You need to take your time, honey," she added, looking at her granddaughter. "My God, you were shot twice." Anissa's stoic father nodded his head in agreement.

Despite her condition and the best-intentioned advice from her friend and family, Anissa rolled her eyes. "Listen, I'm going to get bored in this place pretty quickly if I have to watch game shows all day long. Can you at least get me my laptop?" she pleaded.

"I'll see what I can do." Turning his attention to Cook, Nowitzke barked a little too brusquely, "So, why are you here, Sean?"

"I heard Anissa was injured. I just wanted to stop by to see her," offered the insurance executive with a grin. "In fact, I hope to see more of her once she's released from the hospital."

"Fabulous," replied Nowitzke derisively. Intent on getting out of the room, he hugged Anissa before giving his best to her relatives, hoping to avoid any injuries from hugs or handshakes. "Nis, I'll be in the office today. Call you later to bring you up to date."

Nowitzke had almost escaped when Sean stood from his seat. "Detective, do you have just a minute?" His request drew a curious glance from Anissa. Nowitzke nodded, and they stepped out into the hallway, finding a small lounge area away from traffic. "I understand you investigated the Lockett's robbery."

"How would you know that?"

"From reading the police report filed by Detective Copeland. You were mentioned as 'providing assistance,'" he said, using his fingers to make air quotes.

"I was in the wrong spot at the right time. Strange case, by the way . . . robbers using blanks before stealing millions in diamonds," replied Nowitzke wryly.

"Tell me about it. Anyway, my company is on the hook for that loss too. Combined with the Bateman burglary, WSU owes a fortune in claims just for this week. Our company president is flipping out. I've got directors sending questions to me at all hours of the day. The sky is suddenly falling. These two claims are so bad that even the rank-and-file employees are pissed off that their annual corporate profit-sharing check might be at risk because of my program. Now it's *my* program. Everything was great when all the premium was coming in, but now I'm the schmuck."

"Join the club. We have meetings on Wednesday nights," offered Nowitzke. "Why are you telling me this?"

Sean looked around the area to see if they were truly alone. "I need to show you something." He pulled out his phone and clicked on his messages, then handed the cell to the officer. "I got this text last night."

Nowitzke focused on the screen.

Lockett's and Bateman's are connected.

Staring at the message for a moment, the detective's head skewed before asking the obvious. "Do you know who sent you the text?"

"I have no idea. I even had to look up the area code . . . New Mexico, by the way. I don't know anyone there."

"So how did this person get your number?"

Sean shrugged his shoulders. "I have no clue. I meet a lot of people and hand out my card like its candy. I go to trade shows, visit with brokers across the country, and glad-hand people in both the jewelry and insurance industry. Getting my cell number isn't hard."

"I'm assuming the sender used a burner phone," concluded Nowitzke.

"I even tried to call the number but couldn't connect to anyone," replied Sean, staring down at the phone as if it would magically provide some answers. "Do you think these crimes might be linked?"

"I have no clue," replied Nowitzke, shaking his head. "Right now, I have a dead suspect involved with Bateman's, and there have been no arrests in the Lockett's robbery. Let me take another look into it. Copeland is an old friend. Even though the robbery is out of my jurisdiction, Arturo offered to help if he could. Forward the text to me."

Feeling some hope, Sean shook Nowitzke's hand. "Thank you, Detective," said the distraught young man before angling back toward Anissa's room.

Nowitzke called to Sean. "Hey, you realize that I consider Anissa to be like a daughter to me. More than that, she is my friend. I just wanted you to know that. If you do anything to hurt her, I won't be using blanks. That's assuming her Special Forces father leaves much for me to shoot at."

"I understand," said Sean, still managing to smile.

CHAPTER 29

Upon returning to his office, Nowitzke needed time to think through this latest revelation of a possible connection between Bateman's and Lockett's. He picked a snow globe at random and gave it a shake, watching as the sparkling white flakes floated through the thick, clear liquid before lighting on a can of Spam. Was the text about a relationship between the Milwaukee robbery and Appleton burglary credible? If that was the case, who would even have that information?

Nowitzke gave the globe another shake. He had already spoken to Russell about the potential of a gang doing both the robbery and the burglary, concluding it would be highly unlikely. Robbers use weapons and force to take what they want, while burglars are into stealth and don't want confrontation. It made no sense that the two losses were connected. But this was new evidence, in theory. It couldn't be ignored.

Lost in concentration, he turned to contemplate the beige wall behind the credenza holding photographs of his closest friends. Not that he had many. A wedding photo of his second wife, as well as another with number one, were now relegated to a drawer. His gallery included an obligatory photo with Chief Clark published in a local paper after Nowitzke received a commendation for solving a series of murders involving religious leaders. There was a grainy black-and-white shot of him with Miss Alma standing in her yard. But his most cherished photo was of Anissa flashing her teeth and a shiny gold shield when she was promoted to detective. It was positioned next to a picture of Arturo Copeland taken on a happy summer day at a department outing years before. Conspicuously absent from the gallery were any photos of family members.

Nowitzke put his feet on the desk. His brain rattled through what he knew and what he didn't. Pulling out his cell, he punched in the number of the texter as provided by Sean. Surprisingly, rather than getting an anticipated busy signal, he heard a beep, denoting he could leave a voicemail despite the lack of any introduction. Listening intently, he heard nothing until there was a second beep and the call disconnected. The detective hit the redial button, hoping for a different result, but was not rewarded. *It must be a burner phone.* He would drop the number off with his forensics unit and its new hotshot investigator, Norman McKenzie.

Norm was a former computer geek who ran his own business but turned electronic sleuth on the side. Frankly, Nowitzke didn't care how McKenzie made his living on the outside. He had already performed magic by tracking down suspects and helping build evidence in several tough cases. The thought also occurred to him that Russ might have some additional resources beyond that of the Appleton PD. He made a mental note to follow up with the fed.

The question of the day about the identity of the anonymous texter remained open, for now. More than that, Nowitzke desperately wanted to pick Russell's brain on the issue, but that call also went to voicemail. Hoping to run this situation past Copeland, Nowitzke's luck had not changed after leaving yet another voicemail. *Fucking A.* However, when he called Anissa's hospital room, he got her before the end of the first ring. She was alone and bored now that her family had returned to Michigan, and she was looking for visitors to help pass the time of day. It would be an opportunity for them to catch up on her shooting, Nadia's story, and the curious new development potentially linking the cases.

CHAPTER 30

When Nowitzke arrived at Anissa's room, he found her wearing a plush blue bathrobe, sitting in a chair and breathing heavily.

"Nis, you alright?" asked the concerned detective.

"Yes. The nurse had me on my feet walking the hallway to get me moving. I had a nice chat with one of the officers on my protective detail as we went down the corridor and back." She closed her eyes for a moment and took several deep breaths. "I'm totally zapped from my little workout."

"You know, you were shot a few days ago and had a surgery, for Chrissake. Give yourself a break. You'll work your way back to normal in no time."

"I hope so. My doctor says I'm being released tomorrow. But no work for at least a week."

"Take your time. I'll keep you in the loop on developments. Actually, I have some questions for you, if you're up for it," said Nowitzke, taking a chair opposite Anissa. "What do you recall about the night you were shot?"

Anissa grimaced. "Not much. I've been thinking about what happened for several days without much luck. I remember walking down the hall to Besnik's room with an odd feeling that something was not right. When I pushed his door open, I saw him staring up at the ceiling with his mouth open. Then, when my eyes adjusted to the light, I saw the bullet wound in his forehead. Before I could pull my gun, I felt a burning sensation in my back and passed out." She paused. "Chuck, I don't remember if I dreamed it or not, but I could swear I heard the sound of someone running. That's it."

"The thinking is you entered the room when Besnik's killer was still there. He probably could have killed you too but didn't for some reason."

Tears began to stream down Anissa's face at the thought of how close to death she had come.

Nowitzke grabbed a box of tissues off the nightstand and handed them to the young officer. "I saw video of a larger guy hoofing it down the hallway. But I didn't see anything that could help identify him. Of course, we got no video worth shit from the cameras at the hospital." The detective paused. "By the way, what's the story on your roommate?"

Anissa looked confused by Nowitzke's question before its meaning dawned on her. "Nadia? How did you know?"

"I was worried about your car and brought it to your garage. While I was there, I picked up your mail and went into your place. Let's just say Nadia and I surprised each other. Caught her coming out of the shower."

"Oh my," was all Anissa could muster. "Is she alright?"

"Oh, yeah. I've been looking for a good sketch artist ever since," replied Nowitzke, smiling.

Anissa's head tilted, and her eyes narrowed briefly. "Don't be a jerk, Chuck. Is she out of harm's way?"

"Yeah, I moved her to a safe house."

"The Appleton PD doesn't have one."

"She's at my place under the watchful eye of Miss Alma. And yes, I've been the perfect gentleman," said Nowitzke. "By the way, did you buy Nadia's story about her supposed lack of involvement in the Bateman case?"

"Grudgingly," replied Anissa. "She admitted her brother was involved, having learned the family business from his father. I keep wondering what Nadia knows. There was no doubt she was scared the night she showed up at my apartment. I assume you know about Katallani?"

"Heard the name. Nadia thinks she might have even met him once but wasn't sure. I don't know what she knows either, or if she just wants us for protection."

Nowitzke's phone rang, and he answered. "Hey, that was fast. Before you get too far, Norm, let me put you on speaker with Anissa. Can you hold on for a moment?" Before clicking on speakerphone, Nowitzke gave his partner the sixty-second overview of the Lockett's robbery, his involvement, and the text supplied to him by Sean Cook.

"Hi, Anissa. How are you feeling?" asked Norman.

"I'll live," she responded.

"Chuck, we looked into the number you asked about. Although it does have a New Mexico area code, we checked the time of the actual text and found that it pinged off one of our local towers. According to the tower dump, the text originated about forty miles south of Appleton."

"How close can you get to the actual spot?"

"Within a couple of feet."

"Seriously?"

"Based on what we've been able to find, the text was made off a frontage road near Highway 41. When we brought the coordinates up on Google Earth, we found nothing. I mean nothing around there . . . it's like a driver pulled over and punched in the text. There was no civilization anywhere, meaning no cameras either."

"Where is the phone now?" asked Nowitzke.

"God knows," replied Norman. "The text was not from an Android-based phone. Probably a burner, meaning when it's turned off, we have no way to track it."

"So, the only way we can track this person is when the phone is on?"

"You got it. My inclination is that your guy is reasonably sophisticated relative to what we do."

"Beautiful. Thanks, Norm. I owe you a beer," said Nowitzke as he clicked off the call, thinking through what McKenzie had reported. He turned his attention back to Anissa. "How are you getting along with Mr. Cook?"

"Fine, I guess. But any relationship development has been stymied by a couple of bullets. He's an interesting guy, though. I assume the text in question is what he shared with you this morning?"

"Yeah. He's in corporate panic mode right now. Two large losses on business he brought to his company. Apparently, the natives are getting restless about having to part with more money than he's bringing in."

"Insurance companies are funny that way." Anissa sighed, then gave Nowitzke a small smile. "Please give him a chance."

Nowitzke responded with a combination shrug and an eye roll. "By the way, here's your laptop," he said, handing her a black, soft-sided bag. "I decided to ask the powers that be for forgiveness rather than permission to bring it. Don't use it too much and just get better, okay?"

CHAPTER 31

Nowitzke's Taurus ground to a halt in a cloud of blue smoke next to the steps of his walk-up. It had been a long day. Pulling a brown paper bag from the front seat, which concealed a twelve-pack of beer, he placed it into a box with several books of mug shots and began trudging up the stairs. As he climbed, he noticed the aroma of food cooking. While he could not place the exact smell, it was enough to set off hunger pangs. By the time he reached the top of the stairway, he felt that something was amiss. The front door was askew, with no sound coming from his apartment. Carefully placing the box on the porch, he pulled his Glock, gently pushing open the apartment door with one hand while leading with the barrel of his weapon. In a loud whisper, he called, "Nadia?" Not getting a response, he stepped into the room. "Nadia?" He briefly studied the place with a puzzled look. It had been cleaned and looked better than the day he moved in. Nonetheless, aside from the momentary diversion, his worry grew until he heard the slam of a screen door below and the approaching laughter of a woman.

It was Nadia climbing the stairs. She was wearing a white peasant dress with bare feet, and her dark hair fell over her shoulders. She was astonishing, enough to cause the detective to hesitate for a moment.

"Jesus, Nadia. You scared the shit out of me," exclaimed Nowitzke. "Where were you?"

"I was downstairs with Miss Alma. She's been teaching me how to cook. We're invited to dinner, so put your gun away and hurry up."

"What did you do to my apartment?" asked the detective.

"I cleaned it. I had nothing to do, so I borrowed a broom and some cleaning supplies from Miss Alma. You had a bunch of junk that I threw out. If I'm going to stay here, I just want it to be nice, okay?" she said, looking at him with her hands on her hips.

How could he argue her point? "Well . . . thanks," he replied sheepishly. "I guess the pine scent threw me off. Like I was in the wrong place for a moment."

"After I took care of the mess, Miss Alma kept me busy in her garden. She's quite an interesting woman. Oh, and she said that you should bring your beer down to dinner so she can have one too."

"So much for the rules," said Nowitzke.

"Chuck, she's an old lady, but she's pretty sharp. We spent a lot of time today talking about our family history. She's trying to figure out how we're related."

"Shit. Thanks for the warning." He briefly shook his head like a criminal who had been caught. *What else does Miss Alma know?* "By the way, you look great," added the detective, trying not to make it sound like an afterthought.

Nadia smiled coyly, making her dress sway.

Dinner was everything as advertised by the smell on the staircase. Fried chicken, cornbread, and fresh vegetables. While Miss Alma and Nadia cleaned up after the meal and chattered on about the day's events and plans for the week, Nowitzke sat alone enjoying his beer. Even though the rules were still in place, he had tried to respect them in his own way, limiting himself to three. He could not remember the last time he had a real home-cooked dinner. It was something he missed, even though such a thing had rarely been a part of his life. Miss Alma pulled an apple pie from the oven and asked Nadia to help serve.

As they sat down for dessert, the old lady looked at Nowitzke. "We need to talk, Detective."

Nowitzke froze for a moment. *Jesus.* "What's on your mind, Miss Alma?" he asked, trying to maintain a level of cool.

"Well, several things. I've lived alone for a long time. Things have passed me by. Since my husband died, I think I've missed out on many of life's moments. My husband and I never had kids. But over the last day or so, I have enjoyed spending time with Nadia. It's like she's the daughter, or granddaughter, I never had. It's reminded me of how thankful I am for everything I have."

Nowitzke exhaled and considered what Miss Alma was talking about as he looked around the modest home. "I'm happy the two of you hit it off."

"Detective, I'm old, but don't think for a moment that I've lost it," she said. "There is no way Nadia is your niece. And she for damn sure isn't your girlfriend. So, would you care to bring me into your little secret?" demanded the feisty ninety-year-old woman. "And no bullshit, please."

Nowitzke looked at Nadia sitting next to him. Before he could begin, any smile on Nadia's face disappeared, replaced by a worried look. The detective's demeanor went from uncertain to serious as he stared across the table into his landlord's eyes. "Miss Alma, you're right. Nadia's not my niece or girlfriend. She's my witness. Last week, there was a burglary at a local jewelry store."

"Bateman's?"

"Yes. Anyway, Nadia's brother, Musa, was one of the perpetrators. A couple of days ago, Musa was injured trying to escape when I tried to arrest him. While he was recovering in the hospital, he was shot and killed. The attacker also shot my partner in the back."

"Oh my God, you mean the young woman whose picture I saw on the news?" said Miss Alma, her eyes opening wide at the revelation, aghast that such a thing could happen in her small town.

"Yes, Anissa Taylor. She'll be fine. However, we think the killer might have reason to be after Nadia."

"Why?" asked Miss Alma.

Nadia chimed in, "Because I may have seen the man who contracted my brother to burglarize the store before he murdered him."

Miss Alma reached across the table, taking Nadia's hand.

"I'm sorry for the lie, Miss Alma," continued Nowitzke. "I brought Nadia here to protect her. For no other reason. And I'm trusting you to keep this secret. I don't want to put you in danger either. If you want us to leave, just say so and we're gone."

Miss Alma glanced back and forth at her guests during an extended moment of silence. "What can I do to help?"

"Just keep doing what you're already doing. Nadia needs to stay within the yard and do nothing to call attention to herself. You've lived here a long time. If you see anything suspicious, let me know. Worst case, call 911."

"Like I said," declared Miss Alma, her eyes welling up as she spoke, "the last couple of days have been the best I've had in years. It's nice to have a friend again. If I can help protect her, I'm happy to do it," she concluded, as if she had sworn a blood oath. "Now, would you mind passing me another beer? I can't believe how good it tastes tonight."

With Nadia living upstairs, rule number three was on life support. However, Nowitzke pronounced rule number four officially dead as he reached for another beer. *Jesus, I just hope she doesn't find out about the cat anytime soon.*

CHAPTER 32

The kid had come through, pretty much as he said he would. However, there was one big detail that had not been anticipated. And it stood well over six feet tall with a muscle mass totaling just over three hundred pounds. Charles Hayes, a meat wall of a man, was not supposed to be there, according to the executive's information. Hayes had taken one too many steroids trying to eke out a life as a professional bodybuilder. While the bulk of his time was spent in the weight room, Hayes paid the bills working as a bouncer at a local club. At least he did until he beat two college students so severely that no other bar in town would have anything to do with him. Now he was a supposed bodyguard. But while the man looked like he could snap a spine like a dry twig, Hayes was an amateur to the executive. Someone who could be dispatched of with relative ease.

The real problem was Hayes's partner, BB. Boris Bobrov was also along for the ride. According to the dossier, the former Russian Spetsnaz operator had served for years fighting jihadis in Afghanistan before seeing the capitalist light and beginning to sell protection services to high-paying Americans. Bobrov was a badass known for his foul disposition and a large scar on his forehead.

Hayes and BB together were a little more horsepower than the executive planned for. But he spent the better part of a dreary day observing the rental car containing the two men and his primary target as they moved from one jewelry store to the next. Moreover, he had their itinerary as well as confirmation that the prized item was also in the vehicle. The executive was patient, convincing himself that he had the advantage. Knowing where he could pick up his target again later in the day, he hatched his plan after looking up local hardware stores on his smartphone. Finding one in the area, he made a U-turn to do some shopping.

CHAPTER 33

Through a circuitous route, Eugene Watson somehow managed to become the jeweler to the stars. Known to his friends and clients as Geno, he had risen from very humble beginnings as the firstborn son of a farmer in a small town just outside of Green Bay. Although his father had slated his son to take over Watson Farms someday, Geno resolved to do almost anything short of shoveling cow shit for the rest of his life. Following high school graduation, Geno took what little money he had scraped up from odd jobs and resolved to attend an in-state college as far from home as his budget would allow. There, two things changed the course of his life.

To make beer money, Geno took a part-time cleaning job at a local downtown jewelry store. Carl Barnes, the owner, was the last generation of the family-owned business in downtown Eau Claire. For whatever reason, the kindly old man saw something special in Geno and began to teach him the business. To the detriment of his studies, Geno realized he had been given an opportunity that would pay the bills well beyond anything he could earn by completing his anthropology degree. Observing his new mentor, Geno learned the value of integrity and salesmanship. He entered a new world where he began to rub shoulders with doctors, lawyers, and CEOs, earning the trust of many who had unlimited supplies of cash. As part of his role, Geno also became a regular at several annual charity functions where he met many stunning young women willing to do almost anything to model expensive diamond necklaces and fine jewelry. In two short years, the farm boy confirmed every early confidence granted him by Barnes and was on a path to purchase the business. However, Geno had larger ambitions to take his knowledge and skills and make a bigger impression on the world.

The second disruptive force was James Keegan, Geno's freshman roommate. Somehow, Keegan managed to find his way from his hometown, Los Angeles, to the obscure college in Wisconsin. With a flair for the dramatic, Keegan was pursuing a degree in theatre arts. And, despite their different backgrounds, the two became fast friends by lot, in part because neither fit in particularly well at the university. When Geno dropped out of school during his sophomore year, the pair decided to remain roommates, moving into a shabby little off-campus apartment in a well-worn section of town. While each was busy during the week developing their respective careers, Friday nights were reserved for plotting the future over pitchers of stale beer and popcorn at a local bar.

Keegan's good looks earned him several spots on local television ads. Even though he later recognized the poor quality and cheesiness of the commercials, they became part of his growing portfolio, along with regular appearances as the lead in university stage productions. More importantly, being a small-town celebrity was more than enough to pay the bills. After five years on campus, Keegan graduated by the skin of his teeth. Following his commencement ceremony, Geno took him out to dinner at a restaurant neither could afford just years before. As a final send-off, Geno also presented Keegan with the gift of a luxury watch.

Keegan returned to southern California to become another waiter hoping to achieve stardom. In between serving food to tourists, producers, and starlets, he found sporadic work as an extra on several films before earning a speaking role on another. Fate then smiled kindly on Keegan, who stepped in for another actor who had called in sick on the first day of a major production. Five years into his career, he became an overnight success, earning status, additional roles, and more money than he could comprehend. All the while, Keegan stayed in touch with his best friend.

About the time Keegan found success, Carl Barnes succumbed to cancer after a three-year battle with the disease. During Barnes's struggle, Geno took over the day-to-day operation of the business from his mentor, increasing sales and profits while raising the profile of the store. Geno's final reward from Barnes came during the reading of the kindly old jeweler's will. Without any direct heirs, Barnes bequeathed all his assets, including his business, to Geno. Seeing the prospect of realizing his own dreams, Geno took a risk. He sold the store and Barnes's home while liquidating all but the premium-level merchandise. Geno had done his research about several potential places to light before relocating to the beauty and wealth of Phoenix. There he built a new business from scratch, C. Barnes & Company, as a tribute to his old boss. He also chose to focus on high-end merchandise to attract money to the store while adopting an exclusive appointment-only approach to retail.

As he built his new business, Geno made it a point to get together with Keegan at least monthly. On one occasion, Keegan brought a friend along. When introduced to Keegan's pal, Geno had a sense they had met before, although he could not place where. Following an evening of drinks and dinner, the three of them toured the new store. By the end of the night, the friend asked Geno if he could buy a watch. Geno joked he would be more than willing to provide a discount on the expensive timepiece, valued at over $100,000, never thinking he would complete the sale. However, Keegan's friend accepted. When he pulled out his credit card, Geno recognized the name immediately. The friend did indeed look familiar. He was a primary character on one of television's most watched police investigation shows. Embarrassed that he didn't recognize the high-profile actor, Geno reminded his newest customer to "tell your friends."

And he did. Within weeks, Geno saw a trickle of Hollywood money find its way to Phoenix. His new clientele appreciated Geno's discretion and the quality of his merchandise. Trading discounts for photos which were prominently placed on the store's wall, Geno ultimately saw his business explode. So much so that he altered his original plans.

He began bringing significant pieces from his store directly to his California customers. In fact, Geno was rumored to have sold a million-dollar diamond necklace to an Academy Award–winning actress on the tarmac of John Wayne International Airport in his private jet.

Then, he came into possession of the Pink Monster, a rare emerald-cut pink diamond measuring 5.51 carats with a value roughly at $8 million. Watson had the stone placed into a necklace, which became his signature item. Making it a part of his marketing strategy, Geno would place the Pink Monster on any woman involved in a purchase, take a photo, and email it to her as part of the service. The Monster became the impetus for many exceptionally large sales. In fact, it had become an expectation from his California customers, as well as his growing New York base, to feel the weight and heft of the stone. But the Monster would also cause Geno's undoing.

While the Pink Monster had given him name recognition and publicity, it had also become an insurance nightmare. Given the value of the stone and Geno's travel schedule, his insurance carrier insisted that the Monster be relegated only to the fortress-like security of his Arizona location. Watson tried unsuccessfully to explain to his underwriters the need to travel with the stone. While they eventually relented, Geno paid a hefty premium to continue his schedule. He also agreed that he would have at least two bodyguards with him constantly while traveling, adding to his expenses. The final condition from his insurer was that the diamond must be stored overnight in a safe-deposit box of a local bank.

For Watson, the conditions were worse than the price of the coverage. That was, until he met Sean Cook of Wisconsin Specialty Underwriters. Sean's background, including his experience in the

London market, was all Watson required to switch carriers. Sean seemed to take a much more reasonable approach to how the Monster would be protected. Even though he charged a similar price to the going rate, Sean required only a single armed guard. Also, based upon how Watson did business and the type of luxury hotels he stayed in when on the road, Sean required the large diamond be stored only in the hotel safe at night. The only other prerequisite was that Sean insisted on knowing when and where Watson would be traveling with the Monster. With more reasonable insurance conditions in place, the Pink Monster began to earn its own status in airline miles.

CHAPTER 34

It was an overcast day in Wisconsin. The type where the daylight turns the overhead clouds dark grey, making it impossible to tell whether it is morning or afternoon. Geno had traveled to the state under the guise of showing off the Monster to friends who owned several Green Bay jewelry businesses. However, the actual purpose of the trip centered on attending his father's funeral the day before. Even though they had been estranged for several years, Geno realized he had only one father, who was now gone. And while he felt no real loss, he did recognize an air of finality.

The pressure of a family gathering, most of whom were more like strangers, and the melancholy of the weather combined to add to his grim mood. Worse, he had spent the entire day between stops riding in the back seat of a filthy rental car accompanied by an immense mouth breather and a second man who smelled enough of cheap cigarettes to jeopardize the cleaning deposit on the vehicle. Now, on his way back to the private jet and the warmth of the desert, a full-on rain started about the same time as the bucking sound coming from the right rear tire. Three miles short of the Appleton airport, his massive bodyguard pulled to the side of the desolate road to investigate the problem.

After several minutes of inspection, the tree trunk communicated his diagnosis using the breadth of his vocabulary. "Flat tire," he concluded in a dull tone. Both he and the smoker got out of the vehicle just as a Good Samaritan pulled over to offer his assistance. Although BB tried to wave off the elderly gentleman, this was his excitement for the day, even though he could add little more than coaching for the other two.

"Shit," exclaimed the executive to no one as he watched the senior citizen and the two bodyguards struggle with the tire from the warmth of his own car on the other side of the road. Having slipped a ten-penny nail under the rear tire of the jeweler's car while it was parked at its last stop, he knew this was his last chance to act. He screwed a six-inch long suppressor onto his pistol, pulled a driving cap onto his head, and zipped past the disabled vehicle before spinning his car around and pulling up behind the growing caravan. Stepping from his car, he mentally walked through the batting order.

BB was kneeling in a puddle, wrestling the flattened tire off the car. He had no time to react when the man in the hat and raincoat appeared from nowhere with a weapon. In the pounding rain, the others around the vehicle could hear neither the *pfft* of the bullet as it entered BB's head nor see the pink mist as it exited. With the most dangerous member of the protective unit accounted for, the exec turned his attention to Hayes. He had been holding an umbrella for BB and was slow to react before taking two rounds to the chest and crumpling heavily onto his partner's now dead body. Having witnessed the murders in progress, the elderly man made a break for his vehicle. However, with two arthritic knees, he covered barely ten feet before feeling two bullets tear into his back and out of his chest.

The executive then turned his attention to Watson, who could not hear or see the assault from his position inside the car. However, he was quick to understand what was taking place when the barrel of a gun broke the window next to his seat. With little room to maneuver, the jeweler resigned himself to putting his hands up.

"Where is it?" asked the attacker, opening the front passenger door.

"What?" responded Watson. The insufficient answer earned him a bullet to his left knee.

"Care to try again?" With the jeweler now screaming in pain, the executive commanded, "Where's the Monster?"

"If I tell you, will you leave me alone?" asked Watson, doing his best to negotiate while trying not to lose consciousness.

"Sure," came the less-than-reassuring smug response.

"It's in the glove compartment."

The executive turned toward the hiding spot, away from Watson. Even though the jeweler was in agony, he knew he was in a fight for his life. Gathering all his strength, Watson lunged from the back seat and grabbed at the man's head from behind for all he was worth, eliciting a scream from the exec. Watson dug his hands into the man's eyes, clawing deeply into his face, tearing skin and drawing blood. The attacker swung an elbow wildly, catching Watson in the jaw, knocking out a tooth and sending him fully into the rear seat once more. Then, a second bullet hit Geno's other knee, putting him in so much distress that he was on the verge of passing out. Now, with a moment to search, the exec ignored the warm blood flowing on his face and felt through the glove box before removing a sleek red velvet box containing the large diamond.

Placing the stone into his coat pocket, the exec turned his attention back to Watson, who was writhing in pain. Then, he calmly leveled his pistol before putting two bullets into Geno's forehead.

CHAPTER 35

Nowitzke was excited to help Anissa move back home and knocked off work early. However, his enthusiasm quickly turned to agitation when he saw Sean Cook pushing his partner in a wheelchair down to the curb near the hospital entrance.

"Right on cue, Detective Nowitzke!" yelled Sean as he saw the officer step out of his vehicle into the drizzle.

"What are you doing here, Sean?"

"Just lending a helping hand. Anissa told me you were picking her up this afternoon. But I decided to come and follow you back to her place. I'm making dinner for the two of us tonight."

Even in her weakened state, Anissa shot Nowitzke a stern glare, warning him to back off.

"Thanks for looking out for her," choked out Nowitzke. "She can use all the friends she can get during her recovery."

Sean placed several bags of Anissa's belongings into the trunk as the detective helped the young woman into his vehicle. As they pulled away, Nowitzke saw Sean fall in line behind him in a metallic green SUV. After several minutes of silence, Nowitzke asked, "So, how are you feeling?"

Before Anissa could answer, the detective's phone rang. Nowitzke saw that the number was from the Appleton PD dispatcher, and without a hands-free feature on his ancient Ford, he tossed the phone to Anissa to take the call. Although he could only hear Anissa, her silence and body language indicated it had taken on an ominous tone.

"My God. A 187. Give me the address, please." There was a pause before Nowitzke heard the young woman say, "We're rolling," as she placed the portable bubble light on the dashboard and turned it on.

"A murder?" asked Nowitzke.

"A multiple homicide. Head in the direction of the airport off Highway CB. A passerby stopped and found several bodies near some cars parked off to the side of the road. The guy called it in and is waiting for us. Several patrols have been dispatched to preserve the scene as best they can in the rain."

"Alright. Let me drop you off at your condo."

"Negative, Chuck. Let's move. I might be weak, but I'm not dead."

"Fair enough. By the way, you know your boyfriend is behind us, right?"

Anissa closed her eyes and dropped her head. "Shit. Let him follow us. After I help with the initial part of the investigation, maybe he can take me home."

As Nowitzke neared the site of the murders, he came upon several squad cars blocking the busy road to keep traffic from driving through the crime scene. Recognizing the approaching beater with the bubble, the officers waved the slowing Nowitzke through before stopping Sean. The rain was letting up as Nowitzke parked, and the two detectives, moving at Anissa's pace, deliberately approached an expansive area bordered by bright yellow police tape. They were met by Officer Kenny Hicks.

"Afternoon, Detectives. How you feelin', ma'am?" asked Hicks in his staccato speech pattern.

Anissa winced. "I'm doing much better, Officer . . . thank you. Where's the man who was first on site?"

"Sitting in the wet grass on the bank of the road," said Hicks. "Name's Andy Davis. Seems pretty shaken up by the whole experience."

"Go figure. What do you know?" asked Nowitzke.

"Not much. Four bodies . . . one in the first car. A rental. Two guys piled together next to a flat right rear tire. And an old man who must have been trying to get away. Looks like he took two to the back. Weird thing is nothing seems wrong. I mean, no obvious motive. Don't seem like the type for a drug deal, even though the two lying over there look like bodyguards. No one looks familiar. But hey, I'm no detective," concluded Hicks with a smile. "I've called in the medical examiner, and he's on his way."

Both Nowitzke and Anissa took a broad stroll around the entire scene before she retrieved the camera from the car. As Anissa began photographing the area, Nowitzke turned his attention to Davis.

"Mr. Davis, I'm Detective Nowitzke. I'm told you found the bodies?"

"Yes, sir," he replied, standing. "I was on my way home from work and saw the emergency flashers on one of the cars. I pulled over to help . . ." said Davis, pausing. "Jesus . . . I found the old guy lying facedown in the road, bleeding from his back. Then I realized he'd been shot, twice. As I approached the first car, I found two more people. I didn't touch them, but it was clear they were also dead. I thought that was bad enough until I looked into the vehicle. There was a guy in the back seat covered in blood. In fact, the whole interior was a mess. The poor bastard was shot several times. It's the worst thing I've ever seen in my life," concluded Davis.

"Did you see the shooter?"

"No. And thank God. An animal like that probably would have killed me too."

Nowitzke took Davis's particulars and sent him on his way after making sure he wasn't too shaken to drive. Then Nowitzke poked his head into the vehicle just as another car with bubble lights pulled up.

"What the hell is it with you two finding bodies in shitty weather?" yelled the round, bald man with a greying, bushy beard emerging from his car, recalling their first meeting in a blizzard.

"Good to see you too, Wally," replied Nowitzke. Dr. F. Walter Schmidt had arrived. The long-time medical examiner was a bowling ball of a man, standing roughly five and a half feet tall and at least as wide. "Have you been losing weight?"

"Fuck you, Chuck," said the surly old man. "Oh, hello, Anissa," he added, lightening his tone upon seeing the young detective approaching. "Have they caught the asshole that shot you yet?"

"Nice to see you, Wally. And no, they haven't," she replied, glancing at Nowitzke.

"So, what is it today?" asked Schmidt.

"Well, I'd say your dance card is full," replied Nowitzke. "Four customers scattered in and around the cars."

"Nice. Who is everyone?"

"Beats the hell out of me. We arrived just before you did, so we're still working on that. But my first guess is the two guys near the back of the first car were protecting the one in the back. From what I saw, those two were changing the tire. You can see a big nail sticking out through the rubber. It has the makings of a setup of some sort, but I'll be damned as to why," said Nowitzke, pausing to turn toward the other body. "Looks like the poor old bastard on the shoulder back there was an innocent bystander trying to help. The only real struggle looks like it happened in the car itself. We'll dust the vehicle for prints and try to identify the bodies from any paperwork they were carrying. But the rain has washed away tire marks from any other cars. I can't see any local video cameras, but it's a point to follow up on. You see anything different, Nis?"

"Yes. It looks like the victim in the car fought with his attacker. In fact, I'd like you to look at his hands closely. I would bet next month's paycheck that he scratched the shooter pretty well. I'm sure there's DNA under those fingernails," Anissa concluded.

"Nice catch," replied Nowitzke, nodding. "There should be several slugs available from the victims as well. Looks like a professional hit to me. While I don't know for sure, I'm thinking one guy did all the damage. Hopefully, we can piece together a motive."

"Wow, you guys have improved," said Wally. "I'll see what I can do with the slugs, handle the toxicology, and get you a report as soon as possible. Ballistics can see if the bullets were all fired from the same weapon." Wally began to go about his work, beginning with the body in the car.

"Anissa, you did some great work today," said Nowitzke. "But the rain is picking up again, and you're not a hundred percent. Have Sean pull up and enjoy a quiet dinner at home."

"You sure?" asked the young woman, who was spent but didn't want to leave her partner behind.

"Yeah. Listen, I was handling murders like this when you were a prom queen. I got this." Nowitzke called the officers to let Sean's vehicle through before moving to help Schmidt with the body.

Wally had retrieved one victim's wallet, finding an Arizona driver's license and a business card inside. "Eugene Watson, Jeweler to the Stars," read the medical examiner.

"Shit, another jeweler killed in Wisconsin?" responded Nowitzke incredulously.

Sean's car pulled up slowly to the side of the road before he stepped out into the weather. Anissa started walking towards him when Nowitzke called out.

"Hey, Sean, you got a minute?" he yelled, closing the gap between him and the pair. "Do you know a Eugene Watson? His card says he's a jeweler from Arizona."

Confused for a moment, Sean responded, "Geno. How do you know Geno?"

"I think he's the one in the car. Dead," said Nowitzke matter-of-factly.

"Oh my God. What the hell was he doing here?" he exclaimed. "Where's the Monster?"

"I don't know. We haven't identified the person who shot him . . ." replied Nowitzke.

"No, I mean the Pink Monster," said Sean, panic rising in his voice. "Geno traveled with it everywhere. It's a five-carat pink diamond. Is it in the car too?"

"We didn't find any diamonds anywhere, but we haven't fully searched the car yet," the detective responded, pondering this as a potential motive for the crime.

Sean ran to the car, hoping beyond hope that it was not Watson. But it was. There he sat in the back seat, staring blankly forward with two holes in his forehead and much of his brain on the rear window. Sean barely made it to the wet grass before he started retching.

"How do you know Watson?" asked the detective after giving Sean a moment.

"He's another one of my clients," said Sean, wiping his mouth with the sleeve of his jacket. "These two guys must be his bodyguards." He looked down at the two men stacked on each other. "Geno approached me when he was having trouble getting reasonable insurance coverage for the Pink Monster. We worked out some terms. I knew he traveled extensively with the stone, but he did what we asked him to. So much for armed guards." Sean was pale, on the verge of going into shock.

"What was the stone valued at?" asked Anissa.

"I think we had it insured for $10 million," he said, shaking his head. "Jesus, what the hell is going on?"

"Well, looks like your luck is holding," replied Nowitzke as his phone buzzed. "Russ, I've been looking for you. Let me bring you up to speed on current events in our area." He gave the fed an overview of what had just taken place.

"Wow, the Pink Monster stolen in Wisconsin, tied to a quadruple homicide. I'm in Milwaukee, but I can be in Appleton tomorrow morning."

"Great. I've also got a couple of things to run by you. We got a strange text connecting Bateman's and Lockett's, and I may need FBI resources to help resolve a potential link. See you in the office."

After clicking off the call, Nowitzke mulled over the series of jewelry crimes and their increasing brutality. Ultimately, the detective was left to agree with Sean Cook's observation. *What the hell is going on?* Still, he knew he had been down similar investigative paths in his past and remained confident in himself. But he needed a break. Something that would turn the odds into his favor. Nowitzke knew that eventually it would happen. The open question was whether it would come in time to stop the next crime and any associated pain and suffering.

CHAPTER 36

The following morning, Russell knocked on the glass window of Nowitzke's office door with his elbow to get the detective's attention, not realizing he was using his speakerphone on a conference call. Russ held up two large coffees for the detective to see, prompting Nowitzke to jump out of his office chair and open the door for the fed mid-conversation.

"So, how are you doing, Art? I mean with Muriel," asked Nowitzke, who accepted the coffee from Russ and sat down.

"I'm not going to lie, it's been a five-year struggle," came the voice through the grey box on Nowitzke's desk. "First, her breast cancer metastasized. Somehow, she summoned the strength to work through chemo and all the other treatments. Things that almost killed her. Then, when the doctor said she had beaten the odds, she developed early-stage Alzheimer's."

Nowitzke closed his eyes upon hearing the news and sighed. "Art, I am so sorry. I didn't know how rough you had things. Is Muriel still at home?"

"I couldn't take care of her, Chuck. I've had to put her into a nursing home." The hollow voice cracked before tailing off into silence.

Breaking the pregnant pause, Nowitzke replied, "Please give Muriel my best." He took another moment and then added, "Russ, I'm glad you're here," signaling his friend on the phone that a third party had entered the room, albeit a little late. "I'm on the line with

Arturo Copeland, the investigating officer on the Lockett's robbery and an old friend. Art, meet Louis Russell, FBI."

"Hello, sir," came the response on the other end of the call.

"Well, you've both been busy men," said the FBI agent, who had dropped into one of the chairs in front of the detective's desk.

"Absolutely," replied both detectives simultaneously.

"We were just talking about the Lockett's robbery, the Bateman's burglary, and what happened yesterday in town with the quadruple homicide and presumed theft of a large diamond," started Nowitzke, taking a sip of the warm brew. "Russ, in a little over a week, we've had three major jewelry felonies in the state. Frankly, even though Arturo and I had our run of crimes against jewelers several years ago in Milwaukee, I've never seen anything like this in all my years of law enforcement. What, if anything, do you know about Eugene Watson?" he asked, looking at Russell.

"Not much. I got some intel from New York this morning. Watson was a high roller who made it big with the Hollywood elite since leaving the farm in Wisconsin."

"No shit. I wouldn't have figured. Why the hell was he here?" questioned Copeland.

"I did a quick background check on Watson," chimed in Nowitzke. "Apparently, his father passed away recently in the greater Green Bay area. But I'm not sure why Watson had the big diamond with him. That's the kicker to me. Watson comes from Arizona for a funeral, but someone took a helluva gamble to kill him and three others on the off chance the jeweler had the stone with him."

"You're assuming it was an off chance," offered Russ. "Maybe the killer had some sort of insider information that Watson had the stone with him."

Nowitzke nodded. "You're right. This wasn't a hit on the jeweler, so the killer must have known. As I've thought about the crime scene yesterday, it was clear the robber did some advance planning. He or she must have set a nail under the vehicle's tire at a prior stop, knowing it would eventually disable the car and distract the two bodyguards."

"A nail in a tire?" replied Russell. "You know, for years we had problems with South American gangs trailing jewelry salespeople who used that technique to steal goods. But, almost always, they were distraction thefts, not robberies involving the murder of the victim. It sounds like your perpetrator may be familiar with jewelry theft."

"Or just an expert in disabling a vehicle the simplest way possible," countered Nowitzke. "Listen, I called you both to talk about a text message that was sent to a local insurance underwriter, a guy named Sean Cook. Poor bastard has the misfortune of insuring all three losses." Nowitzke pulled out his phone, showing the copy of the text to the fed but reading it for Copeland.

"Connected, huh? Who was the text from, and how would that person know?" asked Copeland.

"The primary questions, Art," replied Nowitzke. "Sean says he doesn't recognize the number and has no idea who sent it to him. We ran things down with our forensics people. They concluded the phone is a burner. When they did the tower dump, they said the message came from some secluded road off Highway 41 about forty miles south. What they tell me is that unless the phone's turned on . . ."

". . . you have no way to track it," said Russell, finishing the sentence. "Your people are correct."

"Does the FBI have any tools that might help?" asked Copeland.

"No, nothing beyond what you already have access to. Let's put it this way, it would be unusual if the robbery and burglary were connected given the psychological profiles of the typical actors. But, I guess, not impossible," conceded the fed.

"Any luck on your end with the Lockett's robbery?" asked Nowitzke, directed to Copeland.

"Nothing that you don't already know," he replied. "For now, it's a dry hole. We're working leads every day but aren't getting much in return. How are you doing with your investigation of the burglary?"

"Well, you know one of the perps is dead. One Musa Besnik. Besnik was working with the YACs on the Bateman's burglary."

"The YACs are still around?" questioned Copeland.

"Yes," responded Russ. "They aren't what they once were, but Bateman is out millions due to their work."

"Get this, Art," said Nowitzke, "one of the sales associates is an Albanian knockout named Nadia Belushi. And guess what?" he asked. "Turns out she's Besnik's sister."

"No shit," replied Copeland. That revelation even got Russell's attention.

"She dropped off the grid shortly after the crime, but we've now got her in custody."

"Really. She's at the Appleton PD jail?" asked Copeland.

"No. Her story is that someone she refers to as Katallani was responsible for the burglary. Supposedly, her brother contracted with Katallani. But when Besnik fucked up, leaving DNA at the scene, his boss killed him. Nadia says she might have once met Katallani, but she's not sure. Although if she did, she might be next on the hit list. Russ, can you run that name through any of your national databases?"

"Sure enough," replied Russ.

"I'm not sure what you'll find," continued Nowitzke. "According to Nadia, the term Katallani is the equivalent of an Albanian demon. Anyway, I was concerned she was at risk, so I moved her to a safe house here where I can keep an eye on her. But that's the long answer to your question. Art, were you planning on coming this way in the next week for dinner?"

"I was, but I can't leave the office. I apologize. I'd love to see your new digs. Hey, can you give me your new address so I can send you a bottle of scotch as a house-warming gift?"

"Absolutely. But make sure to send the package in a brown paper bag. Between my landlord and porch pirates, I'd hate for someone to steal it," said Nowitzke, giving his friend his particulars. "You take care, Art," he offered as he clicked off the line.

The detective turned his attention back to the fed. "Russ, you are fully up-to-date on our little Wisconsin crime spree. I appreciate the time and the coffee. Would like to see any of the evidence we gathered yesterday?"

Russell stood and shook his head. "Chuck, my impression is you're all over this. Again, if the FBI can provide any help to you, please call me," he added before hesitating briefly. "By the way, who's Muriel, the woman you were talking about with Copeland?"

"His wife of thirty-some years. A beautiful lady. You heard the medical history and can guess the prognosis. In addition to the mental stress, the financial impact must be crushing now that she's in a home," he replied absently. "I thought I had money problems, but my impression is that Art and his wife lived up to and perhaps beyond their means with little to fall back on."

"When you think you have it bad, you can always find someone else who has it worse," the fed retorted. "I'll get back to you on the name as soon as possible," he added, changing the conversation. "Do you need any assistance in protecting the witness?"

"Negative. At this point, I think we're in good shape," concluded Nowitzke, picturing all ninety pounds of a spirited Miss Alma standing up to an intruder.

CHAPTER 37

Kendra Mullins, senior vice president of Wisconsin Specialty Underwriters, was beside herself. Upon joining WSU three years before, she had pitched the idea of creating a series of new niche programs to diversify the sleepy company's portfolio of tired existing products offered by every one of its competitors. More importantly, she promised management new streams of revenue and untold profits. Blessed by the company's president, then ratified by the board, Mullins was given carte blanche to lead the bold, new strategy.

Her first major hire was Sean Cook, an insurance savant with a resumé touting underwriting experience in the London market insuring jewelers. Sean was charged with building a new program from scratch, working with an internal team to support the effort while also courting brokers who controlled large blocks of business. At the same time, Sean immersed himself in the jewelry industry, becoming a regular at high-profile functions and spending money lavishly to earn name recognition and trust. And Sean delivered on his promises to Mullins. His early results were stellar, everything she had foreseen. New accounts were booking as fast as the home office team could handle them. More importantly, income skyrocketed, driving profits to levels not previously seen at WSU. Mullins was confident that her brainchild would punch her ticket to becoming the next CEO at the company.

But after three years of prosperity, the program's direction took a dramatic turn. New business was still coming to the carrier, but the small trickle of expected losses had morphed. Mullins's pet project had just sustained its third multimillion-dollar loss in less than a month, and she was in full panic mode. Shit was rolling downhill from the corner office faster than she could shovel it. Her survival instinct was to steer the mess toward Sean Cook. And now he was feeling the pressure. Sean did his best to explain to Mullins that the accounts he dealt with had high values, took risks, and were always a target for criminals. Even though he followed best practices and tightly managed his accounts, losses would be inevitable. It was the insurance business after all. When the bean counters pointed out that the three most recent claims wiped out all the profits for the program since its creation, in addition to cutting deeply into the earnings of the company's traditional business, both Mullins and Sean knew someone would have to answer.

Not knowing what else to do, Sean reached out to Nowitzke, making an impassioned plea for him to meet with the underwriter and his boss. Sean reasoned that since the detective was the only person with actual knowledge of each loss, he might be able to lend some level of support to the program business. Although he questioned the value of the meeting, Nowitzke was uncharacteristically sympathetic to Sean's plight and grudgingly agreed to attend.

Nowitzke regretted his commitment almost immediately upon entering the plush fourth-floor office of the severe-looking woman wearing a designer business suit and an unusual hairstyle. *Christ, her hair looks almost metallic, except where someone shaved it down to her scalp.* "Ms. Mullins, I'm Detective Nowitzke," he said, drawing only a scowl in return. Mullins remained seated as Nowitzke dropped into the fine leather chair next to Sean and across the desk from the woman.

"How is your investigation progressing with the three serious crimes, Detective?" asked Mullins, drumming her manicured blood-red fingernails on the oak desk. "Are you close to making any arrests, or, more importantly, recovering the stolen merchandise?"

"The honest answer is we are working these files hard every day," replied Nowitzke. Sean cringed, not wanting Nowitzke to share the honest answer with Mullins. "A colleague of mine in Milwaukee is on top of the Lockett's file. Appleton PD continues to get leads, and each case is developing at a different pace. We are also working with the FBI to potentially recover some of the goods." Sean thought the reference to the national crime-fighting organization was a nice touch but then winced as Nowitzke concluded, "The fact of the matter is jewelry is fungible. What was taken was likely fenced in several large southern cities within a day of each loss. The chances of any major recovery are pretty much slim to nil."

Mullins blinked hard at Nowitzke's answer. "So, your answer is no to both arrest and recovery?" she said vacuously.

"That is correct, ma'am."

"So why are you here wasting my time?" she said as she sat back in her chair, distractedly scrolling through texts on her phone.

Nowitzke straightened in his chair and tried to bite his tongue from delivering a snappy comeback. "I was asked by Sean to meet with you and provide an update. As a public servant, I granted the request. Believe me, this is not something I typically do on any open case. In fact, my time is pretty fucking valuable too. It would be better served chasing down the people that stole from your clients or finding the person who put a bullet into the head of one of your jewelers. If I've wasted yours, I'm sorry," he said, resisting the urge to punctuate the sentence with "bitch."

Mullins was caught off guard by the detective's response, not used to having such direct communication with anyone in her office. Sean blanched at the exchange and rose from his seat, trying to signal the end of the meeting, but Nowitzke missed the subtlety of his gesture and remained fast in his chair. "Sean, I need a moment alone with Ms. Mullins."

Sean now looked terrified, wishing he had never suggested the session, and left the office, closing the door behind him. Even though Mullins was in her domain, she was now playing defense. "Please tell me about your jewelry program," asked Nowitzke in a more relaxed tone.

Mullins shifted in her chair, recognizing the police detective was now simply seeking information about her operation. "I guess it's my baby. I talked with our CEO about starting several new niches here to differentiate WSU from its competitors. We've been doing very well, up until recently with these large claims. It's something people here are not used to, and a lot of the staff is on edge, including me," she admitted.

"You've had some bad luck," commented Nowitzke, rising to look at the view out of the window. "How did you come to hire Sean?"

"I found him on the internet through a job search board. Sean had impeccable credentials with experience in London and a broad background in insurance."

"Did you check his references?"

Mullins considered the implications of the question before answering. "No. I was in a rush to get our program up to speed, and I cut that corner. There didn't seem to be any need to with his resumé."

"Did you do any background check on him?" asked the officer.

"Well, no . . . again, I didn't," stammered Mullins. "Is there something I should know about that you aren't telling me?"

"No, nothing at all. Just curious, I guess. I do want you to know that we are working these crimes incredibly hard, Ms. Mullins. In addition to the loss of property, we have a trail of bodies associated with two of them. It is my priority now."

"Please call me Kendra, Detective," exhaled the insurance executive. "I've heard about the murders and am sick to death about them. I know Sean is too. I apologize for my behavior. I guess it's just the stress around here. Many employees are concerned that the board might make some changes to our new programs. Ultimately, my impression is they love the strategy of entering new markets but might want to find someone better to execute it. I would guess I'd be one of the first on the chopping block if things get that far. If you would, please call me with any updates."

"I will," concluded Nowitzke, handing her his card.

It was approaching closing time for most of the employees, and Nowitzke followed the flow of traffic back to the lobby of the building. Cook was sitting alone in a comfortable chair with his head in his hands, waiting for the officer. "You look like you could use a drink, Sean. I'll buy," said Nowitzke. The underwriter said nothing as he stood and they walked to the parking lot. "Follow my Taurus and the trail of blue smoke."

Minutes later, they arrived at The Office, a popular sports bar not far from the business district where WSU was located. While The Office catered to a variety of demographics over the course of a week, the post-5:00 p.m. crowd on workdays was primarily professionals looking to unwind, entertain customers before heading off for dinner, or hook up with others looking for drinks and meaningless sex. More than once, someone had called home to tell their spouse they would be putting in extra time at The Office.

Despite its appeal, The Office was nothing more than a large pole building with a stylish circular metal bar sitting underneath a bank of flat-screen televisions, which allowed patrons to watch whatever game was on at the time. Decorated primarily in Wisconsin Badger red and white, the room contained framed jerseys and signed sports memorabilia. Beyond the bar were rows of high-boy tables and booths, all strategically placed near even more television screens.

Shortly after Nowitzke and Sean sat down, a fetching brunette wearing a tight referee's jersey, cut-off shorts, and a baseball cap approached. "Gentlemen, I'm Olivia. It's beer and wings night. What can I get you?" she asked.

"Olivia, why don't you save yourself some work and just bring us a pitcher of what's on special and two glasses?" said Nowitzke.

In the din of people unraveling from their day, Sean remained quiet, gazing off into space, preoccupied with the meeting that had just ended.

"Chuck, you know Mullins is going to fire me," concluded Sean. "She loved the program when it was printing money, but these losses have killed us. And I'm the guy that's responsible for the current result."

Olivia dropped off the beer and promptly left to wait on other customers. Nowitzke poured two tall glasses and pushed one across the table to Sean. "So what if she does fire you. You'll find another job. I thought you had a big-time resumé working with jewelers. Shit, I've lost jobs before and always landed on my feet."

Sean gauged the paunchy, disheveled detective guzzling his first beer, and the image offered him little comfort. "I'm just not used to this kind of failure. I think the thing that bothers me most is that several people have been killed. That's definitely something I've never had to live with," he said, staring blankly at a European soccer match on one of the televisions.

"Listen, Sean . . . Sean," Nowitzke said loudly, trying to get the young man's attention, which was momentarily hypnotized by the game. "Shit happens. The people who got killed knew the risks of their jobs for the most part, or they should have anyway. You're not responsible for them or how they went about their business. You only provided their insurance, for Chrissake. Imagine how you'd feel had Anissa been killed. It could have easily happened when she was protecting the scumbag thief."

Sean considered the weight of Nowitzke's comment, taking a heavy pull on his drink. "Jesus, that never occurred to me. I was sick when I heard Anissa got shot. Man, I was so worried not knowing if she would live or die." He took another drink of his beer. "By the way, you know I have feelings for her."

"Yeah, I know. I'm a detective, remember. I'm sure she'd like to hear from you now that she's at home."

"So, you're cool with that?"

"Let's just say I've already expressed my position on the matter to you." Nowitzke pulled back his blue, checked sports jacket, exposing his weapon. "Listen, she's a beautiful young woman who I regard highly. But I don't control her. I think she's figured out there's more to life than a career and wants more. Especially now with this shooting business. Any relationship is up to the two of you."

Sean downed his beer, poured another, and lifted his hand to hail Olivia. "Thinking about Anissa, I feel better already."

The second pitcher of beer went down at the same pace as the first.

Nowitzke stared into the bottom of his glass before continuing the conversation. "If Mullins fires you, what's your next gig?"

"Tell you what I'd like to do. Maybe it's the beer talking, but I'd love to ditch the whole nine-to-five thing and open my own bar . . . in Nicaragua," he said.

"Fucking Nicaragua? Wasn't there a war there recently?"

"Yeah, about thirty years ago. In the meantime, it's become quite the vacation destination."

"Well, I guess, if you're into third-world countries and malaria. I don't get it. What's the draw to Nicaragua?"

"Sun, beach, no snow, and lots of tourist money from Europe and the US. It's my dream to own a business. At least at this point in my life, while I'm still young enough to make the leap."

"Is it expensive there?" asked Nowitzke, downing the last gulp in his glass.

"Not terribly. A little tougher without a job, of course. But based on what I've seen online, I could get started with a decent business in a prime location, with an apartment, for less than half a million," replied Cook.

"I'm guessing dollars, not pesos or whatever they use there? Tell you what, I'd loan it to you if I had it, just to say I'd been there and had a beer on the beach. But based on my recent divorce, and the one before that, I'll be a working man until I'm roughly one hundred and three."

Sean laughed. "Nice to see you have a sense of humor about your finances."

"What's the alternative? It's only money. I made some choices that didn't work out. I like what I do, for the most part. But I'm guessing the closest I'll get to Nicaragua is having a fish taco at a restaurant in Appleton."

"Listen, Chuck, I really appreciate you making the time to come to WSU today," concluded Sean. "Thanks for the beer and the discussion. I need to shove off."

"No problem," responded Nowitzke, hailing Olivia for the check. Before Nadia had started living at his place and learned how to cook, he would have stuck around for another beer and tried to strike up a conversation with the young ref. However, he now had better things to do.

CHAPTER 38

The kid assumed his position in the same booth in the back of the dining room at the truck stop. Although he thought about altering his appearance for this meeting, he ultimately concluded there were few options beyond a t-shirt and jeans. Ruling out sunglasses as being too conspicuous for a midnight meeting, the only change he made was exchanging the farm seed logo hat for a camo baseball cap. He soon realized any efforts to disguise himself were for naught when Ruthie spotted him instantly after he got comfortable.

"Didn't see you there with your new camo hat, hon," she joked. "Coffee? Oh, and is your good-looking friend coming by too?"

"Yes, two coffees, please," conceded the kid. He didn't know the executive all that well, but based on his recent handiwork and the rising body count, he was now concerned for Ruthie's well-being if she let on about how good her memory was. Of course, his partner had done everything short of wearing a flashing beacon on his head to stand out from the crowd on his first trip to the truck stop. And history was about to repeat itself.

The exec entered the dining room through the front door wearing a custom-tailored suit and flashing a heavy gold Rolex watch as he ambled past a roomful of bleary-eyed truck drivers. *So much for fitting in.* Beyond the clothing, however, the executive was also sporting two large gauze pads, one on each side of his face. The kid could only shake his head at the visual as the man glided toward him before taking a seat in the booth. Before they started their conversation, Ruthie brought their coffees, doing a double take at the older man's bandages.

"Anything else, hon?" she asked, trying not to stare.

"Nothing, ma'am," replied the kid politely. "This should be fine." When Ruthie was out of earshot, he continued. "Nice disguise."

"Fuck you," came the prompt response.

"Did you lose a fight with a bear?" asked the kid flippantly before making the connection. "Oh shit, was that from Watson?"

The executive said nothing, taking a sip of his coffee, but his body language revealed everything in response.

"Man, I told you to forget about the Monster, but you couldn't leave it alone. Now we've got more bodies and you have two big fucking scars on your face."

"Shut the fuck up. Is someone spying on us? I'm told that there is a text message floating out there connecting the robbery and the burglary. My sources say it originated in the general vicinity of this restaurant," he said, his voice rising.

"I have no clue, but it seems unlikely. Do any of the truckers in here look like they're eavesdropping on us? How could anyone else know what's going on?" questioned the kid. "Or did you just forget to kill someone along the way?"

"You don't think Ruthie is watching and listening too closely, do you?"

"Give me a break. Yeah, our three-hundred-pound waitress who always seems to be working the graveyard shift is probably a cop. We've been here twice. You're paranoid. How could she know anything about our early targets or any of our conversations? Your biggest risk with her is getting a huge piece of ass in a stall in the men's room."

"Hey, the heavy honeys need love too," replied the exec, who had calmed momentarily. "I also hear I'm now known as Katallani."

"Yeah, I'm aware of that too. What does it matter? As far as I know, it's not an alias you've ever used before. I understand Besnik came up with that, and his sister told the detective who is working the cases."

"Well, I'm about to clean up that open item shortly," replied the older man as he tried to scratch an itch under the bandages.

"What are you up to now? The name means nothing . . . Albanian gibberish, for Chrissake. We have one final gig before our partnership dissolves. Can't you leave it alone without calling more attention to us?"

"What do you think? If Besnik told his sister about me, I'm at risk, and so are you," said the executive. "You should be glad. If someone wasn't taking any action, you might be enjoying sex in the men's room of a federal prison."

"Just leave me out of this. I don't want any details," said the kid. "By the way, are we on schedule?"

"We are. I've located my team, and they're locked and loaded."

"You know if you do this right, you and your team won't have to kill anyone."

The exec said nothing. He poured more coffee for himself, then asked, "Were you able to find the device?"

"Got it on the dark web. Here you go." The kid pulled a black suitcase from under the table and slid it over to the older man. "From what I gather, it fell off a truck outside of Moscow. I've paid for it out of my end."

"Does it work?"

"Beats the hell out of me. But it better. My suggestion is to road test it before the job. It comes with instructions in Russian and English, and based on what I've heard, you might want to cover your nuts when you turn it on," said the kid with a laugh. "At least if you're planning on having kids in the future."

"Funnyman. Anything else?"

"Oh, yeah, I got a couple of Serbian party favors in my SUV for your little escapade, just as you requested."

"How come you didn't bring them into the restaurant?"

"Yeah, that would look very inconspicuous. Several large camo-green boxes with foreign writing on the side along with a symbol that screams warning in any language," replied the kid. "One of the rednecks in this joint would shoot you before you got them loaded in your car."

The exec couldn't help but laugh quietly at the kid's observation. "I suppose you're right," he conceded, taking another sip of his coffee. "By the way, we're a go. We have the date and the route set. If we pull it off, it will make the other heists look like we stole chump change. Watch the news and you'll know when it goes down."

"Send my cut to my account. I assume this concludes our partnership?" said the kid.

"It pretty much should," concluded the executive.

"After this job, you can buy all the Neosporin you want for your face."

"Fuck you. I can afford plastic surgery."

The men left out of different doors, one through the front with the other out the side exit, going their separate ways. However, even from their respective positions in the parking lot, they both heard Ruthie's yelp at finding another hundred-dollar tip left behind on the table.

CHAPTER 39

When Nowitzke arrived at work the following morning, he was surprised to see Sean Cook waiting for him in the lobby under the watchful eye of Officer Benson. "We're spending too much time together, Sean. People are going to talk."

The underwriter looked anxious but seemed pleased to see the detective nonetheless. Nowitzke waited for Benson to open the magnetic lock on the heavy door then held it for the young man to enter the office area.

When they were out of earshot from the lobby, but before they made it to Nowitzke's office, Sean began, unable to contain himself. "Chuck, it happened again early this morning. After our conversation about WSU and losing my job, I guess I wasn't sleeping well. Anyway, I heard my phone buzz and saw I had a text from the same number as before. From our mystery man. But this time, I was able to respond, and we had a short back-and-forth. I wanted you to see it but also to find his location, if possible."

"Let me see your phone," said Nowitzke after entering his office and perching on the edge of his desk. The detective scrolled through the exchange that took place that morning at 1:05 a.m.

Katallani was responsible for Watson's murder. He stole the Pink Monster.

Cook – *Who is Katallani? How do you know?*

None of your business. Three down and one to go for Katallani. The final crime will dwarf the others. Then he'll disappear forever.

Cook – *Where will it take place and when?*

Chicago. Soon. A major jewelry hit. There will be blood in the streets.

Cook – *I need more details to help stop him.*

I'm not sure you can. In the meantime, sit tight. More to follow. But share this with absolutely no one beyond your chubby friend and the FBI.

After reading the series of messages, Nowitzke smiled and shook his head. "Nice work on the exchange, Sean. So essentially, your buddy implicates Katallani in all three crimes, intimates another is in the works . . . and thinks I should lose a few pounds."

"Yeah, something big," responded Sean, ignoring Nowitzke's final comment. "Who is Katallani?"

Nowitzke took a deep breath and considered how much information he should give to Sean. "Frankly, no one knows. As told to me, he's a demon of some sort."

"Alright . . ." Sean replied, pondering Nowitzke's response. "Back to the text, how would we ever narrow down the specific target considering the size of Chicago and the number of jewelry stores?"

"How the hell would I know? You're the jewelry insurance expert. Do you have accounts in Chicago?"

"Some, I guess," replied Sean.

"Big ones? Any obvious targets? I mean, anything that makes sense if you were Katallani? Or could it be an account you'd like to pick up?"

Sean said nothing, frozen, unable to isolate any possible clients in his head, let alone fathom what was about to take place.

"Oh, and we can't tell anyone but Russell and his cronies. Interesting," continued Nowitzke, wondering exactly what that meant.

The officer punched McKenzie's extension into his desk phone and put it on speaker. "Good morning, Norm. Nowitzke here. Question. Do you still have the number from the tower dump we discussed the other day?"

"Yes, of course."

"Would you run it again? We got a hit last night with another text. Also, see if there's any chance the burner has been left on."

"Will do. I should be able to get back to you shortly," said McKenzie as he hung up.

Nowitzke moved behind his desk and sat down. "Sean, I need to contact Russ to update him and pick his brain about any Chicago jewelry connections. It almost seems like your new texting buddy thinks we should be able to figure this out on our own. But I don't have any real knowledge about what type of crime this might be or know the area or any obvious targets. How do we figure out Katallani's next objective?"

"Well, maybe I can give it a shot," replied Sean with a level of uncertainty in his voice.

"Please do," said Nowitzke, ending the meeting. "And as soon as possible."

As Sean rose to leave the detective's office, the desk phone rang, stopping him in his tracks. Picking up the receiver, Nowitzke heard Norm's voice. "Let me put you on speaker."

"Chuck, just wanted to give you a heads-up. Since we knew the number we were looking for and the timing, it wasn't a big deal to go back and run it through again. Basically, we have record of a text exchange starting at 1:05 a.m. this morning. Looks like the whole discussion took just about a minute. Of course, the originating phone was then powered down immediately after the conversation was over."

"Of course. Where did the text come from?" asked Nowitzke.

"You're not going to believe this, but within about ten feet from where the first text did, some forty miles south of here."

"Shit," said Nowitzke. "I was hoping someplace different, like where there was a camera in place."

"Sorry I don't have better news," replied Norm.

Listening to the conversation, Sean drifted toward Nowitzke's credenza where he looked at the detective's photos. As the call ended, Sean hesitated for a moment, intrigued by a particularly ugly snow globe.

"Sean, don't even think about touching that one. It's a Halloween Michael Myers collector. We've talked about this before."

"I was just curious about it," replied Sean, looking for an exception from Nowitzke.

"Alright, give it one try, if you must. Just don't break another one, please."

Sean shook the globe. But rather than the traditional white snow he expected, the figure of Myers and his victim were suddenly enveloped in a shower of red flakes simulating the resulting arterial spray after a slashing.

"Jesus, Chuck, you are one sick motherfucker," said Sean, laughing. "I guess I am too, though."

Nowitzke couldn't help but join in the laughter. "Get out of here and come up with your potential hit list in Chicago, and I'll speak to Russ. Now, I've got to get to an appointment."

CHAPTER 40

BBB was a popular lunch place located off a town square in downtown Appleton. Wedged between what passed for high-rise professional buildings in the upper Midwest (ten stories max), BBB was an urban rehab project in a building formerly housing a large retail space. It was one of the few restaurants in the area that businesspeople could walk to before closing the next big deal.

During the day, BBB was referred to as the Better Business Bureau given the amount of work conducted at the café. From a point of fact, each of the B's represented the first initial of the three Jones brothers who owned the property: Barry, Bob, and Bill. For whatever reason, their parents never made it past the B's when searching baby books for names. However, once most of the professionals left for home, the place morphed into a hipster bar featuring live jazz and an eclectic crowd. When the switch took place, the initials signified any number of definitions as identified in the Urban Dictionary.

The Jones boys leased half the first floor of the structure after petitioning the city fathers for the right to allow seating on the public sidewalk during the summer. From 11:30 a.m. to 1:30 p.m., those tables, covered with bright yellow umbrellas, became highly coveted. It was also the perfect site for the executive to conduct his experiment.

From the seat of his 5 Series BMW, the well-dressed man fit in with his surroundings. Certainly much more so than any clandestine midnight meeting at a truck stop. His vantage point gave him the perfect view of roughly two hundred businesspeople eating their lunches. More importantly to the exec were those working their cell phones rather than picking at their salads and sandwiches. He estimated roughly half the crowd either had their device up to their head or were talking using a Bluetooth speaker wedged in an ear. The number did not include the suits who acted like the homeless, walking aimlessly on the streets staring down at their devices while appearing to talk to themselves. The setting was a veritable petri dish for his little research project.

In addition to the upscale café, the executive also had clear view of a four-door mechanic's shop kitty-corner from his position. The shop had a fenced-in parking lot containing luxury cars waiting to be fixed. He surmised many of the people eating at BBB probably enjoyed the convenience of dropping off their vehicle in the morning and walking to work before buying it back after being repaired. From what he could see, the four large electric garage doors were working overtime even during the noon hour as many picked up their rides, making space for those scheduled in the afternoon.

The setting was perfect. With these two obvious targets, the exec also knew there were no medical facilities in the immediate area. That was an important distinction, because attacking one, even inadvertently, would draw unwanted scrutiny from the authorities that he did not need. Pulling the briefcase from behind his seat, he opened it carefully, placing the device on the passenger seat. According to his research, activating the unit was not supposed to put the operator in any danger, but he didn't believe the Russian-to-English instructions. This was especially so, as he remembered the snarky comment from the kid who obtained the unit for him. *Russian technology . . . what could go wrong?* Yet, he also knew the same type of equipment was used by his own government to protect American presidents when traveling to less-than-friendly foreign countries.

The device itself was unremarkable-looking. Colored flat grey, it was the size and shape of the internet modem that sat on his desk in the den. Having read the directions several times, he mentally went through the simple setup process, which amounted to arraying the set of small antennas. Since the case came with its own battery, he didn't even need an external power source. Now, short of hitting the power button, he was ready to go. He was curious if this would work, still marveling at the unit's purported power. As he pushed the large red power button with his right hand, he unconsciously covered his testicles with his left. And then he waited, but not long.

The effect was immediate. Everything and nothing happened all at the same time. The din of conversation hovering over the restaurant stopped as if on cue. The executive watched as those using their phones literally stood in unison with heads rotating back and forth to see if anyone else had the same problem. When they recognized that no one had a signal, they automatically turned their attention to the restaurant staff as if BBB had done something to pull the proverbial plug. With his window down, the exec was close enough to hear the questions from the confused crowd. Then, as if led by an orchestra conductor, the businesspeople went through the process of turning off their phones and letting them restart. Without any luck, the more astute techies in the crowd pulled and replaced the battery in their cell. But there was still no joy. Most had run out of technical solutions and were doomed to having actual conversations with their neighbors.

The cell phone street zombies had a similar reaction. Like a movie, everyone stopped dead in their tracks as if God had hit the pause button on life. The exec smiled, observing each person pull out their earbuds, check the phone power level, and do a reset, all while remaining in place.

The auto shop had a different problem. Productivity ground to a halt as the garage doors stopped working, trapping four vehicles inside. The executive laughed with delight as the mechanics in the shop redirected their efforts to figuring out the glitch. Even the patrons gathered around the control unit felt compelled to offer their advice.

Three minutes into the denial-of-service attack, the exec had the proof of concept. He punched the power button once more, and on cue, life as the businesspeople knew it began again. Immediately, the executive heard the buzz, beep, and song of phone ringers erupting in unison from callers previously cut off. The diners refocused on the issues at hand, the street droids began walking and talking, and there was a general cheer from the auto shop as all the doors rolled up.

The exec calmly lowered the antennae of the device and closed the case before storing it in the back seat. The test had been a success by all measures. He was unconcerned about violating the Communications Act of 1934, which included the potential of an $11,000 fine or imprisonment of up to a year, a law that somehow covered first-time offenders using a cell phone jammer. Small potatoes, given the rising body count he was responsible for. Anyway, he would soon be long gone, leaving law enforcement to put together the pieces while he enjoyed a steady diet of conch and rum punch on a sandy beach somewhere.

As the afternoon progressed, each of the local service offices for the major cell providers received a plethora of customer complaints. Of course, the representatives at each carrier professed to know nothing about the service loss. After analyzing where the complaints originated from, though, the cell companies judged that whatever the problem was had been confined to one square mile. There were no damages, no police reports. However, each of the local Green Bay television affiliates devoted thirty seconds to reporting about the strange occurrence as a filler story that evening.

CHAPTER 41

Nowitzke surmised that his smoke-belching Taurus would bring property values down at the van Berlage as he pulled up to the front entrance. Anissa glided out of the door into the brilliant sunshine on cue as if to hurry the entire process along, minimizing any potential relationship damage with her fellow condo dwellers. However, Nowitzke took the time to park his car and jump out from behind the wheel to open the front passenger door for the young woman. Even though Anissa flashed her typical smile and looked as though she had stepped out of the pages of a fashion magazine, she was moving gingerly.

"Chuck, you didn't have to take me to my doctor's appointment."

"I know. But you're not cleared to drive yet. Didn't want you to have to take an Uber."

"Well, thanks," she replied, wincing as she stepped into the car. "I appreciate it. I just thought you were buried at work."

"I am. Coffee is in the holder for you," he said as he pulled away from the condominium. "By the way, I've been spending way too much time with Mr. Wonderful."

"Seriously?"

"Yeah, going to his office to be abused by his boss and then out for drinks."

"Well, you're seeing more of him than I am. He hasn't called for several days. Maybe he's cooled on me," replied Anissa.

"Really, just when I thought there was hope for the man. He may well be an idiot after all. Any chance he's not hetero?"

Anissa did not take the bait but sat silently, contemplating the surrounding greenery as the vehicle groaned through the city.

"Oh, speaking of the dumbass, Sean got another text from our secret source," said Nowitzke. "According to the texter, Katallani killed Watson, his bodyguards, and a local before taking the Pink Monster." He took a sip of coffee, managing to dribble a trail of the beverage down his shirt.

"Seriously," Anissa replied.

"The text came in early this morning in the same spot as the first, according to Norm. Interestingly, Sean had a back-and-forth with whoever, and in theory, Katallani is planning on a large jewelry theft in Chicago. Not sure when, where, or who the target is. And, according to our texter, the only people who can know about this are Sean, me, and Russell."

"But you just told me."

"You and I are the same as far as I'm concerned . . . Appleton PD. I'll call Russ later." Then, Nowitzke cocked his head and suddenly went silent.

"Chuck, are you alright?" asked Anissa, touching his arm and looking at him with a worried expression.

"Fuck," he exhaled. "The texter limited who we could talk to. It just dawned on me that Copeland is out of the mix. Why would that be?" he asked.

"I have no idea. Maybe the texter doesn't know about Copeland," replied Anissa after taking another drink of her coffee. "Doesn't it seem like we're placing a lot of weight on information provided by someone we don't know? I mean, how credible is this person? The only tips we've gotten are from a potentially unreliable source about the crimes after the fact, with no real details. And now we get a cryptic message about a crime that is supposed to happen in Chicago but with no specifics. The whole thing sounds like bullshit to me."

"You might be right," conceded Nowitzke as his vehicle pulled up to the entrance of Anissa's clinic. "Hey, I'll park the car and come up shortly. Can't wait to catch up on an old edition of *Cat Fancy* in the waiting room." He stepped out of the car to summon a wheelchair for his protégé from the volunteer on duty before finding a space in the parking lot.

An hour later, Nowitzke began to nervously look at his watch, wondering about the length of the appointment. Just as he stood to ask the receptionist about Anissa's status, she stepped out into the waiting room. Large red blotches covered her face. It was clear she had been crying.

"Nis, you alright?"

"Get me out of here. I can't breathe," she whispered as her voice cracked.

Nowitzke grabbed Anissa's upper arm to steady her while directing her toward a wheelchair. When they were alone in the elevator, the only sound was her whimpering. By the time they made the lobby, tears were streaming down her face. As they got into the car, Anissa lost control of her emotions with an inconsolable cry.

CHAPTER 42

"Anissa, what's going on? What did the doc say?" asked Nowitzke. A simple question, yet the hardened detective feared the answer.

"I'm not sure I can tell you. I mean, I don't think I have the strength to say it out loud."

"Are there some complications with your injury?" *Or something worse?*

Anissa wiped her eyes and turned toward Nowitzke. "My overall recovery is going pretty much as anticipated . . . except for one thing. A bullet nicked one of my fallopian tubes, causing some damage to that part of my body," she said between heavy breaths. "Essentially, the doctor told me I might not be able to have children." She finished the sentence with a gasp, turning her head to look away from the driver's seat and out the passenger door window. "It cuts my chances in half, at best."

Nowitzke had nothing. He looked out the driver's window to shield Anissa from the flow of tears running down his nose and quelled the urge to punch the steering wheel for fear of upsetting her even more. After several minutes of silence, Nowitzke composed himself, using the sleeve of his jacket to wipe his eyes before starting the car and pulling into traffic, unsure of the destination. Suddenly, the details of the crimes could not have been further from his mind. He was in new territory. He clearly understood the implications of the injury for his young partner but struggled with what he should do or say.

"Chuck, please don't take me home yet," Anissa asked in a feeble voice.

"I wasn't going to. Just thought we should get out of the clinic's parking lot. Do you have anywhere in mind?"

"No, just drive."

Nowitzke guided the car aimlessly around the city for several miles before turning and coming to a stop in a park near a lake. Almost immediately, the detective regretted his choice. Although the park offered quiet green space, the warm, sunny day had also drawn an army of mothers pushing strollers with young children in tow. "Nis, we need some air. Let's take a walk."

Anissa said nothing but dutifully unhooked her seat belt and climbed out of the vehicle. Nowitzke came to her side of the car and guided her onto one of the cedar-chipped paths cut out of the greenery. Despite Nowitzke's best intentions, every twist and turn on the trail was greeted by shouts from more kids yelling for their mothers to watch as they did tricks on playground equipment or screaming as they chased each other through the grass.

Eventually, the officers took a break, finding a picnic table to sit on. "Jesus, Chuck," Anissa said with a stifled titter, "could you have picked a place without so many little crazed munchkins running around?" The subsequent laugh caused her body to reverberate in pain. "Oh, man, that hurts," she exclaimed.

"Sorry, Nis," Nowitzke said, laughing at his well-intentioned faux pas. "I didn't know where to go. You might not believe it, but I sometimes come here to think. I don't ever remember seeing so many parents and kids here before though." He looked around the park, then back at Anissa. "Do you want to leave?"

"No, I'm fine. You were right. The fresh air and sun feel great," Anissa declared, breathing deeply.

"Hey, there's an ice cream truck down the path to the right up ahead."

"So, your thinking place and ice cream go together?" asked Anissa.

"Ice cream goes with everything, Nis."

They bought cones and found a park bench overlooking the placid lake away from the shrieks of the children. Both sat quietly, watching a sailboat glide over the water. "You know, Chuck, this injury is just icing on the cake. You've joked with me and asked about past boyfriends, but the truth is, I can't seem to sustain any kind of relationship. I'm snakebitten. I'd love to have a man in my life, beyond you, of course. I've often wondered why I wasn't already Susie Homemaker with a bunch of kids. It's like, what am I doing wrong?" She hesitated. "But then I think about how much I love my career. I absolutely do. Then the other day, I get the 'ma'am' greeting . . . something that my head translated to being an older woman. I know I shouldn't take offense, but I guess it just reminded me that the clock is ticking. Now I feel like I'm damaged goods. What if I finally find a guy, but he wants a family . . . what happens then?"

"You know you're talking to the wrong guy," replied Nowitzke, hesitating for a moment. "But here's what a friend might tell you. First, you didn't do anything to bring this on yourself. You were doing a job that you love when some asshole shot you. Frankly, I don't want to think about what could have happened if you hadn't pulled through," he said, choking up. "But when, and not if, you find your guy and the time is right, just be honest with him. If you not being able to have kids is a deal breaker for him, then keep looking. Jesus, Nis, you're just too beautiful and smart not to. And, for the record, doctors aren't always right anyway. But even if this one is, there are now so many ways to have kids, beyond the old-fashioned way." He finished his cone and stared off into the distance at the white sail on the shimmering lake. "By the way, you'll be a great mom."

"That's what a friend might say?" Anissa smiled. "Thanks, Chuck. Do you mind if I come to you for a regular pep talk?" she said as she leaned into him, putting her head on his shoulder.

"Absolutely. Oh, and my other advice, don't marry a stripper," said the playful Nowitzke.

Anissa responded with a belly laugh that sent her body into another painful convulsion. "Jesus, Chuck, you're killing me," she replied, still giggling.

Both were quiet for several moments before Nowitzke broached a more serious subject. "Anissa, do you need some time off from work?"

She shook her head confidently before answering. "That's about the last thing I need. The doc just cleared me. I know I'm having some residual pain, but it's subsiding. Oh, and I might move a little slower . . . like probably your pace," she said, drawing a sideways look and smile from Nowitzke. "The infertility thing is more emotional for me than physical. Just be warned if I lose it from time to time. Frankly, chasing down some bad guys may be what the doctor ordered, literally."

"Alright, you're pretty much up to speed on the jewelry crimes. Sean is working on potential targets for Katallani's next hit. But I really want to run everything past Mr. Russell and get his take on all the developments. We can save that discussion for tomorrow morning," he offered as they stood in unison and began making their way back to the car. "I'm not sure you know, but Miss Alma has been teaching Nadia how to cook. They always make more food than three people can eat. Why don't you come along to dinner? Nadia would love to see you. And Miss Alma would be thrilled to have a real policewoman at her house."

Before Anissa could respond, Nowitzke's phone rang. "I need to take this, Nis. It's Chief Clark." After answering, the detective held the phone to his ear, listening to his boss but saying nothing for almost a minute. Anissa studied his reaction to the conversation as the message was delivered. Nowitzke shrugged and hung his head. Then, just before clicking off the call, he replied, "Yeah, we're on it."

"We need to make a stop before dinner," offered Nowitzke with a grim tone. "It's the final chapter of one portion of our investigation."

Twenty minutes later, the Taurus pulled up to Bateman's Jewelers.

Much like their first visit to the store, the premises was surrounded by several first-responder vehicles with light bars engaged. Upon emerging from the car, the detectives worked their way through a group of gawkers who had gathered on the front walk before ducking underneath a police tape barrier. They spotted Officer Kenny Hicks on the porch.

After exchanging pleasantries, Hicks rolled his eyes toward the detectives with a "follow me" look, leading Nowitzke and Anissa into the structure. Passing a group of employees in the main showroom, Nowitzke noted that several were crying, while one woman lying on a couch was being given oxygen by an attending EMT.

Hicks paused, nodding towards the woman. "She was the one who discovered the body," he said plainly before pushing open the door to Malcolm Bateman's office. Above the massive wooden desk hung the now lifeless body of the jeweler, dressed in a three-piece suit. "There's not much of a mystery here," offered Hicks as the eyes of all three followed the rope from Bateman's neck up to the rafters. "Looks like he climbed onto his desk and stepped off."

"Jesus," responded Anissa, who was studying Malcolm's death face. "My God, he looks almost relieved."

Nowitzke could only shake his head. Then he saw several documents neatly laid out on Malcolm's desk and the "why" became clear. The first was a letter from Bateman's accounting firm advising him that they calculated the burglary loss at $10.15 million. The second was signed by Sean Cook of Wisconsin Specialty Underwriters making a final offer of five million on the burglary claim. It didn't take a math genius to figure out the problem.

Nowitzke studied the room. In the corner, he found a shopping bag from a local hardware store with a receipt for a length of rope printed at 12:18 p.m. On the corner of Malcolm's desk sat an open crystal-cut decanter of what the detective guessed was a fine brown liquor. *He needed to be fortified first.* "Stupid motherfucker. Killing yourself over money. I don't get it," Nowitzke said to no one as he stepped towards the office door. "Kenny, this one looks pretty straightforward. The ME should be here soon."

As the detectives walked back to the car, they met Wally Schmidt. "Nowitzke, Anissa," he greeted them. "I hear one of your clients is hanging around inside," he said with a macabre chuckle.

"Fuck you, Wally," snarled Nowitzke as they passed each other. *Shit, another casualty courtesy of Katallani.* "Nis, as much as I could use a stiff drink, people are waiting on us for dinner."

CHAPTER 43

As the Taurus pulled up to Miss Alma's house, Anissa balked at getting out of the car. "Chuck, I don't know if I can do this. Nadia's in there. Her brother died on my watch. I can't believe she wants to see me, and I'm not sure if I'm ready to face her."

Nowitzke turned off the vehicle and pivoted toward Anissa. "Listen. Nadia knew Musa was working with some bad people. You went above and beyond. Jesus, you took two to the back for the asshole brother. There was nothing else you could have done."

Although not totally sold, Anissa grudgingly agreed to get out of the car. "Not too long, though. My stamina's still way off, okay?"

"Say the word when you're ready, and I'll take you home."

As the officers approached Miss Alma's back door, the aroma of whatever was cooking wafted from the kitchen, making both detectives salivate. "Damn, something smells pretty good," said Nowitzke as he opened the door for his partner. Anissa immediately heard conversation coming from within the house, becoming louder as it approached her. She recognized Nadia's voice and froze for a moment, now having second thoughts about being there. But before she could turn and leave, Nadia appeared in the kitchen doorway. She said nothing as the two women briefly locked eyes, almost like a standoff.

Then, without a word, Nadia approached the detective and gave her a hug. "Oh my God, Anissa, I'm glad to see you," she said with a measure of relief in her voice. "I'm so sorry for what happened to you."

Anissa winced at Nadia's embrace. "No, Nadia. I'm the one that's sorry. I couldn't save your brother."

"Musa made many bad choices, and I put you in jeopardy by even asking you to protect him. I felt ashamed to ask for your help. I know you did everything you could."

Any manufactured tension between the two women was now gone. As they continued to talk, Miss Alma poked her head into the room. With wide eyes, the short elderly lady sidled up to the much taller Anissa.

"Are you the brave policewoman who was shot?"

"Yes, ma'am," Anissa responded. "I'm not sure about the brave part, but I did manage to get shot," she conceded. Nowitzke handled the introductions.

Miss Alma continued. "You know, in my day, a woman couldn't work for the police, except for maybe in the office. We stayed at home and had babies . . . except for me, I guess."

The innocuous remark hit home with Anissa, causing her to blink hard. Nowitzke shuddered imperceptibly as well.

"But you know what, you're my hero," said Miss Alma. "If only I had been born fifty years later and a foot taller, like you, maybe I would have been a cop too." She gave Anissa a gentle hug. "Detective Nowitzke, you might as well get some beer from your fridge and bring it downstairs to have with dinner."

Dinner turned into a homecoming as much as anything else for Miss Alma's new growing family. Her newest long-lost granddaughter, Anissa, Anissa's foreign half-sister, Nadia, and her weird nephew, Chuck. Just as Nowitzke predicted, the women had prepared a working man's feast. Shortly after the meal, Anissa caught Nowitzke's attention, giving him a subtle sign that she wanted to leave for home. She then announced that she was exhausted and scheduled to begin work again the following morning. The evening concluded with more hugs all around.

Dusk had morphed into night as Nowitzke's Taurus pulled out of the yard. It was a clear, cloudless evening lit brilliantly by a full moon. But it was cool, with the last of the spring chill still in the air.

After fifteen minutes of classic rock, Nowitzke broke the silence. "Nis, you okay?"

Anissa peered out the side window and studied the neighborhoods as they flashed by. "I don't know. Right now, I'm an emotional mess. There's just so much going on in my head, I'm not sure I can give you a better answer. I'm hoping a good night's sleep in my own bed will help me get right . . ." she said, trailing off, suddenly searching the car in a small panic. "Shit, Chuck, I left my purse at Miss Alma's. My whole life's in that bag . . . including my badge and gun. I don't know if it's the meds or what, but I've been so ditzy lately. Sorry."

"No problem, and cut yourself some slack," said Nowitzke, making an illegal U-turn on the quiet street. "No one would have it all together with everything you've been through."

When the Taurus came to rest in Miss Alma's yard, Nowitzke had a strange sense that something was amiss. As the detectives emerged from the car, he noted that the exterior lights in Miss Alma's portion of the home were uncharacteristically off. Then, looking up the stairs towards his apartment, he saw that Nadia had also turned off the porch lamps.

Nowitzke looked at Anissa. "Do you have a gun?"

"Sorry, no, I only have the one in my purse," replied Anissa, glancing toward Miss Alma's home.

Nowitzke reached down and pulled up the leg of his pants, along with a Glock from an inconspicuous ankle holster. "You can't be too careful," he concluded, handing her the weapon along with his cell phone. "Something's up. Call for backup and stay here with your head down. Maybe it's nothing, but I don't want to take any chances with Nadia upstairs."

The detective drew the Luger from his waist, closing the door to shut off the dome light. After moving over the open ground, he made it to the stairway up to his apartment. He began to climb the creaky stairs as stealthily as possible, but each step loudly announced that someone was on their way up. When Nowitzke reached his apartment door, he listened carefully for any sound coming from the interior. There was none. He turned the doorknob, now wondering if the developing drama was just his imagination, with the potential of scaring the hell out of his roommate.

The only light filtering into the darkened apartment came from the moon. Then he sensed movement flashing out of the corner of his eye. Nowitzke jumped, his heart racing. But he quickly realized it was only Sinker approaching, so he reached down to pick up the cat. As he did, Nowitzke felt the blunt force of a pistol on the back of his head sending him to the floor and into blackness. Although stunned and disoriented by the blow, Nowitzke never lost consciousness. He lay on the cool wood floor for several minutes, considering what had happened. Then, slowly gathering himself, the detective heard someone tearing apart another room in the apartment. Nowitzke surmised that this goon, whoever he was, was not a burglar, but searching for Nadia.

The detective felt the warmth of blood flowing from his wound, trickling along the side of his face and into his mouth. The taste both revived and enraged him. As his attacker moved back toward the apartment entrance, Nowitzke summoned his strength, rising to his feet. He drew back and hit the intruder for all he was worth. But to the detective's surprise, the heavy punch bounced off his adversary's jaw with no effect. In kind, the thug caught Nowitzke with an upper cut, sending him sprawling backward over a coffee table and into a soft chair.

Time had run out, and the frustrated attacker knew it. Sirens in the distance were getting louder by the second. He bolted out the door and onto the small porch when Anissa yelled from her position crouched behind the Taurus, "Stop! Police! Drop your weapon and come down slowly with your hands where I can see them." The hitman responded with the loud report of two rounds aimed in the general direction of Anissa's voice followed by one metallic ricochet off Nowitzke's car.

The assailant began descending the groaning staircase quickly until he heard Nowitzke from above. "Stop, motherfucker, or I'll shoot." The thug froze. "Drop your weapon and show me your hands," snarled Nowitzke in a loud, commanding voice. "Now!"

Caught halfway down the stairs, the invader stopped as if considering his options. With only the ambient light, Nowitzke got a better look at the profile of the thick man wearing dark clothing, a black leather jacket, and a fedora. *Is this the dickhead that shot Anissa?* Time halted, at least until the exterior lights on Miss Alma's portion of the house went on in response to the commotion.

"Shit," breathed Nowitzke to himself. "Miss Alma, stay inside!" he yelled from his porch, getting no response from the old woman.

Then, in what felt like slow motion, the intruder wheeled deliberately, raising his weapon towards Nowitzke, getting off one round that whizzed harmlessly past the detective's head. With the high ground, Nowitzke was in perfect position to respond, his Glock trained on his target. But before he could squeeze the trigger, he heard what sounded like an explosion erupting from below him, followed by the sting of hot buckshot striking his body. The man on the stairs crumpled without a sound before listing and falling over the railing onto the wet grass ten feet below, landing with a hollow thud.

Anissa emerged from behind the Taurus with an adrenaline-charged sprint toward the downed attacker. After kicking away his weapon, she checked him for a pulse but found none. The man was dead, steam rising into the cool night air from the gaping hole in his abdomen. Then, Anissa heard a curious low moan coming from near the base of the stairs. The blast from the vintage Remington 12-gauge pump-action shotgun had found the center mass of the target. But the weapon's recoil had also blown Miss Alma backward onto the ground with enough force to split her lip.

"Did I get the SOB who was after Nadia?" asked the stunned woman.

"Damn, Miss Alma. You got all of him," Anissa replied. "Are you alright?"

"Now I am, knowing my friend is safe. But my upper lip feels swollen, and I'm not sure about my teeth."

Nowitzke double-timed it down the stairs, approaching Anissa and his landlord. "Miss Alma, I thought you hated guns."

"I do, Detective. But I don't like taking chances either. I've kept my husband's old duck hunting shotgun in the front closet for years, just in case."

Within minutes, colorful emergency lights and the sound of sirens filled Miss Alma's yard. Despite his injuries, Nowitzke bolted back up the wobbly stairs in search of Nadia.

CHAPTER 44

Flipping on the lights in the apartment, the detective saw that the hitman had tossed most of the place while searching in vain for Nadia. Nowitzke gently called out "Nadia" several times, trying not to startle her as he moved through the small flat. "It's over," he repeated to little avail. "C'mon out." Working his way to the bedroom, Nowitzke got down on his knees before finding her stuffed far under the bed in the fetal position, trembling in her satin night shirt. Nowitzke reached for the near catatonic woman. After several minutes of coaxing, Nadia finally looked toward him and took his hand, like a small child would have. Once out from under the bed, the emotion of the moment caught up with her. She wrapped her arms around Nowitzke as far as she could reach and sobbed uncontrollably.

Anissa had made her way up the stairs to find Nadia affixed to Nowitzke. After feeling the relief of finding the young woman safe, the realities of the detective's injuries set in. He grew unsteady on his feet, needing to sit down. "Jesus, Chuck, your head is bleeding, and you're awfully pale," diagnosed his partner, who gently detached Nadia and led her to the couch before maneuvering Nowitzke into a kitchen chair. "What happened?"

Nowitzke described the short brawl with the thug as Anissa gave Nadia the once-over but found no physical injuries. "When I came into the place, the asshole coldcocked me with his gun. It was dark, and I couldn't see much of anything. I felt a big cut open on the back of my melon, but I was lucky. I had bent down to pick up Sinker so the big guy didn't get all of me, thank God."

"Sinker?" replied Anissa. "Who's Sinker?" On cue, the tabby emerged from the bedroom, popping into Nadia's lap with a graceful leap. Nadia was content to stroke the cat while sitting quietly in the corner, absently staring off into space.

"My cat," confessed Nowitzke. "I violated rule five, but I think Sinker probably saved my life. Still, don't mention anything to Miss Alma, please?"

Suddenly, the thunder of heavy traffic was moving up the stairs towards them.

"What the hell happened here?" boomed Chief Clark, leading an entourage of police, EMTs, and a lone fireman. "If I've got my facts straight, there's a kindly little old lady downstairs who used a gun almost as big as her to take out a hitman bent on killing a potential witness to multiple felonies, stashed in a supposed safe house here that no one, including me, knew about." Clark looked at Nowitzke, who was now being attended to by a first responder.

"Chief, meet Nadia," said Nowitzke, "your primary witness." He pointed to the dazed woman who was also being treated by a medic. Even with his head injuries, Nowitzke provided Clark with a lucid report of the chain of events, starting with Bateman's and leading up to that moment. To the experienced detective, the fact that someone had killed their prime suspect, Nadia's brother, justified him in coloring outside the lines a bit and providing for the safety of a witness who could identify Katallani. Nowitzke explained that he had taken a calculated risk considering that their unknown source now implicated the Albanian devil in several murders as well as three felony thefts. Yes, he knew he had not followed proper procedure. But after the incident involving the attorneys at city hall that led to Anissa's shooting, he didn't have complete trust in Nadia's safety in a jail cell, choosing to stash her at his apartment. Also, he explained that Nadia could have been at risk had someone, including Katallani, posted her bail, making her easier to kill. And the fact that there was a dead gangster now fertilizing Miss Alma's lawn below was Exhibit A in support of his reasoning.

Clark patiently listened to Nowitzke's explanation without any interruption, knowing the detective had delivered results in the past. Just as importantly, he was eagerly sharing his expertise with Anissa, adding bench strength to the department. When Nowitzke's soliloquy was complete, Clark looked at Anissa and then at the senior detective. "So, how's your head, Chuck? You don't have too much grey matter to spare," he said, drawing a laugh from both officers. When the EMT finished working on Nowitzke, Clark cleared the room. "Listen, if Nadia is going to stay here, let me get some of our people on watch around the clock to help out. We don't want to have to depend upon Miss Alma as our last line of defense."

"Thank you, sir. The one thing that bothers me about this whole episode is how this asshole found Nadia here at my place. No one, and I mean no one, knew that she was living here," pondered Nowitzke.

"Well, someone figured it out," chimed in Anissa. "Chuck, you should go to the hospital for additional treatment."

Nowitzke grunted and shook his head emphatically. "Thanks for your concern. But unless you earned a medical degree when I wasn't paying attention, I'm staying here tonight."

"We need to figure out who the hitter was and check his known associates," said Clark. "Since our department is involved with this incident, protocol dictates that the county sheriff's department take the lead on investigating tonight's shooting. Wally Schmidt is already downstairs with his meat wagon working the scene too. Based on what I see, Miss Alma should be in the clear as a justifiable homicide. Also, I'll talk personally to the sheriff to keep Nadia's presence on the down low." Before leaving, Clark walked over to Nadia. "Young lady, you take care," he said, shaking the hand of the still frazzled woman.

Nowitzke nodded at Anissa to stay with Nadia in the apartment while he went down to the lawn to see what was taking place. Large portable lamps had been brought into the yard, illuminating the scene as several uniformed officers were busy gathering evidence. Larry Chapman, a sheriff's deputy, was questioning Miss Alma about what she saw. Based on what Nowitzke could tell, his landlord was enjoying the attention, surrounded by several young, buff deputies. She didn't even object when they suggested she go to the hospital via ambulance.

As he surveyed the area, Nowitzke recognized the prodigious ass of the medical examiner sticking out of the back door of his Taurus. "What's up, Wally?"

"Just trying to dig a slug out of your back seat. Miss Alma said she heard the shooter send two toward Anissa, who was behind your car. Anissa heard one bullet ricochet off your vehicle, but no one heard the second bullet hit anything. On a hunch, I checked the back seat, and lo and behold, I found it," he said, holding up the metal bullet in a plastic bag like it was a trophy. "We also have the shooter's weapon, so ballistics can do their magic too." He paused and looked at the detective, eyeing the dressing on the officer's head. "Jesus, Chuck . . . you look like shit. Are you alright?"

"It's just a flesh wound," Nowitzke responded in a British accent, doing his best Monty Python impression. "Can I get a look at our guest before you leave?"

"Sure. He's tagged, bagged, and loaded in my wagon." Schmidt wobbled over to the back door of his vehicle and gave a pull on a lever, engaging the sliding platform that held the body. When the suspect slid out of the tailgate, Nowitzke leaned in, unzipped the body bag, and studied the dead man's face. It was still contorted in pain as if he knew he was going to die from Miss Alma's blast. But no, Nowitzke did not recognize the hitman. The detective pulled out his phone and snapped several photos before zipping the bag shut.

"A friend of yours?" asked Wally.

"Never seen him before."

"Okay. The sheriff's department will get you an identification on the dead guy, but I'll be filling in the blanks with my findings too."

An hour later, Miss Alma's yard had largely cleared of law enforcement. A lone Appleton PD officer had taken up a protective position at the base of the staircase, as promised by Clark. "Goodnight, Detective," he said as Nowitzke plodded slowly up the stairs, holding onto the railing to steady himself. While he had put on a good show for Clark and the medics, he now had an enormous headache and just wanted to lie down. After willing himself up the steps one at a time, Anissa met him on the porch.

"Nadia's calmed down and went to bed," she reported. "Do you want me to stay here?"

"Nis, you're on low battery yourself, and there's no room at the inn. We'll be fine. But would you mind catching one of the uniforms down there to run you home?"

"No problem. You take care, Chuck. We can talk about next steps on this investigation tomorrow morning," she said, floating down the stairs.

Nowitzke quietly entered the apartment. Anissa had straightened up the place, righting the chairs, putting things back where she thought they belonged. Nowitzke went into the bathroom and searched the medicine cabinet for a painkiller. He took two ibuprofen, washing them down with a beer he pulled from the refrigerator. Then, exhausted, he made himself comfortable on a beat-up old leather chair and closed his eyes, still wondering how anyone could have known Nadia was there. He was about to turn on the late-night news to see if there was any local coverage of the shooting when Nadia appeared at the bedroom doorway.

"Do you have any more of those?" she asked, gesturing at his beer as she walked into the room. Nowitzke was half out of his chair to grab one of the cans for her when she stopped him. "I got it, Chuck. Do you need another one?" she asked, pulling a can from the carton.

"No, I'm good for now," replied Nowitzke, taking a long draw.

Nadia came and sat alongside him on the padded arm of his chair. "I just can't sleep thinking about tonight," she said, taking a sip of beer.

"I heard someone coming up the stairs right after you left. The guy must have been watching. I locked the door, turned off all the lights, and hid. I was terrified. I heard him pick the lock and start tearing up the place looking for me. He knew I was in the apartment and started calling my name." Tears welled up in her eyes. "Chuck, I thought I was going to die. He wasn't here long when you came back to the house. I heard the struggle and some shooting from under the bed."

The detective let her words sink in for a moment and took a pull on his beer, waiting to ask a needed question. "Nadia, did you get a look at the guy?"

"No, I never saw him. I didn't recognize his voice either," she said, taking a longer draw of beer.

Nowitzke pulled out his phone, calling up the picture he took in the backyard. Nadia studied the image of the hitman but shook her head.

"So this wasn't the man you thought was Katallani?"

"No," said Nadia firmly. After a brief pause, she looked at the detective. "Anissa told me the man was shot by Miss Alma, God bless her. Who was he, Chuck? Do you know?"

"We're still tracking that down. Do you have any idea how he found you?"

"No."

"Have you stayed at Miss Alma's house since you moved in?" he asked skeptically, eyebrows raised.

"Yes, I haven't left once. I've wanted to get out into town, but I didn't," replied Nadia forcefully.

Truth.

Nowitzke took a deep breath as sleep was beginning to close in on him. "I'm not sure where we go from here. Someone knew you were here, but I don't know how. Chief Clark is providing a round-the-clock officer to help guard you. We just need to be on high alert until I can sort this out." He took the final pull of his beer before crushing the can and tossing it in the general direction of the wastebasket that was lying on its side. But he was too tired to stand and get another beer.

"Thank you . . . for protecting me," Nadia said, leaning over and kissing him gently on his forehead. "You're my guardian angel." She slid into Nowitzke's lap from the arm of the chair and kissed him deeply on the lips. "Chuck, I don't want to sleep alone tonight." She rose and pulled him to his feet before taking his hand to guide him towards the bedroom.

"Listen, Nadia. I don't know what to say. I was just doing my job . . ." He paused when she put a finger to his lips. She wriggled out of her night shirt, revealing the body that the detective had seen at Anissa's apartment and in several subsequent dreams. "You don't have to do this . . ." he said, briefly protesting before she shushed him again. She undressed him carefully, respecting his injuries, but also slowly worked her body like the day she tried to sell him a watch. Suddenly, he was the stray dog that had caught the proverbial car but now wasn't sure what to do. And the car in question could easily have been sitting in the pole position in Indianapolis on a Memorial Day weekend. By the time Nadia pulled the last article of clothing from his body, he was officially outvoted. Nadia was not having second thoughts, and little Nowitzke had already cast the deciding ballot. As she continued to lead him to the bedroom, he mused that since dinner, rules two, three, and five were now history.

An hour later, when Nadia insisted on smoking a cigarette, rule one also bit the dust.

So much for living in a rules-based society, thought Nowitzke as he spooned up to his roommate before falling asleep.

CHAPTER 45

Nowitzke arrived at work in a clean shirt and pressed suit, with an uncharacteristic bounce in his step. Even Officer Benson received a hearty "Good morning" from the detective, who offered her a donut from the dozen under his arm as he went through the lobby. Sitting at his desk, he was careful not to spill his coffee as he dialed Russell for a long overdue conversation, catching him on the first ring.

"Good morning, Chuck," responded the fed on his car phone. "I heard about the little run-in at your apartment last night. Jesus, are you alright?"

"Just a head wound. I've still got a dull headache and some bumps and bruises from the brawl, but I'll live. No casualties but one. Hey, I want to run this and a couple of new developments past you. I might need the Bureau's help."

"Not a problem. I was in Madison last night. Got up early to get to Appleton to see how you were doing. I should be there in twenty minutes."

"See you in a bit," concluded Nowitzke, punching off the line.

Looking up, he saw Anissa and Sheriff Jake Patton through the glass window of his office, awaiting their turn. Patton was dressed in the full regalia of his uniform while Anissa wore a sleek black pantsuit. As Nowitzke waved them in, he stood to formally greet Patton. The two had previously met at a local law enforcement conference and knew each other well enough to be on a first-name basis. The sheriff had been elected to the office for three terms for more than his good looks. Over his eight-year tenure in office, he had built a sterling reputation, and although he publicly eschewed talking politics, he clearly understood that element of his work, causing many to suspect he was interested in serving at the state level. Nowitzke heard that Patton was highly respected by his people for being a technician and a "hard as nails" cop.

"Morning, Chuck. You're looking dapper this morning," offered Patton, causing Anissa to do a double take at the comment. Dapper was not a word that had ever been used in connection with her boss before. But today, she had to agree that the sheriff was right. "How are you feeling?" asked Patton as he and Anissa took the chairs in front of Nowitzke's desk.

"Frankly, Jake, better than I look. Still some stiffness from getting thrown around like a rag doll. Still have a headache," Nowitzke noted, even though a morning headache was typical for him for other reasons. "But life is great." The last comment again caught Anissa's attention.

The sheriff pulled a black portfolio from under his arm and flipped through the pages to find what he was looking for. "We got an ID on the perp overnight. Based on what we know of him, you're a pretty lucky guy. Our stiff is one Alfred Simmons, a badass who originally hailed from Milwaukee. However, it looks like he spent more time in prison in Waupun, Green Bay, and Columbia County than he ever did in his hometown. Quite the rap sheet too. Murder. Armed robbery. Several charges for felonious assault. Look up the criminal code for violent offenses, and your guy did it. Also, as you know, this asshole was fucking massive in size."

"Tell me about it," said Nowitzke, taking a drink of his coffee.

"According to the records, Simmons once hit another inmate who had pissed him off for some reason. Killed the guy with one punch, accounting for another manslaughter beef. And even though Simmons was never a made man with the Milwaukee families, he did some of their serious dirty work. He's been accused of multiple murders but was never brought to trial because no one could locate the bodies."

"Oh my gosh," exclaimed Anissa. "You were in a fistfight with this jerk?"

"In theory, if me landing one punch constitutes a fight. However, I did keep the title belt on a technicality," Nowitzke mused with a smile. "My impression is you know about my houseguest through Clark?"

Patton nodded.

"Were you able to find out why he was targeting Nadia?"

"No. It's an open question. But given what we've been able to find, Simmons wasn't a free thinker. He was a contractor. One that did what he was told to do, and he was very effective up until last night. We don't know who he was working for, though."

"Shit. So basically, Nadia is still a target for whoever," replied Nowitzke, not divulging the name Katallani. "Nadia's brother was involved in the Bateman's heist. He left some evidence at the scene that pissed off his contractor. And you know the rest of the story. I'll spare you the details aside from the fact that I stashed the young woman for her own safety since she may be able to identify the person behind a series of murders and felony thefts. We're working through this with the FBI. In fact, Russ will be here shortly," he said, looking across his desk toward Anissa.

"Thanks. Clark briefed me. Well, the stiff at the morgue confirms you still have work to do."

Nowitzke nodded in agreement. "Anything else, Jake?"

"Yeah, two things," he said. "After our initial investigation, Miss Alma will not be charged with any crime. Just wanted you to know."

"Maybe Appleton PD should give her a medal for ridding the world of a prime scumbag," offered Nowitzke, pivoting back on his chair. "I can't imagine all the assholes Simmons put in the ground, or the water, only to be killed by an old woman who weighed about a third of what he did."

Patton nodded agreement as he pulled out his phone and hit his speed dial. "Hey, Wally, you asked that I call when I had everyone here. You're on speaker with me, Chuck, and Anissa."

The group heard the voice of the ME. "Morning, boys and girls. We're still working through all the forensics, but I wanted to give you an early find from ballistics. We tested Simmons's weapon. He was *not* the suspect who shot Watson, his bodyguards, and the old man. But we did get a match between the slug I pulled from Nowitzke's Taurus and those taken out of Musa Besnik. Simmons killed Besnik and was the triggerman who wounded Anissa."

Anissa gulped at the revelation. In the grand scheme of things, she realized she had also been lucky. Simmons was like a Terminator, killing without any feeling. Had this animal spared her because she was a woman? She would never know, but she was alive, offering yet another perspective on her newly revealed challenges.

"Any more questions?" asked the ME. With no response, he continued, "More to follow if anything else develops." Then Schmidt curtly signed off.

Patton rose to leave the office. "That's all I have as well. I think my department's investigation is officially over."

"Thanks again, Jake," said Nowitzke. "One for the road?" He held up the donut box. The slim sheriff politely declined, closing the door as he left.

Nowitzke and Anissa were both quiet as each processed the findings from Patton and Schmidt.

Nowitzke broke the silence first. "How you doing this morning, Nis?"

"I'm fine," she lied. "I could ask you the same thing. You took a beating from an alleged murderer, including quite the shot to your head. But despite everything, you're in a remarkably good mood. Also, looking sharp today. Both better than most mornings."

"Like I told Jake, I'm good," he responded, putting her off.

"Chuck, the last time you told anyone you were good, Egg McMuffins were two for one," she concluded, then joked, "Either that or you got laid."

Nowitzke said nothing but made a face. One that she had never seen from him before. But as a police officer, she knew a guilty look when she saw one.

"Wait, are you kidding me? Nadia . . . and you . . . doing the nasty?" she said, doing her best not to form any mental picture in her brain.

Nowitzke sat in silence for a moment. "Let's just put it this way. Egg McMuffins are not on sale."

"How did this happen?" she asked, cocking her head, still incredulous at the admission.

The detective offered nothing more than an embarrassed smile for a moment before shifting in his chair. "Nadia and I were each recovering from the attack last night. We talked. She thanked me for protecting her. She gave me a kiss. One thing led to another and . . . let's just say we broke rule three . . . several times."

"Rule three?" asked Anissa.

"Miss Alma's rule. No fornicating," he said, using his hands to make an air quote. "I'm taking the fifth at this point."

"C'mon, Chuck. You can't just leave me hanging," she said with a playful laugh.

"You think you're pretty funny. Well, remember that when it's your turn and I ask for specifics."

"First of all, you'll never know. And if you do find out and ask, it would be considered harassment," chuckled Anissa.

"Do me a favor and keep this to yourself, please," growled Nowitzke. "Fucking know-it-all detectives," he mumbled softly to himself, looking down toward his desk and trying to focus on some paperwork.

Anissa continued to giggle as she stood and excused herself, quietly muttering, "I can't remember the last time I broke rule three."

"What's that?" asked Nowitzke, looking up at his partner.

"Oh nothing, just talking to myself."

CHAPTER 46

Russell arrived at Nowitzke's office looking tanned and typically well-groomed, despite the cheap suit he was wearing. "Chuck, good to see you up and around," he said, shaking the detective's hand after greeting Anissa. They dropped into their respective chairs. "Man, as the facts rolled in about last night's ruckus with Simmons, I became a little concerned for you. I suspect you've been in a scrape or two along the way, but this guy was a stone killer."

Nowitzke nodded, acknowledging the fed, but quickly moved on and jumped into a brief overview of the prior night's details sans any personal specifics about Nadia. "Frankly, Russ, the fact that someone took a chance to kill Nadia seems to validate that they're worried she might be able to identify Katallani. We've now assigned a protective detail 24-7 to the apartment until this is resolved." He took a deep breath. "I need your input on what's been taking place with our jewelry crime wave," Nowitzke continued, sliding a printed copy of the exchange between their texting informant and Sean. "This is a couple of days old."

Russell's eyes quickly moved down the page. "Another midnight text," he said, studying the words a second time. "So, our unknown friend is now claiming Katallani killed Watson for the Pink Monster. Katallani was also responsible for the Bateman's burglary and the Lockett's robbery. By the way, I've run that name through a number of databases, and it's a dry hole. From what I know of jewelry crime, one person being responsible for these different types of theft is totally outside any profile I've ever read. The only thing worse is that each crime is getting more brutal. If it is one guy, killing Besnik would make some sense in a criminal's twisted mind. But from the details from the Watson murders, I'd say we're dealing with a true animal. Someone willing to kill innocent people without a second thought, let alone his real targets. I'm assuming you did another tower dump regarding where the text originated from?"

"Oh yeah," responded the detective. "Turns out the second text was done a few feet from the first. I thought Sean Cook did a pretty good job of keeping our snitch communicating."

"I guess I'd agree. But the mystery guest isn't telling us any more than he or she wants to. It is interesting though that our friend says there will be one more jewelry crime in Chicago that *dwarfs* the others before this Katallani *disappears from the face of the earth*," said Russ, adding emphasis as if he were narrating a movie trailer. "Any ideas on the target?"

"We were going to ask you the same question," piped in Anissa.

"I asked Sean to give me his best thinking on this," added Nowitzke. "Supposedly, he's still noodling on it. Any informed guesses from your standpoint?"

"I can make guesses, but nothing informed. There are thousands of jewelers in the greater Chicago area, and they run the gamut in terms of quality of merchandise. Obviously, there are some incredibly nice retail stores, like Bateman's, and far beyond, a ton of chain locations, mom-and-pop operations, repair shops, and everything in between. You've got diamond dealers, wholesalers, colored stone people, and, well, you get the picture. Even if we had the right city, the odds of us finding the target business without some intel would be against us."

"Thanks for the reality check," replied Nowitzke. "My take was that the texter assumed we would be able to figure this out on our own, as unlikely as that seems."

Russ closed his eyes for a moment, thinking through specific messages from the texter and obvious targets. Ultimately, he shook his head, frustrated that nothing jumped out to him. "Maybe the 'blood on the streets' comment is a clue. Something incredibly outrageous. It suggests a robbery. More guns and violence. But did you know the average take from a jewelry store robbery is less than $150,000? Of course, Lockett's doesn't fit that profile. It's a time and value thing. How much can a robber get away with before the police arrive? Most of the time, the thieves are drawn to high-end watches or diamonds, but most jewelry robberies just don't result in large hauls."

"Thanks," said Nowitzke, now understanding the futility of finding the next target. "Any final thoughts?"

"Only that it's technically not your problem. I can give our Chicago office and the local powers that be a heads-up. However, unless your unidentified friend comes through with more details, I'm not sure what any of those agencies could do but wait and see."

Nowitzke maintained his gaze with the fed, then cocked his head. "Okay," he conceded. "What do you make of the fact that the sender is telling us to limit who gets this information? Our buddy was very specific. But notably, my friend Arturo would be out of the loop . . . if we follow the instructions."

"That is curious," replied Russ. "The texter says the losses are connected but then limits us from talking with another investigator who is working one of the crimes. I don't get it."

Anissa gathered her thoughts as she stood from her chair. "Gentlemen, I've been skeptical of this mystery person from the get-go. First of all, Katallani is a ghost. Russ, you said yourself that no agency has any record of this guy. It's like he appeared for the first time out of thin air . . . in Wisconsin, no less, hardly a hotbed for jewelry crime. Now we have a supposed insider providing us with information about three seemingly disparate cases linked to Katallani. How would this person know that? Oh, and then this person drops some crumbs that Katallani is going to pull off some major heist in Chicago but doesn't provide any specifics, leaving us hanging. Everyone, including Musa Besnik and Nadia, is running scared of Katallani, and for good reason based on the mounting body count. So why isn't *our* informant afraid of Katallani?

And why is the texter supposedly interested in helping us one minute, then denying us potential resources by not including Copeland, who has both experience and a dog in this fight," she said, sitting down, concluding her argument as her phone buzzed. She excused herself to take the call, leaving the two men staring at each other.

"Told you she was good," said Nowitzke.

"Fed material," concluded Russell as Anissa stepped back into Nowitzke's office. "I'm sorry I couldn't offer you both more," he said as he stood, signaling the end of their meeting. Russ turned towards the door, then stopped and looked at Nowitzke. "You know, for a guy who was in a fight for his life last night, you're looking pretty sporty today."

Anissa tittered quietly, drawing a dirty look from Nowitzke as Russ left.

"Who was on the phone?" asked the detective.

"Sean," replied Anissa. "I thought he might have a potential target for us, but the call was just personal."

"Oh?"

"We have a date tonight," she said giddily.

****

As the business day closed, Nowitzke pointed his Taurus toward the Hobart Thompson Memorial Hospital. Miss Alma had been admitted for observation for the injuries suffered from the kick of her shotgun the night before and was due to check out. Walking through the lobby, the detective felt a strange sense of déjà vu, having last visited Anissa there. Although Anissa had been more seriously wounded, Nowitzke had to give Miss Alma credit. It took guts for the slightly built woman who was pushing ninety to level her shotgun at the gargantuan Simmons and pull the trigger. Even without considering her age, she had sustained a concussion, which Nowitzke knew firsthand could be quite serious.

After finding her room number at the front desk, Nowitzke took the elevator to the third floor. He anticipated that picking up Miss Alma would be a quick and dirty trip, earning him some needed brownie points to offset some of his recent high crimes and misdemeanors. Rounding into her room, he found her snuggled beneath a light blue blanket, eating chocolate pudding, and glued to a daytime soap on television.

"Thank you for coming to visit me, Detective," she said happily as he entered the room.

"Thought you were checking out today, Miss Alma?"

"Well, I thought so too at first. But I'm having such a wonderful time here with all the attention. Did you know that if I touch this button attached to my robe, they come running to see what I want? They'll even bring me food. Would you like me to have them get something for you?"

"No, thank you," he replied, smiling. "So, when are you scheduled to leave?"

"I don't know. Tomorrow or the next day." She motioned him to come closer to the bed. "Just to let you know, I'm fine," she whispered. "They were going to send me home today. Then I saw on the daily menu that they were serving chicken with risotto for lunch. I didn't even know what risotto was, but I faked a headache to find out. I loved the meal. And it's taco night for dinner," she said with glee. "Having people bring me my meals is very nice. Oh, and they have a cute young man who is my nurse. I couldn't believe it. A man, no less."

"Well, it is the twenty-first century," concluded Nowitzke.

Miss Alma blushed. "Do you think he would give me a sponge bath if I asked?"

Nowitzke shuddered before responding. "Go for it, Miss Alma." *Some poor bastard is going to earn his ten bucks an hour tonight.*

"Will you and Nadia be alright without me?" she asked earnestly.

"You take as much time as you need to get well. Nadia and I will muddle through."

CHAPTER 47

A heavy June rain set in over greater Appleton the following morning. Nonetheless, Nowitzke offered a cheery good morning and a latte to Anissa, who was in her office staring blankly at a computer screen. For the second consecutive day, Nowitzke was wearing a suit, albeit one that was a little snug and the cut somewhat out of style. It was as much of a fashion statement as he could muster. Still, it paled in comparison to Anissa, who was dressed in a light grey suit with matching shoes and a blue blouse.

"How are you doing today?" boomed Nowitzke as he took a drink of his coffee and slid into a chair across from Anissa, handing her a large cardboard cup of her own.

"You know, Chuck, I think I liked you better when you weren't getting laid every night," she said vacantly. "Thanks for the coffee though."

"So, things didn't go so well with Mr. Wonderful last night?"

Finally looking up from her laptop, she snapped the cover closed and swiveled her chair around the end of the desk to get better eye contact with Nowitzke. "Well, if you must know . . ." she huffed. "I was putting out the vibe, looking fierce in a short green dress. Our date seemed to start well enough. We went to a cool new sushi place downtown and had several drinks."

"The only way to eat sushi, in my book," Nowitzke chirped.

"We didn't even make it through the appetizers and Sean starts with questions. Not about me or what I like, mind you," she said disgustedly, "but about these stupid cases. So, I tried to steer him away from business and started asking about him. But damn if he didn't come back to the progress we were making on the investigation. Do we have any suspects? Is there any chance we'll make any recoveries of the stolen merchandise? Why is the FBI involved, and blah, blah, blah. I think he saw me as a convenient way to find out what's going on. It became pretty apparent he could care less about me and used the date as a pretext to pump me for information," she concluded.

"Sorry, Nis," consoled Nowitzke. "Maybe Sean sustained a permanent groin injury from an IED during the war? Or he suffers from low testosterone?"

"I'm starting to wonder myself. Anyway, it was an early night," said a frustrated Anissa. "I'm not interested in wasting any more time on this guy."

Anissa's desk phone rang. Nowitzke worked on his coffee, hearing only half the conversation. "Yes, Marlene, he's here," she said. "Chuck, it's Benson at the front door. She tried to track you down in your office." Anissa handed him the receiver.

"Good morning, Ms. Benson. What's up?" asked Nowitzke cheerfully. Anissa was now enjoying her coffee and half of the exchange. "Sure, send him up to Anissa's office. He knows the way by now," he said, hanging up.

"Is Russ here?"

"Better." Nowitzke smiled. "It's your favorite insurance executive."

"Shit. Why did you let the asshole in?"

"Says he's here on official business," replied Nowitzke.

"Marvelous."

CHAPTER 48

Following a handshake with Nowitzke and an awkward greeting with Anissa, Sean got right down to business. "It happened again," he said excitedly, trying to control his breathing. "According to the time signature, the text arrived at 2:08 a.m. Same number as before. I was sleeping and didn't get a chance to respond. It's information about Katallani and his final objective, but damned if I can figure it out." He handed the phone to Nowitzke, who drained the last of his coffee and pitched the cardboard cup into the wastebasket.

Major hijack by Katallani. Friday before noon. Bring SWAT. 41.882070, -87.626160. Your last chance. Share with no one beyond your stout buddy and the FBI.

Nowitzke handed Cook's cell to Anissa before turning the desk phone around to face him and punching in a number. He then pushed the speaker button.

"McKenzie," came the voice at the other end of the call.

"Norm, our texter is at it again. Do you still have the number from the first two tower dumps?

"Of course."

"Would you run it again? Oh, and let me know if the phone is on or off."

"Will do. Be back at you ASAP," said the electronics expert.

"So, you have no idea what this means, Sean?" asked Anissa tersely.

"No. None. Why do you think I would?" Cook bristled back at her. "I came here today hoping you both might be able to help, especially with the deadline in just a few days."

Nowitzke whistled loudly, holding up his hands to quell any potential pissing match between the two. "Listen, why don't we separate what we know from what we don't?"

"Chuck, you know I've doubted the credibility of the texter from the start," replied Anissa. "He or she is clear on some things but not on others. We've got a who, Katallani, a when, this Friday, three days from now, before noon. The previous midnight text said it would be a major jewelry hit, so we know the what, sort of. And now there's the term 'hijack,' which makes no sense to me in this context. I mean, what would Katallani be hijacking? Then, of course, we've also got the same warning to limit resources, cutting Copeland out of the picture. Oh, and a jumble of random numbers."

"When I hear hijack, I think of mobsters stealing a truck for the stuff inside it. Or bootleggers from Prohibition," offered her boss.

"Eliot Ness's Untouchables," mused Anissa. "An appropriate reference considering the prior text says the hit will take place in Chicago. But, to Russ's point yesterday, where? Kind of a key detail, especially if we're alerting a local SWAT team."

"Also, how would this hit dwarf the others?" asked Nowitzke rhetorically.

"Any thoughts on the numbers listed?" asked Sean.

"No," said both detectives in unison. Just then, Anissa's desk phone rang. Nowitzke placed it on speaker, assuming McKenzie was returning his call with the findings.

"Chuck, Norm here. We ran the phone number and got a ping at 2:08 a.m. this morning. The text came literally from the same spot as before. And the burner phone must have been shut down immediately after making the text 'cause we're showing no location now."

"Thanks, Norm," replied Nowitzke, clicking off the line.

"The numbers . . ." said Anissa, thinking out loud. "They almost look like a serial number of some sort. But for what?"

"A gun registration number?" asked Sean.

"No, the pattern doesn't fit," replied Nowitzke. "Nis, enter the numbers into your laptop."

After punching in the series, Anissa stared at the output. "Okay, first up is a reference to several parts catalogs, if you need a replacement piece for a riding mower. Next, the number of some legislative bill in Colorado about school funding. But I'm not seeing anything that could even be remotely connected with a robbery or Chicago." Then, she paused, studying the pattern once more. "Wait," said Anissa, shaking her head. "How slow am I? Sean, read the numbers back to me again." He picked up the phone and ticked off each numeral. "Alright, we have the who, when, and what, but not the where . . ." she concluded, her voice drifting off as she reentered the numbers and waited for the output. "I knew it!" she shouted. "Longitude and latitude."

"Fucking A!" shouted Nowitzke. "We know Chicago, but where exactly?"

"According to Google Earth, the corner of Wabash Avenue and East Madison Street," said Anissa. "Does that mean anything to you, Sean?"

The underwriter turned, deep in thought. "Shit. I should have figured this out on my own," he said, sitting down in the chair next to Nowitzke. "That corner happens to be in the heart of Chicago's jewelry district. The district extends for about two blocks between East Washington and Monroe. In between are two high-rise buildings that house nothing but wholesalers. There's something like three hundred-plus different jewelry businesses in a very tight radius."

"Okay, so how does someone hijack jewelry in a pair of highly protected buildings?" asked Nowitzke.

"They don't. But any building security is only effective until you step out onto the street. As soon as you take the goods out of the building, it then becomes susceptible to a hijack," offered Sean. "There is a major jewelry show in Las Vegas coming up next week. Most of the wholesalers in those buildings display their jewelry at the show. Anyway, a couple of years ago, the owners of each of the businesses in the buildings decided that rather than ship their goods to Vegas individually, it would be better to partner up and send everything in one highly protected truck. A semi with a transponder so it can also be tracked. After picking up the merchandise, that truck is escorted by heavily armed guards to O'Hare International where everything is then loaded onto a plane and taken to McCarran Airport on the way to the convention center."

"What kind of value are we talking about?" asked Nowitzke.

"No one really knows for sure. But if even half the wholesalers located in that area are involved, each bringing a million dollars of goods, you get a couple hundred million in a heartbeat."

"So much for the why this is a target," commented Anissa. "But if the semi can be tracked and is accompanied by armed security, how would anyone stop it?"

Sean remained quiet for a few seconds, then finally shrugged. "Beats me. I have no clue how someone might take the truck. There are levels of security in place for the trip to the airport. I will tell you that the thieves have a tight window though. Once the goods get to the airport and reach the show, the bad guys have almost no chance of taking them. While we don't know the identity of our mystery person, at least we've now got some specifics," said the underwriter before adding one final comment. "If someone were to manage the how and successfully take the truck down, it could easily be the largest jewelry theft of all time."

Nowitzke chewed on the end of his pen, taking time to process what Sean had said. As implausible as such a loss seemed, the elements almost made sense. Any thieves would be taking great risk, but it came with the potential of great reward. "Does WSU have any clients with merchandise on the truck?"

"Of course. Off the top of my head, I'd say fifty-plus."

"Jesus, so your company is pretty much all in. We need to talk to Russ now to give him the details of what we've come up with."

CHAPTER 49

"You know we're taking quite the leap of faith with a story based on details provided by some unknown snitch," said Anissa as Nowitzke dialed Russell.

"I understand, Nis. But everything seems to fit," Nowitzke replied. "We'll tell Russell and get his input. We're pretty much bystanders in the whole thing anyway since Chicago is far out of our jurisdiction. But if Russ thinks this is a credible threat, we've at least given the locals a heads-up."

"I suppose," concluded Anissa.

Nowitzke heard several rings, waiting for the call to connect, before hearing a click and a flat reply on the other end. "Russell."

Nowitzke and Anissa laid out the new developments for the fed, from the final text sent to Sean through their analysis of where and when the seizure would take place. "Damn. We've been worried about the potential of a hijack like this for several years now. The merchandise is safe within the fortress of each jewelry building and after it gets to the actual show, where there are levels of security that I'm not authorized to discuss with either of you. The weak link in the chain has always been during the transport of the goods to the show. In the old days, each of the merchants sent their goods on an individual basis by an overnight transport service or the good old post office. Even though it makes sense for these jewelers to work together, the net result is one helluva target . . . assuming this is real and could be pulled off," concluded Russ. "Tell you what, let me make some calls on my end. I imagine Chicago PD would want to take every precaution to prevent such a crime and possible blood bath in one of their premier business districts. Where is Sean, by the way?"

"He disappeared from here just before our call. I think he did the math about the potential loss to his company and is drinking his lunch early today," replied Nowitzke. "Let me know if you need anything from us."

"Will do," replied Russell before he clicked off the call.

"What do we do now?" asked Anissa.

"On this case, nothing. I assume we have other bad guys we can chase down while we wait to hear," offered Nowitzke.

CHAPTER 50

Nowitzke considered Anissa's question. "What do we do now?" was a fair query considering all the energy, and blood, he and his partner had invested in this series of cases. He was acutely aware of his backlog of open files, but working anything else for the time being seemed uninteresting. From his experience, he knew switching gears from one all-consuming case to others was difficult. By late afternoon, Nowitzke gave up the pretext of work and made a list of personal things to do. It was an opportunity to clear his mind, knowing tomorrow would provide him with a fresh start on other important work.

Pulling out his cell, he made a dinner reservation at a local steakhouse. Nadia sounded thrilled to get his call about a night out, if even for just an evening. While she had not grumbled about her confinement, Nowitzke knew she felt housebound. How could she not? He did, and he got to leave the apartment every day for work. Hardly birds in a gilded cage cooped up in Miss Alma's walk-up love nest, but in a cage no less. Nadia had done everything asked of her, including completing a fruitless search for Katallani in all the mug books Appleton PD maintained. As far as Nowitzke was concerned, this date night was Nadia's reward. He considered the risks of taking her off premises but felt they were manageable, judging that the serious action on the jewelry crimes seemed to have migrated south, headed for an apparent showdown. But, ever the cautious one, the Glock in Nowitzke's waistband would be his backup. Now, justified in his mind, a night out seemed well-deserved. Pulling on his jacket, he waved to Anissa on his way out of the office, focused on several other stops before heading home.

As he drove, his brain was at work. He and Nadia were clearly enjoying each other's company, but Nowitzke reckoned he was not as young as he used to be. She had worn him out, not that he was complaining. Beyond their physical relationship, he simply enjoyed her company. This beautiful woman made him realize how lonely he had been. He also knew in the back of his mind that as good as things seemed for the moment, it would not last. His relationships never did. And realistically, this one made no sense at all. Well, he reasoned it did only because of the protection he provided to her. Beyond that, what else was there? Still, he told himself not to spit in the eye of prosperity.

Walking up the creaky steps carrying a large bouquet of wildflowers, he decided not to overthink things. And there she was at the top of the staircase, her hair up, wearing a short, red cocktail dress with matching shoes. *Carpe fucking diem!* He wondered where she had kept this outfit hidden, not that he cared. She smiled at him and gave him a kiss when he made it up to the porch, politely accepting the flowers before retreating into the apartment in search of a vase. Nowitzke remained outside, still stunned by Nadia's look, unconsciously patting his jacket pocket which held his refilled prescription of Viagra.

Hours later, Nowitzke judged that the evening had gone exactly as planned in his head. The ambiance, food, and service had been impeccable. The detective had even ventured into the reserve wine list, throwing a dart, and was rewarded with a quality cabernet that complemented their steaks. Then neither could resist the presentation of the three-tiered dessert cart. It was an expensive outing, but the detective considered it money well spent. Cash neither of his exes would get. But for Nowitzke, the best part of the evening was watching the heads turn, both male and female, as Nadia entered the room on his arm.

Neither wanted the night to end, so they agreed to take the long ride back to their walk-up. Nadia kicked off her shoes, let her hair down, and opened the window, letting the comfortable evening air blow through the car. The sun had almost set, and the streetlights were in the process of blinking on. As they rode through town, Nadia noticed the municipal building with the large carved wooden sign that announced, "Appleton Police Department."

"Chuck, is that where you work?"

"Yeah. My home away from home."

"Would you give me a tour?" asked Nadia. "I've never seen an American police station."

"Jesus, Nadia, it's just four plain brick walls covered in dull paint. There's nothing to see."

"But you work there. It's a place that's an important part of your life. I'd really like to see it. Pleeeease," she said, imploring him with a look he could not resist.

Shaking his head, he wheeled the Taurus around. "Listen, it's pretty underwhelming, but if you must," he said.

The building was largely deserted with the evening shift, a skeleton crew compared to the day watch. Passing through the front door, Nowitzke nodded to the male officer, who barely looked up from his laptop until he realized the detective had a young woman in tow. Nowitzke caught the sergeant in a double take as the shoeless Nadia sauntered by in her short dress.

Nowitzke gave her the nickel tour, just like the ones he did for the local students, complete with a walk-through of the cube farm found in every office building in the world. As a potential area of interest for Nadia, Nowitzke pointed out Anissa's nondescript workstation. True to form, her desk was clear of any work materials, holding only two framed photographs, one of Anissa as a teenager with her father dressed in his Green Beret fatigues and the second a portrait of her grandmother, likely taken for a church directory. Fifteen minutes later, Nowitzke concluded the excursion, leading Nadia to his office.

"I need to use the men's room," he said, excusing himself after pulling out one of the chairs for her. "I'll be right back. Oh, and don't touch anything."

Nadia sat, considering Nowitzke's original opinion of the place. He was right; it was drab and depressing. She scanned his office. In contrast to Anissa, Nowitzke's desk held a laptop and an avalanche of documents. Other files were heaped in the corners of the office. It reminded her of what she found when she moved into his apartment. Waiting patiently, Nadia's eyes were drawn to the officer's collection of snow globes sitting on the credenza behind his desk. Of course, she had seen snow globes before, but the small collection of tchotchke held an uncontrollable draw to most who saw them. Nadia rose from her chair, carefully stepping around the clutter, and examined the lot. She scanned the grouping before picking up one which featured a more traditional holiday scene, Santa holding his pack in front of several evergreen trees. Giving it a shake, she was delighted as the snow shimmered and gently fell. When the blizzard concluded, Nadia turned the globe upside down, setting off another storm.

Watching the display conclude a second time, her attention turned to a handful of photos on the wall above the credenza. The first was an 8x10 of a beaming Anissa holding a gold badge as she stood proudly next to Nowitzke. For whatever reason, Nadia felt compelled to reach out and touch the edge of the cheap frame, smiling back at the pair. It was clear to her why Chuck held the young woman in such high regard. When Nadia scanned to the next picture though, her eyes stopped and her smile vanished. She blinked hard at the grainy 5x7, and her hands and body began to tremble. She stood straight, not uttering a sound, and her eyes grew large before dropping the Santa globe to the floor, where it bounced with a thud. Then, her bladder released. Urine ran down her legs, puddling on the shabby carpeting as Nowitzke returned to his office.

"Jesus, Nadia. What the hell is going on?"

"Are you going to kill me, Chuck?" she asked distantly, her entire body shuddering.

"What? Kill you?" he asked, confused. "Why would I hurt you? What's wrong?"

Slowly, she lifted her right hand and pointed her index finger at a photo on the wall. "Because you are friends with him."

"What are you talking about?"

"Katallani. You are friends with Katallani," Nadia shrieked as she raised her hands and covered her mouth.

The detective looked at the photos, still baffled. "Who?" he asked. "I don't get it."

"Him," she pleaded, taking the photo of Nowitzke and Copeland from the wall.

"Nadia, this is a friend of mine. Detective Copeland from Milwaukee," protested Nowitzke.

"Chuck, he is the man I saw with Musa. He is Katallani!"

CHAPTER 51

"Fucking A" was all Nowitzke could muster. He sat down in his chair and studied the offending photo. *Copeland is Katallani?* While Nadia excused herself to clean up in the bathroom, the detective tried to make sense of what had just taken place. His brain was on fire. *How is this possible?* He counted himself as friends with the man. But not just a friend. His best friend. They had a history, having worked side by side for years, spilling more liquor together than most people ever drink. Arturo had gotten him through many low times, including his two divorces. *A possible case of mistaken identity?* Copeland was the most decorated detective in the history of the Milwaukee PD. *There has to be a logical explanation.* But Nadia was certain. She had no doubt. Nowitzke didn't know Nadia well, but he sensed there was a certain toughness about her. Still, short of an all-consuming fear, no one pees themselves. *Now she's not sure she can trust me. I see it in her eyes.*

Nowitzke's mind kept coming back to Copeland, a man he respected personally and professionally. The detective stood, almost beside himself with confusion. *It just can't be true.* His friend, now *the* prime suspect in a series of felony crimes, including several vicious murders. Even discounting the secret texter who said Katallani was involved in these thefts, Nadia recognized Copeland as the evil person her brother feared. The man she described as having no problem tying up loose ends, people like Musa. *Jesus, Anissa was shot too.*

Playing through the events of the last several weeks, Nowitzke also thought about the attempt on Nadia's life. *No one knew she was at my place.* Then, an alarm bell went off in his head. *Shit, I gave Copeland my fucking address, and he must have pieced it together.* Nowitzke could come up with no other explanation. He remembered his conversation with Sheriff Patton. Someone had sent Simmons to kill Nadia. *Goddamn!*

Nowitzke was in purgatory, unable to call his old friend and straighten out what had to be a misunderstanding. *Was this the reason the covert snitch wanted Copeland out of the information loop?* The more the detective thought about it—the incidents, Nadia's reaction—it almost made sense. Even though Nowitzke was not one hundred percent sold, he knew he needed to act, and now. With the supposed deadline of the hijack only forty-eight hours away, he was back in the game. *Shit!*

Nadia had found her way back to his office and meekly took a chair as the detective picked up the phone. He woke Anissa with his first call to give her this latest twist of events.

"You're kidding me," said a sleepy Anissa. "How well do you know Copeland?"

"He's my best friend. That's the hell of it, Nis. This is killing me," he said, his voice cracking. "My next call is to Russell. I need to get down to Chicago. Can you come to the office and pick up Nadia?"

Hearing her name, Nadia looked up and shook her head. "Chuck, I believe you had no part in this with Katall . . . this Copeland person. I'll be safe with you at home."

"Thank you, Nadia," he said before continuing his conversation with Anissa. "Nis, tell you what. Sit tight for now, but plan on getting in here tomorrow morning at zero dark thirty. We'll see what the feds want to do."

"Got it," replied Anissa.

Nowitzke caught Russell on the first ring and repeated his story. "Seriously? Copeland? One of our own?" queried the agent. There was silence on the line as Russ thought through next steps. "Tell you what, Chuck. I'll talk with my superiors, and we'll set up an early morning conference call to figure this out. If our source is correct, we have a day or so before the loaded semi leaves the jewelry center."

"Way ahead of you, Russ. Also, I just wanted you to know that I want to be part of the team in Chicago to take Copeland down," Nowitzke said before signing off.

CHAPTER 52

Overnight, Anissa and Nowitzke each got a text from Russell announcing that a conference call with interested parties would take place at 9:00 a.m. Nonetheless, both detectives arrived at the office several hours early, each toting a large Starbucks cup. Neither had slept well, lying awake in anticipation of learning the plan to catch a bad cop. Still trying to reconcile what happened, Nowitzke woke up feeling more tired than when he went to bed. Bleary-eyed, the two of them sat in Nowitzke's office to kill time. Then, at 8:00 a.m., Nowitzke's cell rang.

"Detective Nowitzke, this is Kendra Mullins from Wisconsin Specialty Underwriters."

"Good morning, Ms. Mullins," replied Nowitzke. "What can I do for you?" He assumed she was wondering about all the recent jewelry recoveries Appleton PD had made but forgot to tell her about.

"Well . . ." she stammered. "This is about Sean Cook. I wasn't sure exactly what to do, but he's . . . missing."

"Missing? What do you mean missing, ma'am?" Nowitzke asked, pressing the speaker button on his phone so Anissa could hear the conversation.

"Sean hasn't reported to work for the last several days, and, quite frankly, some of his co-workers and I are very worried about him. We've tried to call him on his cell. One of our staff members even went by his apartment. Obviously, we couldn't get into the place, but Sean didn't answer his door. No one has seen him around town. It's like . . . he's dropped off the face of the planet."

Anissa jumped into the conversation. "Ms. Mullins, my name is Detective Taylor. Can you give us any insight into Sean's frame of mind?"

"I think that's an issue that has many of us concerned. I would say Sean has been under great strain lately. You both know that he set up our jewelry program, and our results of late have been, should we say, less than stellar. He's been getting pressure from me and several other higher-ups."

"I understand," agreed Anissa. "We can have a patrol car do a welfare check on Sean. Essentially, the officers would do some of what your employees did, like knocking on his door. But our people would also talk with his neighbors, that type of thing. Do you know if Sean has any close relatives that we could also talk to?"

"No, none that I'm aware of. I think his mother is still in the UK based on what he told me, but I don't know her name," said Mullins. "If I knew of any other family members, I would have called them and not bothered you." She paused, taking a deep breath before continuing. "Officers, you don't think Sean would hurt himself, do you?"

It was a fair question. They knew Sean was concerned for his professional future but never thought it would lead him to commit suicide, à la Malcolm Bateman. "Ms. Mullins, let us start at Sean's apartment, and we'll keep you up-to-date on what we find," said Nowitzke. "Maybe he had to leave town on some personal business that he forgot to mention to anyone. Or maybe he's very ill." *Or he's on an extended boss-inspired bender.* "Who knows? But there are a lot of reasons he might be out of touch," he concluded, trying to ease the woman's mind.

As they hung up the phone, Anissa and Nowitzke exchanged glances. "You know, the timing on this is curious to say the least," said Anissa.

"True, but Sean is just the insurer at the ass end of these claims, and he's under pressure at work. According to your recent date, he's got no insider knowledge and was pressing you for details. He obviously knows about the truck hijacking in Chicago and the potential for even more losses to his company. Frankly, my impression is that he's mentally tougher than I've given him credit for. But it's not like he's a target for Katallani," said Nowitzke.

"You never liked Sean anyway," countered Anissa.

"Just thought something was off with him, but he started to grow on me. Maybe the logical reason for Sean's disappearance is that he skipped town so he didn't have to take any more abuse from Mullins. She ripped me a new asshole, and I'm the one just investigating the crimes. Man, what a bitch."

"But she's a concerned bitch, Chuck," Anissa replied, getting a laugh from her boss. "Eventually, someone will drop a house on her. I agree there is probably a logical explanation here, but the hairs on the back of my neck went up when Mullins said Sean was missing."

"You too, huh?" Nowitzke drummed his fingers on his desk, thinking. "Tell you what. I'll take the call with Russ and fill you in later. In the meantime, you meet a patrol car at Sean's place and see what you can find, if anything."

"Fair enough," she said, rising from her chair.

CHAPTER 53

Precisely at 9:00 a.m., the desk phone rang. Nowitzke answered with the speaker button in anticipation of taking notes of the conversation. "Good morning, Chuck. I've got us on speaker with Captain Archie Andrews of Chicago PD," said Russell.

"Good morning, Detective Nowitzke," offered Andrews.

"Is Anissa with you?" asked Russell.

"No. Something came up that she needed to chase down."

"I've given Archie an overview of the series of jewelry crimes and what we believe will happen in the next twenty-four hours," said Russell. "Archie and I have discussed Copeland and the potential hijacking, and we've agreed to disagree about its priority. There are a couple of local issues, the biggest being the source we can't identify. Archie's opinion is that this is not necessarily a credible threat. The second major problem is CPD resources."

"We've got our people being pulled in multiple different directions with little wiggle room to spare," offered Archie. "Also, we knew about the semi leaving tomorrow. The jewelers in that complex have transported their goods to O'Hare like this for several years without any issues. I'm just not convinced we've got a real problem."

"Chuck, since you've worked this case from the start, I'd like you to get down here today so we can talk further with Archie. We have some time before the semi leaves tomorrow morning. Maybe we can come to an understanding. Oh, and just in case, bring your tactical gear."

"I'll pack an overnight bag and be out of Appleton in the next hour, just in time to add to Chicago's rush-hour traffic," Nowitzke said before hanging up. He tracked down Clark in his office, giving him a three-minute update before heading back to the apartment. The officer on Nadia watch greeted Nowitzke as he passed by and bounded up to his place. Nadia had just come out of the shower, dressed in a plush robe with a towel on her head, and was drinking tea at the kitchen table as the detective explained that he had to drive to Chicago for a meeting.

"You're after him . . . Katallani. Aren't you?" she asked.

"Yes," he said flatly, "I need to see this through, Nadia." Shaking his head, he continued, "I still can't believe Copeland, my friend, is behind all of this." He began to rummage through his closet looking for his body armor, hoping it would still fit.

"Is there anything I can say to stop you?" she asked, already knowing the answer. "Or anything I might do?" She took the towel off her head and opened her robe just a bit. "Please don't go."

It was a tempting offer to say the least. Probably one she never expected him to turn down. Little Nowitzke even offered a salute at half-staff. However, the detective remained quiet, staring at Nadia with an odd sense that it would be the last time he would ever see her.

"Nadia, I don't want you to live in fear of Copeland any longer. He's killed several innocent people, including coming after you, injuring Anissa . . . he's got to be stopped."

She began to cry, closed her robe, and ran to the bathroom, slamming the door behind her. Nowitzke stopped and shrugged for a moment, unsure of what to do, before deciding to finish packing. In addition to his clothes, he tossed an extra box of ammunition and another pistol into his suitcase, just in case. "Nadia, I'll see you in the next day or so," he yelled resolutely as he turned toward the door of the apartment.

As he made it to the porch, Nowitzke heard the bathroom door open. "Wait," Nadia cried as she ran to him, stepping outside and jumping into his arms before giving him a long goodbye kiss. "I have a bad feeling about this. Please be careful, Detective."

"What could go wrong?" he replied.

Just about everything.

CHAPTER 54

Anissa met two uniforms at Sean's address as provided by Mullins. The building was a red-brick fourplex in an older part of town. She had not been to his place before, and her first reaction was that the structure was not one she would have expected to be suitable housing for an up-and-coming insurance executive. Upon entering the building, one of the patrolmen took the lead, tapping lightly on the door of Unit 1 with his night stick, announcing, "Mr. Cook, Appleton Police." There was no response. The officer repeated his greeting a little louder, adding two more forceful raps on the door. Still nothing.

Getting the result they had anticipated, the three cops walked down a dingy, narrow hallway to find a neighbor. Aside from the sunlight streaming through the front glass door to the building, the only other light was provided by a single sixty-watt bulb held in a tarnished brass wall fixture designed to hold two. Reaching the end of the corridor, they found another door displaying a catawampus number 2. Anissa stepped toward the entrance and knocked politely, declaring "Appleton Police." From the hallway, the officers heard what sounded like a game show on television and rustling inside before a male voice called back. "Who is it?"

"Appleton PD, sir. We'd like to ask you some questions about your neighbor," responded Anissa. She heard the tenant fiddling with the door chain and the metallic clunk of a dead bolt lock. As the thin wooden door opened, the smell of bacon wafted into the hall, preceding a short, slim man wearing a stained grey t-shirt, boxers, sandals, and an open black satin kimono. The thirty-something man stood eye level with Anissa's breasts, prompting him to comb over his thinning brown hair with his hand while sucking in the potbelly that was exposed under his shirt. "Well, hello, Officer," he said, directing his greeting toward Anissa before scanning up to her face. "I'm Randy Price. What can I do you for?" He smiled, exposing a dull emerald-colored front tooth.

Anissa, wearing a brand-new cream-colored business suit, flashed her identification and handed it to Price at his request. "Detective Anissa Taylor," Price repeated the name on the cred as if the little man inside his head were carving it in stone. "Wow, you are a breath of fresh air," he said with an inadvertent whistle through his decaying tooth as he continued eying her up and down.

Patiently, Anissa explained that she and her colleagues were concerned about the well-being of Price's neighbor, Sean Cook. "How well do you know him?" she asked.

"Only well enough to pick up his rent check each month. I guess I'm like the manager here." He puffed his chest, clearly trying to impress Anissa. "I do some light repairs . . . can't do too much though on account of my back. Got rear-ended a couple of years ago. I'm in constant pain," he offered with a practiced grimace as his hand automatically moved to the supposed offending area of his body. "But I got my meds and some Jack Daniels to take the edge off. I'm on disability now after blowing my insurance settlement."

When Price took a breath, Anissa chimed in before he could continue with his life story. "Would you happen to have a key to Mr. Cook's apartment?"

"Do you have a warrant?" responded Price just a little too quickly as the two uniformed officers exchanged glances. "Oh, that's right, you said you were just checking up on Sean. Let me go see if I can find my key ring." He used his hand to paste his comb-over once more, then partially closed the door behind himself.

"What are the odds we'd find something interesting in Price's place if we had a warrant?" Anissa quietly asked the uniforms. Both nodded on cue.

"I wouldn't take the under on that bet, Detective," replied the senior of the pair.

"Besides, we don't need the extra paperwork," his partner added. They heard more activity deep from within the apartment, drawers opened, doors slammed, and then the toilet flush before Price reappeared.

"Found 'em in the first place I looked," he said, holding them up proudly for everyone to see. He stepped past the officers and ambled down the hall, scratching his ass as he went. "Sean's a strange dude," he volunteered. "Seems to work during the day but keeps odd hours." Price fumbled with the lock briefly before announcing, "Wallah," like he was a magician completing his best trick as he pushed open the door.

The two uniformed officers stepped to the threshold as Anissa yelled, "Sean? Sean Cook?" Still with no response, she tilted her head and motioned the officers into the shabby room. She excused Price, promising to drop off the key before sending the ass scratcher back to his hole.

Clearly, it was not the typical apartment of a vice president. Stepping into the living room, Anissa's senses were immediately assailed with an all-pervasive, indistinguishable odor, like an animal had died in the walls. The room contained a soiled brown couch surrounded by several mismatched and equally tattered chairs. A ring-stained wooden coffee table held several empty beer cans, a stack of old newspapers, and a half-eaten container of Chinese food that had already drawn the attention of two very large cockroaches. The balance of the place was a hodgepodge of junk, but what some might have regarded as a collection of vintage housewares and furnishings. Anissa judged the fuzzy blue flocked wallpaper to be circa 1970. There were also several large holes torn into the worn brown carpet. Worse, the place was covered in grime. Anissa cursed herself for wearing a new outfit, hoping to get out of the place without brushing up against anything and collecting a stain.

"Anissa," she heard an officer call from another room.

Stepping into what was obviously the bedroom, the detective noted a tangle of foam blankets clumped on a saggy mattress. The windows near the bed were shrouded with a bed sheet, the preferred strategy of a college student trying to keep the morning light at bay.

"What do you make of this?" asked the officer, pointing to Sean's wallet. Anissa opened the billfold and counted twenty-three dollars in cash, also noting several credit cards in Sean's name. Sitting on the dresser was a supposed Rolex watch, a cell phone, and a set of keys. Anissa noticed that one of the keys was identical to the one supplied by Price. The ring also contained a blue plastic key tag promoting a local Ford dealer, along with what looked like the vehicle key. A search of the dresser revealed nothing, aside from some underwear and socks balled together in a single drawer. She then scanned the closet, noting several pairs of pants, two jackets, some shirts, and three suits, one of which she recognized as Sean's.

Then, anticipating the worst, Anissa took a gulp of air before poking her head into the lone bathroom. Her intuition was right on track as she spied a beautiful blue-green pattern of fungus forming on a previously white plastic shower curtain, a tub with a large black ring around the bottom, and a fetid sink. Yet, Sean's toothbrush remained steadfast in its chrome holder on the counter. The medicine chest held no secrets, only a small white bottle of over-the-counter aspirin. "Let's get out into the hall," she told the officers, feeling as if the walls of the place were closing in on her.

"What do you think, gentlemen?" she asked as they stepped out of Sean's apartment.

"Well, there was no sign of any struggle," said the senior officer. "There wasn't a robbery, considering Mr. Cook's valuables were still in the apartment. It looked like his clothes were still here. My impression is he just walked away."

"I agree," chimed in the junior officer, nodding his head. "Who did you say this guy was again?"

"A local insurance executive," replied Anissa.

"Seriously?" the officers said in unison.

"Yeah, I know. Looks like the housekeeper had taken a few years off. I guess you just never know what people are like sometimes. For what it's worth, can you guys check with the occupants in the other apartments upstairs to see if anyone knows anything about Sean while I finish our business with Mr. Price?"

"Just be careful," offered the smiling senior patrolman as the officers started to climb the stairway.

"I'll bet they don't call him Randy for nothing," added his partner.

"Thanks for the warning," Anissa laughed. "Once you get past the tooth, he's probably quite the catch."

She stepped out of the building for a moment and moved toward her vehicle, scanning the small parking area for a Ford. Sure enough, parked under a tree was a familiar-looking metallic-green Explorer covered with a layer of green leaves and bird shit. She called into the department to verify that the SUV belonged to Cook.

"Yes," confirmed the voice on the other end of the phone. "According to the plate number you provided, the vehicle is registered to Sean Cook."

"Thanks. Since I have you on the line, can you run something else for me?" asked Anissa.

Minutes later, she stood outside of Price's unit, taking a deep breath before rapping on the door. "Detective, you're back," said Price cordially as he stepped into the hallway. He had changed into a pair of ill-fitting baggy jeans and a white tank top, revealing wiry arms covered in sleeves of green and red tattoos. "Can I getcha something to drink?" he asked, holding up a can of malt liquor.

"No thank you, Mr. Price. Here are the keys to Sean's apartment. You've been very helpful." She placed the keys into Price's hand and turned to leave.

"Wait, can I get your business card in case I remember something later?" he asked. "Maybe you could give me your personal cell number too? It might be fun to get together for drinks sometime. Who knows where things could lead?" he offered in a suggestive tone, raising his eyebrows and smiling, again exposing his rotting tooth.

"Mr. Price . . . may I call you Randy?" asked Anissa courteously.

"Sure," said the surprised man, unconsciously stroking his thinning hair, thinking he had cracked her armor.

"I'd love to meet you sometime, Randy. I really would. But I have a personal policy against dating felons convicted for drug trafficking, let alone a person with several open warrants. I didn't have time to look for any active warrants that my friends over at the federal building might be interested in, but let's just leave things the way they are . . . star-crossed lovers, Randy. Just like the Capulets and the Montagues."

The man stood in place, blinking rapidly as he sipped his malt liquor with a confused look on his face, waiting for Anissa to finish. "Huh," he grunted in response. "So, is that a yes or a no?"

"Have a nice life, Randy," Anissa replied as she turned her back on her wannabe suitor and moved toward the stairwell after hearing the officers making their way back down. With her eyes raised expectantly, she asked, "Anything?"

"Nothing. No one upstairs even knows the guy," reported the senior officer. "The residents included a little old lady and a single mom with three screaming kids. Sorry."

"Thanks, guys. Why don't you take off while I run down another lead on Sean," she said, exiting the building. Jumping behind the wheel, she remembered that Nowitzke's sixth sense had declared that something about Sean did not feel right. "Chuck and his goddamned hunches," she muttered to herself. But she was gradually buying into this one.

CHAPTER 55

Anissa's Audi came to rest in a visitor parking space outside a four-story all-glass building standing behind a large stone sign boasting Wisconsin Specialty Underwriters. The uninspired stand-alone structure looked like one of several copycats clustered in the business park. The detective made her way into the lobby where she was greeted by a smiling receptionist. After Anissa flashed her badge and asked to see Kendra Mullins, though, the woman's beam faded quickly. The young lady behind the counter gathered herself, calling an unknown person somewhere in the building before overtly plastering on her required customer service smile once again and asking Anissa to take a seat.

Moments later, a trim Mullins emerged from the elevator wearing a striking powder-blue business suit with her platinum-grey hair cut back harshly. Anissa judged that while Mullins had probably paid a fortune to get her coifed, urban look, she thought the same result could have been achieved by a gardener wielding an edge trimmer. The overall effect added to Mullins's particularly hard look. Nowitzke had described the female executive in his typically unvarnished fashion, judging that if Mullins ever went to prison, she would be running a cell block within a week. Nevertheless, Anissa adopted a professional demeanor and put forth her hand to greet Mullins before they stepped onto the elevator. As they walked together through the hallways, Anissa noticed that Mullins's presence had a chilling effect on her coworkers, who seemingly went out of their way to avoid sharing the same air with her.

There was no small talk from Mullins, who guided Anissa to her office and then to the same chair that Nowitzke had previously occupied. Even though Mullins had expressed concern for Sean over the phone, she was now all business, getting right to the point. "What, if anything, did you find at Sean's apartment, Ms. Taylor?" she asked coldly.

The detective took the time to cross her legs, holding the businesswoman's gaze as she seated herself behind her desk. "Well, Sean was definitely not there. The manager of the building let me into the apartment. There appears to be no foul play, and from what I could tell, all of Sean's valuables, his wallet, credit cards, and phone were still in the place, as well as his vehicle. We got no additional information after a quick canvas of the other tenants in the building." She left out details of Sean's housekeeping issues. "Without any next of kin to touch base with, we're at a bit of a dead end."

"I see. Interesting," commented Mullins, who rose and stared out of the window behind her desk. "When Detective Nowitzke was here, he asked what type of background check I had done on Sean. Frankly, I hadn't done any, which was clearly an oversight on my part. So in the last day or so, I tried reaching out to the references listed on Sean's resumé. But I was shocked that I couldn't locate any of them. Phone numbers listed were no longer in service or simply rang without the option to leave a message. Then I tried to talk with former employers at several of the syndicates that Sean listed working for at Lloyd's. I made some early morning calls to account for the time difference in London, but also came up empty. Several people thought Sean's name sounded familiar, but no one could really place him or give me any details. Maybe the turnover at the syndicates accounts for not being able to find someone who could verify his employment," Mullins noted. "My last step was to check with our Human Resources unit. I pulled his file, but aside from his photo, resumé, and job application, it contained nothing else except for details about his social security number. I remember when we hired Sean that he had to work through the embassy in London to get the number issued since he was a U.S. citizen living abroad." She paused a beat. "Beyond that, I followed up with the college listed, Ipswich University in England. But no one there had any record of him graduating or ever attending the school, for that matter. It's almost like Sean didn't exist up until three years ago when we hired him. I know he had knowledge of jewelry insurance and security, but God knows where he learned that officially," she concluded.

Anissa studied Mullins, trying to gauge what was going on in her head. Bottom line, the executive had cut corners, having given the keys of the kingdom to a potential fraudster. *Maybe Nowitzke was right about Sean after all. Mullins had quickly moved on from any personal concern for Sean, skipping ahead to personal damage control. Why didn't I see this coming too? It could have been my lack of experience or . . . did I get too close to Sean to see any warning signs?* "Given the timing of Sean's disappearance as you've described it, we have the basis for a missing person's case," advised Anissa. "Can you go down to the department and officially file a report?"

Mullins responded with an exaggerated sigh, as if she'd been asked to clean the toilets in the building. "If I must," said the clearly perturbed executive, who now had bitten off more time and paperwork than she cared to invest in this growing mistake in her judgment.

"Also, bring the photo from Sean's P-file. It can only help," said Anissa, rising from her chair. "I'll also mention this to a friend at the FBI to see what help they might offer. Would you mind if I looked at Sean's workstation?"

"Not at all," said the executive. Mullins hesitated for a moment before coming around her desk. "Detective, it's a pleasure to meet another local professional. I'm new in town and have had trouble meeting people . . . if you know what I mean." She shook Anissa's hand, holding it a second too long. "Would you be interested in having cocktails with me sometime?" she asked flirtatiously.

"Thank you for the offer, Ms. Mullins. But I'm in a committed relationship," Anissa lied, somewhat taken aback. "Can you direct me to Sean's office?"

"Downstairs, third floor," said Mullins coldly as she returned to her desk. "Ask one of the employees for help if you need it."

As Anissa took the elevator, she saw her reflection in the polished brass. *Jesus, I should be committed. What the hell kind of vibe am I putting out today?*

Two employees walking down the corridor pointed Anissa toward Sean's space. It was a comfortable double cube where the upper panels were clear, serving as windows so the occupant could see the rest of the world. In contrast to Sean's apartment, his faux wooden desk was neat and clean, containing only a closed laptop sitting in front of a reclining metal office chair. Two comfortable-looking chairs sat perfectly aligned on the other side of the desk. Anissa did a quick inspection of a cabinet but found nothing aside from some working files. Interestingly, apart from the name plate on the outside of the cube, Sean displayed no personal memorabilia, certificates, or photos that distinguished his space from anyone else's.

Anissa sat in the office chair for a moment, thinking about anything she could have missed, when a mousy woman wearing large, blue-framed glasses poked her head around the corner into the office. "Are you Sean's replacement?" asked the middle-aged lady.

"No, ma'am. I'm a police officer investigating Mr. Cook's disappearance," Anissa replied. "Do you work with Sean?"

"I did. But the jewelry division started having some big losses. Ms. Mullins came downstairs and regularly chewed Sean out for everyone on the floor to hear. That bitch," she added to the growing consensus. "It was hard to listen to . . . you know, the way she treated him. I've now been assigned to another unit insuring farms. Anyway, the people down here pretty much liked Sean and became concerned when he stopped coming to work. At first, we wondered if he told Mullins to pound sand and quit. But when we found out he hadn't, we just got worried . . . you know, worried about what happened to him."

"Do you have any ideas about where Sean might have gone?"

"Not really," said the woman. "We all knew he was under tremendous stress. Though, the last time I saw Sean, he seemed nervous and all excited at the same time. He never said a word, but he had a big smile on his face. Like he was going to put one over on Mullins and WSU. I thought maybe he had a new job lined up and would compete against us. But you know, as nice a guy as he was, I never had the feeling I got to know the real person."

The woman's words replayed in Anissa's mind as she drove back to the office. Then the detective realized that everything the woman had said about Sean was phrased in the past tense. Several themes were emerging from the various conversations about Sean. The common thread was that no one, including Anissa, ever felt they had met the real Sean.

CHAPTER 56

"You're shitting me. Mullins is a dyke?" Nowitzke belly-laughed as he spoke to Anissa on his phone in the car. "Seriously, how do you know?" he asked, still chuckling for all he was worth.

"Well, asking me out for a drink while rubbing my hand seemed like a big fat clue. How did you not pick up on that, Detective?"

"I have different plumbing. Christ, I must be getting old," he lamented for a moment. "Well, did you accept?"

"Shut up, Chuck. By the way, it was the second time today someone hit on me."

"Who else put the moves on you?"

"At least the other offer was from a guy, but I don't know if it was an upgrade or not," said Anissa. "The man was quite the stunner though, coming all the way up to my boobs before losing an extended stare-down with them. A poster child for every lowlife scumbag in the world, complete with a white tank top, tats, and a stunning green front tooth to go along with his criminal record. Anyway, he managed to pull himself up by the bootstraps and left his trailer to somehow become the apartment manager at the complex where Sean lives."

"Jesus, you're killing me, Nis. So, you turned down two rising professionals in their respective fields," he chortled. "Your standards are pretty high, but at least you're getting some action with a lot of open territory between these two. Aside from your amorous adventures, what did you find out about Sean?"

"Actually, quite a bit, but I'm not sure how much will be useful to us.

For starters, the man lived in a shithole of an apartment. I mean disgusting enough that the health department might be concerned. But while Sean wasn't anywhere to be found, all his stuff, including personal items like his wallet, credit cards, and his phone, was still there. His vehicle was parked at the place. No one there seemed to know anything about him. It was like he just vanished. I got pretty much the same story from my lesbian lover wannabe. She did a background check on Sean after the fact but couldn't locate anyone that could vouch for him or knew him in a professional capacity. The one thing that stuck out to me was what one of his coworkers said . . . that Sean was excited and nervous to be moving on. But no one knows to what. I asked Mullins to file a report. Can you mention something to Russell, by the way? I'm out of bullets on my end."

"Sure," replied Nowitzke. "I'll see him shortly."

"Where are you? You sound like you're in a car."

"I am. Currently stuck in traffic on the Dan Ryan trying to find my exit for the hotel. Our call with Russ and Chicago PD didn't go as well as I'd hoped. The local cops are in your camp, having difficulty believing in the threat of a hijack from an anonymous source. They do know about the truck transfer though, saying the jewelers have been doing it this way for several years without incident. Anyway, Russ asked me to come down and have a discussion with the captain involved to see if there's anything else they can do."

"Do you want me to come down to Chicago?"

"Frankly, Nis, I think you need to sit this one out. You're still recovering and not running at one hundred percent, even though what you bring to the party is more than most. I'm sorry I had to leave Appleton immediately without telling you. We have a meeting set for after dinner to talk this through."

"Anything I can do from here?" asked Anissa.

"Yeah, actually there is. I forgot that Miss Alma is being released from the hospital today. Can you pick her up and bring her home?" he asked sheepishly.

"You owe me big-time, Chuck."

CHAPTER 57

As Nowitzke arrived at his hotel, he received a text from Russell that the late-night dinner had now become an early-morning breakfast. After another night of erratic sleep, Nowitzke walked from his hotel, arriving at Al's Diner just before six. A large, rusted metal sign boasting "Al's" in red neon script hung on the building located in what appeared to be a demilitarized zone. The entire restaurant was no more than thirty feet wide and roughly the same depth. Based on what Nowitzke could see, Al's had likely been decorated in the 1930s, with few capital improvements since. Perhaps the only real updates were the colorful cardboard advertisements for many local businesses attached to the ceiling tiles. Two white grease boards announcing the daily specials stood out from years of accumulated semi-collectibles, along with autographed baseballs and team pennants on the wall near the kitchen. In and amongst the clutter was a collection of yellowed ancient messages to both staff and patrons, many of them decades old and long since expired. A single one-size-fits-all menu was positioned between the boards while another neon sign blinked "Breakfast all day."

A muscular Black police officer sat in a corner of the room at one of the six mismatched tables, reading the morning paper while sipping his coffee.

"You must be Captain Andrews?" asked Nowitzke, catching the cop buried in concentration.

As the paper dropped to the table, the officer stood, unfolding to a full six foot eight. "Detective Nowitzke, I presume," said the jovial man, extending his hand. "Archie Andrews. I'm sorry I didn't see you come in. I was wrapped up in reading about how my goddamned Cubs pissed away another game last night."

"Did you play ball, Archie?"

"College football. Illinois. But I realized early on that I was not going to the pros, so I leveraged my scholarship and focused on getting my degree. Criminal justice," he concluded. "You an early riser too?"

"Yes," lied Nowitzke. "Call me Chuck." The detective slid into the spot across the table from Archie, pulling a paper mat to his place while rearranging the tarnished silverware."

"Chuck, this is the only time of day I have any peace in my life. A quiet cup of coffee by myself along with my sports page. I get here by five thirty every day just as the place opens. Then the shit hits the fan around eight, and I typically lose control of my day by two in the afternoon. Coffee?" He held up the pot, filling the cup in front of the detective after getting a nod back. "That's what happened yesterday, anyway," he continued. "I had to cancel our dinner because of a gang shooting. Dumb kids killing each other over a piece of turf nobody really cares about. Been that way even before I was born, with no end in sight."

Nowitzke nodded his head in agreement. "Things are much calmer in Appleton, but I had my fill of the same thing working at Milwaukee PD," replied the detective as Russell and Anissa entered the restaurant.

Nowitzke snorted, not surprised to see his partner. "I knew you'd make it, Nis."

"You didn't really think I was going to miss Katallani's final act, did you?" she said, smiling back.

"Kitschy place, Archie," commented the fed.

"Been here forever," said Andrews. "Basically, a total dive of a diner that no one knew about for decades. Then some food critic with too much time on his hands declared Al's a local treasure. Hipsters and tourists now flock to the place, which makes getting a table on the weekends next to impossible. My only hope is the owner doesn't succumb to the pressure by offering healthy choices like egg-white omelets and fucking turkey bacon." He refilled his mug. "Let's order our food so you can tell me the story about this supposed hijacking of the jewelry semi."

A relic of a man, presumably related to the original Al, took their orders before Nowitzke launched into the sequence of events that led them to Chicago. The burglary. Besnik's murder and Anissa's brush with death. The robbery in Milwaukee where the perps used only blanks. The cold-blooded killing of Watson. The theft of the Pink Monster. They paused briefly when their food arrived, but the story continued about the anonymous source, ending with the prediction of the hijack by Katallani, a.k.a. Copeland, his former mentor. "And Sean Cook has disappeared," added Nowitzke for Russell's benefit.

"When did that happen?" Russell asked, raising his eyebrows.

"In the last couple of days. That was the detail Anissa was working on yesterday."

"Russ, do you think there's any connection between Sean's disappearance and Copeland?" asked Anissa.

"I have no idea. It's hard to believe the guy who insured the losses would be taken. For now, let's take one crisis at a time."

"Damn," said Archie after hearing Nowitzke's tale. "What the hell got into the drinking water up in Wisconsin?" He looked at the three law enforcement officers sitting with him, then went silent, taking time to refill his coffee again while thinking through the issues. "Here's the deal about the shipment today from my perspective. Essentially, the movement of the jewelers' merchandise anywhere is a private security matter. They ship goods every day without any expectation of police involvement. This is just a matter of scale as far as I'm concerned. But I also know from experience that there is a GPS tracking unit on the shipper's truck, allowing the freight carrier to follow its progress to the airport. And we're talking about Chicago traffic too. Nothing moves quickly between the jewelry center and O'Hare approaching the noon hour."

"What are you saying?" asked Nowitzke.

"My assessment is it would be almost impossible for us to lose a semi full of jewelry even dealing with a guy like Copeland who has knowledge of police tactical operations. Assuming he even tried, CPD can respond at a moment's notice, if we need to," replied the police captain. "Essentially, we're too big to fail."

"How did that thought work out for the banking industry?" responded Nowitzke.

Archie twisted in his chair, stretching his large body for a moment. "Tell you what. Chuck, I'm impressed with your professionalism and passion. And I always want to be thought of as a friend to the FBI as well as my fellow brothers and sisters in blue. I can have some of the cross streets downtown temporarily blocked off to get the semi onto the expressway, where it would seem to be a lesser target. There'll be hell to pay from the locals who'll bitch to city hall, but we're talking about a ten-minute delay, tops. I can also spare a squad car to lead the semi on the route with a motorcycle cop trailing the procession."

Nowitzke smiled upon hearing Archie's decision and what he would bring to the table. *Making the trip was worthwhile after all.* "You don't mind if Nis and I tag along in my vehicle?"

"Knock yourselves out. You can bring up the rear. By the way, I'll even drive the black-and-white despite the fact the trip will be a waste of time," he proposed.

"Chuck, I'll be on your six," said Russell.

Russ, Anissa, and Nowitzke sat in silence, thinking through Archie's observations. Despite early thoughts of having a SWAT team engaged to protect the truck, they knew Archie was correct in his assessment that the trip was a private enterprise. Also, none could make the case that Archie's professional judgment was incorrect. It was his territory, and he knew the lay of the land. That, and only Archie had any authority over local police operations.

"We'll take you up on your generous offer, Captain," said Nowitzke, still feeling like there was a large hole in their plan. As the four began to get their game faces on, Nowitzke considered Al's collection of baseball relics near the kitchen wall. "You know, the thought occurs to me. Have any of you ever heard of the hidden ball trick?"

CHAPTER 58

Nowitzke tugged on his black cargo pants and black t-shirt before taking a deep breath, struggling into his tactical vest, which required him to use the last stitch of Velcro on the closure. Pulling on a black baseball cap emblazoned "Police," Nowitzke stepped out of the men's room into the basement of the jewelry center. Anissa was sitting quietly on a bench waiting patiently for her boss. She was ready for action in the same tactical clothing, aside from having pushed her blonde ponytail through the hole in the back of the fitted cap.

"Goddammit, Nis," snarled Nowitzke. "How is it that we wear the same equipment, but you look like a fashion model waiting to shoot the cover of *Soldier of Fortune* while I look like a bratwurst on a grill about to burst?"

Russell stepped into the basement from the stairwell, looking particularly intimidating in his gear. "Great, another fucking superhero," huffed Nowitzke as he continued to wrestle with his vest.

"Problems, Chuck?" Russell asked.

"I think my body armor shrank since I wore it last," complained the detective.

"I've talked with Archie," said Russell. "He's already positioned in front of the loading bay waiting on the truck. You've got your sidearms, but the man's a planner and has offered some supplemental weaponry." The fed unzipped a large green camo bag he had carefully placed on one of the benches. "Ladies first."

Anissa peered into the bag and smiled before pulling out a

Remington 870 shotgun. "This should work nicely if we have a problem. Where's the ammo?"

"I'll hand it to you as we leave. Chuck, take your pick." Russell pointed to the bag.

Nowitzke groaned as he bent over. "I'll take the AR-15. Between the two of us, we should have every eventuality covered," he said, studying the weapon.

Russell continued. "I've briefed the semi driver and his rent-a-cop on the route. From here, we're heading south on Wabash where we turn right onto Adams. It's roughly twelve blocks to Highway 90, and then it's a straight shot to O'Hare. Based on Google Maps, we should be able to cover the fifteen miles in about forty-five minutes with traffic. We might even do better since Archie will be blocking off several of the major cross streets as we roll through." Russell pulled out a backpack. "Finally, we'll be communicating via headset." He handed one to both Nowitzke and Anissa. "Tune your unit to frequency 460.125. Any questions?" asked Russell, looking at his counterparts. "Let's saddle up."

Anissa put her headset on. "You got me, Archie?"

"Damn, you've got a sexy radio voice, Anissa."

"Would you like me to talk dirty to you, Archie?" asked Nowitzke, trying to ensure his connection.

"I got you both. Are we ready to go?"

"We'll pull in behind the semi and motorcycle officer when we leave," replied Nowitzke. "Any sign of trouble up front?"

"No, it's another beautiful summer day in Chicago," replied the captain.

CHAPTER 59

The caravan left the jewelry center exactly as planned at 11:00 a.m. Archie turned on his light bar to clear the path through traffic, having to occasionally use a burst of his siren to nudge a Chicago driver out of the way. "Keep it tight back there," chided Archie into his microphone as he kept one eye on the semi and the others in the trailing procession.

"Got it," replied the truck driver, Nowitzke, and Russ in unison, all doing their best to keep up. Traffic was heavy but moving, albeit at a much slower pace than any members of the team would have liked.

Nowitzke looked across the seat at Anissa. "What do you think?"

"So far, so good," she conceded with her head on a swivel, looking out for any potential threats. At the same time, Anissa couldn't help but wonder how anyone would be able to stop the jewelry semi, let alone steal the contents, with all the downtown traffic.

The convoy continued past several of the CPD-blocked streets as Archie again spoke into his mic. "We're coming up on our big right-hander. Then it's a straight shot to the interstate and onto O'Hare," he said confidently.

However, as the column got to the corner of Wabash and Adams, a nondescript homeless man camped on the sidewalk of the intersection rose from his pile of rags. Seeing the oncoming parade, he calmly pulled a Serbian M80 Zolja rocket launcher from his sleeping bag. Mindful of traffic, he carefully stepped between the parked cars and moved into the street, sighting in Archie's squad car. When the black-

and-white was within one hundred yards, the man pulled the trigger on the lightweight weapon.

Archie saw the incoming rocket and contrail but was powerless to do anything. Designed for use against armored vehicles, neither the police captain nor the Ford cruiser stood a chance. The Zolja destroyed Archie's vehicle, killing him instantly, and sent the wreckage in a ball of flame twenty feet into the air before the car landed upside down in the path of the semi.

Seeing the carnage, the semi driver white-knuckled the steering wheel but did not stop, bulling past and through the disabled car, sending it spinning on its roof and pinballing it back across the roadway. While panic set in for the businesspeople and tourists on the street, the homeless man watched coolly as the semi made its turn before tossing a spike strip into the intersection behind the truck.

Within the cab of the semi, the driver turned to his rent-a-cop partner, giving him the signal. The uniformed man opened the suitcase that had been on his lap, arrayed the antennae, and hit the power switch. Both men in the truck instinctively covered their testicles with an available hand as the cell jammer provided immediate results.

****

"Jesus . . . Archie," was all Nowitzke could exclaim as he watched the cruiser disintegrate in front of him. Within seconds of the blast, he and Anissa saw the motorcycle officer that was trailing the black-and-white take evasive action to avoid the spike strip. Even though he did, the cop lost control of his bike in the process, sending it skidding down the road on its side. Unable to stop in time, Nowitzke's Taurus became the first official victim of the spike strips, blowing out all four tires. Both the detectives also realized that all the typical chatter in their headsets had stopped, while a general alarm set in for the bystanders within earshot of the massive explosion or who witnessed the subsequent vehicle collisions. Given the destruction, most of the bystanders were also unaware that their cell service was dead.

Russell, who was in the final chase car, was trapped by the remains of the flaming police cruiser and Nowitzke's disabled vehicle. Stuck in the middle of Adams Street, Nowitzke and Anissa watched helplessly at the surreal, movie-like scene of heavy smoke coming from the squad car, a cycle laying in the road on top of an injured officer, and a homeless man running for all he's worth down the middle of the street before catching and jumping onto the back of the semi. Stunned and unable to raise anyone through his headset, Nowitzke tried to contact Russell by switching frequencies. After moving through the entire dial, he yanked the unit off his head in disgust, throwing it to the floor. "Goddamned piece of garbage." In the meantime, the truck was growing smaller, as if part of an urban one-point perspective drawing.

Stepping out of their disabled Taurus, Anissa spotted the police bike. "Chuck, let's go!" she yelled, running toward the downed patrolman. "Are you okay?" she asked the officer on the ground.

"My leg is broken. And I must have damaged my helmet because I can't contact anyone," he said as a crowd began to gather around him.

Anissa carefully wrenched the bike off the downed cop as she announced, "I'm taking your cycle."

"Go for it. I'll be fine," replied the officer.

"Nis, I've never driven a motorcycle before," said Nowitzke, looking at the large blue-and-white Harley Davidson Electra Glide.

"Looks like you get the bitch seat," she replied, swinging her leg over the machine.

"There is no back seat. Just a small, flat panel, like for a laptop."

"I know. It's illegal for you to ride there, but we don't have much choice today. Climb on, grab me tight around the waist, hang onto my shotgun, and you can write me up later."

Nowitzke did as he was told, his feet dangling just above the road. Despite the melee that had occurred, traffic on the street was moving again. Anissa gunned the Harley's engine, guiding it between lines of cars on the busy street in search of the missing semi. "So much for too big to fail!" yelled Nowitzke from the back of the bike, holding on for all he was worth. As they neared the Highway 90 interchange, Nowitzke saw what he thought was the back end of the semi turning the corner several blocks away onto Desplaines Street. He yelled into Anissa's ear while pointing. "That way!"

Anissa missed the turn but squeezed the brakes, making the bike squeal, leaving a trail of rubber on the road. Then she yelled, "Hold tight, Chuck!" She hit the gas, spinning the bike around in a seamless pirouette before screaming back in the direction of the truck. As they found the cross street, they watched as the homeless man pulled a chain to close the oversize garage door behind the semi now parked in a dilapidated building. Even from a block away, Nowitzke recognized the homeless man. "Fucking Copeland," he muttered.

CHAPTER 60

"Shit," scowled Nowitzke as he got off the cycle. "Us against how many in the garage?"

"Chuck, it doesn't matter, remember."

Nowitzke was deep in thought, considering the building. It was an old, free-standing, graffiti-covered cinder block structure that stood alone on an entire block in a desolate part of Chicago. Aside from the garage door that Copeland had closed, Nowitzke counted at least six other similar openings on the side of the building that he could see.

"Okay, Nis. If you just boosted a semi full of gold and diamonds, what would you plan to do, assuming you made it this far?"

"I guess break it down into more manageable loads and scatter, leaving the semi behind."

"Agreed. That requires manpower, maybe a forklift to offload pallets of merchandise, and several other vehicles to escape."

"Well, we don't have too much time before they find out you've ruined their day by removing the jewelry from the semi and sending it to O'Hare in unguarded panel trucks," said Anissa. "I wish I was in there to see the looks on their faces."

"Be careful what you wish for."

"Is it worth us getting into a firefight? You know that no one's coming, Chuck. If Copeland figured out how to block the police radio frequencies, the same principle would apply to the GPS unit on the semi. No one knows where we are. We're on our own."

Nowitzke knew his partner was right as he wiped his brow. He had to assume they were both outmanned and outgunned. His heart was still pounding in his chest, and he could not stop sweating as he tried to decide his next steps. Eventually, emotion triumphed over logic as he looked at Anissa. "I just can't let Copeland escape. It might be our last chance to get the asshole."

"I knew you were going to say that," replied Anissa as she climbed off the bike. "I'm with you." She did her best to look confident. "Do you have a plan?"

"Here's your shotgun back," Nowitzke replied, tossing her the weapon.

They stalked toward the building even though there was no cover between them and their objective. "Pick a door, Nis." Quickly closing the gap, she steered them toward what once may have been an employee entrance opposite the garage door used by the semi. The wooden door was grey with age and blistered from years of being exposed to the elements. Anissa moved to one side of the opening while Nowitzke took the other. He was breathing hard and took a moment to gather himself. "Check your weapon and your extra ammo," he whispered as they heard activity from several men inside, including Copeland, who was now amid an expletive-filled rant after opening the back of the truck.

Using the muzzle of his assault rifle, Nowitzke gently nudged the door. Amazingly, it cooperated without making a sound, opening just far enough for the officers to squeeze through. From what they could see, there were multiple panel vans positioned next to the smaller garage doors in preparation for a quick departure. The semi stood in the middle of the old shop. Taking cover behind one of the small trucks, they listened as Copeland continued to scream. "Goddammit. It's fucking empty. The cornerstone of my goddamned plan. Shit. Shit. SHIT!" he roared in frustration.

From his position, Nowitzke counted ten men, their eyes fixed on the back of the semi while listening to the tirade. Only four were armed, while the others stood around emptyhanded, likely tasked with the heavy lifting of moving the treasure from the semi to the smaller vehicles. The detective could not see Copeland, who was standing in the back of the trailer, but he was positive his old boss would be carrying a weapon too. After listening to Copeland's pointless diatribe and realizing there would be no payday, the natives were getting restless, having sidebar discussions amongst themselves, making plans to leave the garage before law enforcement arrived. Nowitzke motioned with his weapon for Anissa to creep around to the far side of the garage. After she left, Nowitzke decided to force Copeland's hand.

Standing straight, Nowitzke moved toward the group, leveling his AR-15 and yelling, "Police! Drop your weapons!" in his loudest command voice. Caught by surprise, one of the armed men actually complied with the order, while several others raised their hands like criminals do on every television cop drama. "Let's see your hands . . . *everyone*!" thundered Nowitzke. More hands went up.

Still concealed in the back of the semi, the detective heard his former mentor. "Chuck, is that you?"

"Good morning, Art. I don't want this to get worse than it already is," said Nowitzke.

"I knew you'd figure it out. You also know I can't go to prison," shouted Copeland.

"Art, I need to see your hands. Step out of the truck."

As the words left Nowitzke's mouth, a volley of gunfire erupted from Copeland's direction, cutting through the wall of the semi. Nowitzke backtracked behind the truck where he had started. Finding cover, he heard bullets whiz past his head followed by a burning sensation on his temple where one projectile grazed him. Warm blood trickled down the side of his face as he took several deep breaths and regrouped for a moment. The barrage from Copeland sent several of his own associates diving to the floor, not wanting any part of a gun fight. However, two of the noncombatants were immediately cut down by Copeland's own warriors. Those with weapons then turned their full attention toward the detective, who drew fire from at least three. The smell of gunpowder permeated the air while the deafening barrage of automatic weapons clattered off the metal roof and the brick walls, and Nowitzke heard the constant ping of bullets ricocheting off the vehicles surrounding him. Pinned down, he waited for a lull of the incoming rounds when he heard a pair of earsplitting blasts coming from the far side of the room. Anissa had flanked the men firing at Nowitzke, killing two, which helped equal the fight. However, she was rewarded with return fire and was now unable to move.

With the respite he had been waiting for, Nowitzke slammed a fresh clip into his weapon, ready to reengage the fight after making sure his body armor was still tightly closed. But before he could stand, the morning took another bizarre twist.

CHAPTER 61

As Nowitzke remained crouched against the truck, he thought he heard an engine revving outside the building. He tilted his ear towards the approaching sound, trying to get a bead on the unexpected roar. Just as it reached its crescendo, a vehicle suddenly exploded through a wall, shattering the cinder blocks amidst the sound of twisting metal. The impact sent two of Copeland's men through the air into the side of the semi. Russell emerged from what was left of his car, quickly engaging in the fight with his Glock. He put two shots into the last man holding a weapon, and everything went deathly silent. After gauging the lull, Anissa moved quickly toward the middle of the garage to subdue any other would-be gunmen and attend to the wounded.

Nowitzke bolted from his position, running toward the back of the semi. As he turned the corner, muzzle first, he found Copeland sitting slumped on the ground with his back against the garage door. He had been shot multiple times and was bleeding profusely from his gut. Training his AR-15 on his former mentor, Nowitzke kicked away an Uzi lying on the floor and did a quick search of his former mentor.

"Jesus, Art, you look like shit," said Nowitzke, lowering his weapon. "You lose a fight with a tiger?" He stared at several deep gouges in Copeland's face that had not healed.

"Watson's revenge. I deserved what I got," he wheezed. "I need to lay down. Damn, I'm in a lot of pain." Nowitzke gently helped Copeland slide onto the floor. "Man, I fucked this up," he confessed.

Nowitzke eyed his old friend writhing on the floor and beginning to turn pale as he tried to make sense of what had taken place. "What the hell is going on, Art? My God, when I left Milwaukee PD, you were at the top of your game as a detective. Now you're just . . . like one of the criminals we used to track down."

Copeland looked into Nowitzke's eyes. "It started because I needed cash to care for Muriel," he said in a halting pattern, gasping for air. "She needed help round the clock, and I ran out of money. Insurance wouldn't cover everything. We never had much in the way of savings with all the money we blew over the years. Then I tapped out my 401(k). We were destitute, but I still had obligations to my wife," he rasped. Copeland went quiet for a moment before continuing. "I didn't know what to do. I was up late one night and thought of all those assholes we investigated who pulled jewelry crimes. People we knew who stole but we couldn't prove it. So many of them got away, along with the merchandise. I thought I could pressure some of those old outlaws to help me make some quick money. I needed to work on a grander scale, but I also didn't want anyone to get hurt. I contracted with some of the YACs to do the Bateman's burglary. Even though my cut was in the millions, it wasn't enough.

"So then I threatened some ex-cons to pull the robbery in Milwaukee but insisted they use blanks, figuring if one of those fuckers got killed by the police, the world would be a better place." He paused, choking on the blood flowing out of his mouth, then continued. "I had turned the corner financially, but then I got greedy, Chuck. I knew Watson was carrying a huge diamond that was worth a fortune. Enough to replenish all my savings and then some. I stalked him like I was hunting an animal. When it looked like I would lose my chance at millions, I decided to kill him. But I also had to kill his bodyguards and that stupid old man who was just trying to help."

Copeland teared up and began to convulse. "This hijacking was going to be my final job, Chuck. I swear. It would have been more than enough to take care of Muriel and walk away. But when I opened the door to the fucking semi and saw nothing in the trailer, I knew you were involved. Either way, you helped me today. I figured I'd be rich beyond my wildest dreams from my take or get killed in the process. Muriel will get a million dollars from my life insurance policy, so I can die with peace of mind," he finished, his voice croaking.

"Art, you shot my partner, you son of a bitch!" yelled Nowitzke. "I can't forgive that."

Copeland's eyes went wide, realizing he didn't have much longer. "I had nothing to do with that," he said. "You have to believe me. I'm sorry. God, I'm so sorry for everything. And there's something else you need to know," he said, pulling Nowitzke closer before whispering into his ear, as if making his final confession. When Copeland was done, Nowitzke pulled away, his head cocked, thinking through what he had been told. Nowitzke locked eyes with his former boss, giving him an incredulous look. Copeland acknowledged his friend, who nodded back weakly. Then, in a final moment of pain and remorse, Copeland screamed, "Please forgive me, Chuck. I lost my way. Please . . ."

Before Nowitzke could say a word, he heard someone in the garage yell, "Gun!" followed by the hum of a single bullet. The projectile struck Copeland's head, causing it to explode like a pumpkin with a firecracker inside. His face covered in blood and brain matter, Nowitzke looked up to see Russell in a combat stance with his Glock pointed at Copeland's head.

"Jesus, Chuck, I thought I saw him reaching for his gun," said Russ. "Are you okay?"

Nowitzke said nothing but collapsed against the wall, using the back of his hand to wipe away the sweat and tears that rolled down his nose. "Art, you stupid motherfucker," he mumbled to himself. Drawn by the sound of the final bullet, Anissa found her boss. She sat down next to him on the cold concrete and took his hand as the sound of sirens descended upon the garage.

CHAPTER 62

The investigation of the hijacking was complex, moving well into the evening. Nowitzke and Anissa checked back into their rooms from the previous night and agreed to meet for breakfast at the hotel restaurant the following morning. Punctual as always, Anissa found a table for two and was halfway through a pot of coffee before a disheveled Nowitzke dragged himself into the opposite chair.

"How are you doing, Chuck?"

"I've been better," said the detective with bags under his eyes. "I spent last night thinking about Copeland, the good times we had, Muriel, and then what happened yesterday. None of what he did makes any sense to me. He did it for the money?" he questioned. "I just don't get it, Nis. He was a good man and an even better cop. One of the best." He poured himself a cup of coffee.

Anissa said nothing.

"I woke Clark up this morning and told him about Archie's death, our gunfight, and Copeland's confession to me about the various crimes," Nowitzke continued. "He'd already seen it. Looks like we made the network news, by the way," he added, taking a sip of coffee. "I also cashed in some vacation time to get my head straight. Even though we both knew Copeland was involved with these crimes for some time, there's a finality here that I'm struggling with."

"I can understand," Anissa said to fill in the awkward gap in their conversation. "Where will you go?"

"I haven't figured that out yet."

Anissa looked her partner squarely in the face and saw a battered man. She tilted her head. "You're not quitting on me, are you?" she asked carefully.

"Hell, no. I've still got bills to pay. Plus, my Taurus is toast. Those goddamn tires were the most valuable part of my car." He laughed, lightening the mood.

Anissa smiled. "Then I'll head home, and we'll see you when we see you."

"When you get back, see if you have anything further on Sean. Even though Katallani is dead, we still have some open issues to mop up. Oh, and can you give Nadia a call and tell her I'm still working the case down here?"

"Got it. You be safe, Chuck," she said, giving him a hug before heading to the front desk to check out.

Nowitzke sat alone, working on his second pot of coffee, when he saw Russell walking through the lobby with his suitcase. "Hey, Russ, you got a minute?" yelled Nowitzke, flagging down the fed.

Russell took Anissa's open seat as the waitress brought him a clean cup.

After the waitress left, Nowitzke leaned across the table, speaking in a low voice. "Before Copeland died yesterday, he whispered something to me that I thought you should know. He said Sean Cook was the brains of the outfit and that Copeland brought the hammer. Sean provided the targets for the crimes, along with all the details Copeland needed to make them happen. Remember the Bateman's burglary and how the burglars knew exactly what safes to break into? Sean told Malcolm to group his goods in certain safes under the terms of coverage. Then he passed that information onto Copeland, who gave the details to the YACs. Same for when the robbers hit Lockett's. Sean waited for a surge in the store's reported diamond inventory and then told Copeland so his hitters could strike at exactly the right time. Worse, Sean gave Copeland information about where and when Watson was traveling so Art could steal the Pink Monster.

Apparently, there was a screw-up of some sort because Watson was only supposed to have one bodyguard instead of two. That pissed Copeland off, by the way.

"It all makes sense," Nowitzke continued. "We couldn't understand how the crimes were all connected to one person because nothing fit the typical profile. There was no profile since Copeland hired ex-cons and people he knew he could control to handle the dirty work. And Copeland kept the bulk of the take, paying his guys nickels and dimes."

"Jesus," exclaimed Russell, his coffee untouched. "Did Copeland give you any other details?"

"No. He sounded like he was about to right up until you shot him in the head," concluded Nowitzke, looking askance at the agent.

"Sorry," he replied contritely. "I thought you were in danger. I wasn't willing to take a chance with your life." Russ took a sip of coffee and looked around the restaurant. "Copeland told you nothing else that might be important?"

"Like what?"

"Like where we could find Cook?" asked Russell.

"I already know that . . . at least the country, anyway. You up for a trip?" replied Nowitzke.

"Damn straight. Can we leave this morning?"

"If the FBI can arrange the flights."

"I'm on it," said Russell.

"I've got to make some calls before we leave. Oh, and Russ, bring your beachwear," said Nowitzke.

CHAPTER 63

One week later/San Juan del Sur, Nicaragua

Nowitzke stepped into La Taberna de los Sinvergüenzas, a caricature of every middle-aged American tourist that had ever visited Central America. Wearing a straw hat, a colorful t-shirt covered by an open, blousy, floral button-down, and shorts, he captured the look right down to the tender, pink sunburned arms and the black socks under his sandals. Of course, his shirt was stained with salsa, a casualty of lunch. La Taberna, a palapa constructed of four large posts supporting a thatched palm roof with open sides, was close enough to the Pacific Ocean that the beach served as its floor. Because of its location, the tavern was popular with both locals and tourists. Aside from several non-movable barstools fabricated from cement under decorative tile, most of the seating consisted of swings suspended from beams supporting the roof. Jimmy Buffett and Bob Marley were always in heavy play on the bar's sound system.

During the height of the midday sun, the local temperatures climbed well into the thirties centigrade despite the refreshing breeze off the ocean. Even though he could not make the conversion to Fahrenheit, the detective already knew it was beastly hot when he ducked under the thatched roof, took a seat, and began to create a puddle of sweat on the bar. The only bartender was engaged in a lively conversation with two dark-haired, bikini-clad beauties on the opposite side of the watering hole and in no hurry to move. Finally,

Nowitzke cleared his throat and spoke up in a voice loud enough for the young man to hear him. "You wouldn't have a Miller Lite back there, would you, Sean?"

"Chuck fucking Nowitzke," Sean exclaimed even before turning around, a huge smile on his face. "I knew our paths would cross again." He strode toward the officer. "No Miller here. But how about a local brew, Toña, on the house." He grabbed a brown bottle, twisted off the cap, and placed it in front of the detective. "It took you long enough to find me."

"Well, I've been busy spending quality time in every shithole dive between here and Managua flashing your photo, trying to track down a gringo bar owner. If I spoke fucking Spanish, I could have narrowed the search a helluva lot quicker. La Taberna de los Sinvergüenzas. The Scoundrels' Tavern. Nice."

"Under new management," Sean said proudly. "How did you figure out I was in Nicaragua?"

"You gave me most of what I needed. That and some details provided by an old friend. I remembered our conversation about what you wanted to do with your life. Nicaragua. If you weren't a white guy, I might never have found you." Nowitzke slammed his beer and pushed the empty bottle forward, gesturing for another. "What's the story, Sean? I know you were involved with the jewelry thefts. But I need to hear your version."

A smiling Sean reached into an ice chest and placed a fresh Toña in front of the detective. "Well, it goes back about six or seven years ago. I was a disgruntled college student living with my mother in London. I was going nowhere, with no life and no direction. So, I said, 'Fuck it,' and quit school. But I was bored to death, still wanting something more for myself. Then, after years of floundering from one menial job to another, my mother got me a job at Lloyd's sweeping the floors at night. As I would come onto my shift, I saw many of the underwriters leaving for the day. They were always well-dressed, heading off for drinks and dinner, talking smack about their new cars, how much money they were making, the chicks they laid. But the crazy thing is that most of these guys were also about my age. And they were highly respected. It was everything I was looking for. I decided to make a big change, creating the new Sean out of whole cloth.

"One day after everyone left the office, I made copies of several large jewelry account files to learn the terminology, how the security worked, and the expectations of the customers. Man, I studied everything in those files. The photos. The handwritten notes. I even lifted a couple of reference books too. Then I started showing up early for work so I could listen to their conversations with each other and the brokers. I copied more files and kept on studying. It was like I was learning a secret language. At some point, I understood what the underwriters were talking about, even though I wasn't trained on all the details. I was also confident I could bluff my way through anything.

"After about a year of biding my time, I felt like Babe Ruth calling my shot. I decided to move to the States where I was an unknown, aside from my bullshit persona. Before I left, I went down to Savile Row and bought a custom-made suit. Cost me a goddamned fortune, Chuck. But it was all part of an investment and my plan to pass myself off as an expert in jewelry insurance.

"I started posting stuff online about my expertise, getting the word out, just fishing for a sucker to take the bait. That's how Mullins found me. On LinkedIn. What a fucking bitch!" he exclaimed as an aside. "She had an ambitious start-up project with WSU. After our first meeting, I knew I was in. She bought my fake resumé because it had the word 'Lloyd's' on it and just about had an orgasm."

"Probably the first and only time a guy did that for her," interjected Nowitzke.

"You know it. Anyway, she had found a true expert," said Sean. "I started dictating conditions like I ran the unit, and no one could second-guess me. I demanded a piece of the action, a fat salary, commissions, and heavy bonuses. And it worked. She bought the whole enchilada.

"I had no clue what I was doing, but I had time on my side. After writing an account, I was taking the chance that it would not have a major loss early on. My instincts were correct, and we had few, if any, claims. Believe it or not, I started to make a name for myself. I could talk the bullshit talk and walk the bullshit walk for both the insurance people and the jewelers. Life was great. I focused on high-end accounts, undercut the premiums, made the terms of coverage less stringent than any of my competitors, and the business just flowed in. I was making a fortune, spending as little as I had to as part of a plan to pick up and just walk away."

"No shit. I heard about your apartment. And I thought I was a bad housekeeper," said Nowitzke.

"I had peace of mind, especially since I didn't have to worry about paying any of the claims. That was WSU's problem. You need another beer, Chuck?"

"Sure." Nowitzke shook his head at hearing how easy it had been for Sean to dupe the big-time executive. Then he leaned over the bar, closing the distance to Sean, forgetting for a moment that none of the locals cared about the story. "So, you faked your entire background and got lucky when Mullins didn't do any checking?"

"I was pretty confident I could have stalled her if she really wanted to look into my background, or even find a way to fake my references if she ever asked, but she never did. But once I was in, I also had to look like I gave a shit about Mullins and WSU's ridiculous goals and direction. At the same time, I was making serious money, so I went about my business with a 'fuck you' attitude, just daring her to fire me. The company wouldn't have let her. It loved the money too much. And the weird part was that if Mullins had ever grown a pair and cut me loose, I had job offers from several other carriers just begging me to come work for them. Seriously. Me. That's about the time Katallani recruited me for a scheme that was years in the making."

"How did you meet Copeland?" asked Nowitzke.

"He was just part of the team . . . introduced to me as the muscle. A cop with a lot of connections, including some serious bad actors that I wanted nothing to do with. Turns out we both had something in common, piling up money for what we needed or wanted. Like I told you, my goal was to buy my own bar, work on my tan, and kick back. No nine-to-five bullshit. No debt. I think Copeland's wife was sick and he just needed to take care of her.

"Anyway, the way things worked was that I chose the accounts we hit. I knew the businesses, the security, and, most importantly, the values. I targeted diamonds mostly, but if we had the time, I knew we could make a lot of money with stealing gold too. In some cases, I relaxed the terms of coverage or steered a jeweler to do what I needed that made it easier for us. Copeland's role was to find the people to pull the jobs."

"Like the YACs at Bateman's?" asked Nowitzke.

"Yeah," said Sean. "Boy, I stumbled on that one when you asked. Never heard the term before, and I saw it got your attention at the time. Working with Copeland, I was now making money on both ends, from my WSU gig and on my cut of the goods that we took. But I knew almost immediately that there was a hard edge to Copeland. Whether it was his personality or the stress in his life, he was becoming violent and one greedy son of a bitch, a bad combination in this line of work. That's also when the texts started coming in. I was trying to lead you to him."

"You?"

"Yup. I'd meet with Copeland at some truck stop to talk about our operational plans. Turns out he's also one seriously arrogant asshole. I didn't trust him as far as I could spit. The more he talked, the more I became concerned for myself. Like when I stopped providing him with information, someone would find my body in Lake Michigan. After our little meetings, I'd pull over on a side road and send texts back and forth to myself with a burner phone in one hand and my regular cell in the other so I could feed you the conversations. I also told you to keep Copeland out of the loop because I knew you two were friends. I didn't want you tipping him off. It wouldn't have taken a genius to figure out where the details were coming from, and it would be bye-bye, Sean."

Nowitzke took in everything, motioning for another Toña.

"When Copeland told me he wanted the Pink Monster, I knew he had become uncontrollable. He didn't ask. He demanded the info, even showing me his weapon. The asshole shot Watson, along with all those other people. Fucking Copeland. You might not believe it, but that jeweler was a friend of mine. The way things were originally pitched to me was that these were crimes against property. No one was supposed to get hurt or killed. You have to believe me on that, Chuck. I could even live with the fact that criminals might kill another criminal, but Jesus." Sean wiped the sweat that had formed on his forehead. "So then came the hijacking in Chicago. It wasn't a suicide mission, but I got out of Dodge after giving Copeland the specifics. I didn't want to become a loose end that needed tending to. I sent you the text, hoping you'd bring enough cops to kill that motherfucker. Anyway, I saw the satellite news and everything that went down with Copeland dying a grisly death. A fitting end for the asshole. By the way, I assume that having nothing in the back of the semi was your handiwork?" asked Sean.

"Yeah, it was."

"Nice touch."

Nowitzke took a sip of beer and a moment to study the ocean. "Can you answer one final question for me?"

"Sure."

"Was Nadia involved in the burglary in any way?"

"Who? The babe at Bateman's? No, not as far as I know. I understand that Besnik was her brother, but no, she wasn't part of the job."

Truth.

After telling his story, Sean looked Nowitzke in the eye with a quizzical expression. "So why are you here, Chuck? It's certainly not to work on your tan. By the way, put some aloe on those arms, man."

Nowitzke laughed and took a long draw of beer. "Good question. Well, I just wanted you to know that I could reach out and find you."

"Okay, I knew you were good, but you've got nothing on me," protested Sean.

"Hey, you're living on stolen money, for starters. But you're also involved with the murder of Besnik, Watson, his bodyguards, and the old guy, in addition to being implicated in the deaths of Copeland and his associates. At a minimum, you're a thief and an accessory to murder. Most importantly to me, you're also facing charges for aggravated assault on a peace officer, Anissa."

"Chuck, I told you, I had nothing to do with the heavy lifting. I only gave out information. That's it. I also handed Copeland to you on a fucking silver platter. Watson was a friend, and Anissa . . . if things were different, she could have been more than that," he said hesitantly, looking towards the blue hues of the ocean. "You probably already know this, but one of the reasons I bought my business in Nicaragua is because it's a country that has traditionally refused extradition back to the States despite any treaties that say otherwise. Basically, you can't touch me."

"Listen, Sean. I don't think you were involved in the murders. But I have a tough time with anyone connected to shooting Anissa."

"I already told you . . . Katallani did that, not me. My biggest offense is the insurance fraud, and you can't bring me back for that, can you, Chuck?"

"No. But understand that not everyone sees the world the way I do. The government can still make your life miserable, like having a drone drop a bomb on your house. Or maybe a team comes when you're sleeping and kidnaps you back to the United States."

"I'm no legal expert, but seriously. The state of Wisconsin wouldn't do any of those things."

"I know. But what about the feds?" said Nowitzke. "They have resources that other agencies don't." He nodded toward a thin, muscular man sitting on the opposite end of the bar. "Sean, meet FBI

Agent Louis Russell." The bar owner turned around to see the agent smile and nod at the introduction.

Sean laughed out loud before turning back to Nowitzke. "Do I look worried?"

Nowitzke studied Sean's tanned face. "Actually, you don't." *But why? We've got this guy cold if we want to push it.* "Why are you such a cocky little bastard?"

"Because I understand the importance of insurance. Chuck, let me introduce you to my business partner . . . Katallani, in the flesh," said Sean as Russ nodded back toward Nowitzke.

CHAPTER 64

"Russ? What the fuck?" exclaimed Nowitzke, all the color draining from his face. He looked at Sean. "Wait, I thought you said Copeland was Katallani."

"No. You and everyone else just assumed that based on what Besnik's sister said. Apparently, she saw Copeland at a restaurant one night when he was recruiting Musa to do the Bateman's job," Sean replied. "When Besnik went on the run, he mentioned the name Katallani to his sister. She thought Copeland and Katallani were one in the same, and the myth was born. Katallani was far worse than Copeland . . . no offense, Russ."

"None taken," said Russell, who walked around the bar towards Sean and Nowitzke. "Besnik had some skills and quite the set of balls. Copeland put the full-court press on him to do the work, but Besnik held out for more money. So, I got involved. I pulled his rap sheet and got in his face after flashing my badge. I told him I had him dead to rights on several jobs he'd pulled even though he had never been convicted. I threatened to have him deported back to fucking Albania if he didn't cooperate with me. Besnik said he had an attorney and laughed in my face. I told him he would never get in front of a judge. I'd kill his lawyer if I needed to, with him next in line if it came to that. Then, to make a point, I upped the ante, telling him if he didn't help with the Bateman's burglary, I'd fuck his sister before having her deported . . . just for sport. That seemed to do the trick, and Katallani was born. Can I have a beer, Sean?"

Sean pulled a beer and placed it in front of Russ. Still processing this new revelation, the stunned Nowitzke watched Russ's bottle immediately begin to sweat. "How did you recruit Copeland? He was a straight arrow."

"He might have been at one time, but when I found Art, it was easy. I traveled quite a bit in my former job and started keeping an eye out for someone in law enforcement who had an open wound. You know, someone with a potential ethical problem. Like a secret drug habit. Or a tough run of luck at the track and behind on the mortgage. Maybe an officer with a pregnant girlfriend and a disapproving wife. Possibly something as simple as a sick wife and no money to pay the bills," offered Russell with a smirk on his face. "When I was at Milwaukee PD for some reason, I heard a couple of officers saying that Copeland had been shaking down drug dealers for what amounted to nickels and dimes. I had him followed, and my people got all sorts of photos of the man in the act. Once I had what I needed, I carefully approached him. I knew he wouldn't scare easy. So, I went in the other direction. I asked him to lunch and passed him the pictures before our sandwiches arrived as part of a discussion between professionals. For such a tough guy, he spilled his guts about his wife before dessert. I didn't even know her name until that day in your office, though. When I offered him the opportunity, he jumped."

Still putting the puzzle together, Nowitzke refocused on the bartender. "How'd he get you, Sean?" he asked.

"I met Agent Russell early on in my career at WSU. We attended many of the same conferences, industry dinners, and trade shows. After working there for about six months, we were having drinks in Las Vegas at one of the hotels one night. Russ looked at me and point-blank asked who the hell I really was. Russell knew a bullshit story when he heard one. I confessed on the spot, copping to the fact that I was a fraud. But he didn't arrest me or make a big deal about it. I could see his wheels turning. By breakfast the following morning, he had a proposition for me. The rest is history. I was all in, along with the rest of the crew."

A dumbfounded Nowitzke was quiet as he considered the complexity of the plot that had been formulated. Listening to the various stories, everything seemed to make sense. *Damn, should I have been able to figure this out?* Putting his half-full beer on the bar, he turned his attention back to the agent. At that moment, he felt no real animosity toward the man. However, he had more questions. "What's your story, Russ? You're the mastermind of this whole operation? Why?"

Russ chuckled, knowing that if the roles were reversed, he would have asked the same question. "I'm pushing fifty, after having given most of my adult life to the agency. The job consumes most of my days . . . sometimes seven days a week. I live out of a suitcase for the most part, and I'm always on the go. I was okay with that for a long time. Part of the adventure, I guess. But then I saw other agents who were younger and less qualified than me move up in the ranks while I drew assignments in Mobile, and Las Cruces, and Waterloo, and Erie . . . fucking Erie. Never a chance at a big city office. No bite at the Apple. Twenty years of shit assignments with no appreciation or acknowledgement for what I was doing, the sacrifices I was making . . ." he said, his voice trailing off.

Russ pushed his empty toward Sean and nodded, looking for another before he continued. "I started to see the end of the line coming for me. Thinking about living on a government pension with no real home. No family. No real money. No life. No nothing. And it scared the hell out of me. Yeah, maybe I could do some security work like many agents do when they retire, but it wasn't for me. I wouldn't have lasted as long as my friend Sean here, putting up with corporate bullshit. No way. I always wanted to travel abroad, but that didn't even look like a possibility. A life's work . . . wasted. My God, I was worried that maybe I'd swallow a bullet delivered from my agency-issued pistol someday. When the Bureau asked me to get involved with jewelry and gem theft, I thought maybe this was my last chance to make my mark. But if anything, life got worse. More travel, no recognition. Then when I was at one of the jewelry shows, I had a brainstorm. I saw some potential. If I could get the right people in place, I could stage the crimes and make some serious coin. I was patient, biding my time. When I got to know Sean, I found a bigger schemer than me. Since he had an aversion to serving time, he went along with it. He started tilling the soil, looking for the accounts and setting things up until I recruited Copeland a couple of months later. We were off to the races. Everything worked pretty well, at least until you got involved. Man, you pushed us hard, Chuck, just to stay ahead of you."

"Well, that and the lack of an exit strategy," added Sean.

"I thought it was over," said Nowitzke, his head cocking, a questioning look on his face.

"It is now," said a smiling Russell. "The three of us were set to walk away. But I could see Copeland being problematic after that. I wasn't worried about Sean. He was never into weapons. He's harmless. He'll retire a bar owner here in paradise and become the first man in history to die from a combination of skin cancer, alcohol poisoning, and gonorrhea. But Copeland was another story. Even though he now had millions, he also knew who I was. He would always have that over me. You know, like the leverage I initially had on him. Things had turned. Your best friend can become your worst enemy overnight. I knew that if anything ever went tits-up in Copeland's life, like an IRS audit or being arrested for any crime, that he'd shout my name as bargaining power. What is it the Bible says? 'There is no honor among thieves'?

"I spoke with Sean. He was a small fish with a big brain who I could see running scared of Copeland for different reasons. We both had reasons for wanting Copeland dead. So, we concocted the hijacking. We provided him with everything he needed: a cell jammer from Russia, Serbian rockets, funded his crew. Our plan was to have the police do our dirty work and kill the son of a bitch in a hail of gunfire. But when Archie limited our resources, I had to get involved just to be sure. You and Anissa did your best to get Copeland, but there was no way I was going to let him leave that warehouse alive. I certainly wasn't going to prison." Russ shifted on his barstool. "And since I'm in a truth-telling mode, Chuck, I didn't see your friend going for a gun. Sorry for all the grey matter that hit you when his head exploded. Mea culpa."

There was a long silence with only the breeze blowing through the palms. Nowitzke sat back on his stool, contemplating the breakers hitting the beach. He had come to Nicaragua looking for Sean, knowing upfront that he wouldn't be able to bring him to justice. He came because he needed to get the straight story. Russell was now another matter. Even though the detective had established a level of respect with the wanted man, Nowitzke surmised the former agent would have a gun in his waistband. It was now a requirement for Russ going forward, considering the dollars stolen and the embarrassment to the Bureau. The agency would be highly motivated to come looking for him, seeking to bring him to justice. Replaying the drama in his head, Nowitzke took a deep breath and closed his eyes. From a personal standpoint, he was also in a tough spot. *Jesus, I'm a loose end in a fucking banana republic where life is cheap.* He opened his eyes, all thoughts now begging the obvious next question. "What happens now?" asked Nowitzke.

"It's pretty simple, really," said Russ. "You're not armed, and you have no jurisdiction here."

"By the way, Chuck, I was never worried about you coming here and shooting me," interjected Sean. "You're not a killer like Copeland. I actually kind of liked you."

"Anyway," said Russell, retaking control of the conversation, "Sean runs La Taberna. I start living my life like a king in the Caribbean, moving between islands and other third-world countries. No one will find me, so I don't need to worry about extradition. And you head home, close your file, and tell your story. Our little consortium is officially dissolved."

Hearing Russell's summation, Nowitzke shook his head. "Listen, I'm pretty sure no one will come after the kid. Our attorney general might rattle his saber about extradition and all, but the Nicaraguan government will tell him to get screwed. But you . . . you're one of them. You know that the FBI will dedicate resources to hunt you down."

"That's my problem, Chuck. But even though they never thought much of me, I know all their tricks. I'm not concerned."

Nowitzke contemplated the sun as it began to fade on the horizon. "One more question for you, Mr. Katallani."

"Shoot," said Russell.

"Was it you who had Besnik killed?"

"Yes. I needed to keep Copeland out of it, and my best resource was Simmons. A fucking idiot, but he did as he was told."

"So you were behind shooting Anissa as well?" asked Nowitzke, trying to quell a flare of temper.

"Anissa was collateral damage. I told Simmons not to hurt anyone else. But when Anissa went into that hospital room, the stupid asshole had no choice," replied Russell. "I'm sorry. I was relieved that she was okay. I think she has a great future."

Nowitzke swallowed his anger and considered the permanent results of Anissa's wounds. "And then you sent Simmons after me?"

"No. You gave us the address, but Nadia was the final open item, not you. I didn't want her to be able to identify Copeland, at least until our work was finished. I read the police report from that incident. After you left that evening to take Anissa home, Simmons made his move. You walked into the middle of the shitstorm when you came back to the apartment early. In the end, Nadia survived, but it didn't hurt our operation. Plus, your landlady took care of that other big loose thread for me."

Truth.

Nowitzke shook his head, still trying to grasp the long-term planning and detail that had gone into creating pain and suffering for so many.

"You take care, my friend," said Russell, standing from his barstool.

"You're not my friend," snarled Nowitzke, slamming his hand on the bar in a fit of rage.

"Sean, charge whatever Chuck wants to my account. Oh, and have a nice life, Detective," said Russell as he sauntered off down the beach.

Nowitzke solemnly watched the man walk away from the bar until he eventually faded, along with the sun. Then, he turned back towards the bar and snapped, "Give me a six-pack. I have an early flight tomorrow."

Sean handed the beer to Nowitzke with a conciliatory look on his face. "Listen, Chuck, I sent a package to you. Sort of a peace offering . . . for what it's worth."

Nowitzke glared at Sean but said nothing. Looking defeated, he put the package under his arm and wandered back to his hotel. In the distance, the detective saw the lightning before he heard the distant crack of thunder. A storm was coming.

CHAPTER 65

It was over. Russell let out a long exhale as he dropped into a beach chair. Heavy rollers were hitting the shore as the night sky began to churn. No plan is without flaws, he thought, but he congratulated himself on his success as he sipped his beer in the thick evening air. Coming into the hijacking, it was unclear how he would engineer Copeland's death. But even that worked out. Thinking things through, he wondered if he had used his better judgment on Sean's fate. Sean was unfinished business, but following through now would be more trouble than it was worth. The last thing Russell needed was a murder investigation by local police. He resolved to leave things be, concluding that Sean Cook would not be an issue.

All along, Russell had planned to rent a villa on the beach, even before Nowitzke told him about Sean's presence in Nicaragua. It was part of his personal exit strategy. So, he played along with Nowitzke. He smiled, thinking about how he had been so far ahead of the detective. They had spent days searching the countryside for Sean, moving from one dump to another, before Russell nudged Nowitzke to San Juan del Sur.

Russell's new temporary home was a detached house, complete with a private swimming pool, on the property of an exclusive hotel just down the road from Sean's tavern. It included a butler and a cook. However, Russell had given both the night off for his private celebration. Despite all the amenities, the biggest selling point was the privacy. He had not even seen another hotel guest in the area.

Unfortunately, as nice as it was, the place was only a waystation on a path to parts unknown.

He rose, going back into the house to hide his weapon. Bending over, he pulled a suitcase from under the bed and opened it to take another look at his share. He tossed his Glock into the case, nestling it between thick stacks of hundred-dollar bills, walking-around money for the time being. The mother lode was stored safely in several Cayman banks. With the cost of living in this area, he thought he might be able to get by for years before needing to replenish his supply of cash.

Russell replaced the suitcase under the bed. He kicked off his sandals and padded through the small home, turning on subdued lighting to guide his way back to the patio. On the way, he grabbed another beer and a plate of food that had been pre-ordered earlier in the day. With the growing storm, he noticed the interior lights flicker from time to time. *We're not in Kansas anymore.* It was a small price to pay for his financial freedom and for permanently leaving the United States. He had lived in much worse.

Russell put his food and drink down on the table next to his chair as the wind freshened. He breathed in the salt air, tightened the light jacket he was wearing, and relaxed. The view from this chair was markedly different from the one outside the cheap flat he had rented in Milwaukee. Between far-off lightning flashes, he noticed a small fishing boat bobbing in the water. The vessel was anchored a couple hundred yards off the beach. He thought to himself that fishing in those waves was a tough way to make a living. Then, sitting forward in his chair, he studied the old covered wooden ship closely. It was not lighted, and he couldn't see any activity on board. Even though it was his first night at the villa, he didn't remember seeing the boat earlier that afternoon when he left for his conversation with Sean and Nowitzke.

Straining to get a better look at the craft, he saw a flash paired with the loud crack of thunder. However, his brain then registered that it was not lightning, but an explosion emanating from the boat. Feeling a wave of warmth on his chest, he looked down to see blood gushing from his body. By the time his brain commanded him to hit the ground for cover, a second bullet struck Russell squarely between the eyes, throwing his lifeless body back in his chair.

The squall continued to gather as the diesel engine fired up and the craft began to porpoise down the coast in the heavy surf.

CHAPTER 66

It was still dark when Nowitzke found his aisle seat in first class. His biggest concern that morning was the reliability of pretty much everything before getting on his Delta flight home. The dependability of getting his wake-up call. Whether the cab would be on Nicaraguan time or not. The possibility of the overnight storm having cut the power or made the roads impassable because of downed trees or flooding. The last thing he wanted was to spend another day here. But despite all his fretting, he had arrived at the airport early, zipped through the entire check-in process, and was the first person on the plane. Just as he was about to nod off, a burly man prodded Nowitzke, trying to get to the window seat in the row. The detective's eyes opened and he twisted in his seat, allowing enough room for his new seatmate to brush past him. He closed his eyes again, even waving off the flight attendant who was offering drinks. He'd imbibe after his nap.

In the distance of his semi-sleep, he registered other passengers filing past him to get to coach. The plane's engines roared to life. Ignoring the flight attendant's demonstration of how to operate a seatbelt, he burrowed further back into the leather. Then, his eyes still closed, he asked, "Mission accomplished, Matthew?"

"Tough shot, sir, but all is right with the world again," said the former Green Beret sniper. "Most of the time, I don't need to figure in pitch and roll to get my buck in Negaunee."

Nowitzke smiled to himself but said nothing.

"There's no way Anissa will ever find out about this, will she?" asked Taylor.

"Find out what? It's the reason I kept her out of our little escapade. Nothing good would ever result from that. But if things really went to shit down here, I didn't want her implicated," said the detective.

"And you're sure we got the right man?"

"Got a deathbed confession from my friend in Chicago. He gave me all the facts, including the identity of Katallani. Everything I needed before I called you with the story of what had taken place. Then Katallani himself confirmed for me that he was involved in shooting Anissa. Don't lose any sleep over this. As far as I'm concerned, you've done your country another great service, Matthew."

But as Nowitzke finished his response, he heard only loud snoring from his seatmate.

CHAPTER 67

The Audi pulled up to the curb just as Nowitzke stepped out of the Appleton terminal with his suitcase.

"Thanks for picking me up, Nis."

"Good trip?"

"Yeah. A great vacation. Rested. Recharged. Ready to go. Even got you a little something," he said, pulling a gift bag from his backpack. "Hope it fits."

Anissa's eyes got big at the prospect of wearing any article of clothing chosen by Nowitzke. However, she was relieved after pulling it out of its makeshift wrapping. "A black t-shirt. Nice."

"Look at the back," said the detective.

"'If you can read this, the bitch fell off,'" she said, laughing. "I promise to wear it when I wash my car."

After Nowitzke put his suitcase in the trunk, Anissa pulled into traffic. "What have you been up to since I've been gone?"

"Trying to run down anything on Sean Cook. He's still missing," she said, looking at Nowitzke for any kind of reaction.

"Oh, I forgot about him," he lied. "Nis, if you haven't found a body by now, my big gut tells me he's no longer our problem."

"Oh?" Anissa said, her eyes scanning from the road briefly to her boss's face, sensing he had left out a detail or two.

"It's up to you. Keep the file open for six months, and if you don't hear anything, close it. Anything else happen while I was gone?"

Anissa slowed as she approached a red light. "Chuck, you're not going to believe this," she said excitedly. "Agent Russell had also dropped off the face of the earth. Then, his body turned up at an exclusive resort in Nicaragua of all places."

"Seriously?" questioned Nowitzke, looking back toward his partner.

"Yes. Shot twice, once in the abdomen, once in the head. Long-range, according to the web reports. The local police found a gun and a suitcase full of money in his room. Several reporters have speculated that Russ was heavily involved in the drug trade. It made the national news."

"Jesus, Russell trafficking in drugs? Man, you just never know, do you," said Nowitzke. "You said Nicaragua? Is that near Mexico?"

"Central America, Chuck," she replied, looking at him askance. "By the way, where did you say you were on vacation?"

"On a beach."

"Can you narrow that down?"

"No. Isn't it enough that I'm back?" asked Nowitzke, burrowing into his seat and taking a deep breath.

The remainder of the trip to Miss Alma's was quiet. "See you tomorrow at work?" Anissa asked as she pulled up to the house.

"Damn straight. Looking forward to getting back into the swing of things. Can you pick me up since my car is in the boneyard?"

"Got it," she said as Nowitzke pulled his suitcase from the trunk.

He was home. Finally. Bouncing up the stairs, he was excited to see Nadia. The porch door was open, but there was no activity in the apartment. All the lights were off, and there were no sounds of anyone at home. Walking through the place, he saw a mountain of mail on the kitchen table. "Nadia?" he called, getting nothing in return but an echo. Nowitzke put his suitcase on the bed and started to unpack when he heard the door open. Dropping everything, he stepped eagerly into the main room. "Nadia?" he said, turning the corner.

But it was Miss Alma knocking as she pushed open the door. "Nadia's gone, Detective. She left a couple of days ago. She never said goodbye or left any kind of note," she said in a dour tone. "I'm sorry."

Nowitzke stared at Miss Alma without saying a word. He knew it would happen, just not when. It was a regular occurrence after he got close to someone. He had a fleeting thought of Copeland. Another friend who had departed. Different circumstances, but gone nonetheless. And with each, there was zero prospect of seeing either of them again.

"I miss her too. It was nice to have her around," Miss Alma said, breaking the silence. "I know it's not the same, but would you like to have a beer with me?"

"Sure," replied the detective. He moved toward the fridge and pulled out two cans, then grabbed a glass from the cupboard for Miss Alma before they sat at the kitchen table.

"My, Officer, you have a ton of mail," she said. "Oh, and I brought a package up for you. The postman needed a signature." Her tone begged for Nowitzke to open it as she handed it to him.

The detective pulled a knife from the kitchen block and sliced through the heavy packing tape. The writing on the brown wrapping announced that the contents were "frágil." When Nowitzke pulled the box open, a stream of white packing peanuts spilled onto the table and floor. Holding his hand over the open end of the box, the detective carefully slid the contents out.

It was a snow globe. Under the glass dome stood a resolute plastic snowman wearing a red scarf and holding a sign that read, "Keep your hands warm and your beer cold!" Nowitzke laughed, giving his new toy a heavy shake before setting it on the table. He took a long draw of beer as he and Miss Alma watched the show together. For whatever reason, this globe seemed heavier than most of those he displayed in his office. And despite the lack of any card, he knew that this was the promised peace offering.

Miss Alma remained mesmerized by the falling snow, picked it up and shook the globe once more. "Wow, it's just beautiful," she said as they sipped their beer. "You know, Detective, I've seen many globes over my years, but there's something different about this one. It just sparkles. My God, the snowflakes twinkle . . . almost like . . . like diamonds."

Her remark shook something loose in Nowitzke's head. He put his beer down, sat forward in his chair, and picked up the globe to examine it more closely. *Damn.* He chuckled to himself, sliding back into his seat. *Fucking Sean!* He turned it over once more and placed it back on the table, letting the snow fly. He shook his head. "You're right, Miss Alma . . . just like diamonds."

"Who sent it to you?"

"Someone who knows I'm a collector," he exhaled. Nowitzke looked at the elderly woman, her face still delighted by the snowfall. He smiled. "Miss Alma, thank you for being my friend. You know, I have so many of these snow globes already, I'd like you to have this one."

Miss Alma sat up and looked back at Nowitzke, her eyes welling up. "Oh my . . . it's the nicest gift I've ever received. God bless you, Chuck," she said, then pausing. "Can I get you another beer?"

ACKNOWLEDGEMENTS

When I sat down to write my second novel, my daughter Jamie and I discussed several potential stories before she finally told me to "write what you know." It was great advice. After spending a career in property insurance, I reached out to an old friend and coworker, David Sexton, who I had worked with in the jewelry insurance field. Since I had not worked in the niche for some time, Dave gave me a refresher course in security and trends in the industry. Equally important, Dave helped me make some important reconnections to various subject matter experts that were essential to the story.

In addition to David, special thanks go out to John Kennedy, Daniel McCaffrey, and Stanley Oppenheim for their valuable insights into the technical aspects of the jewelry world.

Also, on a local law enforcement level, Arleigh Porter and Bill Larson answered my list of never-ending questions and helped me make a new contact in Chad Mielke, a forensic electronics expert.

If there are any mistakes or errors in how I have presented technical material, they are strictly on me.

Special thanks also to Jim and Lisa Lombard and Kevin and Mikki Fronek for their input, ideas, and critiques. And thank you for all the love I get daily from the MOG Marketing team!

Finally, thanks to the staff at Ten16 Press (Shannon, Lauren, Kaeley) for getting me over the goal line a second time.

Also from J. P. Jordan:

MEN OF GOD

Having reluctantly accepted a job from family friend and CEO Emil Swenson, former pararescueman Nick Hayden quickly transitions from rescuing soldiers in Afghanistan to desk jockeying at Weston, a Wisconsin-based insurance company. He's tasked with closing a failing division responsible for insuring religious institutions, but recent investigations surrounding the murder of a formerly insured priest, a known pedophile, leave Nick feeling suspicious. Without any leads except a cryptic letter found at the crime scene, the case quickly goes cold, but another murder of a previously insured religious leader leads Nick to a chilling realization: a serial killer is on the hunt. When more obscure messages lead him to believe the next target has been chosen, the race to stop the ruthless killer begins.

CPSIA information can be obtained
at www.ICGtesting.com
Printed in the USA
LVHW031242160821
695404LV00016B/1921